Paradise:
A Chronicle of a
Distant World

Books by Mike Resnick

Stalking the Unicorn: A Fable of Tonight
Santiago: A Myth of the Far Future
The Dark Lady: A Romance of the Far Future
Ivory: A Legend of Past and Future
Paradise: A Chronicle of a Distant World

Paradise:
A Chronicle of a
Distant World

MIKE RESNICK

A TOM DOHERTY ASSOCIATES BOOK
NEW YORK

PARADISE: A CHRONICLE OF A DISTANT WORLD

A TOR BOOK
Published by Tom Doherty Associates, Inc.
49 West 24 Street
New York, NY 10010

ISBN: 0-312-93183-2
First edition: May 1989
0 9 8 7 6 5 4 3 2 1

To Carol, as always

And to my friend Daniel P. Mannix,
who is responsible for more of my science fiction
novels than he'll ever know

TABLE OF CONTENTS

FOREWORD

There is a parable that Kenyans, white and black alike, sometimes tell when they sit around a campfire at the end of the day.

It seems that there was a scorpion who wished to cross a river. He saw a crocodile floating a few feet away and asked to be carried across the river on its back.

"Oh, no," said the crocodile firmly. "I know what you are. As soon as we're halfway across the river you'll sting me and I'll die."

"Why would I do that?" scoffed the scorpion. "If I sting you and you die, I'll drown."

The crocodile considered the scorpion's answer for a moment and then agreed to ferry him across the river. When they were halfway across, the scorpion stung the crocodile.

Fatally poisoned, barely able to breathe, the crocodile croaked, "Why did you do that?"

The scorpion thought for a moment, and then, just before he drowned, he answered, "Because it's Africa."

I have exercised my author's prerogative and related this anecdote to you only because it is an amusing story. It obviously has nothing at all to do with this novel, which is about the mythical world of Peponi rather than the very real nation of Kenya.

M.R.

I

Dawn

One

"There were *men* on Peponi back in those days," said Hardwycke, drawing on his pipe and straightening the blanket that covered his legs. "There was Dunnegan, who brought down seventeen Landships in a single day, and Bocci, who used to go out after Bush Devils armed with nothing but a wooden spear. And of course there was Fuentes, who was the greatest hunter of them all. I remember a little fellow, tough as nails, named Hakira, who lived in a cave with a Demoncat for the better part of five years." Hardwycke grinned. "Before the first year was over the Demoncat was scared to death of him. There was Catamount Greene, who went alone among the Bogoda and became their king, and there was Ramirez, who went into the Great Western Desert a pauper and came out a millionaire. Jesus!" he added, a look of surprise on his weathered, wrinkled face. "I haven't thought of Ramirez in half a century." He paused, and then sighed. "And now they're all gone, every last one of them."

"All except you," I replied.

"I haven't got that much longer, either," he said with a shrug. "One hundred and thirteen is pretty damned old, even with all the replacement innards I've got. I've overstayed my welcome by a good twenty years or more." He took another puff from his pipe and watched as the sun filtered through the smoke. "My legs don't work anymore, my eyes don't focus, and as quick as they cure one cancer I get another." He sighed. "Still, I'm lucky to be here at all. Not many men have been mauled by a Bush Devil and lived to tell about it." He paused, staring back across the years. "Did you know that I was the first man to walk through the Impenetrable Forest, and the first to cross the Jupiter Range? They even named one of the mountains after me."

"I know," I said. "Mount Hardwycke."

He nodded thoughtfully. "Of course, it's Mount Pekana now, but it's still Mount Hardwycke on some of the old maps. Had an animal named after me, too."

"I didn't know that," I said. His voice was weakening somewhat, and I leaned forward slightly to hear him more clearly.

"Hardwycke's wildbuck. They're extinct now, but they've got a couple of 'em on display in the museum on Lodin XI, and a whole herd on Deluros VIII." An expression of distaste crossed his face. "Ugly-looking beasts. Terrible eating, too." His pipe went out, but he kept puffing away absently at it. "Well, I suppose I could have done worse. I went out there without a credit to my name, and came away with a mountain and a wildbuck named after me. Maybe it's not much to show for half a century, but it's more than a lot of 'em came back with."

"I think they were splendid accomplishments, sir," I said.

"I always wondered what happened to Catamount Greene,"

he said. "He was a tough little bastard. Always looking for a fight, he was. I remember one night at one of the local taverns, it must have been ten years after he left the Bogoda, he took on five Navy cadets, each of them damned near twice his size, and came close to killing 'em all." Hardwycke shook his head. "Strange man, Greene. He'd give you the shirt off his back, and then pick your pocket when you returned it." Suddenly he sat erect. "And here I am rambling on again. You wanted to know about the Landships, didn't you, Mr. Breen?"

"I'm interested in all of your experiences on Peponi," I said tactfully.

He smiled. "But they're not paying you for any of the others, are they? It's the Landships that everyone wants to hear about."

"They're not paying me at all," I explained again. "I'm gathering material for my thesis."

"That's right," he said, nodding his head slowly. "I keep forgetting and thinking you're a journalist. But they've never been to Peponi, and you have."

"No I haven't, sir."

He stared at me curiously. "Why the hell not? You're writing about Landships, aren't you?"

"There aren't any left," I pointed out.

"Are they really all gone?" he asked, honestly surprised.

"The last one died seventeen years ago."

He sighed. "If you could have seen them when I did, you'd have sworn they'd go on forever." He shifted in his chair and seemed to be staring back across the decades. "There were herds that took a full day to pass by, and you could feel the ground shake three miles away. There must have been ten or twelve million of them on Peponi when I first got there."

"The official estimates are closer to fifteen million," I noted, suddenly wondering how he adjusted to the sterile confines of his room after a lifetime of exploring endless vistas.

He shook his head sadly. "How does something that big and that widespread disappear in one man's lifetime?" he mused.

"You hunted them to extinction," I suggested.

"The hell we did!" he shot back heatedly. "All the Men who ever set foot on Peponi barely made a dent in them!" He paused. "Those damned Bluegills have a lot to answer for."

"Bluegills?" I repeated. "What are Bluegills?"

"The natives," he said. "Couldn't call 'em apes or monkeymen once we found out they were sentient, even though that's what they looked like, so we came up with Bluegills."

"Why?" I asked. "The word gill implies some kind of fish, yet I know that the natives breathe oxygen."

Hardwycke nodded. "Right. But they've got a bluish band of muscle on the side of their necks, breaking up all that red fur. Looks just like the gills on a fish. They were calling 'em Bluegills before I got there, and the name stuck. Until they complained, anyway." He paused thoughtfully. "Pretty useless lot, by and large." He paused again. "Except for the one who's running the show now," he added with a touch of grudging admiration. "*He's* smarter than most of the Men I've known."

"You're referring to Buko Pepon?" I asked.

"That's the one," he agreed. "It sure as hell isn't his real name, though."

"Did you ever meet him?" I asked.

He shook his head. "No. He came along after I'd left."

He fell silent then, and I asked no more questions for fear that I had tired him. For a moment I thought he was sleeping, and then I decided that maybe he had fainted from his exertions. I was about to summon his nurse when he opened his eyes and looked out the window with a wistful expression on his weathered, wrinkled face.

"You should have seen it back then," he said at last. "The

second you set foot on the planet, it was like you were re-
discovering Eden. Everything was so green, and there was
such a wealth of life! Avians beyond number, herds of migrating Silvercoats literally a million strong, the coolest, clear-
est water. Fortunes to be made farming or hunting Landships.
A whole world for the taking." He paused, collecting his
thoughts. "There were thousands of worlds, I know—but this
one was something special."

"Did you go there expressly to hunt Landships?" I asked.

He shook his head. "I didn't even know what a Landship
was. I went there because I was young and full of dreams and
I wanted to see places that no Man had ever seen before."

"And so you did," I said.

"No," he corrected me. "I was about fifteen years too late.
There were a couple of hundred Men there already." He
peered off into the past. "It must have been something when
the first of them landed there." He looked up at me. "I had
a good run of it, but I got there just a little bit late."

"Two hundred Men on an entire planet hardly constitutes
overcrowding," I noted.

"I know," he said. "But some of the animals were already
starting to avoid any sign of Man, and the biggest of the
Landships were already gone. And the Bluegills . . ." He
shook his head. "By the time I got there, some of them were
even wearing clothes, and they sure as hell knew what a credit
was worth. Not bad for a bunch of monkeymen that had never
even heard of money twenty years earlier."

"How had they lived?" I asked.

He shrugged. "Who knows? Some of them farmed. I suppose others hunted and fished."

"Had they ever hunted Landships?"

He smiled. "They'd never even seen a wheel, let alone a
spaceship. How could they know what a Landship was worth
back in the Republic?" He paused. "They learned soon
enough. Learned what a Sabrehorn was worth, too. Finally

learned enough to throw us out. Still," he added, "I'm glad I was there. It was really something to see back then."

"Tell me about it," I urged him.

We knew from the start (said Hardwycke) that our time was limited. A planet operates on a timetable, just like a factory. You've got to open it up, see what it's got and what you can use, look into all the nooks and crannies—but if it's worth a damn, pretty soon the explorers and pioneers and hunters have to make way for the settlers and farmers. It's just the nature of things. Wanderlust, and a craving to see what lies beyond the next hill, may be what gets Man to where he's going, but it takes other virtues to keep him there.

Peponi was different, though. No matter where you came from, no matter what demon was driving you from world to world, you'd set down on Peponi and immediately you'd feel like you were finally home, like God had just been practicing with all the other worlds He'd made, and that He'd finally done the job right with this one.

When I decided to go there, I had no idea what I wanted to do. Farming didn't much appeal to me, and I didn't know anything about mining, so I decided the first thing to do was to learn the terrain. I'd done a little sport hunting on my home world, so I hired on as a meat hunter for old Ephraim Oxblood, who was trading the rivers of the Great Eastern Continent. His real name was Jones, but he was one of those men who went around naming everything he saw after himself, and he didn't think Jones was a distinctive enough name, which is how Peponi came to have Oxblood River and Oxblood Mountain and Lake Oxblood and all the rest of that stuff you can find on the map—or that you *could* find before they changed all the names.

Anyway, Oxblood had been, I think, the third Man to set down on Peponi, or maybe the fourth. He had no use for farming or anything else that would keep him tied down to one place, so he walked off into the wilderness, started learning the local languages, and spent a whole year living with the Siboni, who were the most warlike tribe of Bluegills. He even went on some raids with them when they made war against the Bogoda and the Kia. Rumor had it that he'd taken a Siboni wife for a couple of years, but I never paid any attention to that: even if there was a way for a Man to take a Siboni to bed, I never met any Man who wouldn't sooner have his fingernails pulled out than have sex with an alien.

After he'd lived with the Siboni for a time, Oxblood had a pretty good notion of what the Bluegills would fancy, and he began trading up and down the rivers that ran through the countryside. Before long he got bored though, and decided that he wanted to see more of Peponi, so he began trading with the Kia as well, and then with some of the other tribes, and as he got older and his operation got bigger, he found that he needed a hunter, both to supply trading material to meat-starved natives and to keep his own Bluegills happy and well-fed. He took out an ad, I answered it, and he hired me on the spot. Credentials never meant much to Oxblood, or any of the other Men who opened up Peponi; if you could do the job, you didn't need credentials, and if you couldn't— well, they found out quick enough, and after they buried you they'd just advertise for a replacement.

Oxblood wasn't at the spaceport to meet me. He sent a couple of his Siboni trackers, and let me tell you, everyone else just stepped aside while these two Bluegills, wearing nothing but armbands and ankle bracelets and armed with their distinctive hook-shaped spears (which were always attached to their wrists by grass ropes), walked right up to the reception area, ignoring all the other Men and Bluegills. They couldn't speak a word of Terran, and nobody there understood Siboni, but they held up a crumpled sheet of paper with my name written on it, so I hoisted my single piece of luggage on my back, slung my projectile rifle over a shoulder, held my sonic rifle across my chest, and went off with them. The last thing I remember about the spaceport was a missionary who had flown out with me from Barringer IV, staring at me with a worried expression and crossing himself as I followed the two barbaric-looking Bluegills out into the hot, humid air of Peponi.

We passed through some sun-bleached countryside that was teeming with exotic-looking animals. There were huge herds of shimmering silver herbivores, and smaller groups of long-necked creatures that watched us curiously as we passed by. Off in the distance I could see some enormous brown shapes, but they were too far away for me to make out any details. Now and then we'd pass a catlike carnivore lying in the shade, but although I kept my sonic rifle at the ready, none of them paid the slightest attention to us.

I found it extremely frustrating not to be able to speak with my guides. I was hot and tired and thirsty, and I wanted to know why the hell Oxblood hadn't met me himself, or at least sent a landcar for me. In fact, I was on the verge of turning around and marching back to the spaceport when we came to a large camp set in a wooded glade. There were a number of grass huts that had been constructed in a large semicircle, plus two geodesic bubbles carefully located under the shade of some overhanging trees. A few primatelike animals sat on one of the branches, listening to the noises that were emanating from a landcar that was parked about thirty feet away from them. I could hear the sounds of metal hitting against metal, and I saw two legs sticking out from beneath the vehicle.

"Hello?" I said, and a moment later a large, weathered, gray-haired man pulled himself out from under the landcar.

"You Hardwycke?" he asked, wiping some grease off his face.

I nodded.

"Well, you seem to have got here without any trouble."

He extended his hand. "I'm Ephraim Oxblood. I meant to pick you up myself in the landcar, but we broke an axle." He spat on the ground. "I tell them and I tell them and I tell them, and they still think that the faster you go over the potholes, the less damage it'll do to the damned car." He spat again, and I saw that he was chewing a reddish tobacco. "Well, can I offer you something to drink?"

"Anything cold will do," I said, dropping my backpack on the ground and balancing the two rifles atop it.

"You look tired," he said after barking an order to one of his Siboni, who brought me a container of lukewarm beer.

"I am," I said. "That was a long, hot walk."

I took a sip of the beer, decided that I liked the distinctive taste, and then took a long swallow.

"You'll walk a lot longer than that before you're through with this job," he chuckled. "Still," he added, "you should have had the Bluegills carry your gear. That's why I sent two of 'em."

"I didn't know how to ask them," I replied.

"You don't *ask* 'em, son," he said. "You *tell* 'em." He barked out a few more commands in Siboni, and immediately the camp came to life, with Bluegills scurrying about, lighting a campfire, taking my gear to the bubble that Oxblood had designated as mine, cleaning off the tool kit. The activity caused the primatelike animals to retreat, chattering noisily, to the higher branches, and a number of small, colorful avians fluttered away.

Oxblood turned back to me. "I'll translate for you for two weeks," he said.

"And then?" I asked, lighting up a small cigar and offering one to him, which he refused.

"Then you'd better learn Siboni, or teach 'em Terran." He paused and slapped at a small insect that was crawling up the side of his neck. "It'll be easier for you to learn Siboni."

"How long did it take *you* to learn Siboni?" I asked.

"Oh, four or five months. Not much to it. Simple language, really."

"But you're only giving me two weeks," I pointed out.

"You don't have to learn the whole damned language," he replied, and I couldn't tell if he was irritated or amused. "The only thing you have to learn is what to tell 'em when you're out hunting, or you want something done in camp." He got to his feet. "Ready for dinner?"

"I thought I'd bathe first," I replied. "I'm pretty grubby."

"Take a Dryshower," he said. I must have looked my disappointment, because he stared at me and added: "Water's in short supply around here."

"I passed a river less than half a mile in that direction," I said, pointing back toward where I had come from.

"It's loaded with killer snakes," replied Oxblood. "Besides, that stuff takes three days to purify—and we're not going to be here that long." He paused. "Son, I imagine you're used to soaking in a tub, but you're on Peponi now. We'll be going places where you'll be grateful for three swallows of water a day, and we won't have any to waste on anything frivolous like bathing."

"I understand, Mr. Oxblood," I said.

"I'm not sure you do," he replied seriously. "But you will. And call me Ephraim."

"All right, Ephraim," I said.

"One more thing," he said, looking up at me. "What do you want to be called—August or Hardwycke?"

I shrugged. "It makes no difference."

"Not to you or me, but it makes a difference to the Bluegills."

"I don't understand."

"You're their boss," he said. "They're expected to call you Boss something. It don't matter which name you choose, but take one or the other, so they'll know."

"Hardwycke, I suppose."

"Good enough," he said. He clapped his hands together, and suddenly all of the Bluegills came to attention and turned to him. He then said something in Siboni, the only two words of which I understood were "*Boss Hardwycke*," and the Bluegills all nodded. Then he went back to work on the landcar, they returned to their duties, and I wandered over to my bubble to take my Dryshower.

When I emerged, dressed in a fresh outfit, Oxblood uttered another command and one of the Siboni walked over to my bubble and took my dirty clothes away.

"He'll have them washed by tomorrow morning," explained Oxblood. "His name's Prumbra," he continued, gesturing to the Siboni. "He's yours for as long as you work for me."

"Mine?" I repeated.

Oxblood nodded. "Don't ever tip him, because he doesn't know what money is. Whack the hell out of him when he fucks up, and give him some extra meat when he does good."

I nodded. Then the odor of the sizzling meat reached my nostrils and I walked over to the campfire.

"I've never eaten food that was cooked over a fire before," I remarked.

"If these idiots would learn how to pack the camp stove properly and stop hitting every bump on the trail, you could remain in blissful ignorance," he said. "They've broken three stoves, and I finally just gave up on it."

There were a number of thick pieces of meat cooking on a metal grill, and the sight and smell of it reminded me that I hadn't eaten all day.

"What's for dinner?" I asked.

"Dust Pig," he answered.

"What's that?"

"Closest thing Peponi's got to a wild boar," replied Oxblood. "Ugly as sin. Weighs about six hundred pounds, and spends most of its time rooting around in the dirt."

"It smells good," I said, buttoning my tunic as the air started turning cooler.

"Tastes awful," said Oxblood. "You ever bring one of these back for dinner, you're gone the next day."

"Then why—?"

"The Siboni are mighty warriors," he said sardonically. "They won't hunt anything that doesn't have an equal chance to kill them—and a Dust Pig against a spear is a pretty fair contest."

"What kind of animals will I be hunting for you?" I asked.

"Mostly Silvercoats," he said.

"What are they?"

"I'll take you out tomorrow morning and show you," he answered. He looked sharply at me. "You brought what I told you to?"

"A sonic rifle and a projectile rifle," I said.

"Good," he said, nodding.

"I'm going to miss my laser weapon, though."

"Too dry around here," he said. "Miss a shot and you might set the whole damned countryside on fire." He paused. "Before we go out, we'll set up a target and zero in your weapons for two hundred yards; you're not likely to get much closer than that to a Silvercoat—they're awfully skittish." He looked at me again. "What kind of stuff did you hunt on your home world?"

"Small game, mostly—and a few antelope that were imported from Earth."

"Well, you'll learn."

"I hope so," I said.

"I hope so, too. I hate funerals."

"I thought I was your first meat-hunter," I said.

He shook his head. "My fifth."

"You buried all the others?"

"Two of 'em. One quit."

"What about the fourth?" I asked.

"That's the one you're replacing," said Oxblood. "He's off hunting Landships."

"I've heard of them," I said. "Are they as big as people say?"

"Depends on which people you've been talking to," he answered. "They go about ten tons, give or take."

"I'd like to see one."

"You will. Half the Men on Peponi are here to hunt them." He turned and barked a command into the gathering darkness, and a moment later a Siboni walked up with a small felt bag in his hand. Oxblood took the bag, inserted his hand, and pulled out a beautiful, red-tinted, multifaceted crystal about the size of my fist.

"Here," he said, handing it to me. "Ever see one before?"

"Just in holographs," I said, handling it reverently. "But I've read about them. This thing is really a Landship's eyeball?"

Oxblood nodded. "That's right. We call it an eyestone out here."

"It's beautiful!"

"The jewelers back on Earth and Deluros VIII can't get enough of them. One with the proper shade of red goes almost five thousand credits; even the yellow ones bring a thousand or so." He paused. "I can't figure out why the blue ones are worthless, but I suppose they have their reasons."

"How do you get close enough to tell what color they are?" I asked, handing the eyestone back to him.

"Carefully," he said with an amused chuckle.

"It seems to me that you'd kill them first and worry about the color second."

"That's the way they used to do it," he agreed, "but now the government has stepped in. Costs twelve hundred credits for a Landship license, so you can take a real beating if you come up with all blue eyes, and you barely break even with yellow ones. Hunting Landships has changed from a mass slaughter to an exact science—which isn't to say that they don't get poached like there's no tomorrow." He paused. "Still, a good hunter can obey the law and get rich from it. Fuentes brought down more than two hundred of them last year—one hundred and ninety-seven reds, five yellows."

"I've read his book," I said, peering off through the failing light at the horizon, just in case a Landship happened to be passing by. It wasn't, though a huge herd of large brown herbivores had moved into view, followed at a respectful distance by a smaller group of spotted animals that seemed to be digging for roots. "That was one of the things that convinced me to come to Peponi."

"Ghost-written," said Oxblood with a contemptuous snort.

"Really?"

"Fuentes may be a hell of a hunter, but he'd have trouble just writing his name in the dirt with a stick. Divide everything he says by three and you'll be a lot closer to the truth."

"Do *you* ever hunt Landships for their eyeballs?" I asked.

"Eyestones," he corrected me. "Not if I can help it. It's easier trading for 'em."

"You mean with the Bluegills?"

He nodded. "A lot of them wear eyestones as ornaments."

"You're kidding," I said uncertainly. "No one could bring a Landship down with just a spear."

"They don't," he said. "But whenever they find a dead one, they cut out its eyestones. Usually they'll trade a pair for a side of meat, though some of them prefer salt or copper, and a few want something even more exotic."

Suddenly a high-pitched roar reverberated throughout the little camp.

"What the hell was *that*?" I asked.

"A Bush Devil, probably, or maybe a Demoncat," he said with no show of concern. "They start hunting at dusk."

"Do they ever hunt Men?"

"No, they mostly hang around the outskirts of the big herds

and pick off the young and the sick—though," he added thoughtfully, "I don't suppose they'd pass up a lone, unarmed Man if he blundered into them."

Two Siboni approached and set up a small table and chairs, complete with a tablecloth and an artificial light that seemed invisible to the insects.

"Dinner time," announced Oxblood, walking over to a chair.

"Where do the Siboni eat?" I asked, sitting down opposite him.

"They'll gather around the fire to sing and dance and eat after we're done," said Oxblood. "There won't be a shred of meat left on that Dust Pig's bones by midnight."

"That's curious," I said. "I read in Fuentes' book that they only eat the hearts of animals they've killed, and that they leave the rest for scavengers."

Oxblood chuckled. "There's a difference between *preferring* the heart and refusing to eat any of the rest. Still," he added, "if one of 'em ever does anything exceptional, something you'd really like to reward him for, toss him the heart of whatever you've shot for dinner that night." He paused. "They think it makes 'em brave. Me, I'd rather have the heart of whoever killed it, if it was bravery I was looking for."

"I noticed their huts," I said, gesturing toward the semi-circle of grass dwellings just beyond the glade. "Do they live here permanently?"

"No. They can build one of those things in maybe twenty minutes. They just abandon 'em when we leave."

He issued another command, a Siboni brought the meat over, and a moment later I had my first taste of Dust Pig. It was every bit as bad as Oxblood had said it was: tough, chewy, with a strong gamey taste. I ate about half my portion, and then shoved my plate away.

He said something else in Siboni, and one of the Bluegills brought a dish filled with exotic fruits to the table.

"Dessert," announced the Siboni.

"I thought they couldn't speak Terran," I said, surprised.

"Oh, now and then one of them picks up a couple of words, just to show off," replied Oxblood with an unimpressed shrug. "Hell, give 'em half a chance and they'd be wearing our clothes and drinking our booze. And there ain't a one of them who wouldn't swap his wife and kids for a chance to drive the landcar. Don't know why they're so hot to pretend they're Men; you don't see any of *us* trying to act like Bluegills."

We finished off the meal with some warm beer—Oxblood explained that one of the Siboni had broken his portable refrigerator—and then headed off toward our bubbles. I was sweating so profusely that I took another Dryshower, then climbed gratefully into my bed. The chirping and hooting and screeching of the nearby fauna was broken by an occasional roar from a distant carnivore. I listened, fascinated, for a few moments, but before long I fell into a deep, exhausted sleep.

It seemed that my head had barely hit the pillow when I heard Oxblood barking orders to the Siboni. I got to my feet, slipped on my clothes, and opened the door of my bubble.

"What's the matter?" I asked blearily.

"We're breaking camp," answered Oxblood. "Grab yourself some coffee and then get ready to move out."

"It's still night out," I said.

"Sun'll be up in another twenty minutes. We've got a lot of ground to cover today; no sense wasting any daylight."

I walked over to the table that Prumbra had set up, had two quick cups of coffee, and then loaded my gear into the back of the landcar. Prumbra carefully added my freshly-done laundry to my pack.

"Okay," said Oxblood, approaching me. "The Siboni will head north and make camp where the river forks off, about fifteen miles ahead. We'll meet 'em there for lunch."

"Where are *we* going?" I asked.

"Across the savannah," he said, climbing into the driver's seat and activating the landcar. "It's time to find out what you can do with those guns of yours."

I pulled myself up to the passenger's seat, and a moment later we were headed out toward the seemingly endless grasslands beyond the glade.

"Now ordinarily we'd just pull up to the first herd of game we saw and blow one of 'em away," explained Oxblood. "No sense giving an animal a sporting chance if you ain't hunting for sport. But since you're going to be on foot a lot more than you're going to be in the landcar, I think we'll stop about half a mile away from whatever it is that we fancy for the dinner table and let you stalk it."

We were no more than half a mile into the grasslands when we saw a huge herd of enormous, horned herbivores.

"Thunderheads," he said. "They go close to a ton apiece. Nasty sons of bitches; hard as hell to kill."

"Do you want me to take one?" I asked, reaching into the back for my sonic rifle.

He shook his head. "Too tough. They make lousy eating."

We drove a bit farther, and then he began making a large semicircle around something that was lying in the grass.

"What's that?" I said, holding a hand up to shield my eyes from the glare of the sun.

"Bush Devil," he replied. "Let's get a little closer so you can get a good look at it."

He continued driving in a semicircle, but made it a little tighter, and suddenly I could see a russet and gold catlike creature laying down in the tall grass.

"One of our carnivores," said Oxblood. "Not as big as a Demoncat, but pound for pound he's a meaner customer. Beautiful protective coloration, too; very difficult to spot."

"But *you* spotted him," I noted. "How?"

He smiled and pointed to the sky, where a dozen large avians were circling overhead.

"He's on a kill," explained Oxblood. "As soon as he leaves, *they'll* come down for the leftovers."

He turned away at a right angle to the Bush Devil and headed off across the plain again. Within a few minutes we came to a large mixed herd of grasseaters, containing four or five different species, and the landcar came to a stop.

"All right," said Oxblood, testing the wind with the smoke from his pipe. "See those silver fellows out there?"

I looked, and was able to make out about three dozen delicate silver-coated animals in among the predominately brown herbivores.

"Yes," I said.

"They're Silvercoats," he said. "They make the best eating." He paused. "The males have the big spiral horns; the small straight horns belong to the females. Try to bring down a yearling who's just starting to sprout its horns; they're the tenderest." He paused. "The heart's just behind the left elbow, in the bottom third of the chest."

"How close am I likely to get before they break?" I asked.

"A couple of hundred yards if you're lucky."

I put back the sonic rifle and pulled out the projectile weapon.

"They're too closely bunched," I said. "I'd probably cripple a couple of them if my yearling falls too fast."

He nodded his agreement, then leaned back on the seat while I slipped out of the car and began approaching the Silvercoats. When I got to within 300 yards they started getting nervous, and a moment later two brown herbivores broke and started racing away. The Silvercoats soon followed suit, and I quickly raised my rifle, got a young Silvercoat buck in my sights, and fired. For a moment I thought I had missed, because absolutely nothing happened, but after he had run for perhaps half a mile he suddenly staggered and collapsed to the ground.

Oxblood picked me up in the landcar, and we drove over

to the dead Silverbuck. The old man got out of the car, walked over to the animal, looked at the bullet hole, and nodded.

"You'll do," he said. "Let's get this thing loaded."

"Do you want to skin it first?" I asked.

He shook his head. "That's Bluegills' work," he said distastefully. He leaned down and lifted the hindquarters, waited for me to grab the head, and we heaved it onto the back of the landcar.

"Prumbra's feeling bad because he's working for you now instead of me," said Oxblood as we began driving off. "Give him this fellow's heart tonight, and it'll set things straight with him."

"All right," I agreed.

We spent the next three hours driving across the plains, Oxblood spotting various animals and pointing them out to me, and then, as the sun climbed higher in the sky, he decided that it was time to turn north and rejoin the Siboni. We had been going in a straight line for almost four miles when he suddenly came to a halt and raised his binoculars to his eyes.

"Interested in seeing a Landship?" he asked.

"Hell, yes!" I said excitedly.

"Keep your gun handy," he said, turning sharply to his right. "They've been hunted pretty heavily in these parts. Some of 'em are as likely to charge as to look at you."

He turned to the northeast, and after a moment I could see three huge figures standing out against the stark landscape, right beside a small grove of tall green trees. As we approached to within a quarter mile of them, I was able to distinguish their features.

They were burly animals, standing perhaps sixteen feet at the shoulder, and covered top to bottom with shaggy brown fur. Their heads were enormous, and each had a long prehensile lower lip that seemed almost as adaptable as a human hand. Their ears were small and rounded. Their noses were quite broad (and appeared even broader as they turned to us with flared nostrils testing the wind). They gave an impression of tremendous strength, but I had read in Fuentes' book that they were also capable of speeds of up to twenty-five miles per hour over short distances.

"Well?" whispered Oxblood.

"I never saw anything that big before," I answered. "How do you kill them?"

"There's a big concentration of blood vessels in the shoulder," he explained. "A well-placed soft-nosed bullet will usually kill them from shock."

"What about a brain shot?"

He chuckled. "No bullet ever made could get through all that bone." He paused. "See that little indentation in the skull, just in front of the ear?"

"Yes."

"A blast from a sonic rifle right there will do it. Two inches too high or too wide and all you've got is one mighty annoyed Landship."

"I can't see the color of their eyes," I said, borrowing the binoculars from him.

"Well now, that's the problem, isn't it?" he replied with an amused grin.

"How close do you have to get?"

"Thirty yards should do it—if he's looking right at you," said Oxblood. "Otherwise, fifteen or twenty."

"And what happens if you get to within fifteen yards and find out that the eyes are blue?" I asked.

He chuckled again. "Then you run like hell and hope he's too busy feeding his face to bother with you."

One of the Landships took a few tentative steps toward us and let out a loud bellow.

"Is he going to charge?" I asked.

"I doubt it. He's probably just trying to scare us away so the wife and kiddies can come out from that patch of trees over there."

The animal bellowed once more, and Oxblood began backing up the vehicle very slowly.

"Sudden movements bother 'em," he said. "They're less likely to charge if you back off slowly than if you race off in a cloud of dust."

The Landship kept walking after us.

"Well, if he's dumb enough to leave his friends and come out in the short grass, he probably shouldn't be passing on those genes anyhow," said Oxblood. "I've still got a couple of Landships on my current license. Why don't you pretend you're me, take your rifle, and wait here for him?"

"Where will you be?"

"I'll keep backing straight up, so that he comes right up to you," said Oxblood. "Wait until he's about twenty-five yards away, and then, if his eyestones are the right color, pop him."

"And if they're not?"

"Touch your hat with your left hand, and I'll speed up and start leading him away from you."

"What if he's more interested in me than in you?" I asked nervously.

"Landships have terrible eyesight, and the wind's blowing away from him," said Oxblood calmly. "At twenty-five yards he won't be able to tell you from a tree stump, and mighty few Landships charge tree stumps."

I pulled out my projectile rifle and cautiously climbed out of the landcar, while Oxblood continued backing up. Then I got down on one knee and waited.

The Landship approached to within fifty yards, then forty, then thirty, and I still couldn't see the color of his eyes. I could see everything else, though: the enormous musculature of his shoulders, the incredibly flexible lower lip, the myriad of colorful insects dancing around his massive head. I could smell his strong, pungent odor, and I could hear not just his breathing but the rumbling of his stomach.

Finally, at fifteen yards, I was able to tell that the eye closest to me was a pale yellow-orange. I lined up my sights on the point of his left shoulder where all the blood vessels converged, and gently squeezed the trigger—and then all hell broke loose.

The Landship turned full upon me, howling and screaming at an earshattering volume, while his two companions came racing up to see what had happened to him. He whirled around in a complete circle, then saw me, extended that frightening lower lip toward me, and covered the fifteen intervening yards like some engine of destruction. I leaped to one side, rolling as I hit the ground, then righted myself and fired three more quick rounds into the creature's chest. It raced right by me, oblivious to its new wounds, and charged straight at the landcar. Oxblood began maneuvering evasively, but while it staggered once or twice it matched Oxblood's every move with remarkable agility. Then the car got stuck in a rut, and I thought Oxblood was done for, but just as the Landship got within reach of him, it shuddered once and died. The other Landships pawed the ground nervously, grunting and bellowing, as if trying to work up their courage for a charge.

Oxblood jumped out of the landcar, withdrew a knife that had been specially modified for the job at hand, and quickly began removing the eyestones as the bellowing became louder.

"Do me a favor, will you?" he said calmly as I raced up to him.

"What?" I asked breathlessly.

"His two chums are thinking of joining the party, and I've only got one Landship left on my license. Frighten them away so we don't have to break the law."

I looked at the two ten-ton creatures that had approached to within one hundred yards of us.

"How?" I asked.

"You're a bright lad," said Oxblood, never looking up from his work. "You'll think of something."

I took my rifle and fired three quick shots in the air. One of the Landships raced off in a panic, but the other, still screaming, uprooted a small tree and hurled it away as if it were nothing more than a twig.

"Forty-five more seconds," announced Oxblood.

I fired just in front of the remaining Landship's feet, hoping that the bits of earth the bullet tore up might sting him. I might as well have been trying to draw blood from that four-inch-thick skin with a dull knife.

"It's not working," I said nervously.

The Landship pawed the ground again and bellowed angrily.

"I think he's going to charge," I said. "Do you want me to shoot him?"

"What color has he got?"

"I can't tell," I said. "He's too far away."

"I'm not wasting my last permit on a Blue," he said firmly. "Hold him off."

"I'm open to suggestions," I replied as the creature began approaching us more rapidly.

"Just another second until . . . got it!" cried Oxblood. "Quick! Into the landcar!"

We both hurled ourselves into the car just as the Landship launched his charge. The ignition caught when he was thirty yards away, we began backing up when he was ten yards away, and about two minutes later we had pulled far enough ahead of him so that we could get out of reverse gear, spin around, and start moving forward.

"Well?" asked Oxblood.

"Well what?" I asked, wiping the dust and sweat from my face.

"A hell of a way to make a living, ain't it?" he said with a vastly amused smile.

T wo

Hardwycke was sitting in a corner on a high-backed chrome chair when I arrived. He looked up from the mindless holographic entertainment he had been watching on his computer and deactivated the machine.

"Back again?" he asked.

I nodded. "If you don't mind, sir," I said.

"Not a bit. I like talking about the old days." He paused. "Besides, I slept like a log after you left last night. I owe you something for that, if nothing else."

"You have trouble sleeping?" I asked.

"When you've spent half your life in the bush, you wake up every time you hear the slightest sound . . . or you don't wake up at all. And they clomp up and down the corridors here as if they've got boots on." He paused and took a sip from a glass, then replaced it on a nearby table. "Vitamins," he said confidentially. "I read the label. Even got Vitamin E in it; maybe they're thinking of fixing me up with one of the nurses." He grinned at his little joke. "So . . . what were we talking about?"

"You told me about your first Landship."

He nodded reflectively. "That's right. Hell of an animal, the Landship. Someday, if they ever untie me from all these machines, I think I'll go back and take one last look at them."

"They're extinct, sir," I said, looking at one of the beams of sunlight that illuminated the room and again wondering how a man who had spent so much of his life roaming across Peponi could adjust to this confinement.

"Right," he said, looking out the window with the bored certainty that he would never see a Demoncat or Bush Devil circling beneath it. His gaze finally fell on some semiambulatory patients whose nurses were taking them out for some air, and he frowned and turned back to me. "Well, it's probably all for the best. They outlived their time, just like me. I'm surprised some zoo didn't pick up a few before the end, though."

"They did," I said. "But Landships didn't take well to captivity."

"Not even on a zoo planet like Serengeti?"

"Evidently not."

"Well, I suppose I can't really blame 'em for that," said Hardwycke. He lit up his pipe. "They belonged just the way they were, free to roam Peponi's plains and forests. Mind if I smoke?" he asked, indicating the pipe. "It annoys the staff and keeps the room from feeling too sterile."

"Not at all," I said. "I didn't know that Landships were forest animals."

He shifted his position on his chair. "They weren't in the beginning . . . but after everyone started hunting them, they adapted pretty damned fast." He paused. "You'd be surprised at an animal's capacity to adapt. Take me, for instance: I never had a tent or a bubble as small as this room, and yet I've been here for eight years."

"When did hunting Landships become so popular?" I asked, trying to lead him back to the subject.

"Right after Jonathan Ramsey wrote up his safari," said Hardwycke. "When he announced that he wasn't going to run for another term as Secretary of the Republic, a bunch of museums got together and paid him to go to Peponi to collect specimens for them. Johnny Ramsey couldn't resist the hunt *or* the publicity—I seem to remember that he walked right out of the Secretary's Mansion on Deluros VIII and onto a ship Fuentes had chartered for him—and once he got back, he must have sold ten million copies of his book. Made Fuentes an overnight hero, and suddenly everyone came to Peponi to hunt. Changed the whole industry. Used to be we'd go hunting alone for eyestones, and maybe sell some Sabrehorns to the Pinkies—but now we could make more money leading luxury safaris and letting our clients blow the animals away. So we did," he concluded simply.

"Oxblood, too?" I asked.

Hardwycke shook his head. "No, he just went farther and farther into the bush. I heard that he finally wound up in the Connectors."

"The Connectors?"

"They're a chain of tropical islands, kind of stepping stones between the Great Eastern Continent and the Great Western." He paused and quickly hid his pipe beneath the folds of his robe as a nurse poked her head into the room. He waited until she left, then took another long puff, coughed, and continued. "Still, I had three good years with him, and he taught me things about survival out there that you don't learn in any books. Finally turned over all his Siboni to me, but they weren't to my liking. I took them along on a couple of safaris and finally dumped 'em in favor of the Sorotoba."

"Why, if I may ask?"

"Too damned proud and arrogant," he responded. "They refused to learn Terran, they stole whatever they wanted in broad daylight, they were always taking off in the middle of a safari and then they'd just show up again a few months later as if nothing had happened. Made the clients feel uncomfortable, too; the help ain't supposed to act like it's better than the employers. Mostly, though, I suppose it was because they managed to break almost every piece of machinery that I owned." He paused, staring at a small brown avian that fluttered outside his window. "Even old Prumbra, who tried his damnedest to act like a Man, couldn't pull it off. He used to beg me to let him be my backup when I was out after Landships, but try as I would, I could never convince him that the bullets didn't travel faster the harder he'd squeeze the trigger." He pointed to his left ear, which I now noticed was missing its lobe. "The day he jerked the trigger and did *this* to me, I took the gun away from him permanently. A week later he was gone, and I never saw him again. I suppose he wouldn't have been satisfied that I'd given him a fair chance until he'd shot off both my ears and maybe my nose."

"Yet a member of the Siboni tribe now holds all the marksmanship records on Peponi," I noted.

"Who told you that?"

"I read it."

"Yeah?" He seemed to consider the remark for a moment, then shrugged. "Just goes to show you: there's a hell of a difference between hitting a target and facing a charging Landship."

"What were the Sorotoba like?" I asked him.

"A little more civilized than the Siboni." He paused thoughtfully. "Hell, *everyone* was more civilized than the Siboni."

"In what ways?"

"To begin with, the Sorotoba wore clothes. Nothing special, just rags they wrapped around their middles, but it was *something*. Most of 'em spoke a little Terran; not much, but enough to make themselves understood." He paused, as if remembering his Sorotoba employees. "And they wanted to be paid in credits. Poor bastards didn't have anything to spend it on, and they worked for something ridiculous like a credit a day, but if you didn't pay 'em every morning, they didn't go to work. I mean, you could hit 'em and kick 'em and generally raise hell with 'em, but if they didn't get their credit they just sat there and stared right through you." He shook his head. "Then they'd come in off a three-month hunt, buy a ninety-credit bottle of cheap booze from some Man or other who was willing to sell to the natives, get so sick they'd almost die, and be ready to start off on another hunt the next morning." He shrugged. "Typical wags."

"Wags?" I repeated, not certain that I'd heard the word correctly.

"Bluegills."

"I'm afraid I'm not quite clear. Are wags a particular type of Bluegill?"

He shook his head. "The Republic set up their administrative headquarters at Berengi—it was just a clearing by a river back then, though I'm told that it's a city of two or three million these days—and started passing all kinds of laws. And some of the do-gooders decided that it was insulting to call the natives Bluegills, and decreed that from that day forth we had to call them Worthy Alien Gentlemen. We still called 'em anything we wanted out in the bush, of course, but back in civilized country, we started calling 'em wags."

"An acronym."

"Whatever. Of course, after they threw us out, they decided they didn't want to be wags, either. I don't know what the hell them call themselves these days."

"Peponites, I would imagine," I said.

"Stupid," he said.

"Why?"

"It doesn't make sense."

"In what way?"

"Does Paradise-ites make sense to *you*?"

"You're confusing me again," I said. "What has Paradise got to do with anything?"

"What the hell do you think Peponi means?"

"I don't know," I admitted. "I assumed Peponi was the name of the man who discovered the planet."

"It was opened up by a member of the Pioneer Corps named Edward Ngana. The rule is whoever opens a planet names it. He fell in love with the place and named it Peponi, which means Paradise in Swahili."

"Swahili?" I repeated. "I've never heard of it."

"An old Earth dialect. Nobody ever heard of it, but Ngana found it in his computer's memory banks."

"Very interesting," I said. "Did Ngana settle there?"

"Tried to. Died of fever two months later. They say the Bluegills killed his wife and kids." Hardwycke paused thoughtfully. "Still, you can't blame him for the name: it must have *been* like Paradise back then, before they started farming all the land and killing off the game, and before the government started sticking its nose into everything. Like I say, I got there a few years too late. But I'd sit around camp listening to Oxblood talk about the old days, so I know what it was like then."

"What happened after you split up with him?" I asked. "Did you start hunting Landships for profit, or did you become a safari guide?"

"A little of each. Mostly safaris, though. The way rules and regulations were coming out of the government offices in Berengi, I figured I'd better get some credentials before they started putting all kinds of restrictions on who could and couldn't run a safari."

"It must have been an interesting life," I commented.

"Depended on the clients," he replied. "Some of them were pretty decent folk; some just wanted to blow away any animal they could get in their sights. Not everyone who killed a Landship was a sportsman or a profiteer, you know—some people just like killing things." He paused. "A couple of 'em even made the Sorotoba look civilized by comparison—and that ain't an easy task."

"What were they like?" I asked.

"The clients or the Sorotoba?"

"Both," I said.

Most people (said Hardwycke) think that the Sorotoba are the laziest of all the Bluegills, and Lord knows they can spend whole days sitting around watching the grass grow. But after you live with them for awhile, you realize that it isn't laziness that makes 'em act that way, but inertia.

Sit a Sorotoba down and he'll stay seated all day if you don't tell him to get up and do something. But on the other hand, give him a chore, and he's just as happy doing that as sitting around.

I lost one particular wag when we were hunting Dashers up in the dry country north of Balimora, which used to be the last town you came to before you reached the desert. His name was Penona, and when I left camp in the morning I told him to dig a well, since we were going to be there for a week or so. When I came back he was dead, drowned in his own well. It was pretty deep, a few feet over his head, and since the Sorotoba come from the desert, most of them don't know how to swim. Evidently Penona had been digging most of the day, and since no one told him to stop he just kept it up until the water rushed in and it was too late. Inertia.

The Sorotoba were a pretty superstitious lot, even compared to the other Bluegill tribes. It used to drive me crazy. You could spend half a year teaching one of them to be a mechanic, and if your landcar broke down and he could find the fault immediately, he'd fix it just as good as a Man could. But if he couldn't find what was wrong in five minutes' time, he'd just give up on it and explain to you that there was a curse on the vehicle. And even after you'd fix it yourself and show him what had been wrong, he'd just smile and answer that your magic was stronger than the curse.

Or you could go out on a hunt, alone or with your clients, and if you were successful it was because one of their gods had smiled down upon you. But if your tracker was too hung-over to follow a spoor, or your gunbearer stepped on a stick and frightened off a record Thunderhead, well, there was a curse on the hunt and nothing good was likely to happen until you all went back to camp so they could slaughter one of their domestic animals or pay a few credits to the local witch doctor.

A couple of them even converted to Christianity. It was ludicrous, of course—I mean, imagine an *alien* going to church and carrying a bible around with him. The missionaries would go home happy, and then out would come the Demoncat teeth and the Bush Devil claws, and you knew that the conversion had a lot more to do with getting their hands on another necklace—the crucifix in this case—than with any spiritual awakening. The ones who didn't unconvert the minute the missionaries left used to go right from church to their local witch doctor's, which at least kept them occupied and gave them something to do on Sunday.

Still, if you treated them well and fed them regularly and understood their limitations, the Sorotoba were about as good on safari as any of the Bluegills. And the wild ones—the ones who hadn't had any contact with Men—were the best trackers I've ever seen. Set 'em down in the middle of Berengi or any other city and they'd be lost in two minutes' time—but stick 'em in the middle of the Southern Desert and they'd find the only water hole within 200 miles. Sometimes they'd forget where camp was when they didn't like your clients, but on days they felt like it they could track a billiard ball down a paved road.

My headman was a Sorotoba named Magadi. Big fellow, heavily muscled, used to laugh all the time. Not real long on brainpower, but none of them were. He ran the camp, kept all the Sorotoba in line, even entertained the clients by juggling a bunch of ten-pound rocks as if they were rubber balls. When he had to lay into the other Bluegills, he'd do it with a vengeance; we never had a mutiny or a mass desertion the whole time he worked for me. It got to where he thought he was a Man, and kept complaining about how stupid and unwashed all the Sorotoba were. Even started calling them wags; it was really kind of funny. He'd walk around camp yelling "You bloody wags do this!" and "You lazy wags do that!" and the clients would practically fall off their chairs laughing. After a while I gave him a uniform—a formal waiter's outfit I bought from a restaurant in Berengi, complete with bowtie—and he was so pleased with it he wouldn't even take it off to wash it. Finally it got to smelling so bad we had to get rid of it, and I thought Magadi would die of a broken heart.

My best tracker was a Bluegill named Prinbul. He'd broken some taboo or other when he was just a kid, and his tribe had thrown him out, and he'd spent the next twenty years fending for himself in the bush. You'd look at him and he was just one enormous scar, from the top of his head to the tip of his toes, but I never found a Bluegill who was better at his job. Prinbul had lived with the animals for so long that he pretty much thought like one.

Nothing can ruin a safari quicker than having your client waste his Landship license on a blue or a clear—with eyestones, color is *everything*—and Prinbul was the only wag I trusted to tell me what color we were stalking. He had this trick of rubbing Landship dung over every inch of his body and then crawling right up to them while the dung masked his own scent. He was never once wrong about the color of an eyestone. He might have stunk to high heaven, but I gave him one hell of a lot of Landship hearts over the years.

He had another trick, too—he could teach a Demoncat to come out and get killed by a hunter. I'd send him off into the bush while my clients were filling their bag with less dangerous game, and he'd kill a couple of wildbuck or Silvercoats over the next two days, drag the bodies over a mile or so of savannah so nothing could miss their scent, hang the carcass from a tree, and then blow some kind of native whistle he had whittled. Whatever Demoncat owned the territory was never far behind, and after three or four days the Demoncat would associate the sound of the whistle with the notion of an easy meal. Then Prinbul would rejoin us, lead us to the spot where he'd been baiting the Demoncat, and blow his whistle. Worked just about every time.

I really hated to lose him. He'd been working for me for about four years, but he was still pretty much a wild thing, sleeping apart from the other Sorotoba, never learning a word of Terran, eating his food raw, refusing to wear any clothes. One day we were out on safari with a man named Bates, the owner of one of the spaceship cartels from Spica VI. Bates got to drinking a little early in the day, and at one point during a break he ordered Prinbul to clean his gun. Well, like I said, Prinbul didn't speak any Terran, and he wouldn't have cleaned the gun even if he knew what my client was saying —cleaning guns is a lot lower on the Sorotoba's social scale than tracking—so he just stood there ignoring the man, and then, before I could stop him, Bates walked up to him and slapped him. He'd have been better off slapping a Bush Devil; ten seconds later he was flat on his back, with Prinbul clawing at his face and gnawing on one of his ears.

Well, we couldn't have the wags feeling free to attack Men, even when it was justified; after all, there were a hell of a lot more of them than there were of *us*. The law was right there on the books, plain as day, and it didn't change until a year or two before they got their independence: if a Man killed a Bluegill, he was fined fifty credits; if he did it twice and couldn't show just cause, he was fined 500 credits and told to leave the planet. But if a Bluegill struck a man for any reason at all, the penalty was death.

I was fond of Prinbul, and I didn't think much of my drunken client, so I let Prinbul escape into the bush. I never saw him again, but at least he stayed alive that way. When we got back to Berengi, Bates pressed charges against me, and it cost me my license for eight months. I took a lot of ragging about being a wag-lover, too, but most of the hunters I knew understood why I had let him escape. We hunters tended to stick together, and Bates got turned down three times before he found a guide to take him out on his next safari.

I must say that I didn't lack for action during the time I was without my license. The Sentabels, one of the major tribes on the Great Western Continent, about 200 miles west of the Connectors, had burned down a couple of settlements and were in a state of open rebellion. I never did find out what caused them to do that; I don't think anyone much cared. With Men outnumbered thousands to one, the government had to put the rebellion down fast and worry about the reasons for it later. Even though he didn't know anything about warfare, the government put Fuentes in charge of the human forces, and most of the hunters rushed to join up.

It wasn't much of a war. We went down there with about a thousand Men and a native contingent perhaps twice that size. There were about 200,000 Sentabels when we got there. After we'd marched to the western end of their homeland and back up to the Connectors, there were maybe 80,000 left, and they were as pacified a batch of wags as you'd ever want to see. The whole campaign took exactly five months and two days, and when I got back to Berengi, they returned my license early as a way of thanking me.

One of the interesting things about the campaign was that we used Dorado and Sorotoba recruits to help us. It wasn't hard to get 'em to come along, either; if a Bluegill wasn't a tribal brother, most other Bluegills tended to think of him as a natural enemy. We didn't give them weapons, of course; it might have been damned hard to get them back. But they served as trackers and runners and cooks and bearers and in any other capacity that we needed them. It was the first time the government thought of having one batch of Bluegills to fight another; it wouldn't be the last.

Anyway, after I got back into the hunting business, I found old Magadi, rounded up a new batch of Sorotoba, and went back into the bush. Had some interesting clients, too—not everyone wanted to blow away Landships and Demoncats. First client I took out was collecting avians for some museum, and every specimen had to be just perfect. We were out for nine weeks, we shot only seventeen avians, and he thought the safari was a roaring success. My next trip out was with a botanist who would spend his whole day holographing flowers and most of each night putting sprigs of plants into nutrient solutions. By the time I finally took out a client who was looking for Bush Devils and Thunderheads, I was more than ready for it.

You know, there are a lot of false notions about what constitutes a good professional hunter. The typical romantic view of him is that of a tall, bronzed, immaculately-clad man who knows Peponi like the back of his hand, speaks every native dialect, never misses what he aims at, and usually makes a play for his client's wife.

I see those holos about hunters out in the bush and I have to laugh. You know what's the single most important trait a hunter can have? He's got to be able to hold his liquor. You're only out on the trail for maybe five or six hours a day, and you sleep for another seven or eight, which means you've got at least ten hours of time to fill. Clients fill that time by drinking, and if you don't drink with them, they get offended, as if you think you're too good to associate with them. Even Oxblood, who never did any professional hunting himself, warned me about that before I left him, and he was dead right. When they stop drinking with you, things have already gone from bad to worse, and they're not about to get any better.

As for speaking dialects, a hunter knows the dialect of the wags he's using on safari, and if he's an old-timer who did a little trading before he took up leading safaris, he might know bits and pieces of three or four other dialects. But Peponi had some two thousand tribes of Bluegills, major and minor, and between them they spoke about 1,800 different languages, and nobody could learn them all. Usually if you could speak Bogoda, Kia, Sorotoba, or Siboni you could get by all right, at least on the Great Eastern Continent; there was almost always somebody around who understood them.

As for the outfits they wear in the holos, they're damned foolish. Most of the hunters I knew wore shorts. Our legs may not have been all that nice to look at, but when you're foot-slogging for miles on end in tropical climates, the last thing you need are long pants. A lot of us wore vests, just to have enough pockets. You were always running out of places to hold things, like compasses, pipes, salt pills, hunting knives, bullets, and maps. And I've never seen a holo hunter with an ash bag. We used to dump our pipe ashes into this thin bag and hang it around our necks; then, when we'd be stalking an animal, we'd tap the bag with a finger and see which way the ashes blew; that way, we'd always know if the wind was changing.

Most of us were pretty good shots—you can miss a Demoncat or a Landship once or twice and maybe survive, but you sure as hell can't make a regular habit of it—but our notion of an ideal safari would be one where we never had to take a single shot. After all, it was the client who was paying for the privilege, and we were just there to back him up if something went wrong.

As for the romance part, I won't deny that an occasional hunter would go off with a client's wife, but it didn't happen all that often. For one thing, it was bad for business: word gets around that a hunter is sleeping with his client's wife, and he's going to be a mighty lonely hunter before long. It became kind of an unspoken code with us: you could fool around all you wanted in Berengi or the other towns, but you didn't touch a client's woman (or man, for that matter; we had a number of damned good female hunters). Also, just from a practical standpoint, most of us didn't have *time* for romance on safari. We'd be up two hours before the clients, organizing the camp, and we'd be up two hours after they went to bed, breaking down the kitchen and planning the next day's hunting. Add to that the problem of keeping discipline among your wags, keeping all the machinery in good repair, and drinking with the client, and believe me, the only thing you wanted to do at the end of the day was sleep.

Most of the clients I took out were easy enough to get along with; some of them weren't. When you'd get a real bastard, the kind of guy who drank too much or started taking drugs in the bush, or took it out on your wags when he missed a shot, you only had a couple of choices. You could put up with his behavior, in the hope that it might improve, but it almost never did. You could return immediately to Berengi, which sometimes worked, but you always had to worry about having your license pulled.

Or you could bush him.

There's nothing quite so pathetic as a client who is convinced that he is totally lost in the wilds of an alien planet. You'd just lead him around in a great big circle, keep him moving until he was ready to drop, send a couple of wags ahead to scare off the game so you couldn't shoot anything for the pot, and when you'd finally come to water tell him it was polluted. Three or four days of that would take the spunk out of anyone.

What a hunter really wanted was a client who knew what game he was after, killed it quickly and cleanly, didn't ask too many stupid questions, and understood that the hunter was a middleman between himself and the wags. Lord, you cherished clients like that.

What you didn't cherish were the ones who got so excited when they came face-to-face with a Demoncat or a Landship that they forgot everything they ever learned about shooting. They'd take three shots at a Demoncat, miss two and gutshoot him with the third, and then you'd have to go into the bush after a very angry 700-pound carnivore while they went back to camp for a bath and a shave and some dinner.

Old Dunnegan used to tell me that that was the part of hunting he liked best, going into the bush alone to clean up a client's mistakes. It was just him against the animal, and if the bush was thick enough, it was about as close to a fifty-fifty chance as the animal ever got.

Me, I hated it. No two wounded animals ever acted exactly alike. The Thunderheads were the worst, because they'd race off into the thickest bush around, and then, once they were out of sight, they'd double back and lie in wait beside their spoor. I called it the Triangle Trap: they never charged until you were within ten or twelve feet of them, and no hunter ever got a second shot once he walked into a Triangle Trap. You'd kill him with the first shot, or it was all over for you.

Still, for sheer unpredictability, I'll take the Landship every time. The closest call I ever had came on a safari on a spring day. The long rains had just finished, and I had a client called Lewellan, who had come out with his teenaged son. The father was a pretty decent sportsman, but the kid would just stand there, petrified, every time he saw anything bigger than a Dasher or a Silvercoat.

Anyway, after Lewellan had bagged his carnivores and his Thunderhead, and a couple of the twenty-foot-long millipedes that pass for snakes on Peponi, he decided that it was time to go after his Landship. I suggested that we leave the boy at camp, but both of them insisted that he come along. The father, I know, wanted to make a man out of him; to this day I don't know why the boy wanted to come

Anyway, we set out that morning, and by noon we'd found some relatively fresh Landship dung. I sent a couple of trackers on ahead while we stopped for lunch. They came back about an hour later to report that there was a herd of about fifty Landships grazing about two miles to the north of us.

I didn't see any sense frightening them with the landcar, so we started walking to the north. We caught up with them about two hours later, and I signaled that we should come to a halt about half a mile away.

"I'm going to get a little closer," I whispered. "When I find out which of them are carrying the right color, I'll motion to you to join me."

"Right," said Lewellan.

I turned to his son.

"Are you okay?"

"I'm fine," he said sullenly. "Just point out which one I should aim at and I'll take care of it."

His face was drawn and pale, but his hands weren't shaking, so I decided to let him try to take his Landship.

I tested the wind, approached to within about 300 yards of the nearest of them, then dropped to my belly and snaked my way through the tall grasses until I could finally catch some color. The big bull nearest to me was a blue, but there were two reds and a yellow right behind him, grazing placidly in the midday sun. I crawled back until I was about 250 yards away, tested the wind once more, then stood up silently, turned to Lewellan and his son, and waved them forward.

They joined me a few minutes later, and I carefully pointed out the two bulls with the red eyestones. Lewellan gestured that he wanted his son to have the first shot, and the boy raised his rifle, lined up a Landship in his sights, and fired. The bull went to its knees, but was up instantly, and I could tell that the bullet had entered too far behind the shoulder. He turned toward us and began charging, and I quickly delivered the fatal shot—but while I was doing so I heard five more shots.

Lewellan still hadn't fired his rifle, but the boy had gone a little bit crazy when the Landship began charging, and was firing at everything he could see. I grabbed the rifle from him and told his father to get him away from the herd, then turned back to see what damage he had done.

All hell had broken loose. Four wounded Landships, two bulls, a cow, and a youngster, were screaming in rage and uprooting trees, and the rest of the herd was fast disappearing into a nearby glade of trees. I managed to kill the cow and the baby as they raced for cover, but the two bulls were too far away.

"What now, Boss Hardwycke?" asked one of my trackers. "We shag 'em out for you?"

I shook my head. "No. Let's sit here for an hour or so and give their wounds time to stiffen." I turned to my other tracker. "Make sure Boss Lewellan and his son get back to camp."

"Yes, Boss," he said, and headed off after them at a trot.

I sat about 200 yards from the glade for almost an hour. We could still hear the Landships crashing around in among the trees, and I've have preferred to wait even longer to let the bullets do their damage—but night would fall in another ninety minutes or so, and I decided that it was time to go in after them.

I sent Pelobi—my tracker—around to the back of the glade to warn me if either of our Landships tried to escape, and then, carrying my rifle across my chest, I cautiously approached the trees and began looking for blood spoor.

I was perhaps thirty yards into the glade when I heard some movement off to my left. I dropped to my belly and began wriggling forward, cradling my rifle on my forearms. A moment later I came to a small clearing within the glade and there, not ten yards in front of me, was one of my two Landships, an ugly wound right in the middle of his huge prehensile lip. I waited until he presented me with a killing shot, then took it and put him out of his misery. The explosion of the rifle precipitated some screaming and bellowing from beyond the clearing, and a moment later a second Landship, his left eyestone shattered by the boy's bullet, bore down upon me. I turned him with a shot to his chest, then took a heart shot and heard him drop about twenty yards outside the clearing.

Pelobi worked his way to the clearning a moment later.

"You want eyestones, Boss Hardwycke?" he asked, pulling out his curved knife.

I shook my head. "One of them's a blue and one's a clear," I said disgustedly.

"What about mother and baby?"

"Both blues."

"Boss Lewellan will be unhappy," Pelobi said with a grin.

"Boss Lewellan ought to be happy that I didn't kill his son on the spot," I replied. "Well, let's get back to camp."

I started to leave, and an instant later Pelobi shouted a warning.

I turned and saw yet another Landship silently bearing down upon me. I dove into the bushes to my right, and he shot by me, missing me by less than three feet. When he realized that he hadn't touched me he squealed angrily and wheeled around, testing the air. He was almost on top of me, and I couldn't get a clear shot.

Then Pelobi threw a heavy branch at him, and as he turned to face his new tormentor, I got a clear brain shot and took advantage of it. The ground seemed to shake as the huge beast fell to earth.

"Thanks, Pelobi," I said when I had finally regained my feet and walked over to this latest corpse.

"Look, Boss," said Pelobi, pointing to the Landship's right hind foot. There was a bullet hole in it.

"That's right!" I said, finally comprehending. "There were *five* shots, not four. I thought the kid had missed one of them."

"He missed all of them," said Pelobi.

The eyestones were yellow-orange, but I was damned if I was going to give them to Lewellan *or* his son, so I had Pelobi cut them out and bury them at the edge of the clearing.

When we got back to camp late that night, Lewellan was all apologies, and his son was sullen and silent. I decided then and there that the safari was over, and we spent the next two days driving back to Berengi. At one point the boy asked why I had bothered to go after the wounded Landships. I explained that we couldn't leave them around to kill the next Men or wags who chanced along, that it was a hunter's duty to clean up his client's mistakes. That did it; the boy didn't say another word until I put him and his father on the ship for Binder X.

I filed my report with the Game Authority, which had been upset with me ever since I let Prinbul escape a couple of years earlier. They pointed out that we had killed five Landships but had only been licensed for two. I knew what was coming next: either I could buy three more Landship licenses and pay a fine, or they were going to have to suspend my hunting license again. So I shelled out something like eight thousand credits, which left me barely enough to replace the ammunition I had used on the safari.

Sure was romantic, safari life.

Three

"Legends?" said Hardwycke.

He was sitting up in his bed, looking a little weaker than the last time I saw him, but as always he seemed enthusiastic when we began speaking of Peponi.

"Hell, yes, there were legends galore—and I don't mean any of that crap about Buko Pepon being born with the mark of a prophet on him, or coming down from the mountains to lead his people to freedom. Peponi was still a frontier world when I was there, and we had frontier legends."

"Tell me about them," I urged him.

"Well, most of 'em are probably forgotten by now, but there was a time about sixty years ago when a hell of a lot of people were looking for the Landship Ruby."

"What was that?" I asked.

"I don't know how the story got started, but rumor had it that there was a massive Landship, bigger than any that had ever been seen, up in the high country at the western end of the Great Eastern Continent. He was supposed to carry scars from every type of weapon—projectile, laser, even a molecular imploder—but no one had come close to killing him."

Hardwycke was suddenly seized by a paroxysm of coughing. For a moment I thought I was going to have to call a nurse, but finally it subsided.

"Breathe in all that dust for half a century and eventually it comes back to haunt you," he muttered after he had regained his breath.

"Are you sure you're all right?" I asked.

"I haven't been all right for thirty years," he said wryly. "But I can keep talking, if that's what you mean."

"That was what I meant."

"Where were we?"

"The Landship Ruby."

"Right," he said, nodding. "Anyway, this enormous Landship was supposed to have a ruby embedded in his forehead, a perfect ruby bigger than any eyestone ever seen. Silly, isn't it?" He paused. "Still, a lot of men went out looking for him. Most of 'em never came back. They still say that old Kansas Pierce found him and got killed for his trouble, but nobody ever proved anything." He smiled. "You wouldn't believe how many wags swore they'd seen him, though."

"Had they?"

"Of course not. But lying comes naturally to them. It's not that they're deceitful. They just don't want to disappoint you, so they tell you what they think you want to hear. Same thing with directions. You'd come to a Bluegill village out in the middle of nowhere, and ask where the nearest herd of Thunderheads was, and they'd point you in the right direction, but whether it was a five-hour march or a five-day march to reach them, the Bluegills would always swear that they were just over the next hill. Once in a while I'd get so frustrated when they'd lie about how far it was to water that I'd come back and thrash the hell out of the headman, but it wasn't really their fault; they were just responding the way they'd been trained to respond. Still, you tended to forget that when you followed their directions and found yourself out in the middle of the bush, looking for Landships, and you knew damned well that there wasn't anything bigger than a Mouse Rat within ten miles of you." He reached weakly toward his nightstand. "You want to hand me that pipe?"

"Are you sure you're allowed to?" I asked, still worried about the way he had looked during his coughing spell.

"I'm sure I'm *not* allowed to," he said. "So what? I'm stuck in this damned room, I can't see fifty feet out the window even if there was anything to see, I can't even stand up without help. If indulging in the one pleasure left to me kills me a day or two sooner, it won't be any great loss."

I shrugged, got to my feet, walked over to the nightstand, and handed him the pipe.

"Thanks," he grated.

"You're welcome."

"You know," he continued, holding the pipe up, "this was the most expensive damned habit I had on Peponi. The wags had been brewing their own beer long before the Republic ever discovered the place, and the first factory built in Berengi was a distillery, but for some reason tobacco just didn't grow well there. There were a couple of local brands, but they were so strong you'd swear a Landship could smell the stuff three or four miles away. I always bought tobacco imported from Pollux IV or New Rhodesia, and let me tell you, it sure as hell wasn't cheap. Still," he added, "I don't know what I'd have done without it."

He filled the pipe carefully, tapped down the tobacco, and lit it. "Tame stuff, this," he said, referring to the tobacco. "Still, I suppose it's all I can handle these days."

"You mention tobacco and alcohol all the time," I noted, "but you never speak about drugs."

"I knew a lot of men who could take a rifle and drive a nail into a tree two hundred yards away when they were dead drunk," replied Hardwycke. "Never yet saw a man you could count on when he was full of drugs. And there was an old saying among Peponi's hunters: Everything Bites. We were usually after the Big Five: Landships, Sabrehorns, Thunderheads, Bush Devils, and Demoncats. But even a Silvercoat or a Dasher could impale you on his horns. A Dust Pig could make pudding out of you if you weren't on your guard, and a Treetop had a kick that could kill a Demoncat, let alone a man. You could footslog for three days without seeing a living thing, and the second you relaxed there'd be something hiding behind a bush or up on a tree limb that was just dead set on making you his lunch. Times like that, a man needs his head on right; there was no place in the bush for drugs. I know a lot of hunters started out thinking differently, but sooner or later they all came around to that point of view. A client drinks a pint of whiskey at night, you can pretty much tell in the morning how he's going to react, and if you don't like what you see, you stay in camp for the day . . . but you could never tell what a man would do when he was on drugs. There were more than enough ways to die in the bush without adding stupidity to the list."

He paused. "Couple of Bluegill tribes I know of used to chew the leaves of a plant called the Meridota. It put 'em in kind of a trance." He took a deep puff from the pipe and coughed slightly. "They're still out in the bush, chewing Meridota leaves and living in mud huts and staring at the sun, while the rest of 'em are building cities and pretending to be Men."

"Did any of the animals chew the Meridota?" I asked.

He shook his head. "Animals ain't as stupid as some people think. Only one I ever saw munching on Meridota was a little avian called the Purpletip, and I later found out that Purpletips were immune to it." Suddenly he chuckled.

"What is it?" I asked.

"Look at me," he said. "Here I am, railing on about drugs, and I've got half a dozen tubes carrying all kinds of stuff into my veins."

"But you're not in the bush," I pointed out.

"True enough," he said, his smile replaced by an expression of regret. He remained motionless for a moment, then suddenly looked up at me. "What were we talking about?"

"Legends," I answered him.

"Ah, yes," he said. "Well, there were always lost gold and diamond mines. A tourist couldn't get two steps off the ship before someone was selling him an authentic map to an authentic lost mine. They were pretty well lost, all right," he added with an amused chuckle. "Most of 'em never did get themselves found." He paused thoughtfully. "After I'd been on Peponi for thirty years or so, I started hearing all kinds of rumors about human goddesses living out among the Bluegills."

"Were Bluegills supposed to have produced them?" I asked dubiously.

"Of course not," he replied. "In most of the stories, they were girls who'd been stolen from their parents' farms and raised as Bluegills. Lot of people went out looking for 'em, too; in fact, though not many people knew it even back then, that's what Ramirez was looking for when he discovered diamonds in the Great Western Desert."

"Were all the legends about goddesses, or were there any about gods?"

"Going into the bush after a man ain't quite as romantic," responded Hardwycke wryly. "Funny thing, though—the only one they ever found was a man."

"Oh?"

He nodded. "Nobody ever did find out where he came from or how he got there, but one day Bushveldt Tesio found him living with some Bluegills on the outskirts of the Northern

Desert. He couldn't speak any Terran at all, he lived on raw fish, he walked kind of hunched over and swinging his arms like the wags do. Tesio bought him from the Bluegills and took him back to his farm and tried to raise him like a Man, but he died a couple of months later."

"Were there any stories of feral children?" I asked.

"Kids raised with animals? Yeah, there was supposed to be one up above the polar circle, running with a pack of those shaggy white carnivores they've got up there, but nobody ever found him." He paused. "Had some *men* go feral, but I suppose that ain't the same thing. There was Hakira, who lived in a cave with his Demoncat, and Papagoras, a biologist who wound up building a two-room shack out by the Rashar River and keeping about fifty big millipedes as pets, and I remember a woman called Mercer or Mersin or something like that who actually tamed a pack of Nightkillers. Of course, by the time I left Peponi, there were so many scientists living with the animals while they studied 'em that they were practically tripping over each other, especially out on the Siboni Plains."

"Did *you* ever go off searching for a legend?" I asked.

"Just once," he replied.

I was in Berengi between safaris (said Hardwycke), and I was staying at the old Royal Hotel, like most of the hunters did when they were in town. A bunch of us were gathered around the Thunderhead Bar in the lobby, mostly talking about Fuentes. He'd just left Peponi for good, saying that it was getting too damned crowded, that the farmers and colonists had ruined the place, and we were feeling pretty glum, because he truly was the best of us all and we hated to lose him. It was ironic that he was the leader of Johnny Ramsey's safari, and that Ramsey had put Peponi on the map and made it so popular that Fuentes couldn't stand it any longer.

Still, it wasn't just the safari business that had changed the shape of the planet. All you had to do was go into Berengi every few months and you could practically see it change right in front of your eyes. When I arrived on Peponi, Berengi had maybe three hundred people, and was mostly two blocks of prefab shops and buildings. By the time Fuentes left it had a population of 16,000, and the police were leaning on us not to upset the locals when we came into town to blow off steam. You used to be able to stand by the window of your room in the Royal and pot Landships and Sabrehorns as they grazed on the hotel's lawn; now you couldn't find anything bigger than a Willowbuck within five miles of town. You'd come back from safari, and for the last half hour you weren't even sure you were still on Peponi: there was nothing but farmland as far as the eye could see. Sure, there'd be an occasional herd of Silvercoats grazing by roadside, and the meat farmers complained that there were still a few Bush Devils in the area, but it sure as hell wasn't like the old days. When I landed on Peponi, I walked all the way to Oxblood's camp, because there were only about twenty landcars on the whole planet; by the time Fuentes left, there was bus service among all the nearby towns, and a weekly airplane between the continents. Berengi's streets were getting so full of traffic that they actually had to erect stoplights, and it could take you twenty minutes to walk from the Equator Hotel to the Royal.

There were two brand-new hotels for tourists, and a couple of nightclubs to keep them happy while they were waiting to go out on safari. The Bluegills had started moving into town, too, and maybe 30,000 of them lived in shacks they had erected on the outskirts. They hawked their crafts to the tourists, and set up a big market about half a mile south of the Royal.

Anyway, we were sitting around the Thunderhead Bar, swapping reminiscences about Fuentes, and at one point Jumbo Neysmith asked if Fuentes had ever found the Golden Kingdom. Nobody knew what he was talking about, so he told us that he and Fuentes had been hunting Dashers down by the Connectors when they heard the legend of a city made entirely of gold, that wasn't run by Men or Bluegills but by some humanoid race that no one had ever seen. Neysmith wasn't interested, but Fuentes had a contract for another book, so he began questioning the wags who mentioned the city and started taking notes.

"Did he ever find it?" asked Bocci.

"Never even went looking for it, as far as I know," answered Neysmith. "I guess it'll just be a footnote in his next book."

Someone else asked where it was supposed to be.

"Smack dab in the middle of the Impenetrable Forest," said Neysmith, "halfway across the Great Western Continent, maybe a thousand miles north of where Ramirez found his diamond mine."

"Figures," said Bocci.

"What do you mean?" I asked.

"Anybody makes his way through *that* forest deserves to find a golden city," he said. "There's places there where it rains every minute of every day, and places where the sun has never pierced through the branches to touch the ground."

"You've been there?" asked Neysmith.

"On the edges," answered Bocci. "Terrible place. You can't get warm and you can't get dry, your clothes rot away and your weapons don't work, and they must have five hundred diseases that haven't even got names yet. Ain't worth going there just to find the Balguda."

"You *have* heard of it!" exclaimed Neysmith. "You know their name."

"I've heard there's a tribe of humanoids in there called the Balguda," replied Bocci. "I ain't ever heard of no Golden Kingdom."

"You weren't curious enough to look for it?" persisted Neysmith.

"I told you—I never even *heard* of it," said Bocci. "Besides, even if I had, it ain't worth the effort."

"Since when is plundering a city of gold not worth the effort?" asked someone else.

"You ever *been* to the Impenetrable Forest?" asked Bocci contemptuously. "It's eight hundred miles across, and you need a machete or a panga ten feet into it."

"Use a laser gun."

"And set fire to the whole damned thing?" retorted Bocci with a dry laugh. "A laser gun will set even that wet wood to blazing." He paused. "Besides, get anywhere near the middle of it and you'd be footslogging through two or three feet of water, running blind in the middle of a perpetual thunderstorm."

"Has anyone ever tried to spot it from overhead?" I asked.

"Can't see nothing from up top," said Bocci. "Those trees are a couple of hundred feet high, and there are two or three canopies of interlaced branches. Hell, there's probably twenty species of animal in there that no one's ever seen."

"Maybe twenty-one," said Neysmith meaningfully.

"Bah!" snorted Bocci. "Fuentes had the right idea. He'll make more money writing 'em up than you'll ever make looking for 'em."

"I'm due to take a client out that way next week," I said. "Maybe I'll take a look."

"You'd be wasting your time," said Bocci firmly.

"It's my time," I said.

"And your client's."

"Maybe I'll look around after I send him home," I said. "Or maybe he'll want to come along. He's a camera hunter. This is his third trip here, and he's got most of the holos he needs from the Great Eastern Continent."

"Want some company?" asked Neysmith.

"Not really," I said.

"I could be your meat hunter," he persisted.

"If you're so hot to find this Golden Kingdom, why haven't you looked for it before now?" I asked.

Suddenly a guilty look spread over his face. "I have."

"How many trips?" asked Bocci.

"Five, so far."

"Waste of time," reiterated Bocci.

"I've got time to waste," replied Neysmith. He turned to me. "But I don't have any more money. That's why I need to hire on with you."

I shrugged. "Okay," I said. "Come along as my meat hunter, and we'll spend a couple of weeks nosing around after I send my client home."

"It's a deal," he replied. "And if we find the Golden Kingdom, we split fifty-fifty."

"Sixty-forty," I said. "Don't forget—it's *my* safari."

"Sixty percent of nothing is nothing," said Bocci sardonically.

I shared his opinion, but what the hell, I'd gotten myself out of the chore of meat-hunting for a couple of months, so as far as I was concerned I was ahead of the game already.

I stayed in Berengi another six days, waiting for my client, a pleasant little man named Walker, to arrive. I always enjoyed blowing off steam in Berengi for a day or two, but by the third day I usually got to wishing I was back in the bush. Cities, even small ones like Berengi, didn't appeal to me, and after a couple of days in town a hunter would come to realize that even though the safari business had never been better, he was on the way to becoming a walking anachronism. Cities are built by people who want a permanent home, and farms are worked by people who are tied to the land; those of us with wanderlust in our souls may be necessary in the beginning, but we're just passing through. Some, like Fuentes, leave early, and some, like me, leave a little later, but eventually all of us leave. Every paved street, every house with a solid foundation, every cultivated piece of land, is just another nail in our coffins.

In fact, on the day I left with Walker and Neysmith, the

government gazetted the first national park. They took almost three thousand square miles right in the middle of the Siboni Plains and outlawed all hunting. I think I knew then and there that my days on Peponi were numbered. It wasn't outlawing hunting; it was the damned *fences*, even if they were just lines on a map.

Still, it was easy to ignore all that once you set out across the savannah. It took us a day to fly to Bakatula, the major town on the Great Western Continent, and the next morning we were driving across the grasslands, with Magadi and two of my Sorotoba trackers in tow. The Silvercoats were migrating up from the south, and they brought with them their attendant carnivores and scavengers. In fact, there was so much food on the hoof that even the Nightkillers, which would usually eat anything, were actually getting fussy about which carcass they would take after one of the big carnivores was done with it. The rains had just ended, and it seemed like all of Peponi was green and in flower. Rivers that had been dry scars on the earth just a month ago were filled with rushing water, and most of the grasseaters had young with them. It made me happy that I was out with a camera hunter this time and that Neysmith was in charge of procuring meat for the table; it was pleasant just to lean back and enjoy the scenery for a change.

We spent three weeks getting Walker the holos he wanted, packed him onto a plane back to the spaceport in Berengi, and then set out for the Impenetrable Forest. We drove due west for almost four days, making about 200 miles per day over rough terrain, and finally we came to the forest's outskirts. The land began getting hillier and more heavily-wooded, and before long most of the animals that relied on sight and speed, like the Silvercoats and Dashers, were left behind. There were scattered herds of Landships and Thunderheads, and an occasional Sabrehorn, but mostly we saw various species of wildbuck—I brought one back that had never been classified before, and got it named after myself—and a number of Tree-crawlers, chattering and swinging overhead from limb to limb.

Neysmith pulled out a map and showed me where he had made his unsuccessful forays into the forest, and we eventually decided on a route that would take us south and west. We made it another fifteen miles before the forest became so dense that we had to leave the car and continue on foot. Magadi set up a base camp and remained behind with the car, while Neysmith and I took the two Sorotoba trackers with us.

We footslogged into the forest for two days, probably not making more than ten miles a day. I never saw so many insects or millipedes in my life, and we had to stop every couple of hours to burn some tiny bloodsuckers off our feet. On the night of the second day it started raining, and it didn't stop. We spent a day in our minibubbles before we realized that it wasn't going to stop anytime in the foreseeable future, and so we began walking again. The two wags started complaining about evil spirits, but we proceeded for another day and a half before I decided we had gone far enough.

"What about the Golden Kingdom?" demanded Neysmith.

"To hell with it," I said, pulling the hundredth or maybe the thousandth insect out of my ear. "At the rate we're going, we could spend half a year walking and not even make it the other side of the forest. My own guess is that we haven't traveled thirty miles total. Whoever named it the Impenetrable Forest knew what he was talking about."

Well, he threw a fit and did everything but threaten me with his sonic pistol, but I remained adamant. I'd had enough of bugs and rain and cold.

"Well, *I'm* not quitting!" said Neysmith, picking up his backpack.

"You're free to do anything you want," I said.

"I never wanted to give you sixty percent anyway," he said.

"To quote our friend Bocci, one hundred percent of nothing

is nothing," I said. "We'll wait a day by the landcar, just in case you change your mind."

He just glared at me contemptuously and then turned and went off down an animal trail. I told the wags we were going back, and for the first time in four days they started smiling and singing.

And then the strangest thing happened. My two Sorotoba trackers, who could have found their way home blindfolded from Balimora or even the Jupiter Mountains, got hopelessly lost. They had marked our trail, of course, but nothing stays marked in that damned forest. The rain had obliterated our tracks, and enough animals had rubbed against the trees that all of the marks were gone.

We wandered through that damned forest for close to a week, but there was no way to tell where we were. My compass, which was supposed to be waterproof, had stopped working, and we couldn't see the sun or the stars because of the clouds and the terraced branches.

There was enough game so that we were in no danger of starving, and we certainly weren't about to die of thirst, but it was the closest I've ever come to panicking on safari. We couldn't just sit there, and yet we didn't know for a fact that every step we took wasn't taking us farther from the landcar and deeper into the interior of the forest. I remember thinking at one point that if we were going the wrong way, at least we might wind up seeing the Golden Kingdom before we died, and I decided that I'd have traded the view and the riches for just seeing the sun one more time.

Then one morning one of the Sorotoba pounded on the door of my minibubble, and I walked out to find myself confronted by half a dozen of the strangest-looking Bluegills I'd ever seen. They were half again as tall as the normal wag, skinny as rails, and covered with incredibly complex designs that had been burned into their hides.

It took about half a minute to learn that they didn't speak

any of the common dialects, so we tried communicating by sign language. I managed to convey our predicament to them, and they volunteered to lead us back, if not to the landcar, at least to the forest's edge.

It was then that I noticed that two of them were wearing golden ankle bracelets. I pointed to them and tried to ask where they'd gotten them, but I couldn't make myself understood. Finally, just as a shot in the dark, I gestured at the lot of them and asked, "Balguda?"

It got a reaction, sure enough. I was expecting them either to smile and nod, or to look blank, but instead they began frowning and one of them raised a sharp stick that he used as a spear and threatened me with it. They calmed down after a moment, and I made no further references to gold or the Balguda.

It seemed certain to me that they'd heard of the Balguda, and just as certain that they weren't on friendly terms with them, which was fine by me: all I cared about was getting out of that damned rain forest.

I thought we were in for at least a week's trek, but we actually came to Magadi and the landcar in less than two days. When I activated the car and showed them how it worked, two of them raced off in terror while the other four gathered around and stared at it in amazement. I brought down a Taylor's wildbuck for dinner—the rifle didn't surprise them at all, which led me to believe they'd seen them before—and invited them to stay and share our meal. They spent the entire night with us, and then sat around the landcar in the morning, waiting to watch it speed off.

Through still more signs, I finally got them to understand that we were waiting for Neysmith, and that we'd probably spend a couple of days in this location before we gave up on him and went home. Finally they nodded, bade us farewell, and trotted off.

I spent the rest of the morning cleaning and polishing my

weapons. Then, just after noon, the tallest of them returned and walked slowly across the little clearing to the landcar, carrying something in his hand.

As he got closer, I could see that it was Neysmith's head. I drew my pistol and trained it on him, but he explained, through a variety of gestures, that he hadn't killed him. I asked who did, and he pointed toward the forest in a manner that led me to believe that the killer or killers were some considerable distance away.

"Balguda?" I asked.

He nodded.

I tried to get him to describe a Balguda, or to tell me where they lived, but he just kept grimacing and shaking his head, and finally I gave it up. At last he placed Neysmith's head on the ground and faded back into the forest.

"Well, at least he found his Balguda, whatever the hell they are," I said after a moment.

"Do you suppose there really *is* a Golden Kingdom, Boss Hardwycke?" asked Magadi curiously. "After all, these wags"—he uttered the word contemptuously, as always—"certainly didn't make the gold anklets they were wearing."

"You know," I said, "the answer to that was a lot more important to me before we entered the forest than it is now."

That was true then, and it's true now.

Four

Hardwycke's color was bad, and he seemed to have lost even more weight. For the first time since I'd known him, the curtains were drawn over his window, as if he no longer cared for the sunlight.

"Welcome back, Mr. Breen," he said weakly, when I entered the room. "I was afraid you wouldn't make it back in time."

"In time?" I repeated curiously.

"I coughed up a lot of blood last night. I'm not supposed to know it, but they expect me to die in the next couple of days."

I didn't know what to say, so I merely stared at him.

"No great loss," he said. "It's past time anyway."

"I'm sorry."

"I've made my peace," said Hardwycke. "I brought nothing to Peponi, and I took nothing out of it. But I would have hated to go without answering all your questions. After all, I'm the last—there's nobody left once I'm dead."

"Are you sure you're up to it?" I asked.

He smiled ironically. "It's not as if I've got any other pressing engagements." He paused for a moment. "How's your book coming?"

"It's a thesis," I said. "Though, with your permission, I think I might write a book as well."

"Don't need my permission to write about Landships."

"Not about Landships," I responded. "About *you*."

He tried to shrug, but was too weak. "Suit yourself," he said at last.

"Thank you," I said.

"But try to make it accurate," he continued slowly. "Hunting ain't as exciting or romantic as the holos and the videos make it out to be. In fact, a good rule of thumb for hunting Landships was that you walked twenty miles for every shot you took."

"Really?"

He nodded, coughed once, and struggled to catch his breath. "And any hunter might find his life in danger once or even twice during his career, but anything more than that was either carelessness or sheer foolishness."

I paused to consider my next question.

"Why didn't you stay?" I asked.

"On Peponi?"

"Yes."

"Almost none of us did."

"I know," I said. "But I don't know why. If you'd opened up some other worlds, it would have made sense to me, but you didn't. Fuentes retired to Deluros VIII, Ramirez went to Earth. Each of you seems to have retired rather than started anew—so why didn't you retire right there on Peponi?"

"Catamount Greene stayed behind," he responded, seeming to draw some strength from his interest in the subject.

"But then, he always had an angle; I remember once he bought Mount Krakwa from the Bogoda for six Dashers. Went out and shot 'em all in one afternoon." Hardwicke smiled at the memory, then became serious. "As for me, I didn't like what Peponi was becoming. Oh, it was inevitable that it would get civilized, but that didn't make it any easier to take. Once you've seen paradise, you don't like to watch it become just another world."

"It still had vast tracts of unsettled land when you left it," I pointed out.

He gasped for breath again, then held very still for a moment, and finally answered my question.

"Everything was mapped," he said. "Once you've got maps, you've got boundaries, and once you've got boundaries, you've got titles and deeds. What you don't have is Peponi, not the way I knew it." He paused. "I could see what was happening, and I knew it was time to get out or start thinking about becoming a farmer or a shopkeeper, and settling down just wasn't to my taste."

"Why did so few of you open other worlds?" I persisted.

"Peponi was like a greedy mistress," he replied. "The more you offered her, the more she took. She took your youth, and your energy, and your health—everything you had to give. It takes a lot out of a man to civilize a world, and it's self-defeating in the end, because the kind of man who does it doesn't want to see the results." He paused again, longer this time. "There just wasn't anything left to give to another world. The sun would take all the life from your skin, the diseases would sap your strength, the dust would get into your lungs and never leave them." Suddenly he smiled. "And there isn't a hunter anywhere in the galaxy who's not missing some skin or an earlobe from the days when he was stupid enough to stand in front of his client."

"Once you left, did you ever keep in touch with any of the people you knew there?"

"No," he said. "I ran into Bocci once or twice, and every now and then I'd hear that Johnny Ramsey had made another speech or written another book. But I never sought any of them out."

"Why not?"

"What for? To sit around and moan about what they had done to our planet?" He paused. "You know, I met a couple of youngsters who went there to fight against Buko Pepon a few years back, and it was like they were describing a different world. Nothing sounded like the Peponi I knew."

"When did you make up your mind to leave?" I asked.

"After I came out of the Bukwa Enclave," he said. "A lot of us left then. We knew we'd never have another hunt like that, so it seemed a good time to leave."

"*You* were in the Bukwa Enclave?" I said, surprised.

"Hell, anyone with a gun was there."

"I read Taylor's account of it," I continued. "He never mentioned you."

Hardwycke snorted contemptuously, and his anger seemed to renew his strength. "Henry Taylor was the biggest liar anyone ever met."

"Oh?"

"He never set foot in the Enclave. Got all his stories hanging around bars in Berengi, and then wrote himself up as the Great Landship Killer."

"Who *was* there?"

"Well, there was me, and Catamount Greene, and Hakira, and Bocci, and old Ephraim Oxblood came back from the Connectors for it, and Starmount, and Bailey, and Rashid, and the Paris Brothers, and Gabe Pickett, and—"

"Gabriel Pickett?" I interrupted.

"That's right."

"Wasn't he the father of Amanda Pickett?"

"Yes, he was."

"I've read all of her books," I said. "I *thought* his name sounded familiar."

"Damned good writer, Amanda Pickett," commented Hardwycke.

"I seem to remember that Gabriel Pickett was a farmer, not a hunter."

"He was—but most farmers did a little Landship poaching on the side to help pay off their mortgages." He smiled again. "I noticed that that little tidbit didn't make it into any of Amanda's books."

"Did you ever meet her?"

"Long time ago. She was just a kid back then. Shy little thing, quiet and standoffish. No way in the world you could look at her and guess she was going to become Peponi's most famous writer." He paused. "She came by it honestly, though; Gabe Pickett kept the most thorough diaries of any man I ever knew."

"He did?"

Hardwycke nodded. "You might want to look at them someday. They might be of interest to you."

"I'm sure they would," I said. "Perhaps I'll try to hunt her up one of these days."

"Couldn't hurt," he agreed. "Last I heard, she was living on Barton IV."

A nurse entered just then to refill some of the medications that were dripping slowly down the tubes that led into his left arm and leg, and I turned my head away until she was finished.

"It's okay to look now," rasped Hardwycke when she had left the room. He smiled in amusement. "I'd have loved to watch your face the first time you saw an animal being skinned."

"It would have been worth the price of admission," I admitted, somewhat embarrassed.

"Don't let it bother you," he said. "Different things affect different people. You don't like the sight of blood. Me, I never could stand being confined."

I thought of him spending the last eight years in this tiny room, and I didn't know what to say. He seemed to read my mind, because he said, "Ain't nothing to see out there anyway."

"Are you up to talking about the Bukwa Enclave?" I asked gratefully.

"Might as well," he said. "It was the last great hunt on Peponi." He paused. "I'll say this for us: we sure as hell went out with a bang instead of a whimper."

What you have to understand about the Bukwa Enclave (said Hardwycke) is that everything came together at once. To begin with, the planetary Governor decided that Peponi was too big for one man to keep tabs on everything, so he divided it up into twelve districts, each with its own District Commissioner. Eleven Commissioners were in place within a month, but the twelfth, the one whose territory included the Bukwa Enclave, was in a hospital halfway across the galaxy and wasn't expected to arrive for almost six months.

Also, a little war had erupted on Columbus II, which was less than two light years away, and about three-quarters of Peponi's military personnel were transferred there for the duration.

Then came the news that the Republic's jewelers were so desperate for eyestones that they would now accept blues and clears.

So what you had was a situation in which the military was no longer out there enforcing the law, the Bukwa district had no Commissioner, and you could sell any eyestone you could take, no matter what color. This led to virtually an open season on Landships, and the highest concentration of Landships on the planet was the Bukwa Enclave, a huge savannah between the Jupiter Mountains and the Dust Bowl.

Once the word went out that the jewelers were buying, everyone—and I mean *everyone*—headed up to the Enclave. It wasn't just the hunters; I mean, hell, there were never that many of us to begin with. But hundreds of farmers like Gabe Pickett took off for Bukwa, and they were joined by miners and traders. I never saw them, but I heard stories that there were even some Bluegills up there, operating entirely on their own.

Catamount Greene was one of the first to arrive. He'd been living in Berengi, scrounging for credits here and there, ever since the government made him give up being the Human King of the Bogoda, and he didn't know the first thing about tracking, but old Catamount never let minor details like that stop him. On the way to the Enclave he stopped by his old stamping grounds and picked up a bunch of trinkets and jewelry from the Bogoda, then found one of the few military outposts left in the Bukwa area and explained that he was trading Bogoda artifacts to the wags who lived in the Enclave. He gave a few of the better ones to the soldiers, bought them a couple of drinks, and went on to say that he was terrified of Landships and that he had heard that the Enclave was filled with them—and within ten minutes he had talked them into marking where the herds were on a map so that he could avoid them while he hawked his wares from village to village. He walked into the Enclave with one weapon, three bearers, and his map, and walked out a month later with more than 3,000 eyestones.

Bocci, who had made up his mind to leave Peponi, stuck around just long enough to clean up in the Enclave. He found a water hole way out at the western end, staked it out, poisoned it, and picked up 700 eyestones without ever firing a shot.

Jumping Jimmy Westerly went in with a stepladder, took it out in the shoulder-high grass where none of the other hunters would go, climbed atop it, and potted twenty Landships the first day he was there. Once they cleared out of the area, he followed them, always keeping to high grass. He'd set up his ladder again whenever they stopped, and he kept right on doing it until he had his thousand eyestones.

Other hunters used other methods. Hellfire Bailey brought in a whole tribe of Dorado, who used poisoned spears and arrows and brought down almost three thousand Landships before the new Commissioner finally showed up and the soldiers returned from Columbus II.

After a couple of months, the Enclave began to resemble a war zone, and I don't just mean the piles of Landship carcasses. First of all, a lot of the farmers really didn't know much about hunting, and more than half a hundred of them were killed by Landships. Then, as the Landships themselves started getting harder to find—the ones who survived didn't want to go anywhere near anything that smelled like a Man or a Bluegill—some of the hunters started marking off territories.

Kalahari Jenkins took a dry area, about forty miles square, at the northwestern tip of the Enclave, announced that it was his personal hunting ground, and swore he'd kill anyone who wandered into it. A miner named Kennedy wandered in one day, chasing a couple of Landships, and Jenkins blew him away. What he didn't know was that Kennedy had six sons, and this started a blood feud. Lasted a couple of weeks before they killed him—I seem to remember that he got four of them first—and then the two remaining sons declared that it was now *their* territory. That lasted about five days, until Hakira came up from the south with that damned Demoncat of his. The Demoncat killed the last two Kennedy boys, and Hakira never fired a shot; he just gathered up all of Jenkins' and the Kennedys' eyestones and lit out for Berengi.

Nobody ever found out what happened to the Maracci Sisters. They were damned good hunters, those girls—but one day they just disappeared, both of 'em, and no one ever found the 800 eyestones they were supposed to have taken.

After about five months, word began coming back from Berengi that the price on eyestones had dropped because so many were coming in, so those of us up in the Enclave started going after other stuff as well, Bush Devil skins and anything else that might have a market value. I never did see a Sabrehorn, but they say that Bocci killed the very last one on the planet up in the Enclave.

After a while, even the scavengers couldn't keep up with the abundance of carcasses, and the place became a charnel house, with Landship carcasses everywhere. Some of the Nightkillers got overly bold and started attacking humans, and we damned near had a war on our hands for a while there . . . but after a while the few remaining packs of Nightkillers went back to eating Landships.

Then the District Commissioner finally arrived. He started making all kinds of pronouncements, but he was powerless to do anything until he got his soldiers back from Columbus, and by then there weren't enough Landships left to make hunting them worthwhile.

When the dust had cleared, the best estimates were that less than five hundred men had gone into the Bukwa Enclave, and that in less than six months three million eyestones had come out. It was the last great hunt, on Peponi or anywhere else, and an awful lot of fortunes were made there. Only about half the men who went in came out, but most of them never had to worry about money again.

They took Catamount Greene to court and charged him with poaching. That was nothing new—they were *always* taking him to court over something or other, and he always beat the charges, just like he beat this one. But they took about twelve other hunters to court, including Bocci and Hellfire Bailey, and some of them *didn't* beat the charge. Their money was confiscated, and they were given a choice: five years in jail or take the next ship off Peponi and never come back.

I went to the trials, and as I sat in the back of the courtroom, I realized that we weren't being judged by any jury of our peers. Hell, all of our peers were dead or on trial. I looked around the room, and all I saw were settlers and farmers and merchants, and you could tell just by studying their faces that they found men like Fuentes and Hakira and even Johnny Ramsey an embarrassment. You know how you feel ashamed of the way you used to act when you were a kid? Well, they were ashamed of the men who opened up Peponi. Oh, they knew that what we did was necessary, but you could tell that they had decided times were changing and we had outlived our usefulness.

They even asked the planetary Governor to testify, and he promised in no uncertain terms that he would bring the full power of the government to put an end to poaching. He didn't stop there, either. He announced that he was going to regulate hunting much more carefully, and that Peponi was creating fifteen game parks to go with the one they'd gazetted on the Siboni Plains. He started rattling off the locations, and I realized that I had just been put out of business: every area I had ever hunted was going to become an animal preserve.

It didn't matter much by then, because I already knew it was time to leave. You looked at all those faces and listened to the official pronouncements, and you knew that Peponi was changing too fast. Oh, there'd be hunting for another twenty or thirty years, but it was on the way out. Navy teams were coming in to map out unexplored territories, even the Impenetrable Forest. The hotels didn't want us coming into town and blowing off steam after a safari, and suddenly Main Street was lined with a batch of safari companies that no one had ever heard of, each of them offering their clients seven exotic worlds in less than a Galactic Standard month. They promised to pick a client up at his hotel, fly him right to the edge of a herd of Landships, give him an hour of thrills while he shot his trophy, and get him back to the Royal Hotel in time for a late lunch and an evening of pub-hopping and native entertainment.

I stuck around a few months, hoping I might find something that would convince me I was wrong. Even had a couple of jobs offered to me as a park warden. I almost took one; I got as far as negotiating the right to do some limited hunting, just for my dinner pot, but in the end I turned it down. Nothing wrong with the kind of people who come out to the parks, but they weren't *my* kind of people. I could understand camera buffs like Walker, who I'd taken out four or five times; he'd stand there taking holos of a charging Demoncat and get furious with me if I tried to turn it before it got within ten yards of him, or he'd climb into a tree to get a holo of a Bush Devil eating a Silvercoat it had dragged up there to keep it safe from scavengers. But I had no interest in the kind of camera hunters who would drive across the parks, intent only on the number of animals they could holo in a day's time, and I had a feeling they would outnumber the Walkers by hundreds to one.

Then there was the matter of poaching. A number of wags had set up shops in Berengi and the other towns, and there was no question that their tribal brothers were supplying them with illegal eyestones. In fact, it was the Dorado and the Kia who brought the Sabrehorn to extinction, not Men. And there was no way you were going to close down a poaching operation if the wags wouldn't testify against their tribal brothers. So I just couldn't see any future in the game warden business.

I considered buying a farm in the Greenlands up beyond Berengi, but I was used to walking across the land, not digging in it. I even looked into taking on some younger partners in my safari company and spending most of my time in Berengi, but Berengi was just a town, and I didn't like towns. Besides, I had all the money I needed, and I didn't propose to spend the rest of my life working at a job that I didn't like.

In the end, I suppose I was just wasting a little time, trying to get all the images of Peponi set in my mind, before I left it for good. And there was never any question about coming back: no one ever goes back to Peponi. Whatever it was that brought you there has got to change before you leave, and once it *has* changed, you don't want to see what it's become. It wasn't just the hunters who felt that way; even Amanda Pickett hasn't been back there since Buko Pepon took over —and he tried like hell to get her back. Even named a district after her, and they've never done that for any other human.

I suppose I ought to make it clear: it wasn't Peponi that was dying. It was growing by leaps and bounds, and a steady stream of Men kept immigrating there. What was dying was a way of life that had existed on Peponi. I suppose that the old-timers, the men like Fuentes and Bocci and Hakira and Hellfire Bailey and Catamount Greene and me, were very much like the Landships and the Sabrehorns and the Demon-cats: we were colorful and we created a lot of interest in the world, but now that civilization was spreading across the face of the planet, we simply weren't necessary anymore. You could never tell when one of us, an old hunter or an old Demoncat, might frighten an investor off. And since we were as wild as the animals, they never could quite trust us to behave the way we were supposed to. We were a potential embarrassment at best, a potential source of disaster at worst; they weren't exactly sorry to have had us, but they sure weren't sorry to lose us either.

People still go to Peponi to see its beauties and its animals, and they still enjoy themselves; they visit the cities and the game parks, they ski down the mountains and swim in the oceans, they visit the wags in their villages and their cities, and they go home with wonderful stories to tell.

But they'll never set off on a trip down a river, or through the high savannah, and know that they were the first to ever see this particular place. They'll never know the feeling you get when you see a herd of Silvercoats so big that it takes them a full day to pass by. They'll never see a Landship or a Sabrehorn, except in a museum. They won't wake up in the morning, hundreds of miles from the nearest town, with the knowledge that they're free to go anywhere and do anything they please, that a whole world is there for the taking. They'll smell the air and see the flowers and watch the avians circling overhead, and if they're lucky they might see a carnivore on a kill, but it won't be the same. For one thing, they'll be on a schedule—here in the morning, there at noon, someplace else at dusk—while there were times, back in the old days, when I couldn't even have told you what month it was. If they're late getting back to Berengi, they'll miss their flight connections and panic their travel agents; if I was two or three weeks or months late returning to Berengi after a hunt, anyone who was waiting for me would still be there, drinking in the Thunderhead Bar, or they would have left a note for me on the Message Tree in front of the Equator Hotel. The Peponi I knew didn't have any calendars or clocks or fences, and that Peponi is gone forever.

I arrived on Peponi a few years too late, but I left at the right time. Whatever it's become now, I don't want to know about it.

I brought nothing with me to Peponi; I took nothing out.

I have no regrets.

Well, just one: I wish I could have seen it as Oxblood and Fuentes first saw it, when it was truly Paradise.

II
Noon

Five

It had been two years since August Hardwycke's death.

I had completed my paper on Landships, received my degree, briefly joined my father in his import/export business on Altair III, found it unsatisfying, and quit. I finally sold a highly-romanticized article on Hardwycke's career to a popular magazine, and thus encouraged, I wrote two more articles, placed them with lesser-paying but more prestigious markets, and suddenly discovered that I had embarked upon a career as, if not a journalist, at least a biographer of August Hardwycke. It seemed more interesting than importing wood pulp from the Delta Scuti system—anything would have been!—and I soon obtained a contract to write a book about his life.

Since Hardwycke's death I had reread Amanda Pickett's *Peponi Days* twice, on both occasions marveling at her remarkable felicity of expression and her ability to make even

the harshest of living conditions seem exotic and beautiful. Somehow the fact that she had seen her father die from
overwork, lost her husband in the Kalakala Emergency, and
eventually went bankrupt were passed over so briefly that one
hardly noticed them. She wrote very selectively of the Peponi
she remembered, emphasizing those aspects that she found
praiseworthy and ignoring the less savory events of her life.
As Hardwycke had put it during one of our conversations,
every line of the book was true, but the book itself was one
big lie.

However, it was not only the most moving evocation of
Peponi, but far and away the best-selling one as well (always
excepting Johnny Ramsey's hunting memoir), and I wrote to
her a number of times, requesting permission to interview her
and read her father's journals. At first I received polite replies
from her that she didn't grant interviews, but when I wrote
to tell her that I had finally gotten a contract to write Hardwycke's biography, she sent me a handwritten note, inviting
me to spend a weekend at her home on Barton IV.

I immediately accepted, and now, some two months later,
I stood before the entrance of her angular chrome and glass
home, waiting for her security system to scan my passport.

The door slid into a wall a moment later and I found myself
staring into the catlike, vertically-slit pupils of a female Bluegill. Her appearance was made even more startling by the
human maid's uniform she wore. I was so surprised to see a
native of Peponi here on Barton IV that I simply stood and
stared at her.

"Won't you please come in, Mr. Breen?" she said in heavily-
accented Terran, ignoring my reaction. "My mistress is expecting you."

"Thank you," I said, recovering my composure.

She led me through a circular foyer and down a corridor to
a pentagonal study, one wall of which was entirely glass and
overlooked a small brook that ran through a wooded yard. A

tall, slender, elegant woman in her mid-sixties arose from a high-backed chair and stepped forward to greet me.

"Welcome, Mr. Breen," she said, extending her hand. "I am Amanda Pickett. I trust you had a pleasant journey?"

"As spaceship trips go," I said, taking her hand.

She was stylishly dressed, her brown hair was exquisitely coiffed in the latest Deluros fashion, and her fingers and wrists were covered with rings and bracelets which never came from Peponi. All in all, she was hardly the sturdy former farmgirl that I had expected, nor did she seem to wear the mantle of serenity that I was sure the authoress of *Peponi Days* must possess.

"That will be all, Nora," she said to the Bluegill. "Please get Mr. Breen's luggage and take it to his room."

Nora nodded, bowed, and left the room.

"Does she live here?" I asked.

"She has been my servant for more than forty years, Mr. Breen," replied Amanda Pickett, "as was her mother before her. If her presence makes you uneasy, I can—"

"It doesn't bother me at all," I assured her. "I was just surprised to see a Peponite here on Barton IV." I paused awkwardly. "By the way, I want to thank you for agreeing to see me."

"I don't usually have visitors, Mr. Breen," she said. "This should be an interesting experience for both of us."

"May I ask why you finally consented to my visit, then?"

She smiled. "First, because I admire your persistence. And second, because I took it upon myself to read two of your articles about August. I realize that you had to slant your pieces for the markets, but I decided that if you are really going to write a book about him that I owed it to him—and to Peponi—to help you make it as accurate a book as possible." She paused. "May I offer you a cup of tea?" She gestured to a sterling silver service that had been set out on a matching tray.

I didn't like tea, but I thought it politic to accept her offer. As she filled my cup, I looked around the room.

"I recognize that painting," I said, indicating a three-dimensional portrait. "It's very good."

"Thank you," she said. "It was presented to me by Jonathan Ramsey himself when I won the Sampson Prize. Since then it's appeared on a number of my dust jackets." She paused. "The landscapes on each side of it are by a local painter."

"And the holograph?" I asked, indicating a small holo of a khaki-clad man. "Is that your father?"

"My husband," she replied. "He died on Peponi."

There was only one bookcase in the room. It was made of a beautiful alien hardwood, and held a bible, her six volumes of fiction, her two-volume biography of Commodore Quincy, a number of other books of varying sizes, and a leather-bound gold-leafed copy of *Peponi Days*, which was generally considered to be her masterwork. Scattered here and there throughout the room were various literary awards and plaques, but nowhere could I see any mementos of her life on Peponi.

"Won't you sit down?" she asked, indicating a long leather couch. I did as she asked, and she handed me my tea.

"Thank you," I said.

"You're quite welcome," she replied, seating herself opposite me on a matching chair.

There was a momentary silence as she seemed to be studying me. Finally she said, "I read the Landship treatise you sent me, Mr. Breen."

"Matthew," I corrected her. "What did you think of it?"

"It suffers from a little too much romanticism, but it's relatively accurate, given the few sources you had to work with."

"You felt I romanticized the Landships?" I asked, puzzled.

"The hunters," she replied. She looked directly at me. "Have you ever seen a Landship, Matthew?"

"Only in holos and museums," I admitted.

"I grew up with them."

"I know," I said, not quite knowing what to say next.
She stared at me for a moment. "Tell me a bit about yourself, Matthew."

"Well, there's really not much to tell. I spent my childhood
reading the works of Fuentes and Johnny Ramsey. I majored
in exobiology, and when it came time to write my thesis, I
chose to write about the extinction of the Landships. I met
August Hardwycke in the course of my studies, and decided
that he had lived such a fascinating life that I wanted to write
a book about him." I paused uneasily. "Just before he died,
he suggested that your father's journals might make some
mention of him, and might even have recorded some exploits
that he himself had forgotten. And of course you knew him
personally."

"You must understand that I was still a teenager when
August Hardwycke left Peponi," remarked Amanda. "I only
met him a few times."

"But you do remember him?"

"Certainly," she replied. "He was a very dashing, romantic
figure."

"Even to someone who had been raised on Peponi?" I
asked, surprised.

"You act as though everyone on Peponi went out exploring
new lands and hunting wild animals," she said. "Most of us
simply worked for a living. Professional hunters were every
bit as exotic to us as they are to you."

"I'm sorry," I said with some embarrassment. "I've read
so many accounts of hunting Landships that I tend to forget
that it was a relatively rare occupation."

"I've read most of the literature on Peponi," she said with
some distaste. "It's a common mistake. Hunting memoirs
outnumber everything else by almost two-to-one." She

paused. "I understand why certain types of Men like to hunt animals. I have *never* understood why they feel compelled to brag about their conquests in print."

I decided not to mention the fact that she herself had described some of her own safaris in *Peponi Days*. "Anyway," I continued, "Hardwycke rarely mentioned those people who didn't share his profession."

"There's no reason why he should have given them any thought whatsoever," she replied. "After all, he'd disappear into the bush for two or three years at a time, and when he wasn't in the bush he was usually in the company of his fellow hunters at the Royal Hotel."

"But he knew you and your father."

"He and my father were among the very first Men on Peponi; everyone knew everyone else back then. But as more and more humans immigrated there, they tended to stay within their own tightly-knit social groups." She paused and stared at me. "If you're to write a biography of August Hardwycke, you really should make an effort to learn about the colonization of Peponi."

"That's one of the main reasons I'm here," I assured her.

"It's one of the main reasons I sent for you," she replied. "Peponi was a world of great beauty and even greater contrasts, and you can't understand Hardwycke if you don't understand Peponi." She paused, then continued her brief history lesson. "Even after the Republic officially opened Peponi for colonization, there was no great interest in immigration. It was generally considered to be a dusty, savage little world whose main justification for existence was that ships on the way to Alpha Bismark II could refuel there."

"What about the diamond mines that Ramirez found in the Great Western Desert?" I interrupted.

"They made *him* rich, but they didn't do much for anyone else," she answered. "Alpha Bismark II was the world the Republic wanted—it had all that platinum and uranium. Pe-

poni was just conveniently located." She paused. "Anyway,
I doubt that more than two hundred Men arrived on Peponi
during the first two decades, so it was natural that most of
them knew each other."

"Hardwycke told me that before he'd been there thirty
years the human population was up to a million or more," I
said. "What caused such a rapid growth after such a slow
beginning?"

"Alpha Bismark," she replied ironically.

"I beg your pardon?"

"It got mined out in less than two decades." She smiled
wryly. "So much for the Gem of the Outer Frontier. Suddenly
nobody needed a refueling station on Peponi any longer, and
the Republic had to find a new way to pay for its presence
there, so it began advertising for farmers and homesteaders,
practically giving the land away to anyone who would come
and work it."

"I see," I said.

She shook her head. "No, I don't think you do. You've
never been to Peponi, but take my word for it: most of the
land—everything except the Greenlands, actually—is virtually useless for agriculture."

"Didn't word of that get out?" I asked.

"Of course," she replied. "You can't keep something like
that a secret."

"Then why did people still go to Peponi?"

She smiled. "When you know the answer to that, Matthew,
you'll be well on your way to understanding what made Peponi
unique." She paused. "More tea?"

"No, thank you."

She got to her feet. "You'll have to excuse me for a few
minutes, Matthew, but I have to send a message to my literary
agent on Deluros VIII. Also, I was in the midst of replying
to some personal correspondence when you arrived. I think,"
she added, "that you might be more comfortable in your own

room while I'm working." She walked over to the bookcase and pulled out a very large, very old volume. "This should keep you occupied in the meantime," she said, handing it to me.

"What is it?" I asked.

"Sort of a family scrapbook," she replied. "These are holos from Peponi."

"Are they labeled?" I asked.

"A few of them." She pressed a small button on one of her bracelets, and Nora instantly entered the study. "And now, Mr. Breen—"

"Matthew," I interrupted.

"Matthew," she amended. "Nora will take you to your room. I'll send for you when I'm finished."

"Thank you," I said, falling into step behind Nora.

We walked down a short corridor and came to a single door, which slid back as we approached it.

"This is to be your room for the weekend," announced Nora, in precise but heavily-accented Terran. "I hope that you will find it satisfactory."

"I'm sure I will," I said, setting the scrapbook down on one of the two large beds. I noticed that my luggage had been placed on a stand right next to a closet.

Nora pointed to another door. "The bathroom," she said.

"Thank you."

"Will you be needing anything else, my gentleman?" she asked.

"Not really," I said. "I would like to ask you a couple of questions, though."

"Yes?" she said, turning to me.

"How long has it been since you left Peponi?"

"Thirty-three years, my gentleman."

"Don't you miss it?"

"I miss what it was, my gentleman," she replied. "I do not miss what it has become."

"What *has* it become?"

"I'm sure that my mistress can explain it far better than I can."

"Does the fact that you are still her servant a quarter of a century after Independence ever bother you?" I asked.

"I am not a servant," she replied with dignity. "I am a maid."

I considered asking her the difference, but I didn't want to appear to be baiting her, so I thanked her for answering my questions and dismissed her. I quickly unpacked my bags, then sat down on the room's only comfortable chair, and began looking through the album. Some of the earlier holos were badly faded, as if they hadn't been sprayed with the proper preservatives (as indeed they probably hadn't), but while the colors were poor, I was nonetheless able to make out the subjects quite clearly.

Most of the early holos were simply different views of the farm that Amanda Pickett had made famous in *Peponi Days*; though I had never seen it, I had no trouble identifying the rambling old farmhouse, the butchery, the schoolhouse Pickett and his daughter had erected for their native squatters. There were a number of shots of his Beefcakes, that hardy hybrid meat animal that had been imported to Peponi, and which the natives, who never fully comprehended the concept of a monied economy, soon began breeding and collecting as their own form of currency.

There was only one holograph of Amanda's mother, a tall, slender, truly lovely woman. Amanda herself appeared in almost a third of the shots, as a baby, a toddler, a little girl, an adolescent, a young woman, and finally as the owner and manager of the farm. Gabriel Pickett looked like any farmer anywhere—lean, hard, and overworked. He seemed to age almost from one holograph to the next, and vanished entirely about halfway through the book.

There were holographs of a number of Gabriel Pickett's

friends: most were farmers, but I was able to identify a middle-aged August Hardwycke in two of them, and I learned for the first time that Fuentes and Johnny Ramsey had stopped there at some point during their historic safari. There was also a very little man with a huge hat that a scribbled caption informed me was the infamous Catamount Greene.

Here and there were holographs of Landships drinking from a nearby river, or a Bush Devil that Amanda herself had killed when it tried to kill one of the Beefcakes . . . but most of the animals in the holos were pets: a baby Silvercoat, a lame Dasher, even an orphaned Sabrehorn. At one point the farm must have resembled a cross between a children's zoo and an animal orphanage.

Some of the most interesting holos, however, were those of the Peponites (which, thanks to my association with Hardwycke, I still thought of as Bluegills). There were shots of the household staff, the kitchen staff, the gardeners, and the farm laborers, all clad in immaculate white outfits. They may have worked virtually for free, but there were still an enormous number of mouths to feed.

And then I came to the end of the book, and there were no animals, no natives, not even Amanda. There was just her husband, weapons strapped to his waist and slung over his shoulder, looking grim and hard, and I decided that these must have been taken during the Emergency.

Then, on a whim, I went back to the middle of the book and started looking at the young Bluegill faces, trying to see if I could spot Buko Pepon—but the fact of the matter, I realized uncomfortably, was that one youthful native face looked very much like another to me. If he was there, I couldn't recognize him. In fact, I couldn't even spot Nora, and I had seen her just twenty minutes ago.

I studied the faces further, wondering: What does one look for in a child who will grow up to be the Moses and Messiah of his people, a leader whom the Republic will first equate with Satan Incarnate and then revere as perhaps the greatest alien statesman of his time? A steely glint of eye, a hardened jaw, a face reflecting an inner compassion? He could have been any of those ill-clad native youngsters or none of them; there was simply no way to tell.

I was still staring at the book, thumbing through its pages, when Nora entered the room and announced that Amanda Pickett was ready to receive me once again. I tucked the book under my arm, followed her down the corridor, and was facing Amanda in another moment.

"Did you find it interesting?" she asked, taking the scrapbook back from me.

"Fascinating," I replied. "Is there a holo of Buko Pepon in here?"

She shook her head. "No, he was raised about three miles away."

"You knew him, though?"

"I met him occasionally when I was growing up, and we attended college together on Deluros VIII. I believe he was the first of his race ever to attend an off-world school." She paused. "He was Robert Prekina back in those days. I don't think he actually changed his name until after he graduated from college."

"What was he like?"

"He was a very unusual little wag, and he grew up to be a very unusual big wag." She stopped suddenly. "I hope my use of the term *wag* doesn't offend you. It's a word I grew up with, and it never had any improper connotation before Independence."

"Not at all," I replied. "I'm still trying to stop thinking of them as Bluegills. I suppose it's Hardwycke's influence."

"Please don't use that word in front of Nora," she said seriously. "*That's* a term they might have killed you for, even before Independence."

"So I gathered," I said. "By the way, I noticed only one

holograph of your mother, and you made no mention of her in your book. When did she die?"

"About thirty years after the holograph was taken." I must have looked puzzled, for she continued: "My mother ran away with another man when I was three years old."

"A colonist?" I asked.

"Colonists were the only men she ever met." She paused. "There was a pretty wild crowd that lived about an hour to the north of Berengi. They hunted and they partied, and they vied with each other in creating splendid estates—but with very few exceptions, they were actually subsistence farmers, producing no more than they and their squatters could consume. It was a very attractive life for a woman who always had to work and never knew any luxury."

She fell silent, and I decided that it was time to change the subject.

"I see from your album that Johnny Ramsey visited your farm," I noted.

"Johnny Ramsey was first, last, and always a politician, even when there were no offices left to run for. He stopped at every farm he could find, just to shake hands and pass the time of day. I was only four years old at the time, and I truly don't recall his visit." Suddenly she smiled. "My father used to say that he could have made an excellent living just printing up 'Jonathan Ramsey Slept Here' plaques."

"He must have been one of the most colorful characters ever to set foot on Peponi," I said.

"They were *all* pretty colorful back then," she replied. "Personally, my vote would go to Catamount Greene."

"Not Hardwycke?"

She shook her head. "He spent all his time in the bush. Catamount was always in the thick of things. He made eight or nine fortunes on Peponi, and lost every one of them." She paused. "You knew, of course, that at one time he was the King of the Bogoda?"

"I've heard about it."

"It's a sore point with them nowadays, and they've written it out of their history books, but it's the truth," she said. "The Bogoda were always the major tribe on the Great Eastern Continent, just as they are today . . . but when humans started arriving on Peponi, they refused to have anything to do with us. They wouldn't trade with us, wouldn't work for us, wouldn't even let us pass through their territory. Catamount walked into Bogodaland literally on a bet; he didn't speak the language, and had no interpreter with him." She smiled. "Two years later he was their king."

"How did he manage it?" I asked.

"That depends on whose story you believe. According to him, he found two warring villages, offered his services—and his molecular imploder—to the smaller one, won the battle for them, and proceeded methodically through Bogodaland, ending wars and consolidating territory." She paused. "My own guess is that it was much less romantic than that. A number of the Bogoda were suffering from various minor diseases, and I believe he simply imported enough medication to cure them. By the time I met him, the Bogoda revered him more as a witch doctor than a conqueror." She sighed. "But however he did it, there's no question that he became their king.

"In fact," she continued, "at one point the government ordered his arrest for making treaties with the Bogoda without their authority. They sent a squad of twenty soldiers into Bogodaland to take him back to Berengi, and when they got there they came face to face with 50,000 armed Bogoda warriors. Naturally, they weren't anxious to try to take him anywhere—but then he decided to give himself up, so he walked all the way to Berengi with a few hundred bodyguards, marched them into the courtroom, and demanded an immediate trial. The judge took one look at his retainers and threw the case out of court."

"How did you meet him?" I asked.

"Our farm was *in* Bogodaland," she replied. "You couldn't live there for any length of time *without* meeting Catamount Greene."

"I never saw Bogodaland listed on any map."

"We didn't call it that, but the wags did."

"What did you call it?"

"Oh, there were numerous names for all the tiny towns that sprung up, but the entire area, except for a couple of national parks, is still referred to as the Greenlands."

"The Greenlands? That's supposed to be the breadbasket of Peponi, so to speak."

She nodded. "The Greenlands encompass almost all of the truly rich farmland on the continent—which, I might add, isn't much. After the colonists found out how poor the rest of the land was, they petitioned the government to restrict the Greenlands for human use only, and the government agreed."

"And Catamount Greene arranged that?" I asked.

"No, Catamount was just an adventurer and a scalawag," she answered. "A charming one, to be sure—but he had no more interest in the problems of the farmers than he had in anything else that didn't line his pockets with money." She paused. "No, the man responsible for getting the government to give us the highlands was Commodore Albert Mason Quincy."

"I read your biography of him," I said. "It was the first book you ever wrote, wasn't it?"

"That's correct."

"I'd love to see the statue of him that they erected in Berengi," I continued. "The holographs of it were very impressive."

"They tore it down the day after Independence," she replied with an expression of nostalgia tempered by bitterness. "It used to stand at the north end of Commodore Quincy

Avenue, which was once Main Street and has since become Buko Pepon Boulevard."

"I wasn't aware of that."

She nodded. "He'd been dead for twenty years, but he was still a symbol of everything they hated."

"Did you know him well?" I asked.

"I didn't know him at all," she answered. "I knew *of* him, of course; every colonist did. He was, in a very real sense, our guardian angel. But I didn't receive the commission to write his biography until after he had died." She paused. "Would you like to meet some people who knew him personally?"

"Very much so," I assured her.

"There's a group of about thirty Peponi expatriates on Barton IV," she replied. "I've taken the liberty of inviting a few of them over to dinner this evening."

"Thank you," I said. "I very much appreciate it." I paused. "Is there some reason why there are so many of you here on Barton IV?"

"We tend to be a little clannish," she answered. "And we have a shared experience that no one else can truly comprehend."

"Living on Peponi?"

"No," she corrected me. "*Surviving* on Peponi."

Six

The Peponi expatriates that Amanda Pickett invited to her home were a mixed lot.

There was Wilkes—I never learned his first name—a lean, bronze-skinned man who looked more like a hunter than a farmer. He wore a bracelet of braided hair from the tail of a Landship, which was totally out of place with his formal attire, and yet it was the bracelet, rather than the outfit, that seemed proper. He had lost his right arm in the Kalakala Emergency, and I had a feeling that his left eye, too, was artificial, though I never asked him. I suppose he would have made an excellent and loyal friend, but my initial impression was that I certainly wouldn't want to have him for an enemy.

There was Malcolm Pepper, a neat little man with the affected dress of a dandy, who looked like he had never been within fifty light years of Peponi. He wore more jewelry than

Amanda, every hair was exactly in place, his face had been treated so that he no longer grew hair on it, and I was able to detect slight traces of mascara and rouge. His shoes may not have been the brightest things he owned, but they came close. I had a difficult time picturing him facing a Demoncat or even an unplowed field, but he looked like he would have been right at home at the notorious Dalliance Club in Berengi.

There was Jessamine Gaines, a pudgy, gray-haired woman, as tanned as Wilkes, who had buried four husbands in Peponi's unfertile soil: one had been killed by a Bush Devil, one by a Thunderhead, and two by disease. She wore no jewelry except for a rather garish red eyestone on which had been engraved the tiny likeness of the Landship from which it had been taken.

Finally, there were the Crawfords, an octogenarian couple, both small and very wrinkled, evidence of their years spent working in the Peponi sun. Neither of them spoke much, she from choice, he because he was very sensitive about the lisp made by his prosthetic tongue—his real one had been cut out during the Kalakala Emergency.

They all arrived within a couple of minutes of each other, and by the time introductions had been made, Amanda escorted us into her living room, where we all seated ourselves while Nora brought us drinks.

"So, my dear boy," said Pepper, lighting an Antarrean cigarette and placing it into a long gold holder, "Amanda tells me that you're writing a book about August Hardwycke?"

"That's right," I replied.

"He was before my time," continued Pepper. "A most brutal man, or so I've been given to understand."

"I didn't find him so," I said.

"How else may one describe a man who dedicates himself to a career of butchery?" said Pepper pompously. Then he shrugged. "Be that as it may, he left Peponi before most of us had arrived. I fear that we're not going to be of much use to you."

"I'm not so sure of that," I replied. "You've all lived on Peponi. I'm always interested in the reasons why five people should walk out of paradise."

Wilkes snorted contemptuously. "Paradise? Whatever gave you that notion?"

"That's what the word *Peponi* means," I answered.

"Well, perhaps it *was* paradise," acknowledged Wilkes after a moment's thought, "back when Landships and Sabrehorns roamed the planet and men like Hardwycke were free to wander and hunt where they wanted." He paused, frowning. "But that was a long time ago, Mr. Breen, and a lot has happened since then."

"Commodore Quincy tried to make it a paradise," added Jessamine Gaines, "but the Republic fought him every step of the way."

"It wasn't just the Republic," said Wilkes. "It was those damned bloody wags!"

I turned to Nora, who had reentered the room and was walking from one guest to another, serving drinks, but if she heard what was said she gave no indication of it. They seemed happy to ignore her existence, and she, for her part, seemed quite content to be ignored. I wondered if all Peponites had been treated like this in what everyone fondly referred to as the "old days."

"Whatever it was," said Jessamine, "it ceased resembling paradise a long time ago. Still, I have hopes for it."

"Then why did you leave?" said Wilkes gruffly.

She shrugged. "It was time. Everything was changing. I left the day they buried Catamount Greene. He seemed to represent the old Peponi, and when he died it was as if the last vestige of the Peponi I knew had died with him."

"He was from the old Peponi, no question about it," agreed

Amanda. "And he was the one human they left totally alone during the Emergency."

"They were scared to death of him," said Wilkes.

"No," said Jessamine. "I think they worshipped him."

"Same thing," said Wilkes.

"Maybe I'm writing about the wrong man," I said, carefully setting my drink down on a silver coaster. "The more I hear about this Catamount Greene, the more I think *he's* an excellent subject for a book."

"One more barbarian for the semi-literates to worship," said Pepper distastefully.

"Aren't you being a little harsh on him?" I said.

"My dear boy, he actually *lived* with the Bogoda for three years!" replied Pepper. He leaned back on his cushioned chair, fingers interlaced, as if there was obviously nothing further to say on the subject.

"There's only one man worth writing about," said Wilkes, "and that's Commodore Quincy. The worth of a man isn't how many amusing stories you can tell about him, but what kind of mark he leaves behind him. If Hardwycke and Greene and Fuentes and the rest of them had never lived, it wouldn't have made a bit of difference. If Quincy hadn't been the man he was and gone to Peponi when he did, the planet's entire history would have taken a different course."

"True enough," said Crawford. They were the first words he had spoken since we had been introduced. Then he added, "The stupid son of a bitch!"

"That's your injury speaking, not you," said Jessamine.

"My husband would be a whole man if it weren't for Quincy and his policies," said Mrs. Crawford heatedly.

"We've all been through this a hundred times," said Wilkes, leaning forward intently. "You didn't object to those policies when they were benefiting you. None of us did." He paused. "Your husband lost a tongue; I lost an arm. Others lost a lot more than either of us. It's part of the price we paid to tame a world. And if the Republic had had the guts to back us up, it would have been *worth* the price."

"Rubbish," said Pepper, paying no attention to Nora as she reentered the room and filled his glass again. "If the wags wanted that silly old dirtball that badly, I'm perfectly willing to let them keep it."

"You say that because your life hasn't changed in the least since you left," replied Jessamine. "But most of us loved Peponi. We gave everything we had to it."

"I've heard all this before, my dear," said Pepper with a bored expression. "It usually precedes a three-hour deification of Commodore Quincy."

"The man was a saint," said Jessamine firmly. "An absolute saint."

"The dear old boy used to tear up the Royal Hotel every time he went on a binge," noted Pepper. "I'd hardly call that saintly behavior."

"But he always paid for it," said Jessamine.

"He also shot a couple of wags who had the temerity to enter the Thunderhead Bar while he was there," interjected Amanda disapprovingly.

"What's wrong with that?" demanded Wilkes. "He paid his fine, didn't he?"

"I can see where the wags might have objected anyway," I offered.

"What do *you* know about it?" said Wilkes, turning to me. "You can't possibly know what things were like back then, Mr. Breen. We were colonists on a distant world, outnumbered by tens of thousands to one. We *had* to establish certain rules or we would have been overrun."

"We were anyway," said Crawford.

There was an uneasy pause.

"Only after the rules were suspended," said Jessamine at last, shifting uncomfortably on her chair. "If Commodore

Quincy had lived, there never would have been an Emergency."

"Or if there had been, he would have put it down in less than a week," said Wilkes decisively.

Amanda shook her head. "He'd have been the first one they killed."

"Right," agreed Crawford.

"The Siboni would have protected him," said Wilkes. "He was always doing favors for them."

"There were ten million Bogoda and only half a million Siboni," answered Amanda. "What could they have done?"

"They could have *fought!*" said Wilkes. "One Siboni is worth twenty Bogoda!"

"They wouldn't have had the slightest idea what they were fighting for," said Pepper, downing his second drink in a single swallow. "Most of them still live in their charming grass huts and hunt for dinner with spears and arrows."

"He's quite correct, you know," said Amanda to Wilkes. "The Bogoda run the planet. I don't think any Siboni has ever run for office, or served the government in any capacity."

"That's because they're warriors," said Wilkes stubbornly. "Quincy knew that. That's why he went out of his way to befriend them. If he had been alive during the Emergency, he'd have turned them loose on the Bogoda and we'd all still be on Peponi."

Amanda shook her head again. "The old days were coming to an end even before the Emergency." She sighed. "All those immigrants, all those tourists—it just wasn't the same. Berengi changed so much from one month to the next that you almost didn't recognize it."

Jessamine stared directly at Crawford. "And you can't blame Quincy for *that*."

Nora entered the room and walked up to Amanda, who arose a moment later and announced that dinner was ready. We walked into the large, elegantly-appointed dining room, and I found myself sitting between Wilkes and Jessamine Gaines, facing the Crawfords. Amanda and Pepper sat at opposite ends, and Pepper immediately busied himself selecting the wine for the table.

"Have *you* an opinion about Commodore Quincy?" Jessamine asked me when we were all seated.

"I only know what I've read in Amanda's biography of him," I said cautiously. "I know he managed to get the Republic to decree that only humans could farm the Greenlands, I know he was the political leader of the colonists, I know that his estates were the largest on Peponi, and I know that he died without a credit to his name."

"It was because of his efforts that most of us didn't share his financial destiny," said Jessamine.

"You mean because the Greenlands were so fertile?"

She shook her head. "When the Commodore arrived, there were only two or three farmers on the whole planet. I believe that he even predated your friend Hardwycke."

"By about five years," confirmed Amanda.

"He was an incredibly wealthy man," continued Jessamine, "and he was totally committed to Peponi. He grew corn and wheat and it died. He imported cattle and sheep from Earth and they died. He planted soybeans and they died."

"Why?" I asked.

"Because Peponi isn't Earth, or any other planet. It's Peponi, with its own soil, its own parasites, its own diseases. Crop after crop kept failing, breed after breed of animal kept dying, and the Commodore kept pouring more money into his farms. Finally he imported Beefcakes, and began growing mutated tea and sugar berries, and when they thrived everyone else followed suit—but by then he was already so deeply in debt that he couldn't pull himself out."

"More than that, though," added Pepper, as Nora brought the salad to the table, "he was our cultural as well as our political leader. That much I'll grant the old boy. He could afford to import the latest Deluros fashions, and pretty soon everyone else would follow suit. He would recommend a book, and everyone would read it. And in his dealings with the government, he was the exact opposite of your newfound hero Catamount Greene."

"I got the distinct impression from Amanda's book that he held the colonial government in contempt," I noted. "Since Hardwycke led me to believe that Greene and the rest of his contemporaries shared that view, doesn't that imply a certain similarity?"

"Only in philosophy, not in conduct," said Pepper. "Allow me to give you two examples to show you how they handled similar problems. Who knows? Perhaps you can find some way to use it in your book—in which case I shall expect to see my name in a footnote."

"If I can use it, I'll be happy to give you the credit," I replied.

"One day, about fifty years ago, some soldiers were bringing a herd of Beefcakes through the northern desert into Berengi, to feed the garrison that was stationed there. They came down with some fever or other, and it seemed likely that the Beefcakes would die of thirst before the soldiers were healthy enough to continue their march. Your friend Greene had been poaching Landships in the area, and chanced across them. They offered him fifty credits per head to deliver the herd, and he accepted—but when he arrived in Berengi and presented his bill, the governor decided that his men had made a poor bargain under duress, which was indeed the truth, and offered Greene only twenty credits a head.

"Greene was in his usual foul mood when he left the governor, and he wandered over to the bar at the Equator Hotel." He paused for a moment as Nora began collecting the salad dishes and carrying them off to the kitchen. "Now, it just so happened that some of the local farmers were holding a meeting at the Equator bar that evening to protest the Republic's agricultural policies—and in less than five minutes Greene had them up in arms and ready to march on the governor's mansion. He led them through the streets, and when they reached their destination he told them to wait outside while he presented their list of grievances to the governor.

"He left them lined up at the gate, walked into the governor's office, took the dear man over to the window, pointed at the huge group of enraged farmers, and explained that they were there to protest the government's breaking its promise to pay him fifty credits a head for the Beefcakes. The governor decided that he had a potential riot on his hands, and paid Greene the rest of the money. Then Greene went back to the farmers, assured them that the governor was looking into their grievances, and suggested that they all go home before they did something they might regret." He paused and then grinned. "The next morning he'd bought a new landcar and was back poaching Landships and Sabrehorns."

I laughed appreciatively, amid polite smiles from the rest of the listeners, who were obviously well-acquainted with the tale.

"Now, to contrast that," continued Pepper, as Nora brought out the main course, a local gamefish in a wine sauce, "let's examine how dear old Commodore Perry approached the problem of a hostile colonial administration." He paused to insert a new cigarette in his holder. "When the Republic went to war against the Staghhi, the miners and shipbuilders in the Spica system found themselves short of food, since the war affected the normal transport routes. So the Republic ordered the governor of Peponi—the same beleaguered soul who had had dealings with Greene—to ship all of our exports to Spica II and Spica VI at something less than competitive prices. Do you know what Quincy did when his appeals to the governor failed?"

"No," I lied, for I had of course read Amanda's account of the incident. Still, if her biography of Quincy was as inaccurate

Peponi Days, it certainly couldn't hurt to hear a firsthand description.

"Well, to begin with, this pillar of civic virtue burned down the governor's mansion."

"*That* got their attention," put in Wilkes between mouthfuls.

"Then, since he, perhaps more than anyone else, realized that for the first and probably last time in its history, the Republic actually *needed* Peponi, he led a march on the spaceport, shut it down, and presented the Republic with a list of demands. He refused to reopen it until they agreed to pay top dollar for our exports. They also had to promise that there would be no reprisals after the Staghhi war, and the Republic had to pledge, in writing, that they would never recant their decree that the Greenlands were reserved solely for human use." He paused. "*That's* the difference between men like Greene and a man like Quincy. Greene was a scoundrel and a scalawag who could lie and bluff his way out of almost anything, whereas Quincy never bluffed. He was fully prepared to let the entire planet go bankrupt if the Republic hadn't given in to his demands."

He turned to me expectantly, as if I were supposed to make some comment.

"And did the Republic keep its word about not punishing him after the war?" I asked as a matter of form, for again, I had read the answer in Amanda's book.

"Absolutely! In fact, the dear man became so popular that they actually offered to make him the Governor of Peponi!" laughed Pepper.

"He turned it down," said Wilkes, "or we'd all still be there."

"If it hadn't been for Buko Pepon, he'd still be revered as the most important figure in Peponi's history," added Jessamine.

"I disagree," interjected Amanda, with the air of one who had explained her position time and again. "If it hadn't been for Quincy, there would have been no Buko Pepon. There would have been a subsistence farmer named Robert Prekina."

"Did they ever meet?" I asked, finally remembering to take a bite of my dinner, and deciding that I didn't like the local fish very much.

"Not socially, that's a certainty!" said Pepper, looking vastly amused. "Quincy had no use for any wags except his Siboni pets. But I imagine Pepon must have seen or heard him speak from time to time."

"Probably not," said Amanda. "Pepon was still a child when Quincy died."

"Still, I suppose we couldn't have had one without the other," said Jessamine with a sigh.

There was a momentary pause, which was finally broken by Wilkes.

"We should have blown the little wag bastard away the first time he stepped out of line," he said.

Crawford nodded his agreement. "There's no sense being kind to them; they simply don't understand it. I tried it, and look where it got me."

"If Quincy had known what Buko Pepon would become," continued Wilkes, "he'd have killed him at birth."

"Then there would just have been someone else," said Jessamine. "Pepon was better than some of them would have been. At least we're all still here."

"*Here*," repeated Wilkes angrily. "Not *there*!"

"That's not entirely fair," put in Amanda. "He invited everyone to stay."

"I was there for the death of everything we loved," lisped Crawford, forcing the words out. "I didn't have to stay for the wake and the funeral, too."

"Generosity," muttered Wilkes. "That was our first mistake. Give them a little education, pay them a little money, and suddenly they forgot everything we did for them."

"It was their world," I said.

"It was a goddamned jungle!" snapped Wilkes. "Who do you think built the towns and roads—the wags? *We* sweated blood to tame that planet! A lot of good men died in the process, but we got the job done, the way Men always get the job done. In the process, we showed them how to fight disease, how to make their land productive, gave them all the benefits of a Republic colony—and look at how they repaid us." He paused for breath. "Hell, if it wasn't for us, they'd still be sitting around naked in the dirt!"

"You see, Mr. Breen," said Jessamine, "we don't hate the wags. We never did." Wilkes snorted contemptuously, and she glared at him before turning back to me. "They've re-written their history books to make it look as if we had en-slaved them, but it just isn't true. They benefited from almost everything we did . . . but you can't expect to civilize an entire world of savages in one or two generations. Did you know," she added, "that when Men first arrived on Peponi, there was no word in any of their dialects for '*wheel*'? They'd never seen one! Surely no reasonable man could expect us to hand over a planet to a people who had no written language, who consulted witch doctors and magicians, who worshipped fifteen or twenty gods and tortured domestic animals as a religious ritual. Even Commodore Quincy realized that some-day they would have to control their own destiny . . . but he knew that it would be many generations before they were ready to do so."

"But he was mistaken," I pointed out. "They're doing it right now."

"Are they?" she shot back. "They owe the Republic billions of credits that they'll never be able to repay, they've over-grazed most of their grasslands, and their standard of living is lower now than before Independence." She paused. "Quincy knew that they'd behave exactly like this if they were given their independence too soon. That's why he kept them out of the Greenlands; he foresaw that they'd turn it into a desert if they weren't educated in modern farming technology. You know, there was a time, and not so long ago, when the Greenlands produced enough to feed the entire planet. Now they import more than half their food."

"They make Quincy out to be a demon now," said Wilkes. "They even had a public celebration the day they tore down his statue. But if it hadn't been for him, there wouldn't even have been a city to house the damned statue in the first place."

There was another uneasy pause, as they waited to see if the outsider was going to make any further misstatements about the past.

"I'm very interested in something Amanda said a few moments ago," I said after a moment, when it became obvious that no one else was going to break the silence.

"What was that?"

"That Buko Pepon asked all the humans to remain on Peponi after independence."

"He did more than ask," said Wilkes contemptuously. "He practically begged."

"How many Men took him up on his offer?"

"There were about a million of us on the planet," said Amanda. "I would guess a third of us stayed."

"How have they fared?"

"You'd have to ask *them*, wouldn't you?" said Wilkes.

"There've been no anti-human pogroms or anything like that?" I continued.

Pepper laughed. "My dear fellow, the Republic has a navy of eighteen million ships, and a standing army that numbers in the billions. Surely you don't think they'd stand still for a massacre, do you?"

"They stood still for Independence," I answered.

"That was a totally different matter," said Wilkes. "I don't mean to insult you, Mr. Breen, but you're speaking from ignorance."

"No offense taken," I said. "If I didn't want to cure my ignorance, I wouldn't be asking questions."

· "Oh, very well said!" chuckled Pepper. "Let's see you reply to *that*, Wilkes."

"From everything I hear, most of the Men who stayed behind are doing quite well," said Jessamine, getting back to my original question. "In fact, I've frequently toyed with the notion of moving back there myself."

"May I ask you a personal question?" I said.

"Yes," she replied warily.

"You've been gone for more than a quarter century. If you miss Peponi, why *haven't* you gone back?"

"Because the Peponi I miss no longer exists," she answered.

"Then why consider going back at all?" I persisted.

"Because that's where I was happiest," she replied thoughtfully. "Haven't you asked yourself why such totally different people should spend so much time together, Mr. Breen?"

"The question had crossed my mind," I said.

"It's because we've shared experiences that no one here on Barton IV, or anywhere else in the Republic, can appreciate. Even Malcolm, who can afford to live anywhere he wants, who never worked the land a day in his life and would run for cover if a Silvercoat approached him, has more in common with us than with anyone else on this world."

"True enough," admitted Pepper. "You can't know what it was like, Mr. Breen—and if you visited Peponi today you still wouldn't know. But there was a certain beauty to it back then, a certain feeling that each day promised a remarkable new experience."

"You would wake up every morning to clean fresh air," continued Jessamine. "You did nothing for yourself; you had servants for everything. The countryside was beautiful, rolling green land crisscrossed by rivers and dotted with animals. It could be a hard life when the rains didn't come, or the Landships ruined some of your crops, but somehow you knew that

if God had ever made a planet for Himself, it was Peponi."
She paused. "It seemed eternal and changeless, and even
though we could see change coming on the horizon we had
men like Commodore Quincy to push it back to where we
didn't have to think about it. Even the Emergency seemed
to reaffirm our feelings for Peponi, for now it was no longer
a gift, but a homeland for which we had fought the bloodiest
of battles."

"And then it all turned to dust," said Wilkes. "We fought
and we won, and the damned Republic gave it away."

"It wasn't that simple, and you know it," said Amanda.

"It was exactly that simple," reiterated Wilkes.

"I'm not going to argue with you again," said Amanda. "I
know your feelings about it, and you know mine."

Wilkes glared at her for a moment, but let the subject
drop.

During the meal I heard a lot more about Commodore
Quincy, and not very much about August Hardwycke, who
didn't seem to interest them as much, since he had had no
effect on their lives. Then, as Nora began removing the dessert plates, we adjourned to the living room for a mint-flavored
liqueur that had been imported from Peponi, and which everyone else seemed to relish although it was much too sweet for
me. Finally Nora saw that I wasn't drinking, and brought me
a cup of strong Peponi tea.

As soon as we had finished our various beverages, Pepper
announced that he had to leave, and offered Jessamine Gaines
a ride home. She accepted, and a few minutes later Wilkes
followed them. Then Mrs. Crawford went off with Amanda
to see some new purchase in her study, and I was left alone
with Crawford.

"Did you get your answers?" he asked with a pronounced
lisp.

"Not really," I said. "But I have a lot more questions now."

"Peponi's like that."

"You have no desire to return there?"

He shook his head. "If you found the perfect woman, had an affair with her, and then had to leave, would you really want to see her thirty years later when she was old and fat and toothless and avaricious, or would you like to remember her as she was?"

"I don't know," I said. "If I truly loved her, I think I'd want to see her again."

He shrugged. "To each his own."

There was a lengthy pause.

"It must have been wonderful to wake up to the sight of Landships in the distance," I said, breaking the silence.

"I woke up to many things," he lisped. "Landships, Bush Devils, flocks of avians so thick you could barely see the sky, droughts, monsoons, even the Kalakala."

"I'd love to hear about your life on Peponi," I said.

He checked his timepiece, then shrugged again. "Why not?" he replied.

Seven

We weren't among the earliest arrivals on Peponi (said Crawford), not like Hardwycke and Greene and Quincy. But we got there while it was still a wilderness, when a man had to fight the soil and the animals and the elements to make a living.

I'd been an officer in the Navy for eight years, and when I met and married Christina it seemed to me that it was time to retire and settle down. The Republic was practically giving away land on Peponi to veterans of the war against the Canphor Twins, so we decided to move there.

There were times during the first few years when we were ready to call it quits and admit we'd made a terrible mistake. The drought killed our first crop. Landships trampled our second. Our third crop came in—barely—and then floods washed our fourth away. You wouldn't think you could have drought *and* floods within three years of each other.

Bush Devils and Demoncats and Nightkillers picked off most of our meat animals the first couple of years, until I stopped using wire fences and began using thornbush enclosures like the Bogoda did. Looking back now, I don't know why we stuck it out—except that you'd wake up every morning and look out over the Bzenzi Hills and know you'd never find a more beautiful place no matter how many worlds you visited.

We had four children—three sons and a daughter—and raised them all to maturity, which is a pretty good record for a frontier world. I never thought I'd outlive them all, but I did, which says more about Peponi than it does about me.

Daniel, our firstborn, was the adventurous one. He had a pet Treecrawler that used to ride everywhere on his shoulder. One day a Bush Devil killed it. Daniel never cried, never said a word . . . but that night he was nowhere to be found, and I noticed that one of my sonic rifles was missing. Then, the next morning, just before we could launch a full-scale search for him, he came back dragging the Bush Devil behind him . . . and from that day on, he was the hunter in the family. Nothing could make that boy stay at his computer or do his lessons, but he knew the bush better than most professional hunters, and we never lacked for meat again. To the day he died he was barely literate, but literacy isn't exactly a survival trait on a world like Peponi. And when the drought would come every few years and the banks began demanding their money, Daniel would disappear for a month or two, and when he came back he had enough eyestones to hold the banks at bay until the next harvest.

Thomas was the son every father dreams of having: bright, handsome, hard-working. He always had his chores done, and spent most of his time locked away with his books and his computer, learning things for the sheer joy of learning. I always thought he'd have turned out to be a writer like you if he'd lived. He was a quiet boy, never caused anyone any trouble, got along well with everyone. I was thrilled when he married the girl from the next farm; I even expanded our house and gave him the new wing as a wedding present.

Caleb was our little savage. He was more Bogodan than the Bogoda. I'd yell at him until I was hoarse about keeping his distance from the wags, and five minutes later he'd be back by the squatters' huts, sitting cross-legged in the dirt and listening to all their crazy stories and legends. He even took to wearing a Demoncat's tooth hung around his neck to ward off evil spirits, and the more Christina and I would try to convince him that Men didn't mingle with wags, the more of a wag he became. I threw him out of the house the day he came home from the hospital, his skin all burnt from the brands they applied to him during one of their Rite of Passage ceremonies—he couldn't have been sixteen at the time—but we made our peace and he moved back in a couple of years later. Well, not exactly *in*; but he lived on the land, in his own grass hut. If Men and wags could interbreed, I wouldn't have put it past him to have taken a wag wife.

Jessica was always my favorite, and I spoiled her as much as one *could* spoil a child on Peponi. Probably I gave her too much. I remember when she was twelve we took her to Deluros VIII for a week, and that was probably a mistake; here was a girl who had never seen a three-story building, and suddenly she was on the capital world of the race of Man, rubbing shoulders with—what was the population back then?—eleven billion people, and surrounded by all those interlinked skyscrapers that almost blotted out the sun. I thought most kids would want to see more of the galaxy after being exposed to something like that—and maybe they would—but when she came home she threw herself into every aspect of the farm, and when it became obvious that Thomas would eventually be leaving Peponi to attend a first-class university and Daniel and Caleb had absolutely no interest in the farm, she begged us to let her manage the place. I don't think she ever willingly set foot off of it again. She didn't even like to go into Berengi to shop, and begged off making the trip whenever she could get away with it.

After we'd been there six or seven years, things began changing for the better. For one thing, we had good rains five years in a row, and by the time we hit another drought, Commodore Quincy had already developed a strain of mutated sugar berries that could thrive without water, so all we lost was our tea crop. We had Beefcakes by then, though they took an inordinate amount of work. They weren't native to the planet, and they tended to pick up almost every type of external parasite there was. We had to dip them three and four times a week to keep them healthy, and they tended to attract all kinds of predators.

Still, we finally started pulling ourselves out of debt, and we found that we loved the life we were now living. The three youngest children had so many pets—mostly orphaned animals—that I sometimes thought we were running a zoo, or maybe an animal infirmary, and there were times we almost had to forcibly restrain Daniel from appropriating some of them for the dinner table.

Our social life centered around the old Villa Hotel, a couple of miles from Commodore Quincy's estate on the eastern edge of the Greenlands. Every other Saturday there was a function of some kind—a pet show, a flower show, a concert, a dance—and we'd take the landcar there for the weekend and return home totally refreshed and ready to face the problem of coaxing a living from the land for another fortnight. Twice a year, during the rainy seasons, we'd go into Berengi and spend a week shopping; in the beginning we'd stay at the Royal or the Equator hotels, but when they became overrun with tourists, we joined a private club where we could spend time with our friends. The Dalliance Club is the one that got all the notoriety, but there were half a dozen more respectable clubs, and most of the locals belonged to one or more of them.

When we arrived, our land—it came to about two square miles—was totally empty, but within a day or two the company that sold it to us had erected our house and furnished it, and then called us into their office to select a headman. I wasn't even aware that we needed one, but they assured me that no Man worked his own land. The wages for a headman were something like two credits a week—a mixed drink cost you almost that much in the Thunderhead Bar—but they told me that it was a fair wage, and certainly no Bogoda ever complained to me about money.

We picked a tall, good-looking wag named Bill, and within a week he had brought some fifty or sixty of his relatives to the farm. They spent two days constructing their huts, and then went to work, plowing the fields and planting the seeds. It seemed to me that a tractor could do the job much faster and more efficiently, but it was explained to me by one of my neighbors that it was financially prohibitive to import farm machinery that far out on the Rim, and that even if the machinery were available, we'd be putting all our Bogoda out of work. I couldn't see that it made that much difference, since none of them had been working before we arrived, but they pointed out that the only way the Bogoda could have access to fertile land was if we allowed our squatters to plant kitchen gardens around their huts, and finally we decided that we might as well conform to the established practice, since we couldn't afford the tractors and harvesters anyway.

After we'd been there for about two years Christina set up a small infirmary, since the Bogoda seemed to be completely ignorant of all modern medical procedures, and they kept multiplying so rapidly that a year or two later we built a small schoolhouse on the grounds. We weren't qualified to give them a real education, but we did manage to teach most of them Terran, which made our lives a little easier, and we taught them the rudiments of contour farming and crop rotation. And by the time Caleb was five or six years old he could speak Bogodan like a wag, and we never had any communication problems after that.

Our Bogoda were a pretty decent lot, and we were really quite fond of most of them. We'd seen what happened to farms where the wags were treated badly, and we made up our minds that that would never happen to us. We had to punish them if we found them loafing or stealing, but we never flogged them, and the only wags who ever died on my property died from old age or disease or a millipede bite, never from a bullet or a whipping. (I think Caleb would have led an insurrection if we'd ever raised a hand against them.)

We were good to our Bogoda, and they were good to us. When they'd become so sick, or get so chewed up by an animal, that we couldn't cure them ourselves, we'd send them off to the wag hospital that the government had set up just outside Berengi, and we always took them back when they were healed. We had a couple of houseboys who became such fine cooks that I got them jobs in the kitchen at the Equator Hotel, and I saw to it that they got six credits a week apiece, since it was more expensive for a wag to live in town. The only major fight I remember having was when Caleb fell out of a tree he had climbed and broke his arm, and Bill, our headman, wanted to take him to the local witch doctor to get it fixed. I explained that we had to go to Berengi to get the arm set by a doctor, Caleb sided with Bill, and for a few minutes there I thought I was actually going to have to thrash the pair of them; but finally Bill gave in, and Caleb was in so much pain that after a while he didn't care who fixed his arm as long as it got fixed. The minute we got back from Berengi, though, Bill took Caleb to his tribal magician for some herbs and blessings, just in case the pressure cast didn't work.

That really was an isolated case, though. In fact, when the wags saw that our medicine cured them better than their own witch doctors could, they started converting to Christianity. They didn't understand much about it, but they knew our God was stronger than theirs—or at least that He was a better healer. I never could get used to all those shaggy alien shapes sitting in pews and grunting out hymns, but if it meant that we could keep them alive and healthy and working, I was willing to tolerate it.

Things went pretty smoothly even after the Commodore died. A lot of people had predicted that the Republic's alien-loving liberals would move in and start putting the wags in charge of various governmental departments, but we were too far out on the Rim for the Republic to notice. Besides, they had other problems—like the war against the Tibori.

In fact, if you want to know the turning point in Peponi's history, it wasn't Quincy's death at all. It was the Tibori war. It was only about eighty light years away, and of course most of the able-bodied men and women on Peponi volunteered for service, since the Yaronites and the Raboi were still at war with the Republic in the Core and the Spiral Arm, and most of our forces were needed elsewhere.

The Republic's biggest mistake was allowing us to use our wags. We didn't arm them, but we let them serve as noncombatants—such as cooks, couriers, and the like—since we were so shorthanded. The Tibori were dug in on five or six planets, and the action had degenerated into a ground war, since the Republic didn't want to totally obliterate such mineral-rich planets.

We finally won, but it took us almost two years, and when we came back there was something different about the wags. They had seen Men being killed by the thousands, and had seen another alien race hold us off for almost two years even though we outnumbered them and had more firepower, and suddenly, for the first time, there were signs of discontent.

That's when we started hearing about Buko Pepon. He'd been on Deluros VIII for about fifteen years, trying to drum up support for Peponi's independence, and with Quincy dead he was finally able to get the Republic's permission to organize a political party, even though wags weren't allowed to vote. He called it the Peponi Planetary Union, and he began lobbying the government in Berengi to grant the wags certain rights. Mostly they were little things, like being allowed to walk on Quincy Avenue, or the right to be represented by a wag lawyer in court (which was ridiculous, since there were only two wag lawyers on the whole planet), things like that.

In retrospect, we should have either given him everything he wanted or killed him right then and there, but we didn't. The colonial government granted the wags a few privileges in the hope that that would satisfy them, but Pepon kept lobbying for more. He had even written a book—*The Peponi I Can Almost See*, he called it—and had it published while he was living on Deluros. There must have been half a million copies sold there before anyone on Peponi even knew it existed.

When he finally returned to Peponi, he was arrested—but eventually they had to release him, since he hadn't broken any laws and there wasn't anything they could hold him for.

That was our second big mistake, because it made him a hero, especially among the Bogoda. Pretty soon he was speaking to rallies, and even our own Bogoda were sneaking off the farm to attend them. Some of the other farmers punished their wags for having anything to do with Pepon, but Christina and I could see the handwriting on the wall: bit by bit he was going to get them more and more privileges until they finally wound up running the planet, and since it was our home and we planned to remain there, we decided to make our accommodation with the inevitable.

I even let Caleb drag me along to listen to one of his

speeches, just to find out for myself what he was saying, instead of reading all the scare stories in the newspapers.

I can still remember my first sight of him. He was older than I thought, and he had a cloak made from the skin of a Bush Devil wrapped around a formal human outfit. He held the severed tail of a Silvercoat in one hand, and used it both as a flyswatter and a means of emphasizing his points. He was a totally charismatic figure, and he spoke for almost two hours. My Bogodan was never too good, so I didn't understand much of what he said, but from the enthusiastic responses of the crowd I got the gist of it, and I didn't like it. He wanted independence, which I had already known, and he wanted it *immediately*, which I hadn't known. He never exactly called for armed rebellion, but he made it clear that the Bogoda's patience was at an end. There was a certain urgency in his voice that I found very disconcerting.

Yet, when it was all over, Caleb led me through the crowd to meet him. I felt uneasy, for we were the only two humans there, but Caleb seemed not to notice or care; I suppose that emotionally he was every bit as much a wag as Pepon was.

"Ah, Mr. Crawford," said Pepon in absolutely perfect Terran, "your son has mentioned you frequently to me. How nice of you to attend our little meeting."

"I've read a lot about what you've been preaching," I replied. "I thought I ought to hear for myself."

"And now that you've heard, what is your opinion?" he asked.

"I think you're moving too fast," I answered honestly.

"If we left it to the government, there'd be no movement at all!" interjected Caleb heatedly.

"It is impolite to interrupt your father, Caleb," said Pepon gently. He smiled at me. "On the other hand, I happen to agree with your son. Have you a response to his statement, Mr. Crawford?"

"Yes, I do," I said. "To the best of my knowledge, only

seven members of your race have had a higher education. To be perfectly blunt about it, most of them still live like savages, and have no more interest in self-government than they have in advanced mathematics. How can you reasonably expect to form a functioning government?"

"Let me respond with a question of my own," said Pepon. "There are less than a million Men of Peponi, while there are more than two hundred million of us. How long can you reasonably expect to keep us in bondage?"

"Not much longer," I admitted.

He smiled. "You see? We *do* agree on at least one point."

"But we'll have to educate an entire generation to become civil servants and bureaucrats," I continued.

He shook his head firmly. "We have given you too many of our generations already; we cannot sacrifice yet another."

"No alien race has ever won an armed rebellion against the Republic."

"If you will read my book and study my speeches, you will find that I have never urged my people to take up arms. I have been to Deluros; I know that we could never hope to match the military might of the Republic."

"Let me suggest that passive resistance won't be very effective, either," I said.

"I do not believe in passivity," said Pepon firmly.

"Then I don't see how you can possibly achieve your goals."

"We will achieve them because they are just and honorable," he said. "And historically inevitable. Peponi was well-named; it can be a paradise for all of us, Mr. Crawford." Suddenly his face hardened. "But if the promise of paradise is withheld from my people, then we must convince Man that it will no longer be a paradise for you, either."

"That sounds very much like a threat," I said.

"Oh, no, Mr. Crawford," he said with a sudden smile. "Threats against the state are treasonable. It is merely a prediction."

Then he turned to speak to some of his followers who had come up behind Caleb and myself, and we went back to the farm. I kept a much closer eye on Pepon during the ensuing months, reading his speeches and following his activities through the various media, but after two years had passed it became obvious that he had not been able to carry his message much beyond his own Bogoda followers. A few Sorotoba and Kia joined his party, but most of them paid little or no attention to him, and he made absolutely no converts among the Sentabels, the Siboni, the Korani, or the other major tribes.

It was then that he began changing the thrust of his arguments. No longer did we hear about independence. The Peponi Planetary Union became the Bogoda Political Union, and slowly, almost imperceptibly, his focus of attention became the Greenlands. This, he pointed out, was the Bogoda homeland, and now the Bogoda were forbidden by law to own their own property. The speeches became stronger and more frequent, all aimed at forcing the government to change its position.

And then one morning we heard the news: the McElroy family, which lived about fifteen miles away, had been butchered in their sleep: even the five children, all under ten years of age, had been literally chopped to pieces.

Two days later Jessamine Gaines found that her entire herd of Beefcakes had been mutilated: the genitals had been cut off all the males, and each Beefcake had had its left front foot chopped off.

It was the beginning of the Kalakala Emergency, but nobody knew that for a few weeks. At first we thought these were isolated incidents, perhaps caused by a gang of Bogoda psychopaths. Then they hit the Preston farm, killing old Jim Preston and his two sons, but they left Mary Preston for dead and somehow she survived long enough to tell the police that her houseboy had let the killers in during dinner, and that she recognized four of them, two from her own squatters' colony and two from Wilkes'. She also heard the word "Ka-lakala," but she had no idea what it meant.

Three more families were killed and two farms were burnt to the ground by the time the government finally declared a State of Emergency. They sent an armed squad of soldiers to Pepon's home, but he surrendered without a fight, and they had him on trial within a week. He was defended by a wag lawyer, and much to my surprise and chagrin I saw holos of my own son, Caleb, sitting at his table, whispering advice to him. It was on that day that I disowned Caleb.

Pepon claimed that he had never ordered his people to commit acts of violence, and while the record bore him out, it seemed so unlikely that they would do so without his consent that he was found guilty anyway, and sentenced to thirty years of hard labor in the frontier town of Balimora. He was taken there under heavy guard, and everyone assumed that that would be the end of it.

A week later a group of 200 Bogoda overran a police station in the town of Marracho, mutilating and killing eleven human police officers, and we knew we were in a war.

They were clever, the Kalakala. For one thing, nobody knew what "Kalakala" meant—the word doesn't exist in the Bogoda language. To the best of my knowledge, nobody ever found out the meaning—to this day Pepon swears that even *he* doesn't know—but it was a catchy concoction of sound, and it was easy for people to remember it once they'd heard it.

Also, as much as they terrorized the humans in the Greenlands, they were even worse to their own tribesmen. They made them take fearsome oaths and perform unspeakable acts to prove their loyalty, and they had no compunction about killing any Bogoda who remained loyal to his human patrons.

The problem was that you didn't know who you could trust. You might have 300 Bogoda living on your place, and you knew with an absolute certainty that anywhere between five and fifty of them were Kalakala. It could be your houseboy, with instructions to unlock your doors in the dead of night, or your cook, who had been given poison to put in your food. It could be your stock men, who would mutilate your Beefcakes when the order came through, or even one of the old women, who would drop a vial of poison in your well on her way to the river to launder your clothes.

Even when you caught one of them, it didn't do you any good. Those oathing ceremonies were so hideous and so intertwined with his primitive religion that he'd happily die before he'd tell you anything useful—and a lot of them did. Not a single prisoner taken during the first year ever implicated anyone else in the organization.

By now the authorities realized that they had made a serious mistake when they jailed Pepon. It was obvious, since he had been kept incommunicado, that he couldn't be directing the Kalakala; and it was just as obvious that he was the only wag alive who had the power to call them off. Rumor had it that they offered him his freedom if he would publicly disavow the Kalakala, and that he turned them down, saying that *they* had created the problem without his help and that they could solve it the same way.

The Republic was too busy fighting its wars to give any aid to Peponi, and so a handful of policemen tried to cover the entire Greenlands. And since the Kalakala had infiltrated every farm, it was hardly surprising that there was never an attack on a farm that the police had staked out.

It finally reached the point where most of us sent our women and young children into Berengi. Jessica refused to go—she was more passionately devoted to the farm than any of us— but Christina and my daughter-in-law went into town to work as volunteer nurses, treating both Men and wags who had survived the attacks.

I took to wearing a pistol even inside the house, and every night I locked all our wags into an enclosure. Daniel was off in the Jupiter Range, helping the police hunt for the Kalakala's headquarters, but Thomas, Jessica, and I managed to keep the farm running.

Then one evening, after I had finished dinner, I became aware of a strong odor of smoke. I looked out the door and saw that my outbuildings were burning, and that there were wags running everywhere.

Suddenly Bill raced up to the door.

"It is the Kalakala!" he cried. "They have set fire to the barns!"

"Are your people all safe?" I asked, checking my pistol to make sure it was charged.

"Yes," he replied breathlessly. "But I have been unable to find Boss Thomas or Boss Jessica," he added in worried tones. "Are they with you?"

I called out for them, but there was no answer, and I immediately raced outside to search for them.

An instant later two Bogoda, who had been crouching down below the windows, grabbed and disarmed me, and Bill approached me, a large dagger in his hand.

"I am sorry that I must do this, Boss," he said sincerely, as five or six more Bogoda set fire to my house.

"Where are my children?" I demanded, struggling futilely to free myself.

"All except Boss Daniel are dead," answered Bill. "Even Boss Caleb."

"Caleb?" I repeated. "But he defended Buko Pepon in court!"

"I know," replied Bill regretfully. He gestured to a fencepost, where they had hung Caleb's severed head. His dead eyes stared at me through a cloud of insects.

I looked at my son's head and fought back the urge to vomit.

"Why?" I mumbled uncomprehendingly. "We've always treated you well, and Caleb was as much your son as mine. Why have you done this?"

"Because if we allowed Men like Boss Caleb to live, people would say, Oh, they are merely killing bad Men who have mistreated them. But if we kill Men like you and Boss Caleb and Boss Christina, they will know that we have done it to reclaim our homeland, and not out of personal hatred. I am sorry, but it is even more important that the good Men must die than the bad ones."

"That's crazy!" I said, still in shock. "You're killing off the only Men who might make peace with you!"

"You talk too much!" said one of the wags, and before I knew what he was doing he had pried open my mouth, pulled out my tongue, and severed it.

So much blood gushed out of my mouth that I thought I was going to die right then and there, but suddenly Bill uttered a brief command and they all began running away. It turned out that a police patrol had spotted the flames from my barn and had rushed to the farm, bristling with weaponry.

They killed Bill and eight of the others, and somehow they managed to keep me alive until they could transport me to the Berengi hospital.

They released me a month later, and I went back to the farm. All I found was the burnt skeleton of my house and the charred bodies of Thomas and Jessica. Caleb's head was no longer on the fencepost, and though I spent half a day looking for it I never did find it.

We left Peponi the next day. Daniel was killed about a year after that, while he and Wilkes and some others were tracking a Kalakala war party in the mountains. Thomas' wife remarried and moved to Declan IV, and we've pretty much lost touch with her.

I loved that planet once. I thought I could build a life and a family there, but I was wrong. I thought we and the wags could reason together, but Peponi has no room for reasonable men.

If I were you, young man, I'd stick to writing about people like August Hardwycke and Catamount Greene. Their stories are a lot prettier than ours.

Eight

I walked through the beautifully-kept and pre-cisely-manicured park, following the winding walks and arched bridges, until I came to Wilkes, who was sitting alone on a bench.

"I hope you don't mind meeting me here in the park," he said as I approached him.

"I'm glad that you agreed to speak with me at all," I replied. "I know that it's an imposition."

"Nonsense," he said gruffly. "It's not as if I've got anything else to do with my time these days. When do you have to be back at Amanda's?"

"She told me that she'd be serving lunch at noon."

He checked his timepiece, squinting as the bright overhead sun reflected off its crystal. "Well, that gives us an hour and a half; you certainly ought to be able to learn what you want to know by then." He paused. "I want you to know that this is nothing personal; ever since the Emergency, I invite no one I don't know to my home."

"No apology is necessary," I said, sitting down next to him and wishing I had some crumbs to feed to the avians that were boldly strutting around the bench.

"I wasn't apologizing," he said irritably. "I was explaining."

"The Emergency seems to have changed everyone who experienced it," I noted.

"Watch your own family and friends get cut to ribbons, and and I guarantee it would change *you* too."

"I'm sure it would," I agreed.

He stared at me for a long moment. "I thought you were writing a book about Hardwycke," he said at last. "He was gone long before the Emergency."

"Peponi interests me," I admitted. "I'm considering doing another book about it."

"Then you ought to go there."

"Eventually I suppose I will," I replied. "But as all of you pointed out last night, they've rewritten a lot of the history books since Independence—so I'd like your input as well."

He seemed to consider what I had said for a moment, then nodded his head curtly.

"What's the subject of this new book?" he asked.

I shrugged. "I don't know yet."

"If it's the Kalakala, forget it," he said. "Damned near half the survivors wrote books about it."

"But that was decades ago," I replied. "Everybody's had time to reflect on it now, to see it in perspective."

"The only perspective I ever saw was in a forest on the side of the Jupiter Mountains, with a bunch of wags just out of sight who wanted my scalp as badly as I wanted theirs." He gestured to the neatly-cropped lawn and the gold-tinted trees that had been planted in precise mathematical patterns. "It was as wild as *this* is tame."

"Did you ever meet Buko Pepon personally?" I asked.

He spat on the ground. "If I'd ever gotten close enough to meet him personally, he wouldn't be around now."

"Even though he was in jail during the Emergency?"

"Look," said Wilkes, "maybe he was the leader of the Kalakala and maybe he wasn't—but either way, there wouldn't have been any Kalakala if he hadn't started giving them ideas."

He got to his feet.

"I always take a walk this time of day," he announced abruptly. "If you want to keep talking, you're going to have to walk with me."

"I don't mind."

He headed off at a brisk pace. "Doctor's orders. I've had problems with my legs ever since the Emergency. Comes from spending all those nights out in the cold and the rain, hunting for those bastards up and down the mountain range."

"Why did you confine your search to the Jupiter Mountains?" I asked.

"Because that's where they were hiding, the ones who weren't on the farms or in Berengi." He paused. "Look, they were fighting to throw us out of their homeland. Well, except for the Greenlands, the rest of their homeland *was* the Jupiter Range. Any given day, ninety percent of them were up there in the mountains."

"Crawford tells me that you were with his son Daniel when he died."

Wilkes nodded. "The kid was a damned good hunter, but he thought he was tracking animals instead of wags, and he got careless. Took him a long time to die; I could hear him screaming all night long. We found what was left of him in the morning; there wasn't enough to bury."

"Why were *you* in the mountains?" I asked, absently reaching down to pet an avian, which shrieked and fluttered away from me. "Didn't you have a farm to protect?"

"I had almost a thousand Beefcakes," he answered. "One

morning I found about half of them mutilated—ears hacked off, eyes plucked out, genitals slashed, tendons sliced. They were still alive, and I had to kill them. I decided no one was going to scare me off my place, so I got rid of all my wags and sat up every night, waiting for them to return. It took them a month, but they came back. I shot about a dozen of them, but they just kept coming. I took a poisoned arrow in my arm; it must have been pretty weak poison, because it didn't kill me, though I did lose the arm. About the time the poison knocked me out they gave up charging the house, and I found out later that they settled for killing the rest of my stock and burning my barns." He paused. "It was probably just as well that they did; if the police hadn't seen the flames, they wouldn't have arrived in time to save me."

He sighed deeply. "Well, after I got fitted out with a new arm, I went back and took one last look at the farm, realized that twenty years of work had been undone in a single evening, boarded up the house, packed my weapons, and volunteered for active duty against the Kalakala. The government was short-handed at the time—the Republic never gave us any military support until the third year of the Emergency—and since the police were tied down watching the Greenlands, they mostly used hunters and some of the loyal wags in the mountains." He paused. "Your pal Hardwycke would have had the time of his life there. Tracking the Kalakala in the heavy forest took a lot more skill than walking up to a Landship on the open savannah and blowing it away."

"You mean that you went after the Kalakala with professional hunters rather than soldiers?" I asked, surprised.

"We didn't have any soldiers," he replied irritably. "Just the police. And they didn't have any experience in jungle warfare. The first two units they sent up into the mountains got lost, and the third got slaughtered. That's when they decided that the hunters would at least be more at home with the terrain, and most of them had their own trackers. We even shipped a couple of thousand Siboni up to the Jupiter Range; they hate the Bogoda, and they killed more than their share of them. Problem was, they also started raiding the villages at the foot of the mountains. It didn't make any difference to them who was Kalakala and who wasn't; they were just interested in killing any Bogoda they could find, so we finally had to send 'em back home."

"What was it like up there on the mountains?" I asked.

It was grim (said Wilkes), grim and frightening. Usually when you got to where you thought the Kalakala were, you couldn't see twenty feet ahead of you. Most days were uncomfortably hot; the nights would drop to near freezing, and it rained five or six times a day. You'd see a footprint at the edge of a forest, and you knew that there was a wag watching you, maybe carrying a spear, more likely carrying a laser pistol or a sonic gun he'd stolen from one of the farms, and even your Dorado and Korani trackers couldn't spot him.

Or you'd be walking atop a ridge, and you'd see a party of Kalakala atop another ridge two miles away, and you knew that by the time you'd climbed through the valley separating you from them they'd be long gone, and that one night, when you least expected it, those same wags would sneak into your camp and try to slit you open from stem to stern.

I remember the very first time I went up into the mountains—it was Mount Hardwycke, if that's any use to you, though nowadays I think they call it Mount Pekana. I had about a dozen Dorado and Korani with me; the Dorado were trackers, and the Korani were all armed with projectile rifles. We knew there were Kalakala in the area—the Dorado had seen signs of them—but we couldn't find them, and at dusk we decided to make camp in a small clearing. I assigned two Korani to keep watch, and then I went to sleep.

I woke up in the middle of the night, certain I'd heard a rustling sound in the nearby bushes. I saw that the two lookouts had fallen asleep, so I took my rifle and pumped about twenty rounds into the bush where the noise had come from.

All hell broke loose. The Korani started shooting in every direction, and the Dorado were running around the clearing, screaming and demanding to know what was happening, and avians started screeching, and then a Landship broke cover and ran right through the camp, scared out of his wits.

When everyone had calmed down, I gave my two Korani lookouts hell for falling asleep on the job, and then we all approached the bush I had fired at to see how many Kalakala I had killed.

You know what we found?

A dead Nightkiller, with eighteen of my bullets in him.

That was just another hazard of hunting the Kalakala up there in the mountains. You were as likely to flush a Landship or a Thunderhead as a Kalakala, and they were just as dangerous. I think we must have blown away three animals for every Bogoda we killed, and they took their share of us too, especially in the denser regions of the forest, where we didn't have room to maneuver.

Anyway, it was two weeks before we finally caught a Kalakala warrior, and even after we captured him he wasn't much use to us. We couldn't get any information out of him at all; he finally died during one of the beatings my Korani gave him.

There was a town called Lamaki at the base of the mountains, and we—the colonists, not the police—used to meet at a bar called the Sabrehorn Inn. We'd come down out of the mountains every couple of weeks, exchange information, get warm and dry for a day or two, and then go back to work.

That was where I first met Felicia Preston. She was Jim Preston's sister. She'd been living on Pollux IV when she got word of the massacre up at his place. She came out to Peponi to bury Jim and his family, and stayed to fight the Kalakala.

You just had to take one look at her to know she was something different. She had eyes that could pierce right through you, and hands as coarse and strong as any man's. She was about twenty pounds underweight, but she had an air about her that made you think that if she ever got into a freehand fight with a Bush Devil, you'd be wasting your money if you bet against her. Nobody ever asked her what she had done for a living back on Pollux, and she never volunteered it, but it made you wonder. Those were hard men at the Sabrehorn, men who hadn't seen a bed or a woman for months, but she didn't back down from any of them.

And bit by bit she began bringing information down out of the mountains, stuff that no one else had been able to get. One time it was the name of the Kalakala oathgiver in the Bagenzi District, another time it was a list of all the Kalakala on the Griswold farm, and one night she even told us when and where they planned to strike next.

Now, you have to understand that we'd been trying for almost a year to get this kind of intelligence, and here was this woman, not even one of us, who'd gone right up into the mountains and come back down with it.

Most people left her strictly alone when she was in town, but I finally approached her one night at the Sabrehorn and asked if my wags and I could join her party when she went up the mountain the next morning. She just stared at me for a minute, then shrugged and nodded. She didn't say a word to me all evening, but she was waiting for me the next morning with her two Dorado trackers.

We were well into the forest by noon, and then one of her trackers pointed to a small thornbush. A couple of blue threads had been caught on it, and suddenly our entire party became silent and alert. Her trackers and my six Dorado scoured the area for more signs of Kalakala, but with no success. Finally she summoned her two wags, whispered a terse command, and then sat down propped up against a tree.

She told me to do likewise, but I said that I thought we should keep looking for the Kalakala.

"Forget it," she said. "They're gone. If they weren't, our Dorado would have found them."

"Then let's try to pick up their trail," I said.

She shrugged. "You do what you want. Just don't make too much noise as you go up the mountain. I'm not in the rescue business."

"Do you just plan to sit here all day?" I demanded.

"Most of the day, anyway," she answered. "Their trail's too well covered. I'll catch up to them tonight."

"How?"

"Even Kalakala have to drink. I told my wags to hunt up all the nearby water holes."

"And if they drink from a stream?" I said, annoyed. "What will we do—stake out all two or three miles of it?"

"There isn't any running water around here, Wilkes," she replied. "That's why I chose this part of the mountain."

"How do you know? It's never been mapped."

"Yes, it has," she said. "*I* mapped it the first two weeks I was here."

"What else did you map?" I asked.

"All their hideouts. Mostly they live in caves, but now and then they'll camp out in the woods."

"Then why don't we just move in and hit 'em?"

"Because they never stay in the same spot for more than a day or two, and I found more than fifty of their hideouts." She shook her head. "No, Wilkes, there's no sense wasting effort and energy and letting them know we're here. My wags will find out which water hole they're using, and with a little luck we'll pick them up tonight."

I stared at her for a minute, and she matched my gaze, unblinking.

"We've all caught Kalakala parties at one time or another," I said at last. "I want to know why you're the only one who can make them talk."

"Perhaps my methods are more effective," she said. Then

she pulled her hat over her eyes to shield them from the sunlight and folded her arms loosely across her chest. I didn't know if she was asleep, or merely tired of talking to me, but the end result was the same: I sat in silence for the next three hours, ignoring the heat and the bugs, until one of her Dorado came back and whispered something to her.

"All right, Wilkes," she said, rising quickly to her feet. "We're in business. My wags found the place where they drank this morning."

"Where's the other one?" I asked.

"He's got it staked out, in case they come back before we get there."

Without another word she began following her Dorado, and my wags and I fell into step behind her. The water hole was only four miles away, but between the altitude and the terrain it took us almost three hours to reach it. The moment we arrived her missing Dorado dropped lightly out of a tree and indicated that no one had come while he was on watch.

We took up a position in some thick bushes, about thirty yards from the water hole, and waited. It started raining, and the temperature dropped about thirty degrees. I sat with my back propped up against a tree, cold and wet and shivering, but she never seemed to notice it.

Shortly after nightfall I heard what seemed like an avian trilling, and she poked me with an elbow.

"What is it?" I whispered.

"They're coming," she replied softly. "There'll probably be a dozen or so." She paused. "Shoot to maim the three closest. Kill the rest."

"What about females and children?"

"If you see any, kill them," she said emotionlessly.

We waited in silence for another two or three minutes, and then the Kalakala broke cover. There were nine of them, and I zeroed my sights in on the nearest, then felt her hand on mine.

She mouthed the words, "Not yet," then returned her attention to the wags. Six of them had reached the water hole, and the other three positioned themselves around it, peering intently into the bushes, obviously acting as sentries as the first six filled their gourds and carrying skins.

Then, before I realized that she was even aiming her rifle, three explosions rang out and the three sentries dropped to the ground. I shot the two closest in the legs, then looked for another target and found that Felicity had taken care of them. Two other Kalakala lay writhing on the ground, while the last two were perfectly still.

"Good work, Wilkes," she said, rising and walking over to the scene of the carnage. She withdrew a hunting knife and carved a crude "F" on the torsos of the five dead warriors.

"So the Kalakala will know who did it," she said, anticipating my question.

She whistled once, and her two Dorado entered the clearing, and I signaled my own wags to do likewise.

"Tie 'em up," she ordered, and a moment later her Dorado had thoroughly trussed up the four survivors. All four had been shot in the legs; two had shattered kneecaps, another had most of his foot blown away, and a fourth was bleeding profusely from two wounds in his upper thigh.

"Now tell them that I only need information from one wag," she replied. "The other three are meat for the Nightkillers. Tell them that the first one who tells me where John Pragranzi is hiding gets to live."

The Dorado translated her message into Bogoda. All four captives stared sullenly at her, their jaws set, their mouths tightly shut.

"All right," she said. "Tell them they can talk with one eye as well as two."

"What are you going to do?" I demanded.

"Just what I said," she replied coldly. "I'm going to find out where Pragranzi is. He's responsible for the butchery at the Blandings farm last week." She turned to the Kalakala. "Any answers?"

They continued to stare at her.

"This is going to hurt you a lot more than it hurts me," she said, grabbing one of them by the fur atop his head.

"You're actually going to cut his eye out?" I said.

"Did you see what they did to my brother and his family?" she responded. "If it bothers you, don't look."

She reached forward with the knife, and I watched, fascinated, as she removed his left eye and the Kalakala gave vent to a hideous scream of agony.

"Your turn," she said, approaching the next one.

By the time she walked up to the third, he told her everything she wanted to know about Pragranzi's whereabouts and future plans.

I expected her to let them go then, but instead she pulled a small pistol out of her pocket and fired one shot into each of their heads. Then she nodded to her Dorado, who immediately cut off the hands, feet, ears, and genitals of all nine dead Kalakala and tossed them into the water hole.

"You look pale, Wilkes," she said when the mutilations were done.

"I'm fine," I assured her gruffly.

"You'd better be," she replied, "because the only way to fight fire is with fire. You're not going to beat a bunch of savages by being an officer and a gentleman; there's no conventional way to fight a guerrilla war in these mountains and in this type of cover. And you won't frighten them with the threat of long jail sentences; most of them will be warmer, drier, and better-fed in prison than they ever were out here. You've got to show them that Man can be more brutal and more savage than any enemy he has to face. If they chop off an ear, you've got to chop off two arms and a leg; if they burn a farm, you've got to burn a village. You may not like it, but it's the only way to fight something like Kalakala, and those who aren't up to it had better pack their bags and find themselves another world."

It was the longest speech I ever heard her make. The truest, too.

Once we got back to Lamaki and word got out about her success, we all began applying her methods. It was grim, bloody work, work that made you forget what being a Man was all about, but it was effective. Within a year the Kalakala were as scared of us as we were of them. We asked no quarter on that damned mountain, and we gave none. If we couldn't find them, we'd poison their water. If they took to hoarding water, we'd butcher their meat animals. If they went off on a raid and left their females and children behind, and we found them, they had a pretty hideous surprise waiting for them when they got back. They'd spent three years killing any Bogoda who wouldn't join their cause; we started killing any Kalakala who wouldn't recant his oaths—and if he did recant and there were no authorities around, we killed him anyway.

They used the name of Buko Pepon as a rallying cry; we began carving an "F" on every wag we killed, and before long they started thinking that Felicia Preston was everywhere. If Pepon was bigger than life to them, than Felicia was bigger than death.

Then, after another year passed, the Republic was finally able to spare us a few divisions, and that was the beginning of the end. They started making daily bombing runs on the Jupiter Range, blowing thousands of Kalakala and tens of thousands of animals to pieces. One by one the various gangs of Kalakala would come down out of the mountains and surrender, but there were a few holdouts, and we went back into the mountains after them.

We caught Krajna and Bzanti on the very top of the mountain, damned near freezing to death in their rags, and finally we captured James Praznap when he sneaked into a local village for food. He was their top general, and the holos of his hanging even made the Deluros papers.

That broke the back of the Kalakala, taking Praznap. The State of Emergency continued officially for another five years, but for all practical purposes it was over. We'd won the war, and life should have gone back to normal.

But it didn't.

The Republic had gotten a little too greedy, had tried to colonize too many worlds, and suddenly what happened on Peponi was happening all over the galaxy. The Canphor Twins revolted again, and the Lodin system became a war zone, and before long the Navy was spread so thin that the Secretary decided that he'd better start making the best bargains he could with some of these worlds or in a few centuries his successors would be presiding over an empire that controlled just two planets: Deluros VIII and Earth.

So, one by one, the Republic began giving each recalcitrant world its independence, trying to get rid of the problem planets before all the others got the idea of rebelling. It worked, too: they granted Independence to twenty-six worlds, and kept the other thousand-plus in the fold. They had to grant certain social and economic rights here and there, but they avoided a galaxy-wide revolution.

Peponi was fifteenth in line for Independence, once they took care of the real trouble spots like Canphor VI and VII and Lodin XI. Then, a year before Independence became official, they looked around to see who was likely to become the President of the planet, and they didn't like what they saw: every potential leader was a veteran of the Emergency and had been radicalized to the point where there was a very real possibility that they would massacre the human population and withdraw Peponi completely from the Republic's sphere of influence. There was Bago Baja, who was the *pro tem* leader of the Bogoda, and Sam Jimana, a fiery speaker from the Kia who had been educated on one of the Canphor Twins, and finally they decided that Buko Pepon, even though he was probably responsible for the Kalakala, was the most moderate leader they had, so they commuted his sentence and turned the old devil loose.

And that was it. We'd seen our people mutilated and butchered, finally beat the bastards into submission and went back to our farms—and the goddamned Republic turned the planet over to the wag who had started it all.

A year later they gave him permission to form a provisional government, and three months after that the Secretary of the Republic himself officially recognized Buko Pepon as the President of Peponi.

Suddenly Men began leaving the planet, and every time a Man left, a wag moved into his place. They not only held every position in the government, but they started moving into the Greenlands. Before another year had passed my two closest neighbors were wags, and my own wags, once they moved back, refused to work unless I tripled their wages.

Pepon even started forming an army and a navy. I don't know who the hell he thought would *want* to invade his goddamned planet; the only people who ever wanted to live there were Men, and he was driving us out.

Anyway, I went into Berengi one day to pick up some supplies, and once I got there I stopped and looked—really *looked*—at what was going on. Half the stores were run by wags, all the police officers were wags, looking like buffoons in their human uniforms, there were wags walking everywhere, bumping into Men without apologizing, driving landcars, even drinking in the Thunderhead Bar.

We *won* the damned war with the Kalakala. I know—I was there.

The Republic gave us three years to enjoy our victory, and

then they pulled the rug out from under us. They took a wag who had been found guilty of treason—and instead of killing him, they turned the whole planet over to him and treated him like a statesman instead of a convicted felon.

It made me ashamed to be a Man, and that's when I knew it was time to leave Peponi forever.

Nine

"It's lovely out here," I commented.

"Isn't it?" agreed Amanda Pickett, as Nora served us our soup. We were sitting outside, on her shaded backyard patio, which was surrounded by carefully-tended shrubbery and a variety of avianhouses. "Did you have an interesting discussion with Wilkes?"

"Yes," I said. "He's a very bitter man."

"He has a right to be. He spent four terrible years in the mountains." She paused to sip a spoonful of her soup, then nodded her approval, which seemed to be a signal for Nora to return to the kitchen. "I assume that's what you talked about?"

I nodded. "He seems more upset about the aftermath."

"Well, from his point of view, the Republic encouraged him to fight for his land, and then gave it away to the wags."

"The others didn't seem as outraged."

"Others?" she asked curiously.

"The people I met last night," I said, taking a spoonful of soup. "I assume each of them was involved in the Emergency?"

"You couldn't live in the Greenlands and *not* be involved," replied Amanda. She paused long enough to take a piece of a cracker and throw it on the ground, where a small blue-and-white avian swooped down, picked it up, and strutted off holding it proudly in its mouth. "Even Malcolm Pepper got involved in the fighting."

"He certainly didn't strike me as the type."

"When your house and land are under attack, you become the type very quickly," said Amanda, breaking up another cracker and tossing it onto the ground, where a variety of tiny avians happily fell to eating the pieces.

"I meant that he would seem more at home at an opera or a literary tea than climbing up a mountain looking for savages." I suddenly became aware of the fact that Nora was staring at me, but it was too late to retract what I had said, so I did my best to pretend that I didn't notice her. She stood motionless for a moment, then took away our soup dishes and replaced them with a plate on which there were a number of little triangular sandwiches.

"Not everyone fought in the mountains," said Amanda. "One of the first things the government did was increase the security around Balimora."

"Balimora?" I repeated.

"The frontier town where Pepon was imprisoned. Malcolm volunteered for duty there, and spent the next few years living with hundred-degree heat and dust. Six separate attempts were made to free Pepon during the Emergency; Malcolm took a spear in the leg and a bullet in the shoulder while defending the jail." She paused. "When it's wet or cold out, you can see that he still has a very slight limp."

"Such a dapper little man!" I mused. "I wouldn't have believed it."

Nora returned with some wine. Amanda took a sip, nodded her approval, and then continued: "When he finally returned to the Greenlands, he found that his house had been burned down, his wells had been poisoned, and all his animals were missing, either dead or stolen to feed the Kalakala."

"So he emigrated?" I asked.

She smiled. "You don't know Malcolm Pepper. He liquidated his assets and went into the insurance business."

"I beg your pardon?"

"The major insurance companies blacklisted Peponi after the Emergency," she explained. "But Malcolm suspected that, with Independence in the offing, the Bogoda would be on their best behavior—so he began insuring the larger hotels and stores in Berengi, quickly expanded his business to other cities and towns, and made a fortune before the big companies decided that it was safe to reenter the market. *That* was when he finally left."

"Fascinating!" I said.

"He traveled around the Republic for the next decade," she went on, "dabbling in a little of this and a little of that, and finally he heard that Jessamine and I were living here in the Barton system, came to visit us, and decided to make Barton IV his home—though he's still away on business more than half the time."

"What was Jessamine's role in the Emergency?" I asked between mouthfuls.

"She's a very interesting woman," replied Amanda thoughtfully. "She outlived four husbands, all of whom were dead before the Emergency. I believe that the Crawfords named their daughter Jessica in honor of her. Anyway, after the killing started, she refused to leave her farm. She made her Bogoda leave, though, and replaced them with Siboni. The Kalakala made three raids on her farm during the Emergency; Jessamine and her Siboni held them off all three times. I'd estimate that she personally shot and killed about fifty Kalakala. She stayed until Independence, then legally sold her farm to her Siboni—I think that all of ten credits changed hands; she was never going to let it fall into Bogoda hands—and left for Deluros VIII. But she learned what we all learned: once you've lived on Peponi, you can't be happy on a planet like Deluros. You need water and green things, not streets and skyscrapers, and finally she came to Barton IV."

I finished the last of my tiny sandwiches, looked around for more, couldn't find any, and felt awkward about asking, so I simply sipped my wine and considered my next question.

"Where did Felicia Preston wind up?" I asked. "Ever since Crawford told me his story last night, I've been toying with the notion of putting together a book of reminiscences about the Emergency. Not political or sociological or anything like that; just expatriates telling their stories in their own words." I paused. "I think I might like to interview her."

"Didn't Wilkes tell you?" asked Amanda, surprised.

"Tell me what?"

"She died about two years into the Emergency."

"No, he didn't say anything about it," I replied. "Did the Kalakala get her?"

Amanda shook her head. "She contracted pneumonia up in the mountains, and while she was trying to fight it off she contracted another disease, something that was carried by the mites she picked up in the forest. One of her Dorado trackers ran to Lamaki for help, but she died before they could get back to her."

"I wonder why Wilkes didn't tell me that?"

"Perhaps because he's used to keeping secrets," said Amanda.

"I don't understand."

"It was decided not to let the Kalakala know that the Great

Human Sorceress was dead," explained Amanda. "They buried her in secret, and Wilkes killed her two Dorado trackers so that they could never tell what they knew. Later he told everyone that Felicia had been ambushed and wounded on the mountain. I think that was when they all began carving Felicia's initials on the Kalakala corpses, though they may have started doing it even earlier."

"If it was such a secret, why did Wilkes tell you?" I asked.

"He didn't," she replied. "Not while we were all on Peponi. But twenty years after a war is over there's not much need for military secrecy, and he let it drop one day when he was visiting me here. Until that day, most of us thought Felicia had fought until the end of the Emergency and then gone back to Pollux IV, though no one was ever able to track her down to give her the medals that she had been awarded."

I finished my wine and leaned back comfortably on my chair, sorting out the various things she had told me. Then another question occurred to me.

"You know," I began cautiously, "you speak about everyone else, but you never mention your role during the Emergency."

"My role was rather ambiguous," she replied.

"In what way?"

"I had become friends with Buko Pepon while I was at college on Deluros, and I had set up inoculation and education programs for not just my own Bogoda, but for most of those who lived in the Greenlands. Also, as you could doubtless tell from my biography of Commodore Quincy, I thought his policies, while they temporarily benefited the colonists, would ultimately lead to disaster. In fact, I had been one of the very few colonists to lobby for the rights of the native population prior to the Emergency. When the reason behind the Kalakala outbreak became known, my loyalties were divided: I disapproved of their methods, but not their goal. I didn't want to see them slaughtered, and I didn't want to be killed by them, so I left the planet and sat out the Emergency on Roosevelt III." She paused. "My husband elected to remain behind and fight. He was killed on Mount Hardwycke about four months after I left."

A cool breeze swept across the yard, and Amanda suggested that we adjourn to the study for coffee. I followed her inside, where we seated ourselves on a long sofa and she continued her story.

"I corresponded with Buko Pepon throughout the Emergency." She smiled reminiscently. "He later told me that my letters were the only ones he received that weren't censored."

"What did you write about?" I asked as Nora entered the room with a silver service and poured coffee for us.

"I wrote a few letters about the brutality being exhibited by both sides in the conflict, and some others about the kind of government I hoped one day to see on Peponi," she replied. "But mostly they were about little things, the things I missed on Roosevelt III and that I knew he missed in prison: the magnificent sunsets in the Greenlands, the way the entire world seemed to come to life once the long rains began, the lame wildbuck I had raised as a pet, the senseless slaughter of the Landships . . . I wrote about memories and feelings that we had in common. Many of these memories later became bits and pieces of *Peponi Days*."

"And Pepon?" I said. "What did he write to you?"

"He wrote about many of the same things, but of course he was more concerned with the direction Peponi would take after the Emergency was over. Almost everyone expected him to die in that hot little prison cell, but he always seemed to know, deep in his soul, that his work wasn't completed yet, that he would survive to lead Peponi to independence. There must have been times when that belief was all that kept him going."

"Do his letters still exist?" I asked.

"I turned them over to the Berengi Museum some years ago."

"I'd like to see them someday."

"You'll be disappointed," she replied. "He speaks Terran much better than he writes it . . . and of course, the letters were heavily censored." She paused, as if deciding whether or not to tell me something more. Finally she added: "I destroyed the last four that he wrote."

"Why?"

"They were written after I told him that I probably wouldn't be coming back to Peponi. He urged me to return so fervently that I thought they could be misinterpreted, so I burnt them."

"Why was he so insistent that you come back?" I asked.

"I think it was because he, alone of the Bogoda, could foresee what would happen if all the colonists were to leave after Independence. We had abandoned other worlds in the past—agricultural worlds where there were serious climactic changes, mining worlds that were played out—and each of them reverted to semibarbarism once we took our technology away with us." She paused. "Because I had written the Quincy biography and some other books, I was perhaps more visible than most of the human settlers, and of course I was a second-generation colonist. I would have made a very nice symbol that he could point to, a human whose family had been here almost from the beginning and who was willing to stay here under a native government." She smiled. "And there was something else . . ."

"Oh? What?"

"He wanted me to write his biography."

"Is he that much of an egotist?"

"What politician isn't an egotist?" she replied. "Also, a biography written by a wag would never be marketable anywhere except on Peponi; however, a biography written by a human would circulate throughout the Republic and possibly encourage more investment and immigration—especially if it was written *after* the Emergency, and most especially if it absolved him of all complicity."

"What was his reaction when you turned him down?" I asked.

"He never officially asked me. There were some strong hints, but then he was freed and he was too busy lobbying for independence and forming a government to give it much thought. We still correspond from time to time, and he still hints at it on occasion, but he knows that I'm not going to do it, and I think he suggests it more as a courtesy than from any serious expectation that I might reconsider."

"Why *didn't* you write it?" I asked. "After all, you accepted a commission to write Quincy's biography, and you disagreed with *his* policies."

"I didn't write it because I feel an author should know her subject: any book about Buko Pepon must necessarily be about Peponi, and I no longer know Peponi. It's been more than thirty years since I last set foot on it, and the Peponi I remember is not the Peponi that exists today. *My* Peponi exists in *Peponi Days*, and my holograph albums, and my father's diaries." Suddenly she stood up. "Which reminds me—those diaries are your reason for being here. Let me get them for you."

She left the room for a moment, then came back with four thick leatherbound volumes cradled lovingly in her arms. She brought them over to the couch and handed them to me.

"The writing is blurred in places," she warned me, "and his handwriting isn't the most legible." She took the top volume from me and began thumbing through it, then stopped about a third of the way through. "Do you see this?" she said, pointing to a tiny pawprint. "It's from a Demoncat cub that my father brought home after he'd had to shoot the mother, which had been killing our livestock. We kept it for almost

five months before it died. I don't think any Demoncat of any
age has ever survived longer in captivity."

She turned the pages again, and stopped at a crude drawing
of a native face with an intricately-designed pattern overlaid
on it. "This is a Siboni with his facial hair shaved in a war
pattern," she explained. "He was a minor chief named
Chachma, and he became a close friend of my father's. I used
his grandson as my headman for a few years, just after I returned from college on Deluros VIII."

She went through the books, showing me tidbits from Peponi's history: a drawing of the incredibly rare Hardwycke's
wildbuck, which was now extinct; some bloodstains from the
time her father had killed a Bush Devil that attacked him on
his own veranda, and had then written up the episode before
even washing the blood from his hands; the actual faded red
and gold feather, pressed between two pages, of an avian her
father had shot and had never been able to identify. In the
back of the first diary were her father's phonetic translations
of Bogoda, Siboni, and Sorotoba, written down during the
period when he was trying to learn the various native dialects.

"I'm afraid I can't allow you to take them with you," she
said apologetically. "But I can have Nora make copies of them
for you, if you will sign an agreement to use them only for
research and never attempt to publish them."

"I'll be happy to sign the agreement," I said. "But given
their historical importance, don't you think they *should* be
published someday?"

"They will be," she answered. "I've made an arrangement
with my publisher to bring them out in a matched edition
with my own diaries after my death."

"It should provide fascinating reading," I said.

"Only to scholars with an obsessive interest in Peponi's
history," she replied. "Neither of us expected our Peponi
diaries to see print, and they lack a certain felicity of expres-

sion. I have an almost irresistible urge to rewrite them, but that would completely destroy whatever historical significance they might possess."

She called for Nora, handed the diaries over to her, and instructed her to make copies of them.

"She'll be working in here," said Amanda, "so why don't we move to the living room?"

I got up and followed her.

"May I offer you a drink, Matthew?"

"Not right now, thank you," I said, seating myself on a large, cushioned chair.

"You seem preoccupied," she noted after I had been silent for a few moments.

"I was thinking about Nora," I admitted.

"What about her?" asked Amanda.

"She puzzles me."

"In what way?"

"I keep wondering why she should be content to remain a servant when she could be totally free on Peponi?"

"She's totally free here," answered Amanda.

"But she works at a menial job," I said.

"She *works*," repeated Amanda, emphasizing the word. "There is every possibility that she would be unable to find work on Peponi, and she certainly couldn't earn as much there as I pay her here."

"Why couldn't she find work?" I asked.

"Because most of the wags are still subsistence farmers, and their attitude toward females is, shall we say, unenlightened."

"Oh?"

She nodded. "Even as gifted a leader as Buko Pepon can't move an entire society out of the bush in one generation," she said. "And it will be many more generations before females achieve equality in Peponian society."

"I see," I said.

"There is just so much one man can do," she continued.

"Or one wag. And of course, he's hindered by his culture, just as all of us are."

"Hindered in what way?"

"He has four wives," she said. "You can hardly expect him to view females as equals."

"Did he treat *you* as an equal?" I asked.

"Yes . . . but I'm a member of an alien race. I don't think he really differentiates between men and women. To him, we're all Men, with a capital M."

"What *is* his attitude toward Men?"

"Personally or politically?"

"Both," I said.

"I really don't know what he thinks of humans personally," she replied. "I know he numbers some of us among his friends, but he has a very complex and secretive nature, and most of his true feelings are closely guarded."

"What about politically?"

"He knows he needs us, and he's willing to do almost anything to keep us," said Amanda. "When the Emergency was over and he was given official permission to form a government, most of the colonists, especially those in the Greenlands, were very uneasy. There were rumors of mass deportations, and even renewed violence. Finally Pepon called a meeting at the Sabrehorn Inn in Lamaki—he uses symbolism whenever he can, and the Sabrehorn was the counterinsurgents' headquarters—and went there by himself, with no aides, no bodyguards, and no media. He told them that both sides had made serious errors and suffered greatly, but that that was all in the past. He said that he was willing to forgive and forget all previous abuses, including his imprisonment, if they would do the same, and that he wanted them to stay and help him create a planet that would provide opportunities for *all* of its inhabitants. The human colonists were free to retain their land and their various business holdings, and he wanted their input in creating a constitution they could all live with. He then announced that the new slogan for his political party was the word *Karabunta*, which means '*Together*' in Bogoda."

She paused, smiling at the recollection. "You can't imagine the effect this speech had on his audience. They had come there half-expecting to be dispossessed, and they wound up being asked to stay on their farms and to offer suggestions about the nature of the new planetary government. They gave him a standing ovation and unanimously pledged their support."

"How many of them actually stayed?"

"Almost all of them, at least in the beginning," answered Amanda. "Those who had made their plans to leave didn't bother to attend the meeting." She paused again. "I would estimate that half of them are still there, which isn't all that bad, given Peponi's economy and its other problems. A number of others still keep vacation houses on the planet; hunting may have been disallowed, but there are still game-viewing safaris and thousands of miles of untouched beaches all along the coasts."

"Which brings up an interesting question," I said.

"Oh?" she said curiously.

"Why did you never go back?" I asked. "You weren't there for the fighting, so you couldn't have any bad memories of it."

"Other than losing my husband, you mean?"

"I apologize," I said promptly. "I had forgotten."

"It's all right, Matthew," she replied. "The truth of the matter is that it had nothing to do with my husband. I knew when I left that I would never return."

"Then let me ask you again," I said. "Why have you stayed away all these years?"

"The Peponi I left was not the Peponi I had learned to love. Everything was changing. The mornings when you could wake up and see Sabrehorns and Landships ambling across

your property, when there were huge chunks of unexplored territory for men like Fuentes and Greene to tame, when Berengi was a small town filled with colonists rather than a city filled with strangers . . . they were all gone long before the Kalakala. Peponi was a world on the road to adulthood, and it had lost the innocence of its youth, as all worlds must."

She sighed and looked out a window, staring into Peponi's past, as I had seen Hardwycke do so many times.

"I have had my fair share of success as a writer, and I enjoy the trappings of luxury," she said at last. "I've lived a full, productive, active life, and I am ashamed of nothing I've ever done." She slowly turned to me. "But do you know something interesting, Matthew? I'd trade it all to have been on Peponi when August Hardwycke first set foot there, when there was a young world spread out before him, all his for the taking."

She paused.

"Isn't that the strangest thing?" she said with a bittersweet little smile.

III

Midafternoon

Ten

Three years had passed since I had visited Amanda Pickett at her home on Barton IV.

In the interim, the Hardwycke biography had come out and died a very quick death. To this day I don't know why. Some critics claimed that, despite the charm of some of his stories, it was very difficult to empathize with a man who made his living by killing animals, and who, by his own admission, may very well have shot the last Sabrehorn on Peponi. But whatever the reason, the book itself appeared only on Deluros VIII and quickly vanished without a trace. Even the disks and tapes never made it out of the Deluros system before being remaindered, and that—or so I thought—was the end of it.

My next project fared considerably better. It was entitled *The Expatriates*, and was a collection of verbal memoirs of those humans who had survived the State of Emergency on Peponi. I began it with a brief historical summary of the period, then segued into a series of firsthand reminiscences, which included those of Crawford, Wilkes, and some twenty-one other Peponi expatriates who had agreed to speak to me about their experiences. I had originally hoped to get Amanda Pickett to read the manuscript and add her own comments to the final chapter, but before I could do so I received word that she had died in a traffic accident on Barton IV. Nonetheless, the book garnered considerable critical acclaim and was a commercial success, even without her hoped-for contribution.

Then my first publisher decided to capitalize on the publicity surrounding *The Expatriates*, and reissued the Hardwycke biography with a new title—and it, too, began selling well.

And suddenly, despite the fact that I had still never been within 200 light years of Peponi, I found myself in great demand. Requests began piling up for articles on Landships, on Hardwycke, on hunting, on the Emergency, on virtually all aspects of Peponian life. I accepted four assignments from the most prestigious markets, sent them off, and, feeling that I had earned a vacation, I closed down my apartment and took off for a month of sun and sea on the Inner Frontier planet of Brandywine.

When I returned home, I found a most interesting message waiting for me on my computer. The Office of the President of Peponi had offered to transport me there at its own expense to discuss a project that I was assured would be to our mutual benefit. If I was interested, I was to contact a human named Ian Masterson, who would make all my travel and lodging arrangements and would act as my personal guide for as long as I was on the planet.

I accepted at once. I had been planning to visit Peponi anyway—I felt increasingly guilty about being considered an expert on a world that I had never visited—and a week later I was notified by the local spaceport that my ticket was waiting for me, and that my flight departed in three days. There was also a list of all the various inoculations and pills I would need, as well as the name of a local doctor who had been instructed to bill the Peponi government for his work.

I felt a bit like a walking pincushion by the time I boarded the spaceship, and I spent most of the first two days sleeping before I felt well enough to examine the recreational facilities. I found a trio of young women who had just returned from Northpoint, a world on the Inner Frontier, and were infatuated with an alien game they had learned called *jabob*. They taught it to me, and I spent an enjoyable few days playing it with them before they departed on Barsoti V. I then elected to go into Deepsleep for the remaining week of the trip.

I was awakened about five hours before we were due to land on Peponi, and I suddenly remembered what it was that I hated about traveling in Deepsleep. Your body's metabolism slows down to a crawl, but it doesn't stop—if it did, you would be dead—and upon waking up you are literally starving to death. However, your muscles have atrophied just enough so that it takes you about ten minutes to be able to move around without any pain or stiffness, by which time you're seriously toying with eating the ship's bulkheads. You invariably overeat once you get to the dining room, and spend your final four hours in the ship's infirmary, where the doctor invariably gives you an amused lecture about self-control before he relieves the agony in your stomach.

By the time I was feeling healthy again, the passengers were transferred to the planetary shuttle. I tried to pick out the various continents as we descended—the Great Eastern, the Great Western, the Ice Bowls, and the Dust Bowl—but there was too much cloud cover for me to identify any of them except the Northern Ice Bowl. Before long we began braking, and a few minutes later I stepped through the airlock and followed my fellow passengers, most of them vacationers laden with expensive holographic cameras, down the ramp to

a nearby slidewalk, which soon deposited us in the main re-
ceiving room of the spaceport.

I then stood in line while a pair of natives in impressive
uniforms examined each passport, and frequently inspected
the travelers' luggage as well. Most of the native passengers
were passed right through, but off-worlders usually had a bit
more difficulty. One of the inspectors found a new type of
telescopic lens that he obviously hadn't seen before, held it
up, turned it every which way to determine what it was, and
finally pressed a button on his computer panel. Another gaud-
ily-uniformed native bearing a Spaceport Security insignia
came over, the second passport inspector joined him, and the
three of them spent about ten minutes looking at the lens and
discussing whether it might be a sniperscope smuggled in by
a would-be assassin.

Finally they returned the lens to its owner and let him
through, and then I stepped up and handed over my passport.

"Welcome to Peponi," said my passport inspector in broken
Terran.

"Thank you."

"Are you here for business or pleasure?"

"Business."

He stared at me, as if trying to determine the nature of my
business, then shrugged and stamped my passport.

"Next!" he called, and I passed through to the main reception area. Three natives came up to me, none of them
speaking Terran, but all obviously determined to carry my
luggage for me.

"No, thank you," I said, looking around for anyone who
might be Ian Masterson.

They persisted, and one of them actually got into a brief
tug-of-war with me when he tried to take my overnight bag
away.

"I'm waiting for someone," I said, yanking the bag back
and walking to a chair.

They followed me, still speaking in their own language, and remained with me for about five minutes, until they finally realized that I had no intention of leaving the spaceport. Then, one by one, they drifted away, looking for some other tourist with luggage.

A number of tour guides were walking through the area, holding large printed signs over their heads. One represented an outfit called Sabrehorn Tours, another was Landship Vacations, a third was Mount Pekana Excursions, and so on. As they progressed they were joined by various tourists who recognized the names of the companies with which they had contracted.

Finally a lean, wiry blond man in his fifties, wearing a pair of tan shorts and a matching shirt, approached me.

"Matthew Breen?" he asked.

"Yes?"

"I'm Ian Masterson," he replied, extending his hand. "Sorry I'm late, but traffic was just terrible outside the spaceport." He looked down at my two suitcases. "Is this all your luggage?"

"Yes."

He barked out something in a dialect I had never heard before, and two natives immediately approached us. He gave a further order, and each of them picked up one of my bags.

"I've arranged for you to stay at the Royal Hotel," he said. "We've got newer ones, but they're a blight on the landscape. The service is terrible, and you get none of the special flavor of Peponi." He paused. "You'll be staying in the same suite of rooms that Johnny Ramsey once stayed in." He smiled. "Of course, they've been remodeled four or five times since then, but they still have the *feel* of the old days about them."

He led the way to a large parking lot, then stopped beside a landcar and pointed to the back, where the two natives loaded the luggage. He gave them each a one-credit note and sent them back to the spaceport.

"Couldn't one of them have carried the bags just as easily?" I asked as we climbed into the landcar.

"Unquestionably," said Masterson. "But then the other one probably wouldn't have eaten tonight; yours was the last shuttleflight due in today." He turned to me. "When you were in the spaceport, didn't you notice all the locals performing menial jobs that a machine could do better? What Peponi needs are *more* unskilled jobs, not less."

"I see," I said carefully. "By the way, what do you call the natives? I gather that *Bluegill* and *wag* are no longer acceptable."

He smiled. "They're acceptable only if you're criminally overinsured and walk around with a death wish. No, these days we call them pepons."

"Pepons?" I repeated curiously.

"Buko Pepon is supposed to be the Father of Freedom— so, since they're all Pepon's children, figuratively at least, they decided that they want to be called pepons. Causes all kinds of confusion."

"I can imagine," I said.

He activated the landcar and began maneuvering it through the heavy airport traffic, and suddenly I could see the city of Berengi a few miles ahead of us, rising up out of the savannah that encircled it.

"Impressive," I remarked, as we drove past a small herd of Silvercoats that stood at roadside, displaying more boredom than curiosity as they stared at us.

"It used to be," said Masterson, "back before we became a mecca for aging businessmen and their camera-crazed families." He grinned. "You're partially responsible for that, you know."

"I am?"

"Nobody ever heard of August Hardwycke before your book came out. Now everyone wants to see the locations you mentioned."

"Do I apologize for it, or proudly take all the credit?" I asked.

"It all depends on who you happen to be talking to," replied Masterson noncommittally. He pointed to a lone Thunderhead grazing about fifty yards from the road. "When I came here thirty years ago, you could still see an occasional Demoncat prowling the streets, and you might pass a hundred Landships on the way from the spaceport to the city. The tallest building in Berengi back then was the Deluros Bank, which went all of four stories." He grimaced as he looked ahead. "Now look at it! All high-rise hotels and office buildings." He snorted contemptuously. "You could just as easily be on Sirius V or Roosevelt III or Goldenrod as on Peponi. I hope they'll let me show you the *real* Peponi while you're here."

"Which brings up a question," I said.

"What is it?"

"Why *am* I here, and at whose request?"

He looked surprised. "Don't *you* know?"

I shook my head. "I just know that the Office of the President is footing the bill, and that you're to be my guide and, I gather, my companion. I had rather hoped you might be able to tell me something about it."

"Not a thing," replied Masterson. He shot a quick glance at me. "Are you in the habit of hopping halfway across the galaxy without knowing who sent for you?"

"No," I answered. "But I've been planning to visit Peponi and this seemed like the perfect opportunity." I paused. "I don't want to sound impertinent, but don't you know who you work for?"

"I work for Buko Pepon," he replied.

"In what capacity?"

"Bodyguard."

"Does he need one?"

"He hasn't yet," answered Masterson. "But sooner or later one of the wags is going to decide he could do a better job than Pepon, and then he'll need all the bodyguards he can get."

"I notice that you just used the term *wags*," I said. "I thought it was frowned upon."

"I don't use it to *them*," he replied. "Just to Men."

We drove in silence for a couple of minutes, as I studied the countryside, spotting an occasional animal among the sparse bushes, and a solitary native herding his Beefcakes. Such dwellings as I could see were either grass huts or dilap- idated old shanties, most of which lacked windows and even doors. There was no garbage anywhere, and I concluded that the local vermin—Nightkillers, Supper Storks, and the like —ate it all every evening, perhaps with a little help from some of the hungrier pepons.

"You know," said Masterson at last, "I'll bet the Old Man sent for you himself."

"The Old Man?" I repeated.

"Buko Pepon."

"I thought *everyone* objected to calling a native a Man."

"Any other native, yes," Masterson assented. "But not Buko Pepon. He's the one wag who wouldn't be a bad addition to the race of Man." He grinned. "Besides, he likes to hear himself called the Old Man, God knows why."

"And you think that Pepon himself wants to see me?"

"It's an educated guess."

"Didn't he tell you?"

"He's got better things to do with his time than talk to his security staff," replied Masterson. "I get my orders through channels."

"Then what makes you think that Pepon sent for me rather than someone else?" I persisted.

"The fact that we didn't roll out a red carpet for you, or meet you with ten thousand pepons trying to play at being soldier in some idiot ceremony." He paused. "The Old Man is very confident of his power, so he tends to do with a lot less pomp and formality than many of his underlings." Masterson laughed. "You should see one of his cabinet meetings. Everyone except him looks like they're attending a masquerade ball, with all their neatly-pressed military uniforms and their rows of medals, as if they'd ever seen action except as a bunch of spear-carrying outlaws. One of them even forgets which of our centuries he's supposed to be from, and occasionally attends in a powdered wig!"

"What about Pepon?"

"Usually he just wears a suit. The only time he wears that Bush Devil cloak of his is on ceremonial occasions. Makes sense," he added. "The damned thing is awfully heavy. He must sweat up a storm whenever he puts it on."

"Have you any idea what he wants me for?" I asked.

Masterson shrugged. "Who knows? He doesn't even confide in his cabinet, let alone his alien bodyguards."

"When will I see him?" I persisted.

"He'll send for you," replied Masterson. "Always assuming it *is* the Old Man that sent for you. For all I know, the Minister of Culture wants to organize a book fair."

We reached the outskirts of Berengi, and began driving through some of the worst slums I'd ever seen.

"Ready-made slums," commented Masterson.

"I beg your pardon?"

"All this that we're passing through was savannah twenty-five years ago," he explained. "It's only been since Independence that the wags have taken to moving off the farms and into the city to look for work." He snorted again. "You wouldn't think anything could get this run-down this quickly, would you?"

"How many natives live in Berengi?" I asked.

"About a million," replied Masterson. "Plus about sixty thousand Men and another five thousand members of other races. Most of the off-worlders are what the locals call Two-Year Wonders."

"What are Two-Year Wonders?" I asked.

"Businessmen who are transferred here for a couple of years. They never learn the languages, never see anything but Berengi, never socialize with the residents. They just put in their time, take their money, and leave." Suddenly he pointed to a small stone cross in the middle of a city park that was in desperate need of relandscaping. "See that?"

"Yes."

"That's Catamount Greene's grave."

"Really?" I replied. "I've read and heard a lot about him, but I never learned how he died."

"After the women and children moved into Berengi during the Emergency, he realized that there was a need for milk, since all the animals were up in the Greenlands. So he started a milk delivery business." Masterson chuckled. "It was quite a sight, this ninety-year-old man riding shotgun on a milk wagon as it made its way to Berengi." He paused. "They say he made eight or nine fortunes on Peponi. However many it was, this was his last one. One day, about two years after Independence, an old Bogoda witch doctor told him he was going to die within a week. He disposed of all his property, sold his business, said good-bye to all his friends, and went into his house to wait. Died three days later, or so I'm told. Most of the Bogoda didn't want a marker on his grave, because they were still sensitive about the Emergency and feeling cocky because of Independence, but the Old Man said that they couldn't turn their backs on their history, and like it or not, Catamount Greene had been a big part of it. So they buried him here in the slums, surrounded by his Bogoda, and named the place Greene Park."

He swerved and muttered a curse as a child ran into the street, then continued. "Most of the humans thought it was a pretty rotten thing to do, burying Catamount in the poorest part of the city. But wherever he is, he's got the last laugh. It turns out he owned the ground where the park is, and he's got a couple of nieces on Alpha Prego III who get a yearly rent from the government."

"An opportunist to the end," I remarked.

As we entered downtown Berengi, which resembled any large city, Masterson began pointing out various landmarks to me: the Equator Hotel, the store that had been built where the old Dalliance Club had stood, the former governor's mansion (which was now a museum), a number of other buildings that had existed back before the Emergency, and finally we pulled up to an old but meticulously-kept two-story building.

"Here we are," he announced, whistling out the window and waiting for two pepons to come out and take my luggage.

"So this is the Royal Hotel," I said, staring at the cavernous entrance and the small outdoor restaurant.

"Starting point for more safaris than you can imagine," he replied. "Come on in and we'll get you registered."

"Are you staying here too?" I asked.

He shook his head. "I've got my own place, out in the suburbs," he answered.

"Then I'll just check in, and you can go about your business," I said.

"Out of the question."

"Why?"

"First, because you *are* my business, and second, because although Terran may be the official language of Peponi, I'd be surprised if more than five percent of the natives know ten words of it."

He walked up to the registration desk, let the computer scan my passport and identification disk, said something in what I assumed was Bogoda, had a brief conversation with two of the clerks, laughed once, and then came away with an amused smile on his face.

"You're in room 215," he said.

"What was that all about?"

"What?"

"What was so funny?" I asked.

"Oh, that. The head clerk doesn't think you look like a writer."

"Oh?" I said, surprised. "What do writers look like?"

"The only one he can remember was Damien Duarte, who wrote a couple of best-sellers about the Kalakala. He was a big, brawny, suntanned guy who looked like he'd be at home wrestling Demoncats. So, since that's the closest the clerk's ever been to a book, naturally he thinks all writers look like that. Also, Duarte had a long, drooping black mustache, and he wants to know when you'll be old enough to grow one. That was what I laughed at." He paused. "A couple of the pepons will put your luggage in your room. Come on and I'll show you around."

"Thanks," I said. "I've written so much about this place that it will be a pleasure to finally walk through it."

"It's not all that luxurious as hotels go," said Masterson, "but once upon a time it was the only one on the whole damned planet."

He led me through a series of interconnected courtyards, showing me the plaques commemorating the famous leaders of the Republic who had stayed here, and then took me to a special room where the sonic rifles of Fuentes, Hakira, Johnny Ramsey, and Catamount Greene were on display, as well as a cartridge belt that had been worn by August Hardwycke. Throughout the hotel, interspersed with the gift shops and bars and restaurants, were the heads of numerous varieties of plains game that assorted hunters and sportsmen had donated to the Royal.

Finally, when we had come full circle, we stopped at the Thunderhead Bar.

"Care for a beer?" he asked me.

"In the Thunderhead?" I replied. "I wouldn't miss it for the world."

We walked into the barroom, which was decorated with old prints, not of Peponi, but of Earth and Deluros VIII and Sirius V and Terrazane and Far London, as if the first residents needed the constant image of home. It was crowded, but finally we found an empty table at the rear and sat down, and a moment later an immaculately-clad pepon walked over and took our orders.

"I've noticed something," I said.

"Yes?"

"Except for two Lodinites and a party of Canphorites, all the patrons seem to be human," I said.

"That's right."

"I can't believe that pepons are still excluded from the Royal," I continued.

He laughed. "Not at all. But except for a few important government officials, none of them can afford it." He looked around. "That's why I like coming here. It reminds me of the old days."

"Were you a settler?" I asked.

He shook his head. "No. I came to Peponi to fight the Kalakala."

"You volunteered?"

He chuckled. "My mother never raised any children dumb enough to volunteer for anything," he said. "About a year into the Emergency, long before the Republic was able to send any troops, the colonial government advertised for mercenaries. I'd spent two years fighting against the Zaberi out in the Quinellus Cluster, and I figured this had to be better than getting into my snow suit and chasing the enemy over glaciers in sixty-below-zero weather, so I signed up . . . and I've been here ever since."

"How did you become Buko Pepon's bodyguard?" I asked.

"Originally he had Bogoda bodyguards, but one of them tried to kill him; it turned out that he was on the payroll of one of Pepon's rivals. So Pepon, who's no fool, got rid of all his wag protectors and hired a human mercenary named Belinda Morales to run his security staff, with the stipulation that she hire no wags at all."

Masterson paused long enough to nod to a well-dressed man who had just entered; the man smiled and waved at him, then joined some companions who were crowded around the bar.

"I had a bit of a reputation as a Kalakala killer," Masterson continued, "so once the Emergency was over I took a good look at the situation and decided that if I wanted to stay on Peponi, I'd better find something to protect me once they got their independence. When I heard that Belinda was hiring Men, I applied for the job and I got it, which is probably the only thing that kept me from being assassinated once the wags took over. They didn't kill *many* Men after Independence— it wouldn't have looked good when they applied for aid and advertised for tourists—but they killed some of us, the ones they held the biggest grudges against. I'd almost certainly have been one of them if I hadn't been working for Pepon himself." Suddenly he smiled. "They spent three years hunting for Felicia Preston before they would finally believe that she was dead. The Old Man tried to call them off, but even *he* couldn't stop them. That lady really put a bug up their collective asses."

"Did you ever meet her?" I asked.

He shook his head. "No. I arrived here one morning, and that same afternoon I was up in the mountains with a squad of Sorotoba warriors, none of whom spoke Terran, hunting for Kalakala." He chuckled. "Good thing I didn't find any for the first week. I wouldn't have known the difference between them and my own wags."

"Where did you learn the language?" I asked, as our beers finally arrived.

"On the job."

"You mean they sent you into the mountains with no knowledge of the territory or the language?" I asked, taking a taste of my beer, which I found to be a little too bitter.

"They were desperate," he replied. "Besides, Sorotoba's not difficult to learn. It only took me about five weeks."

"What did you do in the meantime? How did you make yourself understood?"

"It wasn't that complicated," said Masterson easily. "When you hear gunshots, you yell 'Duck!' and throw yourself to the ground. The slow learners usually weren't around the next day anyway."

"And you went right from that to being Buko Pepon's bodyguard?"

"Not exactly," replied Masterson. "He wasn't freed until three or four years after the fighting stopped. I tried my hand at a number of jobs: tour guide, game warden, road construction, anything that struck my fancy and paid well. But when Pepon was released, it was obvious that the Republic was going to pull out and had hand-picked him to run the planet, and as I said, I knew that if I was going to stay here I needed protection."

"Why aren't you guarding him now?" I asked, noting that two natives, both carrying government briefcases, had entered the bar as customers and were now being escorted to a table.

"His security force numbers about eighty, maybe ten off-world aliens and the rest of us Men. Except when he's out in public, he doesn't need more than half a dozen of us at any given time, and when we're not guarding the Old Man, we get assigned to other duties." He smiled at me. "You're my current assignment."

"Surely my life isn't in danger," I said, suddenly realizing that one of the better killers on Peponi had been chosen to be my companion.

"Not at all," he replied, amused. "But when you work for the government, you do what you're told, and I've been told to make myself and my vehicle available to you until they send for you. And," he added as an afterthought, "to pick up all your bills."

"Well, I certainly appreciate it," I said. "I just wish I knew why I'm here."

"Enjoy yourself while you can," said Masterson. "Whatever it is, once they meet you, you'll probably find yourself buried up to your chin in work." He finished his beer. "Would you care to take a walk around the city?"

"Is it safe?" I asked.

"I'm not talking about the part we drove through," he replied. "I thought I'd take you through Tourist Heaven. I suppose everybody ought to see it once."

"Why not?" I said, getting to my feet.

"You didn't finish your beer," he noted.

"I had enough of it."

"It *is* pretty awful stuff, isn't it?" he said.

"Then why do you drink it?"

"It's the only brand you can get here," he answered.

"A competitor could really clean up," I remarked.

He chuckled. "A competitor could get his testicles cut off," he said.

"I don't understand."

"Buko Pepon owns the brewing company."

"Oh."

We walked to the front entrance of the hotel.

"One thing," said Masterson, just before we stepped outside.

"What is it?"

"If you've got any questions that might be construed as political, keep your voice down if there are any wags around.

They may call this place a democracy, but it isn't—and the wags are just a little bit sensitive about criticism from the race they like to believe they threw out of here."

He walked out into the warm sunlight, and I followed him, wishing I had worn a lighter outfit. We turned left, and I could see the huge hotels and office buildings rising from the flat ground about a mile away.

"Why was the Royal built so far from the center of town?" I asked.

"It wasn't," answered Masterson. "It was here first." He paused. "The original spaceport used to be about six hundred yards in that direction," he said, pointing. "Then, as the shuttlecraft started getting larger and larger, they built the current spaceport, and the town began expanding toward it. Personally, I think its location gives the Royal a nice rural feeling. At least you don't feel claustrophobic when you walk through the courtyards. I'd hate to see some of these ugly buildings towering over it."

I saw a large building across the street, with hundreds of pepons walking into and out of it, and asked what it was.

"Buko Pepon University," replied Masterson. "It graduates about two thousand students a year."

"That many?" I said, impressed.

He nodded. "Then they go back to their grass huts and try to figure out how to apply their educations."

"I thought you told me there was a lot of work here," I said.

"I told you they were trying to *create* jobs," replied Masterson. "And I also told you that it was menial work." He snorted. "Hell, we haven't got two thousand jobs for college graduates on the whole planet, and that damned school keeps turning them out every year. One of these days the Old Man is going to wake up and discover that he's got a very disaffected group of scholars on his hands."

"Does he own the university?"

"No. Why should you think so?"

"Well, he owns the beer company, and his name is on the main lecture hall there," I said, pointing to the inscription on the arch over the doorway.

Masterson shook his head. "No profit in it," he answered, moving to his left to avoid a trio of students who were approaching us. "The Old Man doesn't believe in philanthropy. You'll see his name all over the city: the Buko Pepon Spaceport, the Buko Pepon Coliseum, the Buko Pepon Library, the Buko Pepon Stadium, and the like—but that's just the wags' way of honoring him, or his way of feeding his ego. When he puts money into a business, he keeps his name out of it."

"You make him sound like a very interesting character," I said, gazing at all the privately-chartered landcars that were passing by on their way to the Royal.

"He is," agreed Masterson.

"What kind of President is he?"

"I don't think he's in a class with Johnny Ramsey or most of our other Secretaries, if that's what you mean," said Masterson thoughtfully. "But the old boy is certainly the best wag they could have chosen for the job. He's got a head on his shoulders, and he really does care about Peponi, unlike all those flunkies he's got surrounding him. All they care about is lining their own pockets." He paused. "Which isn't to say that he hasn't got some major problems."

"Such as?" I asked, as we crossed a major thoroughfare and entered the official downtown area.

"Well," he said, lowering his voice as a couple of natives approached us, "for starters, he's got twenty or thirty million wags starving to death out in the countryside," answered Masterson. "Maybe even more than that. He's got a terrible balance of trade, he's still losing humans to other worlds, and his government is corrupt from top to bottom." Masterson smiled and waved to a redheaded woman who was walking in the opposite direction on the other side of the street, and she waved back. "And he's still got the old problem of tribalism on his hands. The Bogoda don't think too much of the neighboring tribes that didn't join the Kalakala, the Sentabels want their own government on the Great Western Continent, the Kia hate the Sorotoba, the Sorotoba hate the Bogoda, and the Siboni hate everyone. He's kept the peace so far, but it gets more difficult every day."

"I see," I said.

"And, in the category of minor problems, I wouldn't suggest walking around Berengi at night unless I'm with you," added Masterson as an afterthought. "Especially on Sunday."

"What happens on Sunday?" I asked.

He grinned. "Ninety percent of the wags claim to be Christians, which is ridiculous, of course—almost every one of them goes right from church to his witch doctor. But because they give lip service to Christianity, they don't work on Sundays —and that includes the police."

"You're joking!" I said, astounded.

"I wish I was," he answered. "From one minute after midnight on Sunday morning until one minute before midnight on Sunday night, it's a thieves' carnival around here. If you're out in the bush, or at the game parks, there's nothing to worry about; but here in Berengi, and in the other cities, you lock your door and don't go outside unless you're well-armed— and even then you're better off staying inside, because they're just a little sensitive about Men who kill wags, even in self-defense." He watched my shocked reaction, then added in amused tones: "It's changed just a bit from the days when Hardwycke used to come to town."

We walked in silence for a block, and then I stopped to look at the window of a gift shop that displayed beautiful wood carvings of various Peponian fauna.

"They're exquisite!" I exclaimed, pointing to a Sabrehorn and a Landship, each about eight inches at the shoulder.

"They were carved by the Baroni, a tribe about four hundred miles southwest of here," Masterson informed me. "They're about the best woodworkers on the planet."

There was a pricetag plainly visible on the Sabrehorn, but the figures on it made no sense to me.

"How much is that in credits?" I asked.

"About six hundred," he replied. "But if you like Baroni carvings, don't buy them here in Berengi. Everything is tripled for the tourists. Get a couple of hundred miles out of town and you can get the same thing for two hundred credits—or if you find an exceptionally hungry shopkeeper, you can probably haggle him down to a hundred and fifty."

We walked a little further, and finally came to the Equator Hotel, with its famed Message Tree standing right in the middle of its outdoor restaurant.

"Back in the old days, all the settlers and hunters used to leave messages for each other tacked onto the tree," explained Masterson. "An early historian could have gotten all the research material he needed just by reading the tree every couple of months."

"There are still messages on it," I noted.

"Mostly advertisements for prostitutes," he said contemptuously. "Not quite the same thing."

"The blessings of civilization," I said sardonically.

We began walking again, and soon came to a small restaurant run by a haughty-looking Canphorite.

"This is a piece of the new Peponi's history," remarked Masterson, gesturing toward the restaurant.

"Oh?"

He nodded. "Sam Jimana was probably the brightest and most articulate of the younger politicians on Peponi. He didn't like Men much; I gather he'd been to college on one of the Canphor Twins. He was probably the most popular politician on the planet, except for Buko Pepon, and it was pretty much assumed that he'd become President when the Old Man died or retired. Jimana only had one serious problem: he was a Kia instead of a Bogoda." Masterson pointed to a table by the window. "He was sitting right there when he was assassinated five years ago. The Kia tried to put the blame on Pepon, but they never came up with any proof."

"Did they ever catch the killer?" I asked.

"Not really. Oh, Pepon got some poor Sorotoba bastard to confess to it and had him executed, but nobody believed that he was the real assassin."

We continued our walk, stopping frequently to window-shop. Masterson continued pointing out locations of historic importance, and then, after another two hours, the sky began clouding over and we returned to the Royal Hotel, beating a tropical cloudburst by less than five minutes.

I went directly to my room, while Masterson stopped by the front desk to see if there were any messages for him and to make some vidphone calls. The security scanner quickly identified my thumbprint, and the door slid back into the wall, revealing the interior of a small but very clean parlor. Colorful holographs of Landships and Demoncats framed the windows, and above the fireplace was a rather crude carving of a native dancer. A small table held a basket of fruit, with a note—in beautiful Terran calligraphy—that this was a gift of the management.

My bedroom was off to the left, and contained an oversized bed, a desk and chair, and a holo screen. Beyond it was a bathroom, and after a week of using nothing but a Dryshower on the spaceship, I decided to allow myself the luxury of a long hot bath in real water.

After I emerged from the tub and stood in front of the heatblower, I heard a knock at the door. Wrapping myself in a towel, I walked into the parlor and ordered the door to slide back.

Masterson entered the room, took one look at me, and grinned.

"What's the matter?" I asked.

"I hope you've got something a little more formal to wear," he said. "Buko Pepon has just sent for you."

Eleven

The President's Mansion was located in the heart of Berengi, opposite the twenty-three-story cylindrical structure that was the brand-new Vainmill Hotel. Four uniformed native guards, each sporting gold braid and epaulettes, signaled the landcar to stop as we pulled up. Masterson got out, nodded to them, and they immediately saluted.

"End of the line," he announced, and I got out and followed him up an impressive staircase into the main reception area —an elegant octagonal room with a thirty-foot ceiling and a pair of crystal chandeliers imported from the Atria system. There were more guards, also natives, and I asked Masterson where the human security team was.

"They're around," he replied.

"I don't see them."

He smiled. "You're not supposed to."

He led me to a small elevator.

"If you weren't with me," he said, "you'd be seeing them right about now."

We ascended to the fourth and top floor, and emerged into a marble foyer. The ceiling was domed, and had bas-reliefs of natives in their different tribal dress. An enormous stuffed Sabrehorn, looking remarkably lifelike, guarded the foyer, its head lowered, its long curved horn poised to defend the planetary President's private quarters. The walls were lined with original paintings and holos, each the gift of politicians or celebrities who had enjoyed Peponi's many charms. A nonrepresentational sculpture by Morita, a major artist from far out on the Spiral Arm, especially caught my eye, as did a solid gold bust of Buko Pepon, but almost all of them were impressive.

Masterson gave me a moment to look around, then escorted me to a door at one end of the foyer.

"This is where I leave you," he announced.

"You're not coming with me?" I said, surprised.

"One doesn't visit the President wearing shorts and a dirty shirt," he explained with a smile. "Also, I wasn't invited."

"Where will I find you when I'm through?"

"If you're still my assignment, I'll be waiting for you right here."

"Well," I said, extending my hand, "if not, it's been a pleasure meeting you."

"Oh, I'm sure we'll meet again," he said. "I don't know what he has in mind for you, but I expect you'll be on Peponi for quite some time. The Old Man can be very persuasive when he wants to be."

"We'll see," I said noncommittally, then approached the door, which dilated to let me pass and immediately closed behind me.

I found myself in an immense office. The back wall was glass from floor to ceiling, and overlooked Buko Pepon Boulevard. The other three walls each had a life-sized hologram of Pepon, and were clearly labeled in Terran. One was "The Exile," and showed him standing on a Deluros VIII street-corner, exhorting his human listeners to free his people from the bondage of colonialism; the second was "The Incarceration," and showed him sitting in his tiny prison cell in Balimora; and the third was "The Triumph," and showed him in his suit and Bush Devil cape, taking the oath of office before an audience of hundreds of thousands of his cheering people.

Pepon himself sat on a comfortable chair behind a large, polished hardwood desk, a small cigar between the fingers of his right hand, a hand-carved quartz ashtray in front of him. Though I knew that he was close to one hundred years old, his barrel chest and broad shoulders made him appear strong and vigorous, despite the white that permeated his facial fur. He was dressed in a conservative business outfit, and his personal jewelry—rings, a timepiece, a small pin—all glittered with diamonds. Somehow his reddish color, the vertical slits of his pupils, and the blue gill-like patterns on his neck seemed less jarring than I would have thought.

"Mr. Breen," he said in a deep, cultured voice, getting to his feet and approaching me with his huge hand extended. "I have been looking forward to meeting you. Thank you for coming."

"I've never addressed a planetary president," I said, taking his hand. "I'm not quite sure what I should call you."

"Mr. President or Mr. Pepon, whichever you prefer," he replied, his entire iris contracting as he moved into a brighter area of his office to greet me. "Hopefully I shall be simply Buko to you by the time you go home. Please be seated."

I sat down on a leather chair facing the desk, he returned to his seat, and a pair of liveried servants immediately entered, one bearing a bottle of Alphard brandy, the other a pair of large glasses. The one carrying the bottle showed the label to Pepon, then poured a glass for each of us. Pepon nodded, and both immediately turned and left without saying a word.

"I can't tell you how pleased I am that you accepted my invitation, Mr. Breen," he said. He lifted his brandy glass. "To your very good health."

"And to yours, Mr. President," I said.

He took a sip. "Very good," he said appreciatively. "Many people prefer the vineyards of Valkerie, but I have always preferred a good Alphard brandy."

"I have only recently been able to afford either," I admitted, "but I think it is a taste that I can cultivate without much difficulty."

He chuckled, a deep, rich, alien, but somehow comforting sound, and I began to understand what Amanda Pickett had meant about his charisma. The large office should have felt almost empty, but he seemed to fill it with his presence.

"Tell me, Mr. Breen, what do you think of our planet?"

"It's very lovely, at least the little I saw of it."

"It is beautiful," he agreed. "While you're here, I hope you'll have time to see some of our game parks. We're very proud of them, and our tourist facilities are second to none."

"So I've been told."

"I hope you're not a dedicated hunter . . . ?" he said questioningly.

"No, sir. I have no objection to other people hunting, but killing animals has never appealed to me."

"I'm glad you feel that way, Mr. Breen, because recently I signed a decree outlawing all hunting on the Great Eastern Continent, and allowing only very limited hunting elsewhere." He paused. "Our game was being decimated, and I simply couldn't allow it to continue. Not only is it a priceless heritage, but, on a more practical note, it brings tourists to Peponi, and tourists are absolutely vital to our economy."

"I'm glad to hear that efforts are being made to save the game," I said sincerely.

"I only wish I had been in a position to do something before we lost our last Landships and Sabrehorns." He took a puff on his cigar. "By the way, I was desolate to hear of Amanda Pickett's death."

"I only met her once," I said, wondering when he would get to the point of my visit, "but she was most hospitable to me."

"A good friend," he said. "And a fine writer. Her *Peponi Days* is a true work of art." He paused. "You, too, are a fine writer, Mr. Breen."

"Thank you," I said.

"I've read your biography of August Hardwycke, and found it a very evocative description of life in a bygone era of Peponi's history."

"I appreciate that, sir," I said. "But I'm not in a class with Amanda Pickett."

"Don't belittle yourself, Mr. Breen," he said. "I've also read *The Expatriates*, which is an excellent presentation of one side of the Emergency, a side that tends to get overlooked on Peponi these days."

"I'm glad it didn't offend you," I said.

He smiled easily. "We were all younger and more emotional in those days," he answered. "No, I wasn't offended."

I didn't know what to say next, so I settled for taking a sip of my brandy and waiting for Pepon to continue speaking.

"Excellent books, both of them," said Pepon. "And do you know what impressed me most about them?"

"No, sir."

"That the author was absolutely invisible."

"I was?" I replied, startled. "That's not necessarily a good thing."

"You look distressed, Mr. Breen," said Pepon. He noticed

that his cigar had gone out, unwrapped a fresh one, and lit it. "Perhaps I should explain my statement. What I mean is that, although you wrote an entire book about one of Peponi's great hunters, and included an exceptionally evocative section on the slaughter in the Bukwa Enclave, I truly did not know your own feelings about hunting until you expressed them to me just now. And to this moment, I do not know your opinion about the Kalakala." He paused. "Oh, I know you feel that their military campaign was doomed from the start—but I don't yet know if you feel that their actions were justified by their grievances." He stared at me. "In other words, you report the facts as you find them, but you leave the reader to interpret them as he sees fit. I approve of that."

"Thank you," I said.

"Let me ask you a question, Mr. Breen."

"Certainly, Mr. President."

"If some member of the Kalakala had told you *why* they felt the need not just to go to war but to commit certain, shall we say, questionable acts, would you have reported that statement fairly and impartially?"

"That wasn't the focus of my book, sir," I answered. "I was only concerned with interviewing the human survivors."

"All right," he said, and I sensed that he was trying to hide his impatience. "Let me put it another way. What did you, personally, think of Felicia Preston's methods?"

"I think they were very efficient."

"That is what you think of them militarily," he said. "What did you think of them *personally*?"

"I don't think torture and mutilation are ever justified," I replied.

He smiled. "*That* is the answer I had hoped you'd give."

"I'm glad it pleases you, Mr. President," I said, wondering exactly where the conversation was going.

He stared at me for what seemed a very long time. "I think you're the right man for the job," he said at last.

"What job?"

"Mr. Breen, I have had seventeen biographies written about me since Peponi achieved its independence and I became its President," said Pepon. "I would be less than candid with you if I didn't say that all of them were laudatory to one degree or another." He paused. "However, each of them was written by a native of Peponi, and they have had almost no distribution beyond our planet." He smiled at me. "*You*, on the other hand, are a Man with two successful books to your credit, both of them about various aspects of Peponi, and you are not without some literary cachet. Were you to write my biography, there is no question in my mind that it would appear all across the Republic, and especially on those worlds from which we must coax either aid or technological assistance. Do you see what I am driving at, Mr. Breen?" he concluded, grasping the end of the huge desk with his massive hands and leaning across it in my direction.

"You want me to write a biography of you."

"That is correct."

"Why did you choose me?" I asked. "There are better writers."

"Perhaps," he said, "but between your literary credentials and your willingness not to make value judgments, there is none better suited to my purpose."

"You keep mentioning my personal opinions not intruding in my books," I said. "What, exactly, am I expected to refrain from expressing personal opinions *about*?"

"May I speak frankly, Mr. Breen?"

"If I'm going to be your biographer, it would be an excellent habit to get into," I agreed.

"Peponi is not the Republic's typical colony planet," began Pepon. "Your race found no sophisticated, technologically advanced, starfaring civilization when you landed here. What you did find was a primitive world with primitive peoples, many of them properly defined as savages. We had no written

language, no techology beyond the ability to build a fire and fashion crude weapons, we had not even discovered the wheel. Now, in less than a century, we have had to undergo perhaps one hundred generations of social and scientific evolution." He paused. "There was a time when our lives were simple, when we lived in harmony with Nature, and Peponi was truly a paradise to us. There will come a time, hopefully in the not-too-distant future, when it can be a paradise again, though of an entirely different kind. But right at this moment in our history, we are in a state of transition, a transition such as perhaps no other race has ever been asked to make." He finished his brandy, put his cigar back in his mouth, and continued: "If you accept the assignment, Mr. Breen, you will be given complete freedom to travel anywhere on Peponi, and to ask questions of anyone. In the course of your research, you may well encounter serious criticism of myself and my government. Some of these criticisms will displease you; a few may appall you. You will hear the truth and you will hear lies and rumors, and you will not have the background to separate one from the other. Therefore, I want a man who will simply observe and report and make no value judgments. I will help you in any way that I can, and will open my files to you. All that I ask is that before you write anything that may seem detrimental to either Peponi or myself, you discuss it with me first, so that I can help enlighten you."

"But you won't censor me?"

"You have my word, Mr. Breen."

"Let me make sure I understand your offer," I said. "I can speak to anyone, human or native, without reservation?"

"That is correct."

"I will have access to your private papers?"

"Except for those dealing with planetary security."

"All my expenses will be paid?"

"Absolutely."

"Will I have the use of Ian Masterson as my guide and interpreter?"

He paused for a moment. "I had in mind a member of my own race. There are numerous pepons who will not speak freely to a pair of human beings, especially if one of them is the notorious Ian Masterson. However, if you insist upon him . . ."

I shook my head. "No. I'll be guided by your judgment in the matter, sir."

"Have you any other questions?"

"Yes. Have you a publisher already lined up?"

"No," said Pepon. "But I can use my influence to find one if you run into any difficulty."

"How long do I have to write this book?"

"I am quite old," he said, "and I have numerous physical ailments. I should like to see the book completed and published within my lifetime."

I wanted to ask how long he expected to live, but it seemed a terribly inappropriate question.

He stared at me again. "Well, Mr. Breen—have we an agreement?"

I considered his offer for a moment, then nodded. "We do," I said.

He uttered a delighted laugh. "Excellent!" he said. "Allow me to offer you a Peponian delicacy before you leave."

"I'd be honored."

He pressed a button on his desk, and another liveried servant entered, bearing a single silver plate with some tiny pieces of grilled, rolled meat on it.

"Have you ever eaten any of our native game animals, Mr. Breen?" he asked.

"No, I haven't."

"Then please indulge yourself with some specially prepared Silvercoat, Mr. Breen," he said magnanimously. "You're not likely to encounter any meat except Beefcake for the rest of your stay on Peponi."

"Is there some reason for that?" I asked, taking a bite of the Silvercoat. I found it a bit gamey, and far too heavily spiced.

"There are two reasons, Mr. Breen," said Pepon. "First, most members of my race prefer domestic animals to wild game. Second, hunting has been outlawed on this continent."

"I'd forgotten," I said, and then, before I could stop myself, added: "Then how did you get *this*?"

"A Presidential prerogative," he said.

"It's excellent," I remarked with more enthusiasm than I felt.

"I *knew* you'd like it," he replied, obviously pleased with himself. "When I was a small child, I used to hunt the Silvercoat with a spear that I had fashioned myself."

"I thought you said that your people preferred Beefcakes," I noted.

"I was always different." He nodded and the servant placed the tray on his desk and left the office. Pepon looked at his jeweled timepiece. "I must attend a budget meeting in about twenty minutes, Mr. Breen—but in the meantime, since you are to be my biographer, I am at your disposal. Have you any questions you wish to ask me?"

I decided to start with a simple one.

"Why did you change your name from Robert Prekina?"

"Robert is a human name; I am not a human. Buko was my grandfather's name."

"And Pepon?"

He shrugged. "An affectation. I spent fifteen years on Deluros VIII, speaking out for Peponi's freedom, so I chose a name that people would associate with my world."

I stared directly into his large, catlike eyes. "Sooner or later I'm going to have to ask you if you had anything to do with the Kalakala."

"No, Mr. Breen, I had nothing whatsoever to do with them. We had the same goal, but I disapproved of their methods."

"What does *Kalakala* mean?"

He shrugged eloquently. "I have no idea."

"It's not a Bogoda word?"

"It's not a word in *any* Peponi language."

"That implies that someone created it," I said. "Who?"

"I truly don't know. Perhaps it was James Praznap; he was their military commander in chief."

"The same James Praznap that Praznap Avenue downtown is named after?"

He nodded. "The people need their heroes. He was a great freedom fighter."

"I thought you disowned the Kalakala."

"Their methods, not their goal, Mr. Breen," he repeated. "You know, I have read and reread *The Expatriates* with interest, and there is one absolutely vital fact that you omitted."

"Oh? What was that?" I asked.

"Less than five hundred humans were killed during the Kalakala Emergency, while more than eighty thousand Bogoda were slain."

"My understanding is that more than half of them were Bogoda who were loyal to the colonial government and were killed by Kalakala," I pointed out.

"*That* is precisely why you must believe me when I tell you that I am ignorant of all facets of Kalakala, including the meaning of the word itself," said Pepon. "I would never encourage one Bogoda to kill another."

"I haven't said that I don't believe you," I replied, noticing that I hadn't finished my brandy and taking another swallow of it. "It has been suggested to me that the word *Kalakala* was created because it was so easy to remember. Can you think of any other reason?"

"Yes, I can," he said. "Since it doesn't exist in any tribal dialect, I believe it was meant to serve as a rallying cry for all tribes."

"But that didn't happen," I said.

"No, it didn't."

"How much residual bitterness remains because the other tribes wouldn't join the Bogoda?"

"Too much," admitted Pepon. "I've done my best to integrate my government, but I shall have to do more." He paused. "My own people are somewhat distressed that I have invited members of all the tribes to participate in government, and that I have never had a Bogoda vice president." He sighed. "Someday I will make them understand that I am no longer a Bogoda, but a citizen of Peponi who happens to have been born into the Bogoda tribe."

I was about to ask if he knew who killed Sam Jimana, the young Kia politician whose assassination Masterson had described to me earlier in the day, but I decided that that would be a bit too audacious, and so I spent the next few minutes asking him about his plans for communal farms, irrigation projects, tourist bureaus, and the like.

Finally he looked at his timepiece again.

"I'm afraid I must bring our discussion to an end, Mr. Breen," he said.

"Will we be able to continue it tomorrow?" I asked.

He shook his head. "No. I have to fly to the Great Western Continent. We will speak again when I return."

"When will that be?" I asked.

"Hopefully a week; certainly no more than two." He stood up and escorted me to the door through which I had entered. "And now, Mr. Breen, I'm afraid I must bid you farewell. Let me say once again that I am very glad that you have accepted my commission."

"Where will I meet my new guide?" I asked.

He smiled. "Just beyond the door. He has been waiting for you."

"Oh?"

"Even energetic men such as Ian Masterson require some rest," he said. Then he added: "I should warn you that your new guide's appearance may startle you, but he is an intelligent and competent youngster with a very bright future ahead of him."

"Why will he startle me?"

"A number of my people have joined what is called the Purist Movement. They feel that Peponi has been contaminated by our continued association with Men, and they have adopted various modes of tribal dress as a form of protest."

"He's not dangerous?" I asked nervously.

Pepon laughed. "My dear Mr. Breen, he drives a vehicle that was manufactured on Spica II, his apartment is filled with technological marvels that were created by Men, and he received his education on a human world." He paused. "No one in the Purist Movement actually wants to go back to living in the bush; they merely want to exhibit an outward manifestation of pride in our race. Their dress is merely an affectation; they'll outgrow it eventually."

Then the door opened, I stepped through it into the foyer, and it closed behind me.

I found myself facing a stocky native who seemed, to my still-untrained eye, to be in early middle age. His face was shaven in a distinctive pattern, and he seemed to be wearing nothing but a colorful robe and leather sandals. Hanging about his neck were a pair of beaded necklaces. Strangely enough, he looked somehow *proper*, certainly more proper than most of the natives—always excepting Pepon—looked in their human outfits.

"Mr. Breen?" he said, approaching me.

"Yes?"

"I am Nathan Kibi Tonka. President Pepon has asked me to act as your guide and interpreter. I am at your disposal until he returns from his forthcoming trip." He paused awkwardly. "Please call me Nathan."

"Fine, Nathan," I said, extending my hand. "And you can call me Matthew."

"Would you like me to return you to your hotel?" he asked, taking my hand in a powerful grip. "Or perhaps you would like to sample some of Berengi's night life? There are many clubs that cater to Men."

"Actually," I said, "what I'd really like to do is get something to eat. Why don't you join me and we can get to know each other a little better?"

He nodded his head and led me to the lift, which took us down to the main floor. As we walked out the door, a luxurious black vehicle, elegant and expensive, pulled up. A uniformed officer emerged from it and saluted Tonka, then ordered the back door to open for me.

"I'd rather sit in the front seat," I said.

He looked concerned, as if it was a request he had never heard before.

"I can see better from there," I explained.

Tonka nodded, and while he climbed into the driver's seat, the officer ordered the back door to close, and commanded the front door on the passenger's side to swing open for me. I entered the vehicle, and a moment later we were cruising down Bakatula Avenue. I had driven down Bakatula with Ian Masterson earlier in the day, and it had seemed a bright, colorful street, filled with gift shops and native vendors. Now, at night, in a car driven by an alien, the shapes of the buildings seemed irregular, and the pedestrians faded into the shadows, and I realized, perhaps for the first time, that I was truly on an alien world.

"Is there any restaurant that you prefer to visit?" asked Tonka.

"I've been on Peponi for less than a day," I said. "Why don't you choose?"

"I would ordinarily recommend the cafe next to the Equator's Message Tree," he said, "but even though my vehicle is clearly labeled as government property, I feel uneasy about leaving it parked downtown at night. Why don't we go to the Royal Hotel? It has a number of restaurants, and that way when you get tired you can simply go to your room."

"That sounds fine to me," I agreed, and about four minutes later Tonka pulled up to the front entrance of the Royal. One of the doormen helped us out, and then took the vehicle to a private parking area.

"Is there much crime in Berengi?" I asked as we walked into the smaller of the hotel's two restaurants.

"Some," he said with a shrug. "It does seem to be getting worse."

"Why should that be?"

"Not because of the nature of the people. I would not want you to go home thinking that all pepons are thieves." He signaled to a waiter. "Berengi's economy simply cannot accommodate its million-plus citizens, and there are thousands more pouring into the city every week. Many are destitute, and have no choice but to steal if they are to live." He paused, trying to order his thoughts. "The average pepon is generous to a fault. He would never refuse to share his quarters or his food with you, nor would he steal from another citizen. But he sees tourists—and some government officials—spending more money in a day than he makes in a year, and the urge to possess some of that wealth must become almost irresistible." He paused. "You will spend as much in the next half hour, just on dinner, as the average citizen of Berengi earns in a month."

The waiter finally approached us and led us to a secluded little table at the back of the room. I noticed that Tonka was the only pepon in the restaurant, but despite his tribal dress none of the other diners seemed to take any notice of him.

"What did you do before you entered government service?" I asked.

"I was a teacher," replied Tonka. "Since I alone of my people had been to missionary school, I felt it was my duty to pass on what I had learned. We had a tiny schoolhouse near Lake Jenapit." He paused, remembering the scene. "The roof was made of grass, and we had to cut windows in the walls to let the light in. I taught all ages and all subjects in a single classroom."

"Why did you leave?"

"Three of my students were accepted by the University of Berengi," he said. "After they graduated they came back to our village to toil as fishermen, because there were no jobs in Berengi that could utilize their education. It was then that I decided that all I was doing was filling their heads with useless facts and false hopes for a better future. I decided to go into politics to make that future a reality rather than a broken promise."

"I find that most admirable," I said. "How long have you been in the government?"

"Three years," he replied with a touch of bitterness. "As you can see, I have not yet reached a position where I can accomplish anything for my people." He paused. "But my time will come," he added with a sudden air of determination.

"Doesn't Buko Pepon have any programs for creating more jobs?" I asked.

"Certainly. But the first thing required to create jobs is money, and money has always been in short supply on Peponi. The President tours the Republic five and six times a year, trying to interest investors in our planet, but we still need far more capital than he has been able to raise."

"I see," I said. I stared at him for a moment. "Incidentally, I see no tribal insignia on your outfit."

"I am a Begau. This necklace," he added, fingering one of them, "is my tribal totem."

"I don't believe I've ever heard of the Begau."

He smiled. "Most off-worlders haven't. We are a very small tribe: There are only six thousand of us. We are fishermen, and we live on the shores of Lake Jenapit."

"What college did you go to?"

"I attended the University of Barios IV on scholarship." He smiled. "It was a disconcerting experience for someone who had spent all his life living in a grass hut and had never worn a pair of shoes until the day before he boarded the spaceship."

"It must have been," I agreed.

He nodded. "I had been to Berengi twice, so I knew what a city looked like, but knowing what it looks like is very different from living in one. Sometimes I feel as if there are two of me: one, the naked child who rose with the sun and boarded his fishing canoe every morning, and the other, the adult who has been to the stars and now serves in the government of Buko Pepon. There seems to be no connection between the two, no single point of reference that both share."

"Both live on Peponi," I suggested.

"If you could see my village and then my office, you would have difficulty believing that both could coexist in the same galaxy, let alone the same world."

"I'd like to visit both," I said.

"Then you shall," he responded. "Where else would you like me to take you?"

"I have been given complete freedom to go wherever I choose," I said. "But I have no idea where to go." I paused. "I suppose since I'm writing Buko Pepon's biography, I should also see the places that are important to his personal history: the village where he grew up, the cell where he was imprisoned during the Emergency, the Sabrehorn Inn, places like that."

He nodded. "When do you want to begin?"

"Tomorrow morning?" I suggested.

"I shall be waiting for you in the lobby."

The waiter returned, and I ordered a Beefcake steak and a cup of coffee. Tonka merely shook his head when the waiter looked at him.

"Aren't you having anything?" I asked.

"I am not very hungry."

"You're sure?"

"I will eat later."

"Why not now?"

"I mean no offense, but I do not eat human food."

"I thought Beefcakes were a native food," I noted.

"They were originally imported by Commodore Quincy."

"You should have mentioned it sooner," I said. "We could have gone to a restaurant that served something you could eat."

"You would not like it," he said.

"You don't know that," I said. "Next time we stop for food, I insist that we eat at a native restaurant."

"You are sure?"

"I'm sure."

He smiled. "I think, Matthew, that we are going to become friends."

Twelve

Nathan Kibi Tonka, still dressed in his Begau tribal garb, picked me up in a more rugged vehicle than he had used the previous night. We left the city and drove north for almost an hour across the flat, dry savannah, and then began a gentle ascent. The foliage became somewhat greener, the air cooler, the landscape more rolling.

"We are approaching the Greenlands," announced Tonka, as we passed a number of tiny tenant farms, each with numerous children playing around their huts. "Buko Pepon's village is about eighty miles north and west of here."

"I haven't seen so much as a Silvercoat in the past thirty miles," I remarked.

"Animals aren't stupid," replied Tonka. "It doesn't take them very long to learn the boundaries of the parks and reserves, and they tend to stay where it's safe."

"But I saw some on the land I passed between the spaceport and Berengi," I said.

He smiled. "It's bad for business to shoot the animals when a tourist may be passing by. But not many tourists come to the Greenlands, except to climb the mountains or go to the game parks, and this road leads to neither. Therefore, any animal that is sighted here is almost certain to be killed." He sighed. "It is a pity, because unlike the Greenlands, this land is very fragile. Do you see those Beefcakes?" he asked suddenly, pointing to a small pasture where a dozen Beefcakes were grazing under the bored gaze of a tall, slender Bogoda youth.

"Yes."

"I could put fifteen Silvercoats and twenty Dashers there, and they could reproduce and live in that single pasture in perpetuity, for they are part of Peponi's ecological system. But put twelve Beefcakes there, as this farmer has done, and in a year's time all the vegetation will have been pulled out by its roots, the entire pasture will turn to dust, and nothing will grow there again for a generation."

"Why don't they try game ranching, then?" I asked.

"These are Bogoda and Sorotoba," he said. "Like the Siboni, they measure their wealth by the number of Beefcakes they own. Wild game has no value."

"Do you mean that some of these Beefcakes will never be eaten?" I said, surprised.

"Eventually they will all be eaten, but first they will be bartered many times. They will be used to pay a bride price, or for a magician's charm, or for any number of things." He shook his head. "No, they are so integral a part of the economy that they will never be replaced by game ranching."

"If the Greenlands have better soil, why don't they graze the Beefcakes there?"

"There are six hundred million Beefcakes on Peponi," answered Tonka. "They graze *everywhere*. Besides," he added, "the farmers in the Greenlands have problems of their own. They don't need to share their land with the Beefcakes."

"I've been told that the Greenlands are the most fertile area on the planet. What problems can the farmers possibly be having?"

"Too many people, not enough Greenlands. You will understand better when you see it for yourself."

As we continued ascending, the character of the countryside changed again, becoming more heavily wooded, and then, suddenly, we were on a high plateau, perhaps 8,000 feet above sea level, and we were driving through the kind of flat, lush farmland that one expects to see on an agricultural planet. The air smelled rich with growing things, and even the huts and shacks seemed to be in better condition than those on the savannah.

The vehicle slowed down and Tonka pointed to a group of twelve thatched huts that were neatly arranged in a large semicircle off to the left, about fifty yards from the edge of the road. "Do you see that?"

"What is it?" I asked. "A village?"

He shook his head. "A family. Originally the farmer may have had ten acres; but as his children matured and his relatives moved in, the land was divided and divided again, and now you have twelve families each farming less than an acre."

"But what about all the land surrounding the original ten acres? It seems to be planted in sugar berries."

"It is—but it is a large tract, and that almost certainly means that it belongs to a government official in Berengi, or to one of the Men who remained here after Independence."

"Who is the largest landowner in the Greenlands?" I asked. "Buko Pepon?"

He nodded. "Yes. The Vainmill Syndicate and the Court-noy Cartel, both of them Republic conglomerates owned and controlled by Men, are the next largest landholders, followed by most of Pepon's cabinet. Pepon himself owns all of Commodore Quincy's old estates, plus a number of other tracts of land."

"How did that happen?" I asked as we increased our speed once again.

"He spent fifteen years among Men on Deluros VIII," replied Tonka with just a trace of irony. "Obviously he learned his lessons well."

"And nobody has objected?"

"He is the Father of Peponi. No one has objected."

"What about the corporate holdings?" I continued. "Surely someone objects to that?"

"Everyone objects to that, even Pepon," answered Tonka. "But those two corporations are also two of the biggest investors in Berengi, and he cannot afford to offend them. If he takes their land away from them, they might very well close their hotels and factories."

"So what happens to the normal Bogoda, who *isn't* a government official?" I asked as we drove by an enormous farm that was separated from the surrounding subsistence tracts by a high barbed wire fence.

"As the colonists left the Greenlands after Independence, the government appropriated their land—and if there was an exceptionally desirable farm where the human owner *hadn't* yet left, the government would offer him fair market value for it and insist that their offer be accepted. Once all the officials had taken what they wanted, they began subdividing the land into five- and ten-acre holdings, and gave one to each family—for as long as the land lasted. But you must remember that there are almost twenty million Bogoda, and there was simply not enough land to go around. Those who were fortunate enough to be given a piece of land immediately became subsistence farmers, which they had always been, though on someone else's land. Unfortunately, they are far less productive now than they were in the colonial period, since the farmers cannot afford fertilizer or insecticide."

"Can't the farmers pool their resources to purchase what they need?" I asked.

"Their only resource is the land," responded Tonka. "The farmers had no money to begin with, and they have had no surplus to sell since they moved here. And do not forget," he continued, "that as each new generation comes to maturity, the plots are divided. Many families now have less than half an acre upon which they must grow enough food to sustain themselves for the entire year." He paused and sighed deeply. "So Peponi, which used to export food to our neighboring planets, now can no longer feed even itself."

"You have obviously given the problem of food production a considerable amount of thought," I said. "How would *you* go about solving it?"

He shrugged. "It is not a simple problem; it will not yield to a simple solution. The solution must reach into all aspects of Peponian life. For example," he continued, "this may sound cruel and unfeeling, but the introduction of your medicine to our society has contributed greatly to the situation."

"It doesn't sound cruel so much as puzzling," I replied. "What do you mean?"

"Infant mortality has been practically eliminated on Peponi, and our social customs have not yet responded to this new circumstance. The average Peponi female has seven children. This was practical, even necessary, when she could reasonably expect five or six of them to die in infancy, but now, thanks to human medicine, we are undergoing a population explosion at the very time that our land is becoming less productive. We *must* limit our population growth." He paused. "The next thing we must do is eliminate our economic and dietary dependence on off-world crops and animals. Just as Beefcakes, which are not native to Peponi, are destroying the savannahs, sugar berries, which we do not even eat but grow only for export, are not a part of Peponi's ecology. They do not belong here. They take certain minerals from the Greenlands and other farming areas, and the land becomes less fertile each year." He sighed. "Only after these two problems are solved would the redistribution of the land be at all meaningful."

"Has Pepon addressed these particular problems yet?" I asked.

"Buko Pepon has four wives and twenty-three children, and owns more than three million Beefcakes," replied Tonka, increasing our speed again. "Does that answer your question?"

"I'd say so," I said wryly. "Does Pepon know your feelings about the Greenlands?"

"Certainly."

"Curious," I mused.

"What is?"

"Somehow I didn't think he'd give me a guide who would criticize him."

"You misunderstand, Matthew," said Tonka. "I think he is the very best President we could have. He fought the battle for Peponi's independence alone and unaided, when most of his people were content to live as Man's servants. It was he who went to Deluros to lobby for our freedom, and he who has almost single-handedly brought a primitive people into the Galactic Era. No, he is unquestionably a great leader." He paused. "He is just not perfect."

"Don't the other tribes object to the Bogoda owning the Greenlands?" I asked.

"Why should we? It is their homeland."

"It just appears to me, as an outsider, that a case could be made that Pepon was favoring his own tribe."

He shook his head. "You do not know him. Perhaps his greatest single quality is that he favors no tribe over another. The Greenlands belong to the Bogoda because they have always belonged to the Bogoda, and that is just and proper. But he is the President of all Peponi, not just the Bogoda." He slowed down again so that he could turn to me. "I do not think you can conceive of the problem of tribalism he faced when he became President. For centuries the Siboni had raided the Bogoda, stealing their females and their cattle. The Korani killed any member of another tribe who set foot in their territory. The Sentabels wanted the Great Western Continent to secede because a Bogoda was named President. My own Begau tribe, which is related to the Bogoda, once hunted the Dorado like animals, and were in turn decimated by the Siboni and Kandabera." He pulled over to the side of the road and came to a stop. "Men can change worlds the way they change clothes, but we are bound by birth to remain a part of our tribe."

He unwrapped his colorful robe and exposed his chest and belly. Burned into his flesh, as if by a branding iron, was a pattern consisting of two parallel lines, a hexagon, and three circles. "This is the mark of the Begau," he explained. "The two lines represent the two rivers that border our territory. The hexagon stands for the six warriors who saved us from the Siboni almost three hundred years ago, and the circles are the Bogoda, the Kia, and the Braggi, to whom we are related. The same pattern appears on *this*," he added, holding up the larger of his two necklaces, and now I could see that it was carved onto one of the larger pieces.

"This is what I am," he continued, gesturing to his brand. "I am a Begau from now until I die. I was twelve years old when the mark was burned onto me, and from that day on I have been obligated to defend my tribe and my village, and to kill my hereditary enemies. I must trust no one who is not a Begau. I must never favor another over a Begau, nor give evidence against a Begau to an outsider, no matter what his crime."

"And the pattern that you've shaved on your face?" I asked.

"Theoretically, I must not allow it to grow out until the last Siboni is dead," he said.

"And this is the doctrine of the Begau?"

"Yes," he said. "I keep the symbols of my tribe for the

sake of my people, but I have forsaken the substance of tribalism for the good of Peponi, as have all members of the
government—but tens of millions have not. That is why we
must have Buko Pepon as our leader."

He covered himself up, then pulled the vehicle back onto
the road and began driving again.

"There was a time, about ten years ago," he continued,
"that four Sorotoba families moved to the Maracho area, just
below the Greenlands. The Bogoda who lived there did not
want them, and threatened to drive them out. The very next
day Buko Pepon showed up, dressed in the tribal robes of the
Sorotoba, and told the Bogoda that if they planned to kill the
Sorotoba they would have to kill him too. Of course they did
not raise a hand against him, and the Maracho Sorotoba were
never harassed again."

"That really happened?" I said. "You're sure it's not just
an apocryphal story?"

"I know two Sorotoba who were there," he assured me.

"You've got a very courageous President," I said, wondering
if any Secretary of the Republic since Jonathan Ramsey would
have willingly placed himself in such a situation.

"He is very brave and very wise," agreed Tonka. "The
same Men who called him a devil now pay him homage as a
great statesman." He smiled. "Do you know why the crime
rate in Berengi is not even worse than it is?"

"Why?"

"Because once every two or three weeks Buko Pepon walks
through the slums, alone, at night. Occasionally he wears his
Bush Devil cape and speaks to the people, but sometimes he
dresses just as an ordinary citizen would. The residents know
this, and the rate of violent attacks has dropped off markedly,
since no one wants to be the one to kill the President."

"That seems to border on foolishness," I said. "Surely
someday he's going to bump into someone who wants to kill
him. A Kia, perhaps, or a Sorotoba."

"No one will kill him," answered Tonka, as if the idea were too farfetched to consider. "He is the Father of Peponi."

"That may not impress somebody who is poor and disadvantaged."

"We are *all* poor and disadvantaged," replied Tonka sardonically.

"Doesn't anyone blame him for that? After all, he's been in office since Independence."

"They blame his underlings, they blame their neighbors, they blame the colonists, they blame the weather," said Tonka. "But he himself is above blame."

"That's difficult for me to comprehend," I admitted.

"The people understand the problems he faces. When your Jonathan Ramsey became Secretary of the Republic, he took over the reins of a working government, one that had laws and policies and allies and revenue bureaus and a military. Buko Pepon took over a planet that had been systematically plundered by its human colonists, and had to create a set of laws and policies and revenue bureaus for a government that did not exist until he took office. The remarkable thing about Peponi is not that we are such a poor planet, but that we have survived at all."

We came to a low brick building in the middle of an open field. It was surrounded by a number of sheds, and Tonka, explaining that once a week this was a very busy native market, stopped to refuel our vehicle, while I wandered about, looking into the dark, cool interiors of the little buildings. Most were empty, except for a framed holograph of Pepon in his Bush Devil cape, the same one I had seen in the lobby of the Royal Hotel. I had the distinct impression that these were supplied by the government, and that it would be very bad for business for the shed owner not to accept one.

Only two of the sheds seemed to be open for business: one was selling warm beer and the other displayed a number of pots and gourds that were obviously not intended for tourists.

The two proprietors, dressed in colorful robes that I assumed were the tribal garb of the Bogoda, greeted me with friendly smiles and tried to sell me some of their wares, but, as Masterson had warned me, once out of the cities and game parks, Terran was virtually unknown. I smiled and shook my head as each in turn approached me, and they took my refusal in good humor.

"Are you ready to go?" asked Tonka, walking over to join me.

"Yes."

"Would you care for a beer?"

"They don't look very cold," I observed.

"They aren't," he agreed. "But they're wet, and it's going to be a long, dusty drive before we reach Balimora."

I shrugged. "You talked me into it."

He handed some coins to the shopkeeper, took two containers of beer off a shelf, opened them, and handed one to me. It was even worse than I had anticipated, and I really had to struggle to avoid making a face that might offend the shopkeeper. A moment later we were back on the road.

"Tell me about the holographs," I said.

"What holographs?" he asked.

"Of Pepon. They were in every shed."

"Oh, yes, they are supplied by the Department of Information," he replied. "Every public business must display at least one of them."

"I also notice that Pepon's likeness is on every denomination of your currency."

"Why not?" countered Tonka. "He is the President."

"What happens when he dies? Will you issue all-new currency bearing the image of his successor?"

It was obvious from his surprised reaction that the question had never occurred to him before, and he silently considered it for some minutes. Finally he shook his head. "It would be wasteful to replace currency that already exists."

We drove in silence, and I spent most of my time observing the changing countryside. We were now in the heart of the Greenlands, and while I saw an occasional colonial farmhouse, it seemed that every hundred feet or so we passed yet another hut or shack. Most were surrounded by numerous children, many of them totally naked, and I began to understand the magnitude of the problem that was facing Peponi if it couldn't bring its population under control.

Every now and then we would pass a landmark of sorts, and Tonka would dutifully point it out to me: this was the farm where the Preston family was slaughtered by the Kala-kala, this was the spot where Catamount Greene first made contact with the Bogoda a century ago, this was the farm where Jessamine Gaines held off twenty Kalakala warriors, this was where a party of colonial counterinsurgents were ambushed and killed by a small war party led by James Praznap, greatest of the Kalakala generals.

Finally we drove up a long, bumpy driveway and parked about fifty feet from a ramshackle old farmhouse. The glass was out of most of the windows, there were no longer any doors, what had once been a kitchen garden was now covered with what seemed a year's supply of garbage, and the beautiful old trees that lined the driveway had died from lack of atten-tion. Some fourteen children were playing, unsupervised, in the front yard, and off in the fields I could see three grown females bent over, harvesting sugar berries by hand.

"I thought you might like to see this," said Tonka.

"What is it?"

"Amanda Pickett's home."

I looked more carefully. Yes, there was the old weathervane that I had seen pictured in Amanda's holograph album, and out front was the stone well from which her father had drawn water prior to getting a pump, but the rest of it was completely unrecognizable.

"I would never have recognized it," I admitted.

"The government declared it a national monument almost twenty years ago," said Tonka. "But they could never find the money needed to refurbish it, and they turned it over to a Bogoda family about twelve years ago."

"What a shame," I said, looking at the decaying building and the many signs of neglect. "I've seen holos of the way it used to be. It was beautiful once." I paused. "I appreciate your bringing me here."

"I read your books. I know that you were a friend of hers." He paused. "She was the best human friend that my people ever had. I have brought you here because you knew her, and because you must see it if you are to understand our problems." He pointed to the children. "These are not savages here, laying waste to a once-beautiful property. They are Bogoda, trying their best to make a life for themselves under very trying conditions. If the house has fallen into disrepair, it is because there are only so many hours in a day, and it is more important for them to produce food from their few paltry acres than to refurbish parlors and kitchens that serve no purpose." He stared intently at me. "There are very few Men I would bring here, but if you are to understand Pepon and Peponi, you must see it."

"I thank you for your trust," I said.

"You can thank me by writing the truth," he said, activating the vehicle and backing out of the driveway. "If I read that Amanda Pickett's house has become a rural slum simply because it is now home to some Bogoda, I will know that you are no different from most other Men."

I made no answer, and we drove another four miles, stopping finally at a group of huts and shanties. Up on a hill overlooking them was a large colonial home, and I could see some children playing on the lawn. The huts themselves seemed almost deserted, except for one very old native who sat on a decrepit wooden stool in the shade of a large tree, eyeing us curiously.

"Where are we?" I asked, as Tonka deactivated the vehicle.

"This is the birthplace of Buko Pepon." He pointed to one of the huts, which had a plaque on it.

"Where is everyone?" I asked.

"Many of them were killed in the Emergency," explained Tonka. "Only three families remain, though the people are very old and their children have long since left to find work in Berengi."

"Why didn't they stay and farm the land?"

He pointed to the broad, cultivated fields. "Pepon owns all the land that you can see from here."

We got out of the car and approached the old native. Tonka greeted him in what I assumed was Bogoda, then turned to me.

"He says that he is honored to be visited by the Man who will write Buko Pepon's story, and will answer anything you would like to know. He speaks no Terran, but I will act as interpreter."

"Please thank him for me," I said, "and ask him if he remembers Buko Pepon as a small child."

Tonka translated the question.

"He says that even then everyone knew that Robert Prekina—that was his name back then—would be the savior of Peponi. He says that his face glowed at night with a holy light, and that when he was four years old he could read and write and speak Terran better than any colonist." Tonka smiled. "I think we may safely assume that he is embellishing his answer."

"I don't know what to ask next," I admitted. "I wanted to learn about Pepon's childhood, if he exhibited any signs of leadership or ambition, but if I'm to be told that he was blessed by God at the age of four, I don't think I'm going to get any useful answers."

"Would you permit me to formulate some questions?" asked Tonka.

"Certainly."

Tonka said something to him, listened politely to a lengthy answer, and then turned to me again.

"I asked about Pepon's family, who did not glow with a holy light," he said with another smile. "There were six brothers, all of whom died before reaching maturity, and two sisters. One of them is still alive in Berengi; the other died in infancy. Pepon himself attended a missionary school about seven miles from here, and left home for Berengi when he was only twelve."

"Did he convert to Christianity?" I asked.

"I can answer that myself," replied Tonka. "He converted as a child, and unconverted when he returned from Deluros VIII, just before he was jailed."

"Ask him if he ever expected Pepon to survive his incarceration."

The old native smiled and nodded.

"He never doubted it," replied Tonka. "Pepon was chosen by God to throw the colonials out and return the Greenlands to the Bogoda."

"Not the most useful interview I've ever had," I said. One final question occurred to me. "I'm going back to the landcar," I said. "Wait a minute or two, then ask him, as if you are asking for yourself rather than for me, if he finds life better now than before Independence."

"He will say that he does."

"Ask him for details," I said. I smiled at the old native, shook his hand, and walked off to the vehicle.

Tonka joined me a few minutes later and activated the motor.

"What was his answer?"

"He says that life is much better now," replied Tonka. "He admits that his children have been unable to find work, and that he can barely raise enough crops to feed himself on the small piece of land Pepon had allowed him to retain, and that his radio, which I gather is his pride and joy, no longer works and he cannot afford to fix it—but he is free, and sooner or later Buko Pepon will supply every single Bogoda with a huge farm and a new radio and a landcar."

"Has he ever been promised that?"

"No."

"Has he any idea where those huge farms will come from?"

"He is an ignorant old Bogoda," said Tonka, seemingly unaware that he had used *Bogoda* the way someone might use *peon*. "Please do not ask me to justify his statements."

"I'm just surprised to find that after a quarter of a century of poverty he still believes everything's going to get better."

"He must believe in something," responded Tonka with a shrug.

"That sounds rather callous," I said.

"Perhaps," admitted Tonka. "The truth of the matter is that we are faced with enormous problems, but they are *our* problems, and *we* shall solve them." He paused. "If we are to have freedom and problems together, or be rid of both, we will choose the former."

"Does everyone on Peponi feel that way?" I asked.

"Possibly there are some who don't," he admitted. "But nobody has ever suggested that we invite Men to once again rule Peponi. They can profit at some other world's expense."

"Speaking of profiteering, does it bother anyone that Buko Pepon seems to have accumulated quite a fortune?"

"By law, all his money must be invested on Peponi," explained Tonka. "It is illegal to take more than two hundred credits' worth of our currency off-world. They must have told you that before you disembarked here."

"All right," I said. "So he invests his money on Peponi. But that doesn't mean that he isn't the richest single being on the planet."

"He is the greatest member of his race," said Tonka. "Why should he not also be the wealthiest?"

"But—"

"When we lived in tribal villages, before the advent of Man, the chief was always the wealthiest member of the community," continued Tonka. "Nobody found anything wrong with that; after all, that was one of the reasons why he was the chief, and nobody ever resented his wealth." He paused. "Buko Pepon is the chief of the entire planet. It is only natural that he is richer than anyone else."

"You're saying that it goes with the job?" I asked, trying to understand his lack of moral outrage or even envy.

"Of course. Why else would one want to rise to power?"

"Pepon told me before I met you that you were not only bright but ambitious. Do you also want to be wealthy?"

"Certainly. I did not educate myself and work all these years so that I could go back to my village and live in a hut and catch fish for a living." He paused. "I want to improve the lot of my people, but I expect to improve my own lot as well. In certain circumstances, that would mean I would want more cattle or more wives, but I have been educated by Men and I work in a government that is patterned after your institutions, so that means I want more wealth." He turned to me once again. "You are a wealthy man, Matthew."

"Not really," I said.

"You have had two best-selling books," he continued. "Surely you could afford to write Buko Pepon's biography for free, or to donate your entire fee to charity. Would I be correct in assuming that you have not seriously considered either alternative?"

"You win," I said with a sigh.

"You see?" he said with a triumphant smile. "We are not so different after all."

"I'm not the one who wears my tribal dress to remind me of the differences," I said.

"I wear it to remind me that we are already equals, and that I do not have to wear a human outfit to prove it."

"Well said, Nathan."

"Thank you, Matthew," he replied, looking quite pleased with himself.

The landscape started changing again about an hour later. The vegetation grew sparser, the hills flattened out, and suddenly I felt much warmer. I remarked upon it to Tonka.

"We are leaving the Greenlands, and are now at a lower elevation. This road will take us to Balimora."

"How long will it take?"

"We should reach the outskirts of the desert in about two hours, and Balimora is another half hour."

I spent the next few minutes looking at the dull brown grass and bushes, trying to spot an animal anywhere in the landscape which once teemed with life, and then I must have fallen asleep; for the next thing I knew Tonka was shaking my shoulder and telling me that we had arrived.

Balimora was a charming little town, a combination of old and new. The brick colonial buildings were whitewashed and sparkling, while the newer structures were somehow alien, filled with strange angles and odd slopes, yet not at all unpleasing to the eye. The wide streets were in good repair, and the native populace, whether in tribal garb or human outfits, seemed well-dressed and affluent, as did three human women I saw walking into a butcher shop. There were almost three dozen stores and shops, including a fascinating boutique that specialized in native cosmetics, and they all seemed to be doing a thriving business. I asked Tonka why this town appeared so much more prosperous than some of those we had driven through earlier in the day.

"We are on the Korani tribal lands," he answered. "They are related to the Siboni, and unlike the Bogoda, they have never taken up arms against Men. As a result, a number of colonists who were forced to sell their Greenlands farms to the government chose to relocate in Balimora after Independence. Some of them built a large food processing factory which hires many Korani, and the rest find work in the gold mines that are just beyond those hills," he concluded, pointing to some rocky outcroppings to the north.

"Who owns the mines?"

"My understanding is that a number of Men lease them from the government."

"So the locals work for former colonists?" I asked. "I thought you disapproved."

He shook his head. "You misunderstood me. I would disapprove of Men coming from off-world to plunder our resources and take their profits back to the Republic with them," he responded. "But *these* Men are citizens of Peponi, and they believe in Buko Pepon's rallying cry of *Karabunta*, which means *Together* in Terran. They have lived here for decades, many of them were born here, they carry Peponi passports, they work here, and they invest their money here. I am sure that when Pepon met the colonists at the Sabrehorn Inn at Lamaki and asked them to remain after Independence and work together with us for the future of Peponi, this was what he envisioned."

"Do they promote your people to positions of authority?"

"Certainly," answered Tonka. "The law requires it."

He seemed unaware of the inherent contradictions of what he had said, and I didn't see the sense of pointing them out to him, so I accepted his answer and began following him as he walked through the town. Finally we stopped before a white brick building that had numerous plaques next to the door, most with engraved impressions of Pepon. I found that I could read none of the writing.

"This is the old courthouse," announced Tonka. "It is a monument now. The new courthouse is on the next street." He pointed to the plaques. "It was here that Buko Pepon was tried by the colonial government, and condemned to thirty years' imprisonment. Each plaque commemorates his trial and incarceration in one of the major languages."

I followed him inside, where we were greeted by a uniformed native curator. Tonka paid our entry fees and then led me to a narrow staircase. I followed him down to a basement that contained two tiny cells, each no more than six feet on a side. It was incredibly hot, and the air was stale and difficult to breathe.

"Pepon was kept in the cell on the left," said Tonka. "The other was never occupied during all the time he was here. His sentence called for thirty years at hard labor, but after his followers made their first raid on the Balimora jail during the Emergency, he was never permitted out of this cell until his sentence was commuted after eleven years."

I entered the tiny cell, and tried to imagine how long I could remain imprisoned there before I went completely mad. One year at the outside, I decided; more likely six or seven months.

And yet Buko Pepon had spent more than a decade here, where no sunlight and no breeze could reach him, where he saw his human jailer for perhaps thirty seconds each day, and had not only survived with his mind intact, but had actually forgiven his captors and asked them to remain on Peponi.

What was a little profiteering compared to that?

Despite all I had read about him, despite the impression he had made on me at our meeting the previous night, despite the stories of his personal courage that Tonka had related to me, it wasn't until I stood inside the prison cell that I finally began to understand the greatness of this remarkable being.

Thirteen

We spent the night in a small Balimora hotel, toured the food processing factory in the morning, and then began heading back toward Berengi before the sun was too high in the sky and the heat became too oppressive.

"August Hardwycke told me that Balimora was the starting point for most of his Landship hunts," I remarked.

Tonka nodded. "That is true. The last Landships were poached about twenty miles northwest of here, at the Balimora game park."

"It seems such a sparse, barren country. You would think anything as large as a Landship would require more food than it could have found up here."

"You would be surprised at how many animals this terrain can sustain," he replied. "Would you care to go to the game park?"

I shook my head. "It's too hot out, and the dust gets inside the vehicle even though you've got the windows sealed. No, let's head back."

"Would you like to break our journey by stopping in the Jupiter Range?" he asked. "We can be there for a late lunch or early dinner, and there is a very nice lodge where we can spend the night."

"That's where the Kalakala's headquarters were?"

"Yes."

"I'd like that very much," I said.

"The game-viewing lodge is atop Mount Pekana," continued Tonka, "which used to be Mount Hardwycke. Perhaps you would like to see the mountain that you have written so much about?"

"I would indeed."

We sped across the flat, sunbleached, almost featureless countryside in silence. At one point Tonka slowed the car down and pointed off to his left, and I saw a lone Nightkiller skulking behind a bush, but I couldn't see what it was hunting. Now and then we would pass through small villages, most of them quite impoverished, and I noticed that the focal point of each seemed to be the well around which the huts had been built.

We also began passing a seemingly endless procession of young natives tending their Beefcakes, moving from one ungrazed patch of ground to another. Most of the animals seemed to be in poor condition, as did a number of the natives. Even the insects that encircled the faces of both the Beefcakes and the natives seemed to become lethargic as Peponi's sun beat down on the landscape.

Finally, as we put still more distance between ourselves and the desert, the land became slightly greener, and the Beefcakes' condition seemed to reflect it. Vehicles were rare out here, and most of the natives walked on the side of the road. Almost all of them were males; the few females carried enormous loads of firewood on their backs, nor did any unencumbered male offer to help them.

"Where are they all going?" I asked, after we had passed what seemed to be hundreds of natives walking in both directions. "The nearest village is almost ten miles up the road."

Tonka shrugged. "Who knows? They might be going to a neighboring village, or to market, or to meet a friend."

"So many of them?"

"They have nothing better to do with their time."

"Why aren't they working their farms?" I asked.

"These are Braggi and Korani," he explained. "They believe that it is a female's lot to work in the fields."

"And what does the male do?"

"He is a warrior," answered Tonka. "He protects the land while the female works it."

"But there's no need for warriors any longer," I said. "Peponi has an army and each district has its own police force."

"True," agreed Tonka. Suddenly he smiled. "They would tell you that they are very fortunate to have been born males."

"What does Buko Pepon feel about all this?" I asked.

"He would like to initiate social change, and have all the people become productive," said Tonka. "But he must move very slowly and carefully. These are not Bogoda, and he must make sure that he does not force change on them so rapidly that they reject his leadership."

"What about the Bogoda?" I asked. "What changes has he wrought in his own tribe?"

"There he has a different problem," replied Tonka. "He had no difficulty convincing the males to work on the farms —it was one of the preconditions he made before subdividing the Greenlands. No, his problem with the Bogoda is convincing the males to allow their wives and daughters to become educated and to work in the cities."

"Why should they resist it?" I asked. "At least the females can find work when the farms become too small."

He smiled. "Ah, but you are looking at the problem like a Man, and not like a Bogoda. You see, every Bogoda father wishes for daughters, for then he will receive the bride price from their suitors, and this will keep him from being impoverished in his old age. But when his daughters move off the farm and into the city, then he is denied their bride price."

"I wasn't aware that fatherhood was supposed to show a profit," I said.

"Look at them," said Tonka, gesturing to the ragged-looking natives. "Look at the land. What else have they to sell?"

I had no answer for him, so instead I asked another question. "What's the unemployment rate on Peponi?"

"That is a meaningless question, Matthew," said Tonka.

"Oh? Why?"

"Because it presupposes that we are able to care for our unemployed, and we are not. There *are* figures available in the cities—Berengi's unemployment rate is fifty-eight percent—but are *these* people"—he gestured out the window again—"who hold no jobs, earn no money, and take nothing from the government, unemployed? They live as they have always lived: off the land." He paused. "What about the village where I grew up? When they are hungry, they catch fish; when they are cold, they build fires; when they are thirsty, they drink from the river; when the river floods, it takes them less than a day to build another dwelling higher up the bank. Some of them have never seen either colonial or Peponi currency. Are they employed or unemployed?"

"You have a point," I admitted.

We soon entered another small town, and Tonka pointed out a large statue to me. It portrayed Buko Pepon, standing between a Lodinite and a Bokarian. He had an arm around each of their shoulders (which was especially difficult given the Bokarian's physical structure), and there was a triumphant expression on his face.

"This commemorates the peace treaty between Bokar and Lodin XI," said Tonka, lowering the window and letting in a gust of hot, dusty air. "They had been at war for almost five years, and neither trusted the Republic enough to allow it to act as an arbitrator. Finally Buko Pepon volunteered his services, brought the rulers of both planets to an estate he owns about five miles from here, and arranged a lasting peace between them."

"I wasn't aware of that."

"Oh, yes," affirmed Tonka. "In fact, he has been the architect of three other peace treaties between warring worlds."

"Really?" I said, impressed. "I knew he was considered a great statesman, but to be perfectly honest, I thought it was because he had imposed order on what could have been a chaotic situation on Peponi."

"If he were a Man, there would be monuments to him on ten thousand worlds," said Tonka with just a hint of bitterness.

"If he was a Man," I replied, "he wouldn't be your President."

"True," agreed Tonka. "I would not want to be the politician who succeeds him," he added earnestly.

We passed through the town, and in another hour were ascending gradually through the foothills of the Jupiter Range. The air became cleaner and cooler, and I could hear the singing and squawking of hundreds of avians. In the distance I could see an ice-topped peak that towered above the others, and asked if it was Mount Pekana, which had originally been Mount Hardwycke.

"That is Mount Buko Pepon," answered Tonka. "Mount Pekana is to our left."

"Where did most of the fighting take place?" I asked.

"It was spread throughout the Jupiter Mountains. The greatest concentration of Kalakala was probably on Mount Pekana." He paused. "That is where we are going now, but because of the terrain, the route is indirect."

When we reached an elevation of about 5,000 feet we entered a thick forest that seemed to extend almost to the peak, some two miles above us. The mountain was not exceptionally steep, but I could see where the altitude must have taken its toll of those colonists and soldiers who, unlike the Bogoda, were not bred or adapted to this terrain.

Finally, at about 7,000 feet, Tonka pulled the vehicle off the road, and we got out. There was a small marker at roadside, and he translated it for me; it marked the spot where Horst van der Gelt, a prominent settler, had been killed in hand-to-hand combat by a Kalakala leader bearing the unlikely name of Commander Arcturus.

"Commander Arcturus?" I said, unable to repress a smile.

"Many of the Kalakala officers took such names in the mistaken belief that the colonists worshipped various celestial bodies as they themselves did. There was General Andromeda, General Aldebaran, Captain Deluros, and a number of others. The commander in chief, though, kept his own name: James Praznap."

Suddenly he stood perfectly still and motioned me to silence. A moment later he relaxed.

"What is it?" I asked.

"Thunderheads," he said, pointing to a patch of brush about ten yards away. "Three of them."

I stared into it.

"I can't see anything," I said.

"Wait."

I continued to stare, and after about thirty seconds I saw a tiny motion. It was just an ear flicking, but suddenly the whole animal seemed to take shape, and a moment later I could see its two companions. They were standing about thirty yards into the brush, staring at us curiously.

Finally one of them snorted and turned away, and I could hear numerous heavy bodies moving through the forest.

"How many were there?" I asked.

"Perhaps forty," answered Tonka. "They're protected here, so they have no reason to be aggressive. They were just seeing who we were."

"Forty?" I repeated, surprised. "How close were the rest of them?"

"Fifty yards, maybe sixty."

I suddenly realized that I couldn't see sixty yards in any direction; even the road disappeared around a curve in half that distance.

"How did they ever fight up here?" I said. "The cover's so thick they could spend years searching for each other."

"They found each other more often than you might think," said Tonka. He paused. "Actually, the forest was even thicker during the Emergency. The only road was a dirt track on the other side of the mountain."

I tried to imagine Wilkes and Daniel Crawford and Felicia Preston climbing up through the forest, never knowing which tree might be hiding a Kalakala, walking through cover so thick that the sun couldn't break through it. The entire mountain had been teeming with Kalakala warriors, each far more at home in this environment than they were, and yet they might go a day or a week or a month without seeing any sign of them—until the moment they relaxed their vigil. Then, too, there were thousands of Thunderheads and Nightkillers, even a few Landships, all of them nervous and irritable because of the incessant fighting, ready to attack the first living thing they saw.

Finally I sighed and shook my head.

"Is something wrong?" asked Tonka.

"I don't know how they could fight a war here," I said. "They must have been crazy to come up into the mountains."

"Or desperate."

"Or desperate," I agreed.

"Actually, if you are fighting with spears and arrows against modern weapons, this becomes the very best battleground one could wish for."

"And if they're burning farms and mutilating your neighbors," I said, "I suppose you have to come up here after them, terrible conditions or not."

"The conditions became worse after the Republic joined the battle," said Tonka. "They made daily bombing runs, which didn't do much damage to the Kalakala, but drove the animals berserk with fear. There were perhaps fifty thousand Thunderheads on the mountain back then, and possibly a million over the entire Jupiter Range, to say nothing of Bush Devils and Nightkillers."

"What about Demoncats?" I asked.

He shook his head. "They live on the savannahs; there were never very many of them up here." He climbed back into the vehicle. "Are you ready to continue?"

"Yes," I said, joining him.

The forest became even thicker as we ascended, until finally, at about 9,000 feet, we reached a small plateau. There was an old stone farmhouse in a clearing near a water hole where a number of colorful avians were drinking and wading, and Tonka explained to me that this was the game lodge where we would be staying. He pulled into a large, almost empty parking area, ordered two Bogoda wearing the uniforms of the parks system to remove our luggage, and led me to the veranda.

"This used to be a colonist's farm," he explained. "A 'gentleman's farm,' I believe you call it, since the owner grew only enough food to feed his staff, and used it primarily as a hunting lodge during his vacations here."

"It seems to be almost empty," I noted. There were only two couples—one human, one native—sitting in the spacious dining room, and the only figure I could see walking around the grounds was an elderly man with a very expensive camera who was avidly taking holographs of avians.

"It is a pity," said Tonka. "I think this is the most beautiful of our national parks, but it is the least frequented, because it has the fewest animals—or, at least, the animals here are the most difficult to see, because of the terrain."

As we finished the gentle ascent up the lawn to the lodge, I found myself gasping for breath.

"The altitude," explained Tonka.

"But it didn't bother me at all until now," I said.

He grinned. "You were sitting in a landcar; now you are walking. Just don't overexert yourself and you'll be fine." He led me to a table on the broad terrace. "You'll feel much better if you sit down."

I took his advice, and he walked over to the bar, handed a couple of coins to the native bartender, and returned a moment later with two very cold beers.

"Thank you," I said. Then, looking at him, I added, somewhat petulantly I fear, "The altitude doesn't seem to bother you."

"This is *my* world, Matthew. I belong here." He handed me my beer. "I took the liberty of ordering lunch for us, since they have a very limited menu. It will take about twenty minutes to arrive."

"Thank you."

A moment later a tall, casually-dressed human approached us. He had thick gray hair, a bushy mustache, and a proprietary manner about him.

"Good afternoon," he said. "I hope my friend Nathan is showing you a good time."

"It's been very informative, Mr. . . . ?" I responded.

"Wesley," he replied, extending his hand. "Mike Wesley. I'm the manager here."

"I'm Matthew Breen. Won't you join us?"

"Happy to," he said, pulling up a chair. "Well, Matthew, what brings you to Peponi—business or pleasure?"

"Business," I said. "I've been commissioned by Buko Pepon to write his biography."

"Really?" he said. "Is the old boy going to publish it himself?"

"The current plan is for me to find an off-world publisher."

"Good," said Wesley. "About time someone else found out how well we're doing here." He turned to Tonka. "Nathan, I hope you're telling him everything he needs to know."

"I am endeavoring to," replied Tonka.

"If I can be of any help, Matthew, just ask. Peponi is a wonderful world; more people ought to know about it."

"Were you born on Peponi, Mr. Wesley?" I asked.

"Call me Mike. No, I came here with the Republic's armed forces to fight the Kalakala. Fell in love with these mountains and decided to stay on. When I heard that the government had no intention of building a lodge in the park, I bought this old place and refurbished it, and got a license to open it to the public." He leaned over to Tonka and gestured toward his beer. "Nathan, if you're not going to drink that, how about giving me a sip?"

Tonka shrugged and shoved his container over to Wesley, who picked it up and drained it.

"God help me, I think I'm developing a taste for Buko Pepon's beer!" he said with a laugh. Suddenly he pointed to the water hole. "Take a look, Matthew. You won't see anything like *this* on Deluros."

I turned to the water hole, and saw a large mixed herd of Thunderheads and Silvercoats coming out of the surrounding woods for their midday drink. The longer I looked, the more animals I saw, including a trio of Dust Pigs and a pair of Willowbucks, which pranced nervously and continually tested the wind.

"Lovely, isn't it?" enthused Wesley.

"Very."

"You know, I visited another world on my last vacation—Hamlet II. Two centuries ago it had even more wildlife than Peponi had in Fuentes' time. Then some of their leaders visited Deluros and Earth and Sirius V and decided that they couldn't consider themselves truly civilized until they destroyed all their animals the way Man has done. Terrible world to visit these days: big empty place. The whole damned world looks like a deserted butcher shop, since they killed off the scavengers too. I'll give the Old Man credit for that much: he knows the value of wildlife. Too damned bad he couldn't have saved the Landships and the Sabrehorns, but at least he got his programs in place before they could kill off anything else."

"*We* did not kill off the Landships," said Tonka. "*You* did."

"Me?" chuckled Wesley. "I've seen two Landships in my whole life. Damned impressive brutes, they were; never saw anything like 'em anywhere else in the galaxy."

"I meant that your race destroyed them."

"Come on, Nathan," said Wesley easily. "Both our races slaughtered them with equal enthusiasm and you know it. In fact, your people killed a lot more than mine did."

"We killed them for profit, just like you," said Tonka. "There is no difference."

"There's one difference, Nathan," replied Wesley. "We found their eyestones lovely, so we killed them to please members of our own race." He paused. "Thirty million eyestones were taken off this planet. How many remain on Peponi?"

"We had no jewelers," said Tonka defensively.

"I never said you did, Nathan," said Wesley. "I just said

we *both* killed them. Hell, at one time it must have seemed like there would never be an end to the Landships. I don't blame either race—but if you're going to insist that someone's responsible, then you'd better realize that your people were equally culpable."

"It is better that we leave the subject alone," said Tonka.

"Fine by me," said Wesley. He turned his attention back to me. "What have you seen of Peponi so far, Matthew?"

"Not very much," I responded. "I've only been here two days. I've walked around Berengi, and I've driven through the Greenlands and seen Amanda Pickett's home and Buko Pepon's birthplace, and I've been to Balimora."

"You should try to visit some of the other game parks while you're here," he said. "The Silvercoats are migrating on the Siboni Plains right now."

"If I can work it into my schedule, I'd like to," I said.

"Impressive spectacle," he replied. "The plains aren't as scenically beautiful as the mountains, but the migration is one hell of a sight."

"How long have you lived in the Jupiter Range?" I asked.

"Since I got here," he said. "I've never left. When the Emergency was over I built a place over on Mount Pepon and worked as a warden in the park until I took over the lodge." Suddenly he grinned. "Very first thing I did was hunt up Joshua and hire him as my assistant."

"Joshua?" I asked.

"Didn't Nathan tell you about Joshua Buchanka?"

"No."

"Shame on you, Nathan," he said jokingly. He turned to me. "Joshua was the best damned field commander the Kalakala ever had." He paused. "I spent three years chasing him up and down this damned mountain. Even had him in my sights twice, but I never could take him."

"You mean you hired a Kalakala warrior you fought against to help you run the lodge?" I said, surprised.

"Why not?" answered Wesley. "He was the most efficient wag they had." Suddenly he turned to Tonka. "Sorry about that, Nathan."

"I will overlook it," said Tonka. "This time."

Wesley shook his head. "I don't think I'll ever get used to calling you people pepons. To me, 'pepon' means just one thing: the Old Man." He turned back to me. "Anyway, I sent word out that I was looking for Joshua. Took me almost half a year to track him down, but I finally found him farming a little three-acre piece of ground on the outskirts of the Greenlands. That's no way for anyone to live, and especially not someone like Joshua, so I drove up to his house, told him who I was, made sure he didn't still harbor an urge to separate my head from the rest of me, and we were in business."

"Where is he now?" I asked, looking around.

"Last time I saw him he was in the kitchen, fixing one of our freezers." He barked an order in Bogoda, and the bartender immediately walked out from behind the bar and headed off toward the kitchen. "He'll join us in a minute," said Wesley.

"I look forward to meeting him," I said.

"There was a time when I looked forward to it more than anything," said Wesley. He rolled up his pants, revealing that his left leg was artificial. "*He* did that to me. Got me with an arrow at long range." He shook his head. "Didn't think I was going to get back to camp. I finally made it, though. They cut off the leg, gave me a new one, and I was back on the mountain two months later."

"I'm surprised that you don't bear a grudge," I said.

"He was just doing his job, fighting for his homeland," replied Wesley. "Can't blame him for that." He smiled. "I'm surprised that he doesn't still want to kill *me*."

"Why should he?"

"I killed his oldest son in an ambush." He pointed to a

spot about fifteen hundred feet above us. "Right up there, it was. Waited in a ditch through two days of freezing rain and killed the first six Kalakala who came along; the last of them was Joshua's son." He sighed and shook his head again. "Good-looking lad, too. Looked a lot like his father."

A stocky, powerfully-built, middle-aged native, wearing a pair of shorts and a matching shirt, walked up to the table.

"Have a seat, Joshua," said Wesley. "This is Mr. Matthew Breen, who's here to write a book about the Old Man."

Joshua Buchanka shook my hand, greeted Tonka, and then sat down opposite Wesley.

"I hope you are enjoying yourself on Peponi, Mr. Breen," he said. His Terran had a thicker accent than Pepon's or Tonka's, but I had no difficulty understanding it.

"Very much so," I answered. "Mike was just telling us about his experiences during the Emergency."

Buchanka smiled. "Mike is a great liar." He leaned over to me. "I could have killed him three different times."

"Hah!" laughed Wesley. "Then why didn't you?"

"I feared they might put someone competent in your place," said Buchanka, returning his laughter.

"I'm amazed that neither of you feel any bitterness," I said.

"Why should I feel bitter?" responded Buchanka. "We won what we were fighting for. One of my sons is a chemist in Berengi, and another is a teacher in Balimora. My daughter works for a bank in Maracho. I did not fight for *my* future, but for *theirs*, and it has been secured."

"But don't you feel any personal enmity toward Mike?" I persisted.

"Because he killed my son?" asked Buchanka. "No. My son was a soldier, and every soldier must risk his life in a war. I do not blame Mike for defending himself, any more than he blames me for trying to put an arrow through his heart when he was my opponent on the field of battle. But when the battle is over, it is time to make peace. If Buko Pepon can forgive the race of Man, then I, who have suffered far less, can forgive one man."

"That's an admirable attitude," I said.

Buchanka stared at the Thunderheads for a long moment, then turned back to me.

"And there is one more thing," he said.

"What is that?"

"Although Mike is the manager of the lodge, neither the bartender, nor the cooks, nor I have to call him Boss." He smiled. "That alone is worth everything that we went through."

"Agreed!" said Tonka passionately.

Fourteen

Tonka had retired early, but the night was so beautiful, the air so cool and fresh, that I decided to sit out on the veranda of the Mount Pekana Lodge. A Bush Devil stationed itself by the water hole in late afternoon, hoping for an easy meal, but the lodge's spotlights came on automatically at dusk, illuminating the entire area, and eventually the carnivore became discouraged and wandered off into the forest. About an hour later a pair of Dust Pigs emerged from the heavy cover for a brief drink, but beyond that I saw nothing but an occasional avian. I could heard the coughing roar of a Bush Devil off in the distance, and the high-pitched screams of a pack of Nightkillers, but eventually even these stopped and the night became utterly still except for the sound of the insects.

I had been sitting there for perhaps three hours, getting up every forty minutes or so for a refill of my Cygnian cognac, when Wesley emerged from the interior of the lodge and approached me.

"Mind some company?" he asked.

"Not at all," I replied.

"Lovely up here, isn't it?" he said, pulling out a pipe and stuffing it with tobacco.

"Yes, it is."

"Makes you understand why they fought so hard to get it back from us," he said, sitting down and positioning his chair so that he could continue looking at the water hole.

"If it was mine, I'd have fought too," I agreed.

He lit his pipe and sighed deeply. "Too bad it can't stay like this forever."

I looked at the shadows that Peponi's single moon threw on the landscape.

"Why can't it?" I asked.

"Rich black earth and lots of rain," he replied. "One of these days they're going to chop down the trees and start farming and grazing their Beefcakes here." He paused. "With a little luck I'll be dead and buried before it's all gone."

I stared through the dark at the barely-visible outline of the Jupiter Mountains.

"Do you really think they'll do that?"

"You've seen their farming methods," he said. "Slash and burn, slash and burn. They could hold their population in check and still starve to death at the rate their farmers and their Beefcakes are destroying the land."

"Can't Buko Pepon do something about the problem?" I asked.

"You're his biographer, Matthew," said Wesley. "What do *you* think?"

"I don't know," I admitted. "I haven't spoken to him about it."

"He's a great President, the best they could have chosen, but he's got his limitations. He's spread himself too thin, taken on too many projects, and there's no one else in the whole damned government who even understands what's happening to the land, let alone cares."

"You don't sound like you have too much faith in Peponi's future," I said.

Wesley took a puff of his pipe. "With the best intentions in the world, it's going straight to hell," he said sadly.

"Are you joking?" I said, though I saw that he was not. "Why should you say that? I was in Balimora this morning, and it seemed like a prototype for a prosperous Peponi city."

"It's an exception, not a prototype," said Wesley. "A lot of humans moved to Balimora after Independence. They had managerial experience and money to invest. Do you know how rare that is on Peponi?"

"No."

"Then let me tell you. Eliminate Berengi, and I doubt that there are twenty thousand Men left on the whole planet."

"Don't you think the natives are capable of managing their own businesses?"

He shook his head. "Not really. First, most of them can't afford to start a business, and second, they have no experience in running one. And then you have the problem of tribalism. Even if he had the money to start a business, no Bogoda would ever promote a Kia or a Sorotoba over another Bogoda, even though the Bogoda was far less able to do the job." Wesley paused. "So if you're a youngster from one of the minor tribes, and you've got any brains or talent, the first thing you want to do is get the hell off the planet and find work somewhere on one of the Republic's worlds. Even if you're a Bogoda or a Sentabel or a Sorotoba, you probably want to leave; there just aren't enough jobs."

"I thought Pepon was putting an end to tribalism," I said, confused.

"He's stopped them from killing each other," said Wesley. "That's an enormous accomplishment—but even *he* can't stop the kind of extended nepotism that goes on in the planet's daily business. Which reminds me: do you plan to fly anywhere while you're here?"

"I don't know."

"Well, if you do, make sure you get a human pilot, or at least a pilot from a minority tribe."

"Why?"

"Because no native who sits on the pilots' licensing board will ever refuse to pass a tribal brother, no matter how badly he fails the test." He smiled. "It makes every commercial airline flight a death-defying proposition. If you've got enough money, or if the government is picking up your expenses, charter a human-owned plane whenever you fly, and you just might live long enough to finish writing your book."

Suddenly the stillness of the night was punctuated by a roar and then an agonized bleating. Then there was silence again.

"Bush Devil," announced Wesley.

"What did he catch?" I asked. "It sounded terrible."

"Probably a Silvercoat. Could have been a Willowbuck, but I doubt it; they're awfully quick. Usually it takes a pack of Nightkillers to run one of them down."

We sat in silence for a moment. Wesley leaned back, reveling in his surroundings, while I waited for a repetition of the roar and the scream, though they never came.

"What other problems do you foresee?" I asked, wishing that I had my notebook or my recorder with me.

"You name it, Peponi's got it," said Wesley. "Take the army, for instance."

"What about it?"

"The Old Man's got a standing army of more than a million wags."

"Really?" I said, surprised. "What does he need them for?"

"Nothing . . . but it employs a million unemployables and keeps them off the streets. It's also his pride and joy, because he's got them tribally integrated."

"Then what's the problem?" I asked.

"The problem is that he's got no one to fight, and he has to feed a million idle mouths. This isn't a national army; it's a planetary one. That means it was put together—theoretically, at least—to defend Peponi from attack, or to attack other worlds." Wesley paused to relight his pipe, which had gone out. "If he has to use them to defend Peponi against an attack, then the battle's already lost, because they don't have any weapons that can stand up to a sophisticated technology like the Republic's—and even if it came down to using them against an invading force that had already landed, he hasn't the capacity to disperse them. You've seen our roads. How in the world is he going to move a million soldiers from Berengi to a coastal city like Capatra, let alone to the Great Western Continent?" He paused again. "If, on the other hand, he plans to use them to attack other worlds, then he's got an even bigger problem: the army only has two spaceships, neither of which can carry as many as a thousand soldiers. So either way, it's a huge drag on the economy, and absolutely useless as a military force."

"Then why does he have them?" I asked, puzzled.

"I suppose he created the army in case some of the tribes, especially the Sentabels on the other continent, tried to secede because Peponi had a Bogoda president. Maybe he feared a civil war—or maybe he just liked to see a million uniformed wags marching down Buko Pepon Boulevard and saluting him on holidays. The point is, now that he's got them, he has to keep them. If he disbands the army, he's just thrown more than a million wags out of work, and supplied them with a chain of command for making their displeasure felt."

"So what can he do?"

"I don't know," admitted Wesley. "If there was an easy solution—or even a complicated one—the Old Man would have found it already." He paused again. "Anyway, the army's just one of his problems. He's got a society that still kills babies when their witch doctors tell them to, that burns tribal symbols into adolescents' bodies, that cuts domestic animals open and reads their entrails to decide what to plant in their fields and when to plant it. If he had two centuries, I don't have the slightest doubt that he could make Peponi a viable cog in the Republic's economic machine, but he's already lived longer than most wags. What can he have left? Five more years? Ten? He can't do it in the time that's left to him."

"Maybe his successors can."

"His potential successors have this unfortunate habit of vanishing into thin air," said Wesley.

"Tell me about that," I said.

"There's not much to tell," answered Wesley. "The Old Man doesn't like rivals."

"I've heard and read a lot about a very popular young politician named Sam Jimana," I said. "Did Pepon have him killed or not?"

Wesley shrugged. "Who knows? Jimana was a Kia. If Pepon didn't order his assassination, you can at least be sure that he didn't lose any sleep mourning Jimana's loss."

"What did the courts find?"

"The courts never got their hands on it. A Presidential Commission hunted up a Sorotoba who confessed to the killing and sentenced him to death. Probably just as well."

"Why do you say that?"

"You've never seen the Peponi court system in action," said Wesley. "*I* have."

"I take it that it doesn't work very well?"

He chuckled in the darkness. "It doesn't work at all. Let's say a Siboni gets accused of a crime—let's say theft and aggravated battery—against a Kia, and there are twelve jurors and three of them are Siboni. The only result you'll ever get is a hung jury. Walk up to the three Siboni and point out that the evidence was overwhelmingly against the defendant, and one of them will say that the defendant owes him three Beefcakes and couldn't pay him if he were in jail, the second will tell you that a Siboni can't commit a crime against the Kia because the Kia used to make raids on the Siboni's cattle, and the third will tell you that his witch doctor cast some bones in the dirt and declared the defendant was innocent."

"Maybe they shouldn't allow a defendant's tribe on the jury," I suggested.

"That'll guarantee a hundred percent conviction rate, regardless of evidence," replied Wesley. "Take our same hypothetical jury. Every other member of it will vote against the Siboni, not because of the evidence, but because of past offenses, real and imagined, that the Siboni committed against their tribes."

"What about the pepons like Tonka who have settled in the city and given up tribalism?"

Wesley smiled. "Tonka hasn't given it up. He just happens to be a member of a tiny tribe, so he's careful about what he says in public."

"So you're saying that justice doesn't work on Peponi?"

"No, I never said that," answered Wesley. "But *human* justice doesn't work. In fact, most human institutions don't work here. Hell, there's no reason why they should; this isn't a human world, and it's not populated by humans." He paused, tinkering with his pipe. "It's the clash with human values that's causing most of the problems. They used to grow food and eat it and that was that; now they've got an alien animal, the Beefcake, that's ruining their land, and with the little fertile land they have left, they grow sugar berries, of all things. I know they have to export them to get hard currency—but ninety percent of the populace has never seen a Peponi coin, so what the devil do they need hard currency for anyway? Pepon's got an army he can't equip and can't mobilize. Landships and Sabrehorns would have tripled the tourist industry, but all the Landships were killed to make jewelry for humans and all the Sabrehorns were slaughtered to make sword sheaths for the Pinkies."

There was another roar, followed by some high-pitched growling.

Wesley smiled. "The Nightkillers have found the Bush Devil," he explained. "They'd like to be invited for dinner; he'd rather eat alone."

Suddenly there was a loud yelp.

"One of them got a little too close to the table," said Wesley.

The yelping continued.

"Well, at least the Bush Devil didn't kill him. Probably just gave him a lesson in table manners."

"If he's been badly bitten, won't he die anyway?" I asked. "After all, he won't be able to hunt."

"If he lives through the night, he'll be all right," said Wesley, peering out into the darkness as if he could actually see the scene he had just described. "The Nightkillers take care of their own. If he's crippled up at all, they'll leave him in charge of the nursery when they go hunting, and feed him when they come back to feed the babies."

"Why does their nursery need guarding?" I asked. "They're carnivores, aren't they?"

"Baby anythings—even baby carnivores—are at risk until they're big enough to defend themselves. Bush Devils will eat them, and there are a lot of raptors sitting up on top of those trees, just looking for something small and helpless to swoop down upon."

"That reminds me of something Hardwycke once said about Peponi: Everything bites."

"Hardwycke?" repeated Wesley, suddenly interested. "Isn't he the fellow the mountain was originally named for?"

"That's right."

"I thought he died half a century ago," continued Wesley. "Did you actually know him?"

"I wrote his biography," I replied.

"Is he still alive?"

"No," I said. "He died a few years ago."

"Must have been an interesting old guy," said Wesley. "I'll bet he had a lot of stories to tell."

"I could send you a copy of the book," I offered.

"I don't read very much anymore," he said apologetically. "I used to, but now I prefer just to sit out here and enjoy myself." He paused. "Still, you might send it along if you think of it. Maybe I'll get back into the habit."

Once again the stillness was broken, this time by the most fearsome scream I had ever heard.

"What was that?" I asked, half-ready to move to the interior of the lodge.

"It's a Bluecrest. He's lost his ladyfriend and he's calling to her."

"What's a Bluecrest?"

Wesley smiled. "The Bluecrest is the most inoffensive avian on the mountain. God forgot to give him any means of defense, so instead He gave him a voice that turns Bush Devils and Demoncats into frightened little kittens."

"You can add human writers to the list," I said fervently.

"Your glass is empty," he noted. "Can I get you another cognac?"

"If you'll stay out here for a while and keep talking to me," I said.

"I'm not going anywhere," he replied, walking over to the bar and pouring me a refill.

"You're not drinking?" I asked when he returned.

He shook his head. "Have to be up with the sun, and I don't sleep too well when I drink after dinner, so I do my tippling in the afternoons." He handed me my drink and sat down. "What were we talking about?"

"You were telling me what was wrong with Peponi," I said.

"I don't want to sound *too* critical," he replied. "I love this planet. That's why I'm still here."

"But you don't think much of its future."

"No," he said with a sigh. "I wish I did, but I don't." He paused. "You know, if every road and car and factory vanished from the face of Peponi tomorrow, it wouldn't make a shred of difference to nine tenths of the populace. How can even a Buko Pepon deal with that? He's trying to create a human society, but he's not dealing with humans. Most of them would be better off living in the bush; hell, most of them have never left it."

"I disagree," I said. "Why don't you try telling Tonka, or even Joshua, that they should go back to wearing loincloths and living in grass huts?"

"I can't," he admitted. "We've got an entire class of schizophrenic wags who don't know who they are or where they belong."

"Give them time," I said, the memory of Balimora still fresh in my mind. "We yanked them out of the Stone Age and asked them to become model citizens of the Republic in one generation. Maybe it takes two or three, or even ten . . . but the fact that the transition isn't smooth or complete doesn't mean that it's a failure, or that it shouldn't have begun."

He shrugged. "Well, you're a writer, so you know a lot more about people and societies than I do. I just know what I see. I hope to hell you're right, because they've already destroyed too much of this world for it to ever go back to being the way it was."

"They?"

"Us, too," he assented. "But I'll be damned if Man has to take all the blame. We may have showed them why Landships were valuable, but they killed a lot more than we did. We imported sugar berries, but nobody is forcing them to use most of their fertile land to keep growing a crop they can't metabolize. No," he concluded, "Man can take his fair share of the blame, but he doesn't have to shoulder the whole thing, no matter what Nathan Tonka says."

"Tonka hasn't said anything about it."

"He'd like to, though." Wesley smiled and shook his head sadly. "Poor Nathan. He's got all the brains and ambition in the world, but he was born into the wrong tribe, so he has to be very careful of what he says, even to an outsider like you. If he was a Bogoda or a Kia, he'd probably be vice president by now." He paused. "It's probably just as well. If he were vice president, he'd probably be listed among the missing."

"That doesn't make sense," I said. "Pepon knows that the people literally worship him. Why does he feel it's necessary to eliminate potential political rivals?"

"Who knows? Maybe he thinks he'll live forever, and he's smart enough to know that he won't stay popular forever. Whatever the reason, he's seen to it that there has never been an obvious successor in line during the entire time he's held office. They rise to the top, and then they either vanish or get booted back down the ladder." He paused. "You know, Bago Baja is on his third time around. He was Pepon's first vice president. Then Pepon accused him of plotting with Canphor VI and VII to overthrow the government, and tossed him in jail. He let him out four years later, and the next thing anyone knew, there was Baja again, this time as Secretary of Agriculture. Then Pepon declared that Peponi would only have one political party, and since Baja didn't belong to it, he was out on his ass again. So he joined Pepon's party, worked his way back up through the ranks, and now he's vice president again."

"Well, I suppose it's better than vanishing," I said.

"The only reason Baja hasn't vanished is because nobody likes him except Pepon. Let him get a following and he'll disappear just like the rest of them." He refilled his pipe, and began packing the tobacco down. "Still, as long as they leave me and my mountain alone, they can all do anything they want to each other. All I want to do is live out my life up here."

"That's really the way you feel?"

"I know it sounds selfish," said Wesley, "but yes, that's the way I feel. I love this planet and I love these people, but they've got their problems and I'm not the one to solve 'em —if they *can* be solved, which I doubt. All I want to do is keep this lodge and this park intact until I die. Then they can do what they want with it."

"That sounds very cynical," I noted, as the Bluecrest shrieked for its mate again.

"You say it's cynical, I say it's practical. Either way, it's sincere."

"Well," I admitted, "you sound like a man who's made his choices and has no regrets."

"Just one," said Wesley. "I wish I'd been born a little earlier."

"Let me guess," I said. "You wish you had been here at the opening of the planet."

He shook his head. "So I could be eaten by hungry natives or die of some tropical disease? No, thanks." He paused thoughtfully. "But I'd like to have been here when Amanda Pickett was writing her books and the wags were content with their lot, back before the Kalakala and the Emergency." He looked out over his beloved landscape and sighed deeply. "It must have been just about perfect back then."

Fifteen

We returned to Berengi the next morning, and I spent the following eight days researching Pepon's biography. The bookstores and libraries were full of material about him, but it was so slanted and worshipful as to be almost useless. His office was a better source, but although he had promised me free access to all his papers, his secretaries and advisors decided that certain files and materials were off limits until Pepon returned from the Great Western Continent and personally handed them to me.

I spent most of my evenings alone in my suite at the Royal Hotel, although one night I did allow Ian Masterson, who knew that I was back in town, to take me to a couple of night clubs. One featured native entertainers, dressed in feathers and animal skins and performing dances and gyrations that they had never performed in the bush. The other had a human singer from Sylaria who seemed to have developed quite a following among the resident humans. I found neither of the clubs very interesting, and politely refused when Masterson called the next evening, volunteering to take me to still more tourist traps.

Then, on my ninth day in Berengi, Tonka approached me at breakfast to announce that Buko Pepon had returned and wished to speak to me in his office at two o'clock. I spent the remainder of the morning selecting the material that I wished to return to his staff, had a light lunch, and walked to his office.

Now that I was better acquainted with Berengi, it didn't seem quite so exotic or alien as it had when Masterson first drove me through it. I nodded to the occasional human tourist that I recognized from the Royal Hotel, tried out my newly-acquired Bogoda on a news vendor, and wound up with a book I didn't want—I had requested the *Bulletin*, one of Berengi's two daily papers, and had been given *The Secret Bullet*, a murder mystery set in colonial times. Since I didn't know how to tell him he had misunderstood me, and he seemed so delighted to have sold this book that had obviously been gathering dust for some years, I decided not to make an issue of it.

I arrived at the President's Mansion about twenty minutes early, found a trash atomizer in the foyer where I got rid of the mystery novel, spent some time wandering around looking at the art and artifacts, and then, at three minutes before two, I walked to the elevator. The officer in charge of it was obviously expecting me, because he simply stepped aside, gestured for me to enter, then followed me inside and ordered it to ascend to the fourth floor.

I emerged in the domed marble foyer with its stuffed Sabrehorn dominating the premises, where another aide greeted me and took me into Pepon's immense office.

Pepon was immaculately clad in a formal human outfit, as he had been during our previous meeting and in every holograph I had ever seen of him. The officer shifted his weight uncertainly, and finally Pepon seemed to notice him and dismissed him. The door closed behind him, and I found myself face-to-face with the President of Peponi.

"Well, Mr. Breen," he said in his exquisite Terran, "how has your research been going?"

"Very well, Mr. President," I said. "I trust your trip was successful?"

He shrugged. "At least things are no worse than before I went there. The Sentabels can be a very stubborn people."

"I'm not aware of the nature of the problem," I said.

"I've created a new game park, and they claim that it infringes upon their grazing land—which, of course, it does. But they desperately need a new source of revenue, and since most of our tourist industry is concentrated on the Great Eastern Continent, this seems to be the best way. The government has even offered to build two large lodges, and to lay a one-hundred-and-fifty-mile road from their local airport and spaceport to the new park."

"It sounds very generous to me," I said.

"It is," he agreed. "But if they had their way, the park would be in the middle of the Great Southern Desert, or perhaps in the center of the Impenetrable Forest. They need the revenues, and they're in no financial condition to construct the road or the lodges, but they cannot see why they have to give up some of their land." He sighed. "I don't know how many times I had to explain to them that you must create parks where the game is, rather than where the Beefcakes are not." He leaned back on his chair, obviously exhausted from his journey, and for the first time I thought he was starting to look his age. "Please sit down, Mr. Breen. It makes me tired just to see you standing."

"Thank you, sir," I said, pulling up a chair.

"I hope Nathan Kibi Tonka has performed his duties as guide and translator to your satisfaction?" he said, pulling a small thin cigar out of an ornate box on his desk and lighting it.

"Yes, he has," I said. "He's a very interesting young person."

Pepon nodded. "And a very ambitious one. If you had seen the tiny village he comes from, you would find it difficult to believe that he has advanced so far." He paused. "I am glad to hear that he has served you well. Was my staff here equally cooperative?"

"There are certain files and documents—which I assume are sensitive in nature—that they will not let me see without further instructions from you," I said. "Beyond that, they have been most cordial and helpful."

"Well, there are certain matters of planetary security that must remain confidential, Mr. Breen," he said. "I'm sure you understand."

"I do."

He puffed his cigar and smiled at me.

"Good. Now let me ask you: how does your research go? When do you expect to start writing the book?"

"When I get the answers to some difficult questions, sir," I said with some hesitancy, "some of which only you can supply."

"I told you during our first conversation, Mr. Breen, that I would hide nothing from you. I always keep my word. You may ask me anything you wish."

"I must confess that I don't know quite how to go about this, sir," I admitted. "You are the President of an entire planet and must be treated with the respect due your office, yet some of the questions I must ask you are . . . well . . ."

"Shall we say that, under other circumstances, they would be considered indiscreet?" asked Pepon with an amused smile.

"Precisely," I answered.

He lit his cigar and stared at me.

"Forget about indiscretion, Mr. Breen," he said. "I want a true biography circulating among the worlds of the Republic. If you were to write the type of worshipful tome that you can find in any Berengi bookstore, no member of your race would give credence to it. Peponi needs tourists and it needs investors, and it can't get them by lying." He took a puff of his cigar and blew a thick cloud of smoke at the ceiling. "You must understand, Mr. Breen, that nothing you can say in this book can possibly damage my standing with my own people. First, if it is in any way detrimental to me, they would not believe it; and second, I do not foresee a market for your book on Peponi."

"Are you saying you won't permit it to be distributed here?"

"I am saying that it is being written to publicize Peponi, and hence would serve no useful purpose by being sold here."

"You never mentioned that in our first discussion," I said.

"You never asked," he replied. "Never fear, Mr. Breen: neither your bank account nor your reputation shall suffer from writing this book. Now, ask your questions and I shall answer them."

I considered arguing with him, but realized that it was useless. No matter what publisher finally brought out the book, if Pepon didn't want it distributed on Peponi, that was that. There was no higher power to whom I could appeal. I could either write it under his terms, or walk out of his office—and since my reputation was based almost entirely on Peponi, I knew that I couldn't walk away from this assignment, no matter how much he had changed the conditions.

"Do you mind if I record your answers?" I said, placing my device on his desk.

"Not at all."

I activated the recorder and began by asking him the date of his birth, since I had found four separate dates in the various materials I had gathered. He admitted that he didn't know.

"I was born into a family of illiterate squatters who had no calendar of their own, let alone a knowledge of the Republic's calendar," he said. "In fact, the Bogoda's year starts and ends with the rainy season, and since it rains twice a year, I am about one hundred and eighty years old by their reckoning. However, since I must have a birthdate, I have arbitrarily chosen 1798 G.E."

"Is there any reason why you chose that particular date?" I asked.

"In a society where so many die young, my people have developed an enormous respect for anyone who can live to old age. Therefore, I chose a date prior to the turn of the Galactic Era's century." Suddenly he grinned. "It *sounds* older."

I next asked him about his schooling, both on Peponi and Deluros VIII. He told me that on Peponi he had studied all of the limited number of subjects permitted to natives, but that once he reached Deluros he had majored in politics and alien history.

"Why alien history?" I asked.

"Because I wanted to see how other subjugated races had achieved their freedom." A quick smile flashed across his face. "You can imagine my disappointment when I learned that most of them hadn't achieved it at all."

"Why did the government arrest you when you returned?"

"The first time? Because they realized that there was general unrest among my people, and they thought they could put an end to it by jailing the most visible leader. Do you know," he added, "that when they could charge me with no other crime, they claimed that I had stolen funds from the Peponi Planetary Union? They dropped the charges and released me about a week later, when the government auditors confirmed that my net worth was about eight hundred credits."

"What is your net worth today?" I asked, studying his face for a reaction.

"I have no idea," he replied easily. "Anyone who *does* know his net worth isn't worth very much."

"Would you say that it's more than one hundred million credits?" I asked.

"Definitely."

"Half a billion?"

"I really couldn't say," he answered. "I should imagine so."

"How do you justify such enormous personal wealth in view of the fact that Peponi itself is a poor planet, and that millions of its citizens live in abject poverty?"

He leaned forward, placing both his elbows on the large, polished desk and clasping his hands together. "Mr. Breen, there is a difference between robbing the people, as so many tyrants have done in your Republic, and investing in them, as I am doing on Peponi. I have no secret accounts on Deluros VIII or Earth. My money is right here on Peponi, and it is working for the people."

"Could you explain *how* it is working, Mr. President?" I asked, surprised that he was so forthright in his answers thus far.

"Certainly. I'm sure you have learned by now that I own the only brewery on the planet. We have nineteen branches on the two major continents, another one in the Connectors, and we'll soon have one on the Dust Bowl. The brewery employs almost thirty thousand of my people, and another eight thousand are employed in related industries which cover everything from printing the labels to manufacturing the containers to shipping the finished product."

He paused, ordering his thoughts, since he knew that his answer was being recorded. "If an off-world corporation had built the brewery, the major managerial positions would be forever denied to my people. With local ownership, just the opposite is true: we do not employ a single human. Also, if it were owned by off-worlders, the profits would be channeled into other enterprises, most of them on Republic worlds. But because I may not, by law, invest my profits on any other world, I reinvest them on Peponi, and by doing so I create even more industry and more jobs." He smiled. "Does that answer your question?"

"Not entirely," I said. "It seems to contradict the conditions I saw in Balimora, where your people are working in mines and a factory owned by Men."

"It's a completely different situation, Mr. Breen," replied Pepon. "They have promoted my people to key management positions in the food processing plant, and the mines are actually owned by the government of Peponi and merely leased to the human management, each of whom is a Peponi citizen." He paused. "I spend many months of each year on other worlds trying to encourage just that type of investment. I've had some limited success, but most corporations want their own people to manage their concerns, and very few of them are willing to lease property from an alien government. *That* is one of the reasons for this book, Mr. Breen: to convince them that Peponi is a stable world that merits their consideration."

"*Is* it that stable?" I asked. "You mentioned the problems you are having with the Sentabels."

"Those problems have been solved."

"I get the distinct impression that they have been solved because of the forcefulness of your personality and the esteem in which you are held by your people," I said. "Will the solution outlive you?"

"The rule of law will not end with my death, Mr. Breen," he said firmly.

"I wasn't thinking so much of the rule of law as the re-emergence of tribalism."

"That is the area where I truly feel we have made the greatest progress," he said with a note of pride. "I have fourteen ministers in my cabinet, and they represent twelve different tribes. I have never had a Bogoda vice president. If I do nothing else during my presidency, I will mold the tribes of Peponi into a single, unified people. They will retain their tribal identities and customs, but they will act for the common good of the planet."

"Yet not a single Siboni has ever held any office, elective or appointed, in the government."

He sighed. "The Siboni have been remarkably recalcitrant, but I have not yet given up on them. The day will come when a Siboni sits on my cabinet."

"And you are convinced that this policy will be continued after your death?"

"All of my subordinates share my worldview," he replied. "And we have many talented young politicians who have vowed to carry out my policies."

"But the best of them seem to disappear," I noted.

He stared at me, the blue, gill-like lines on his neck deepening in hue. I had never noticed that before in any member of his race, and I didn't know how to interpret it.

Finally he smiled a very alien smile, and his catseyes glittered brightly. "Are you accusing me of murder, Mr. Breen?"

"I'm not accusing you of anything, sir," I answered. "I just wonder if you can offer an explanation for their disappearances."

"Certainly," he replied, and I had the feeling that he was repeating this answer by rote. "You must understand that I fear no political rival. I am President for Life, and my security force is without equal. I can aspire to no higher office or greater power, and I have absolutely no fear of assassination." He paused. "However, because there was an attempt made on my life prior to my taking office, many of my followers fear that more attempts will be made, and that eventually one of them may be successful." He paused again, and shot me a quick glance to observe my reaction to his answer. "I do not know what happened to the six politicians who disappeared. I suspect that they were murdered and their bodies disposed of. I suspect that these crimes were perpetrated on my behalf by some loyal but very misguided followers of mine. In every case I put the entire power of my office behind those in charge of the investigations, but the criminals were never apprehended."

I wondered how these answers would be received on Deluros VIII or Earth, or if *anyone* would believe that a secret could be kept from Buko Pepon on his own planet.

Pepon puffed his cigar thoughtfully, and then continued: "In the case of Sam Jimana, whom I loved like a son, we *did* find the culprit, a minor Sorotoba official who was tried, found guilty, and executed."

"An expatriate on Barton IV," I said, so as not to implicate Masterson or Wesley, "suggested that the Sorotoba was innocent and was tried and executed as a matter of expediency, since if a Bogoda had been connected with the crime the Kia might have withdrawn their support from the government."

Pepon frowned. "That is a fabrication, Mr. Breen," he said severely. "This government can function with or without the support of the Kia. The criminal confessed, and before you leave the planet I will have a copy of his signed confession delivered to you."

"Thank you, sir," I said, feeling that any further question on the subject would be interpreted as harassment rather than research. If that was his answer, that's what would go into the book, and the readers could decide for themselves whether to believe him or not.

He stared at me, his slit pupils expanding and contracting, his face just a bit too alien for me to tell whether he was annoyed with me or simply amused.

"Come, come, Mr. Breen," he said at last. "Surely you have not run out of difficult questions."

"No I haven't, sir," I responded. "You are the major landholder in the Greenlands, are you not?"

"Yes, I am," he said with no hesitation. "The Vainmill Syndicate is the second largest, but one day I hope that the government can buy them out."

"How many acres do you own?"

"I don't know," he replied. "I would estimate that my holdings come to perhaps twenty percent of the whole."

"How do you reconcile that with the fact that fully half the Bogoda have been denied plots of their ancestral land?"

Pepon stared at me for a long moment.

"Let me ask *you* a question, Mr. Breen," he said at last.

"All right."

"What do you think would happen if I turned over my property to those Bogoda who currently are without a plot of ground in the Greenlands?"

"I imagine they'd be very grateful," I said.

"You are being purposely obtuse, Mr. Breen," he said without irritation. "I will tell you exactly what would happen. First, they would move onto the land. Second, with no knowledge of crop rotation or contour farming, they would begin to work the land. And finally, as their children reached adulthood and their extended families moved onto the land, they would subdivide it." He paused and stared at me once again. "And in another ten or fifteen years, the Greenlands—the most productive farmland on the entire planet—would be nothing but an endless row of two-acre plots in the hands of subsistence farmers who cannot begin to afford such basics as fertilizer or insecticide, let alone purchase the hybird crops that can produce a far higher yield."

He paused again, taking another deep puff of his cigar. "Mr. Breen, I have never made any secret of the fact that some twenty million of my people are currently starving, most of them on the Great Western Continent. If I did not ship them the crops from my landholdings, that number might well be thirty million."

"I don't wish to contradict you, sir," I said cautiously, "but I've seen your farms, and most of them raise nothing except tea and sugar berries."

"The tea is sold to the Republic, and the profits are reinvested on Peponi," he said. "But the sugar berries are traded to nearby worlds in exchange for the foodstuffs that my people need."

"Can you document that, sir?" I asked.

"Don't you believe me?" he asked gently, but as I stared at his great bulk and glittering alien eyes, I got the distinct impression that his question was not prompted by gentle feelings.

"The question is not what *I* believe, Mr. President," I said, choosing my words very carefully, "but what the readers will believe if this is the extent of your answer."

"I see," he said slowly, the blue marks on each side of his neck turning a deep, rich purple. "Very well, Mr. Breen; I will consider providing you with documentation."

"Thank you, sir."

"Next question?"

I led him into a discussion of Peponi's economic difficulties. The planet had too few exports, imported too many vital goods, and could barely pay the interest on its massive loans from the Republic. He admitted the gravity of the problem, and speculated on ways in which Peponi might be able to cope with it and eventually solve it: massive development of the Great Western Continent and the Dust Bowl, a loose economic alliance with four other recently-independent worlds, various austerity programs. All of these were merely stopgap measures, however; ultimately, he felt, Peponi could become solvent only if it made better use of its farmland, and found ways to reclaim that land which had been ecologically degraded.

Did that mean getting rid of Beefcakes and subsistence farming? Eventually subsistence farming would have to go, he agreed, but his government couldn't throw the Bogoda and the other tribes off their land while so many millions of his people were already hungry. If he could just find a way to reclaim and irrigate the Dust Bowl, it could feed the entire planet—but even human technology wasn't up to that task at the present time, and he had serious misgivings about giving humans too much power to remake his planet, although he realized that might be Peponi's only option in the long run. He was less adamant about the Beefcakes; he understood the harm they caused to the land, but they were so much a part of Peponi's daily life and economy that I could tell he hadn't truly come to grips with the need to remove them from what was, in truth, an alien environment.

I asked if he had considered farming the seas. He had taken some steps in that direction, but the cost of building the number of aquaculture stations needed to make more than a marginal difference to Peponi's hunger problems was prohibitive. Then, too, additional capital would be required for the creation of a system of roadways that would allow efficient distribution of the end product. Also, he had seen Landships and Sabrehorns become extinct during his own lifetime, and that had had a profound effect upon him: He seriously doubted that aquaculture could supply sustenance to the billions who would shortly be needing it. If Landships could vanish from Peponi, he argued, so could fish.

We paused for a few minutes while Pepon rang for one of his liveried servants and requested a brandy, and then began the final segment of the interview.

"I've heard about some of your exploits from Tonka and others," I said, "and I wonder if you could relate them to me in your own words."

"I would be happy to."

"Let's begin with the time when you appeared in Marachi in Sorotoba tribal garb."

He smiled, and seemed to relax as he related the experience

to me. He also told me of his incarceration in Balimora; of the loneliness and frequent sense of futility he had felt while fighting a solitary campaign for Peponi's independence during his fifteen years on Deluros VIII; of his role in the various peace treaties that had been signed under his auspices on Peponi; of his memories of a childhood in the Greenlands; of the terrible sense of guilt he had suffered when he learned that the last Landships had been poached by his own people during his Presidency; of the joy he had felt when his lifetime of lobbying had resulted in independence for his planet.

The entire time I was listening to him, I was trying to reconcile *this* Pepon with the one who was undoubtedly profiteering from his holdings in the Greenlands and had probably ordered the deaths of seven of his political rivals. Ultimately I decided that the only way to judge him was to balance the good he had done against the evil—and by that criterion, he came out better than most Men.

"We were not the first planet to be given independence by the Republic," he was saying, "and I thought it might be instructive to learn from the mistakes others had made before us. A number of them had disenfranchised or dispossessed their entire human populations, and invariably their economies had suffered. Lodin XI found itself so short of technology that it actually begged Men to return, and created a tax situation so favorable that a number of them did indeed go back." He paused. "I was determined that this would never happen to Peponi. The Men who had moved here had done so at the instigation of the Republic, and I decided that we would never hold them personally to blame for the colonial period in our history. If they were willing to stay and work for the good of Peponi, to invest in our economy and share their technological expertise with us, we would welcome them and offer them full citizenship." His cigar went out again, but this time there was enough left that he simply relit it. "About half the Men eventually left, but half of them are still here more than a quarter of a century later. They have done very well in the new Peponi, and Peponi has made excellent progress with their help."

"That's an extraordinary attitude," I said sincerely, "given the treatment you received at their hands."

"What's past is past," he said with a sincerity that would have sounded false coming from any Man I ever met. "I had time to think and to plan a new society while I was in prison—and at least, incarcerated as I was, no one can claim that I was responsible for the Kalakala atrocities."

"I think you are truly remarkable, sir," I said. "I stood inside that cell for perhaps five minutes, and I felt claustrophobic. I truly don't know how you survived it."

"The vision of what Peponi could become sustained me," he answered.

"And now you have achieved it," I said.

He shook his head. "No, Mr. Breen. I may have a large ego, but it is not *that* large. We still have our problems. We are an underdeveloped world, and we must learn how to feed all of our people. We must teach them to read and to write, and to forsake tribalism, and somehow, *somehow*, I must find a way to make them preserve the land which gives sustenance to us all. But, given time, none of these problems is incapable of solution." He sighed once again, and once more I was suddenly aware of his advanced age. "But I would live no place else, and face no other set of challenges. Edward Ngana, the Pioneer who first landed here, chose very wisely when he named this world Peponi."

"You feel it is Paradise, then?" I asked.

"Not yet, Mr. Breen," he replied with a confident smile. "But if the God Of All Things can see fit to give me just twenty more years, it will be."

IV
Dusk

Sixteen

The Peponi spaceport hadn't changed much in fourteen years. There were a few more beggars, and the paint was starting to peel in the darkened corners, but there was still a long line of tourists waiting for two passport officials to check their papers and luggage. It felt familiar, inefficient, and strangely reassuring.

I had spent almost two years writing *Pepon of Peponi*, and it had won the prestigious Artistotle Award for the best biography of the year. It hadn't sold quite as well as I had hoped—and, as Pepon had promised, it never appeared on Peponi at all—but the award more than compensated for the lack of a best-seller. Suddenly my services as an "expert" on undeveloped and newly-independent worlds were in demand. I began traveling extensively and wrote seven more books during the next twelve years, concentrating upon such diverse planets as Kabara III and Riverwind.

Then my publisher decided that it was time for me to return to Peponi, which had provided the background for my first three books, and see how it had fared since the death of Buko Pepon some ten years earlier. When I began doing my preliminary research, I was surprised to discover that there had been two military coups since Pepon's death, and absolutely amazed to learn that the current president was Nathan Kibi Tonka.

My research had suggested that Peponi had fallen upon hard times. Corruption was supposedly far more widespread than when I had first visited it, and they still had not managed to halt their population explosion. The 200 million pepons of fourteen years ago had become 340 million, and the only remaining question was not *if* the population would top the billion mark, but *when*.

Peponi's economy was a shambles, but that was nothing new for undeveloped worlds. It continued to depend on aid and loans from the Republic, and was now importing almost ninety percent of its food.

On the other hand, it remained a major port on the tourist circuit, and was reputed to be one of the very few alien worlds where citizens of the Republic could expect a cordial welcome and could walk the streets in relative safety.

I had completed my research, and now I was here to evaluate the situation for myself. I had arranged to stay at the Royal Hotel, which I remembered very fondly, but this time I would also be visiting some of the game parks and touring some of the smaller cities. I was just vain enough to think that the name Matthew Breen might secure special treatment for me, so I let no one know that I was coming, since I had had previous experience with governments that wanted only certain portions of their planets to be seen.

I looked ahead, trying to determine why the line was moving so slowly. The inspectors were methodically going through every piece of an elderly native's luggage, asking questions about everything from a pocket computer to a pair of shoes.

Finally I saw some currency change hands, the native was passed through without any further trouble, and then the next native's luggage was subjected to the same intensive scrutiny. It was obvious that he would ultimately be approved for entry, and just as obvious that the only way to get approved quickly was to bribe one of the inspectors. The native currently being examined had a stubborn, stoic expression on his face, and finally the human who was in line behind him got tired of waiting, passed a couple of credit notes to the inspector, and both of them were instantly approved.

It was a nice racket. Even if they met a recalcitrant tourist who didn't believe in bribery, there was every likelihood that someone standing behind him was in a hurry and would pay the bribe on his behalf. The treatment given the natives was worse, in degree, than that given the off-worlders, but almost no one of any race passed inspection in less than ten minutes without slipping some money to the inspectors. Since the amount of the bribe was usually just a credit or two, and the inspectors were probably being paid only two or three credits per day, I decided that I really couldn't blame them too much for displaying such enterprise.

I had waited patiently for almost half an hour, moving up from the back of the line until there were only ten or eleven people ahead of me, all but one of them Men, when a uniformed native bearing a security badge approached me.

"Mr. Breen?" he said.

"Yes."

"Come with me, please."

"Is anything wrong?" I asked as I picked up my luggage.

"You will follow me, please," he said politely but noncommittally.

I fell into step behind him, and we walked through the large public area into a narrow corridor. We passed a number of doors, until finally he stopped before an unmarked one.

"You will enter this office, please," he said.

He stood aside, effectively blocking the corridor through which we had come, and I had the feeling that he was prepared to stand there all day if I didn't obey his request.

"Should I knock first?" I asked, looking for a buzzer or a retinal scanner but finding none.

He shook his head. "You are expected."

I took a step toward the door, which dilated to let me pass through, then snapped shut behind me.

I found myself in a small, remarkably neat office. There was a row of file cabinets along one wall, and a pair of computer terminals on another. Holographs of Buko Pepon and Nathan Kibi Tonka stared down at me from above the cabinets. There was a small, uncluttered desk near the room's only window, and sitting behind it was a human whose bronze, weathered face looked vaguely familiar to me.

"Come in, Matthew," he said. "Pull up a chair. Can I offer you something to drink?"

I continued to stare at him. "Have we met before?" I asked.

He smiled. "Many years ago."

"Ian Masterson!" I exclaimed, finally recognizing him. I walked forward and extended my hand.

"I wasn't aware that I had changed all that much," he said.

"Your hair's much thinner," I said. "And I seem to remember that you were about thirty pounds lighter."

"A pound every six months," he said with a chuckle. "It doesn't sound like much, until you start adding up all the years." He pressed a button on his desk, and part of the wall receded, revealing a well-stocked bar.

"What'll it be, Matthew?"

"Anything but the local beer," I said.

He laughed. "You've got a good memory. It's *still* pretty awful."

He poured us each a Cygnian cognac, then gestured for me to sit down at the opposite side of his desk.

"It's good to see you again, Matthew," he said. "I've been following your career."

"You have?"

"You're the only writer I know. I especially liked your book on Riverwind."

"Thank you," I said. "I wish you had been able to read my Pepon biography."

"I did."

"I thought it wasn't sold here."

He smiled. "It wasn't."

I decided that his smile looked more self-satisfied than friendly.

"How did you know I was coming to Peponi?"

"It's my job to know," he replied easily.

"The last time we met you were Buko Pepon's bodyguard," I said, taking a sip of my cognac. "What are you now?"

"Oh, I'm still in the security business," he replied.

I put my cognac down on the desk and stared at him for a moment.

"I have a question, Ian," I said.

"What is it?"

"Why am I here?"

"On Peponi?"

"In your office."

"I thought I'd save you the trouble of standing in that interminable line," he said. "Besides, it isn't often that I get to say hello to an old friend or have an excuse to drink on the job." He paused. "How long will you be staying here?"

"Don't you know?"

He smiled again. "As a matter of fact, I do. If you'll tell me which game parks you plan to visit, I'll see to it that you're not charged for them."

"That's very thoughtful of you, Ian," I said, "but my publisher has agreed to pick up my tab."

"How generous of him," said Masterson. "I wish someone would give *me* an all-expenses-paid vacation."

"Write a few books and maybe someone will."

"Perhaps when I retire." The smile vanished. "You're not as naive as you used to be, Matthew."

"Thank you. It comes from visiting so many dictatorships."

"I still have to know, though: are you here for business or pleasure?"

"What if I told you it was for pleasure?"

"I'd say you were lying," he stated flatly.

"Then I might as well tell you the truth," I replied with a shrug. "I've been commissioned to write a follow-up to the Pepon biography—sort of a Peponi Revisited."

He nodded. "I thought as much."

"Why should it concern you?"

"Anything that concerns Peponi concerns me," he said seriously.

"That's the kind of statement I'd expect to hear from President Tonka."

"You will—once he learns why you're on the planet." Masterson paused. "You've put us in an awkward position, Matthew. More to the point, you've put *me* in an awkward position."

"Why?" I asked. "I thought you worked for Security."

"I'm in charge of it, in fact," he said.

"I have no weapons," I said. "I'm not here to assassinate Tonka or overthrow the government."

"I know," he said. "The problem we have is that Security does not mean today what it meant in the Old Man's time."

"Why don't you tell me about it?" I suggested.

"Just a moment," he said, pressing a pair of buttons on his desk. "All right," he said. "The scanners don't pick up any recording devices."

"They're in my luggage," I said. "Deactivated."

"Keep them that way whenever you're around me," said Masterson.

. "All right."

"I mean it," he reiterated. "The day I discover you're recording me is the day I revoke your visa and ship you out of here."

"I understand," I said.

"I hope so." He paused. "All right, Matthew—let me lay the situation out for you."

"Please do."

"Your old pal Tonka is no Buko Pepon. The only reason he's in office is because the Bogoda and the Kia don't trust each other, so they settled on a Begau. On his behalf, I'll admit that he's got problems even Buko Pepon couldn't have handled: the Sentabels are trying to secede, the Siboni won't keep their Beefcakes out of the game parks and they're destroying the ecology, a quarter of the goddamned planet's starving to death, the Greenlands have had three years of drought, the navy—he's got a navy now—has already tried to depose him, and we've had to build two new jails in Berengi just to hold our prisoners." Masterson paused and stared at me. "Fourteen years ago it was Security's duty to protect the President. Today it's our job to protect the Presidency. Do you understand the difference?"

"I think so," I said. "Who's in the new jails?"

He smiled. "You understand it just fine," he said. "You know, the Old Man knew what to do about political enemies. One day they were there and the next day they weren't, and he only had to do it eight or nine times. Tonka hasn't got that kind of power, so he simply tosses *his* enemies in jail— and since they know that nobody's going to kill them, they keep multiplying."

"How much control does he have over the press?" I asked.

"Total."

"Even on the Great Western Continent?"

"There isn't any press on the Great Western Continent."

"None at all?" I said, surprised.

"Let me rephrase that," said Masterson. "As we sit here speaking, there are probably five or ten newspapers on the Great Western Continent. By next month they'll all be gone."

"To be replaced by five or ten more," I suggested.

"Well, it does create work," said Masterson with a smile. "An industrious wag could make a full-time career out of building printing presses. Tonka destroys fifty or sixty a year for the good of the planet."

"Why are you willing to be a part of this?" I asked.

"The pay is good and there's no heavy lifting," he replied easily. "That's very important for an old guy like me."

"Seriously."

"Seriously?" he repeated. "You may not know it to look at me, Matthew, but I'm the second most powerful person on the planet—and when Tonka gets thrown out of office, as he will sooner or later, I'll *still* be the second most powerful person on the planet." He paused. "It's an ideal job. No alien can be president, so I'm the only person the current president, whoever he is, can trust."

"And you don't mind the fact that it's a dictatorship?"

"What do you think it was under the Old Man?" he retorted. "A democracy? Pepon never ran for reelection, he murdered his opposition, and when he died he was worth three billion credits on a planet where the *per capita* income is four hundred and thirty-three credits a year. He was the best president they'll ever have, but the only difference between him and his successors is that he was a benevolent tyrant, and they're just tyrants."

"That's an enormous difference," I said. "He *cared* about this world."

"So do I," said Masterson. "It breaks my heart to see what's happened to the game parks and the forests, but my job is to keep order while the wags try to solve their problems, and I've done a damned good job of it. Tourism has more than doubled since Pepon's death. You can't do that if you haven't got order."

"All right, you're a wonderful man and you're holding Peponi together despite the natives' best efforts to tear it apart," I said sardonically. "Now let's talk business."

"Yours or mine?" he asked.

"Both," I said. "Are you going to try to stop me from doing my research?"

"Not unless I'm ordered to. I might even help you if I can get a nice mention in your book. You never can tell what might bring in a good job offer."

I frowned. "That doesn't make sense. Does Tonka control the press or not?"

"Are you the press?" asked Masterson easily. "I thought you were an off-planet writer who was here to research a book."

"In other words, as long as I don't write it here, you won't hinder me?"

"Oh, I might *hinder* you a little, just to convince Tonka I'm doing my job," he replied. "But I won't *stop* you."

"Why not?"

"Because you're a Man, and it would be a bad precedent to throw a Man into a wags' prison. Peponi needs every Man it can get. Besides," he added with a grin, "let the local wags think they can get away with jailing Men and one of these days they might even throw *me* into prison."

"There are no Men in any Berengi prison?" I asked, surprised.

"None."

"Surely Men commit crimes on Peponi?"

"Start jailing Men, and pretty soon you don't have a tourist business," explained Masterson. "And tourism is just about the only viable industry we've got here. So if I find that a

Man has broken a law, one of my people has a little talk with him, we collect an unofficial fine, and we send him on his way. If it's a major law, we throw him off the planet."

"And if he's a resident?"

"Either we deport him, or else we jail him somewhere far away, like in the Dust Bowl, or in Bakatula. Usually, though, we just fine him."

"You collect a lot of unofficial fines, I take it?"

"We do." Masterson leaned back on his chair and clasped his hands behind his head. "I know it sounds corrupt, but just about every judge on this planet is for sale. If our human lawbreakers went to court they'd just buy their way out. This way at least the money goes to the people who have to enforce the laws."

"Except when they're collecting fines," I noted.

"Matthew, when Skyblue arrested three Men for murder, proved the case beyond any shadow of a doubt, and executed them, tourism dropped off almost seventy percent for the next five years. You can't go around jailing or killing Men on a world that depends on their goodwill for its income."

"Well," I said with a sigh, "I'm here to find out what's happening, not to argue with you."

"This book of yours," he said. "Do they plan to distribute it on Peponi?"

"I don't think so," I said. "Besides, from what you've told me, Tonka would never permit it."

"If he's still in charge," agreed Masterson. "But the next president, depending on how he comes to power, might be delighted to see a book that makes Tonka appear to be a petty and corrupt dictator with delusions of grandeur."

I didn't make any reply.

"You look puzzled," said Masterson at last.

"I am," I admitted. "I didn't know Tonka all that well, but he didn't strike me as a potential dictator such as you've just described."

"Maybe the office makes the officeholder," suggested Masterson. "I don't think that Tonka's basically a bad wag, any more than Pepon was—but sometimes the exigencies of your job make you do questionable things."

"Like imprisoning thousands of political enemies?" I said.

"Exactly."

"Pepon never imprisoned anyone."

"Pepon never had to, not after the first few disappeared. Besides, he was the Father of Peponi—and he also had the good fortune to be a member of the most politically powerful tribe on the planet. Tonka is just a politician from a tiny tribe of maybe six thousand wags. He's only got one other Begau in the whole damned government. There isn't a member of his cabinet who wouldn't happily slit his throat just because he's a Begau, let alone because they don't think his policies favor their particular constituencies. The only reason he's survived this long is because no one has been able to accuse him of playing favorites; he made sure that the one tribe that hasn't gotten a damned thing from the government is the Begau."

"He must be doing one hell of a balancing act," I said.

"He is. The trouble is that none of the problems facing the planet are going away while he's trying to protect his back."

"Well, I thank you for filling me in," I said. "And now, if you don't mind, I think I'd better go check in at my hotel."

"Are you staying at the Royal?" he asked.

"You know I am."

"Actually, I hadn't bothered to check yet," he admitted. "I'm afraid you're going to be disappointed in it."

"Oh? Why?"

"They've bought out the human management. It's run by wags now." He paused. "It's still a good hotel, but it's changed."

"In what ways?"

"They've removed every piece of memorabilia from the colonial era, and they've completely refurbished the place.

All the flavor is gone. It's just another expensive tourist hotel now, and not a very efficient one."

"I'm sorry to hear that," I said sincerely. "I have very fond memories of the Royal. Is the Thunderhead Bar still there?"

He nodded. "Yes, but it's called the Nathan Kibi Tonka Bar now, and the place is overrun with wags."

"I thought they couldn't afford it."

"Most of them can't," he affirmed. "I'd say ninety percent of the wags are worse off now than they were under the colonial government—but the other ten percent are making money hand over fist, and they like to be seen at the Royal and the Equator, if only because those are the two remaining institutions from the days when they couldn't even walk on Commodore Quincy Avenue."

"I see."

"What else are you planning to see while you're on Peponi?"

"I haven't decided."

"You might as well tell me, Matthew," said Masterson. "I'm going to find out anyway. Besides, maybe I can open some doors for you."

I considered what he had said, and decided that I might as well be honest with him, especially since there was no way that I would be able to keep my whereabouts a secret.

"All right," I said. "I thought I'd go back up to the Mount Pekana Lodge and see if it's changed much."

"I can save you a trip," he said. "It's gone."

"The lodge is gone?"

"The whole damned park is gone," said Masterson. "They still call it a reserve, but most of the animals are gone, too. The Bogoda have overrun the Greenlands, and they've been clearing the forest up there for the past three years. There isn't much left except some bald mountains and a bunch of Beefcakes."

"How could they do that?" I asked. "I thought it was a game park."

"It's Bogoda land. They can do anything they please with it."

"But—"

"Our two military dictators were a Sorotoba and a Sentabel, and *they* didn't give a damn what the Bogoda did to the park. Tonka *cares*, but he hasn't got the power to stop them."

"Poor Mike Wesley," I said. "I hope he died before they started chopping down the trees."

"Wesley?" repeated Masterson. "He was killed seven years ago. So was that old wag who worked for him."

"Joshua Buchanka?"

"That's the one. They were chopped to bits by some poachers they surprised."

"I'm sorry to hear it," I said. Then a question occurred to me. "All the Landships and Sabrehorns are extinct," I said. "What's left to poach?"

"This particular gang was after Bush Devils," replied Masterson. "There's a big illegal market for their pelts. Those wag bastards have got it down to a science now: they catch them in traps, transfer them to cages, and then kill them by sticking a red-hot iron up the anus so the pelt isn't damaged." He grimaced. "I'd like to do the same to them," he said earnestly.

"Did you ever catch the ones who murdered Wesley and Buchanka?"

"Officially, yes," he replied. "Unofficially, I don't know."

"What do you mean?"

"We picked up about seven or eight parties of poachers on the mountain during the next couple of days and charged 'em all with murder. Got thirty-seven convictions out of it. Even if we didn't catch the murderers, that's thirty-seven wags who never went out poaching game again." He paused. "We're a lot more lenient on poachers down on the savannahs," he added. "If they don't overdo it, we tend to look the other way."

"Why?"

"Because they're starving, and they're poaching meat for the pot. Go after every wag who's ever killed an animal illegally and you'd need an army of more than a million game rangers and officers, so we have to draw the line somewhere." He paused. "Of course, sometimes they go overboard, and then we have to step in. Usually it's too late, though—like that park the Old Man created a few years before he died, on the Great Western Continent. The Sentabels thought it was their private meat shop, and five years ago we finally had to close the whole thing down. There probably weren't two hundred game animals left in the whole three hundred square miles. Now their Beefcakes have pretty much ruined what's left of the land."

"Maybe I'll go to the Siboni Plains, then," I said. "If I remember correctly, the Silvercoats should be migrating this time of year."

"Forget it."

"I *know* the Siboni Plains Park still exists," I said adamantly. "I picked up a guidebook before I left for Peponi, and it's on all the maps."

"Oh, the park exists, and you can see a variety of animals," he replied. "But no Silvercoats."

"What happened?"

"*People* happened," he replied. "Wags and humans both." He took a deep breath, then continued. "The park still belongs to the government, but the surrounding farmland is all privately owned, and as of seven or eight years ago, it was all fenced." He paused again. "The Silvercoats didn't migrate to provide the tourists with a photo opportunity, you know. They migrated because their normal range dried up every summer, and they moved to the Siboni Plains to find water. The farms and fences blocked their path." He stared across the desk at me. "Two million of them died of thirst the first year, and most of the rest died the next summer. There are about two thousand of them left, and they don't migrate any more."

"Didn't anyone point out what was happening?" I asked.

"Lots of people did," responded Masterson. "We've got almost as many scientists and ecologists in the parks these days as tourists. But it's hard to convince a starving, unemployed wag that he should care about a Silvercoat's future when his own future is so uncertain."

"What a waste," I said sadly.

"That it is," agreed Masterson.

"I suppose I'll visit Mount Pekana and the Siboni Plains anyway, just to see firsthand what's been happening to them."

Suddenly a curious smile crossed his face.

"What is it?" I asked.

"Matthew, before you see Mount Pekana and the Siboni Plains, would you like to see what Peponi was like in the old days?" he said.

"The old days?" I repeated.

"I'm not talking about Hardwycke's time, or even Amanda Pickett's—those days are gone forever—but would you like to see what things were like when *I* came here?"

"Very much," I said sincerely. "Is it possible?"

He nodded his head. "I'll arrange it for you."

"Where am I going?"

"The Keringera Park, about one hundred miles north of Balimora. I'll warn you now: it's uncomfortably hot up there. But almost no tourists go there, there's only one very primitive tribe in the area, and it's as close to being an untouched park as you can find. I doubt if it's had as many as five hundred visitors a year since the Landships vanished."

"What will I see there?" I asked.

"Thunderheads, Bush Devils, Nightkillers, about twenty species of herbivores, and a large variety of avians," he replied. "You won't see the immense herds that used to roam the savannah—but this land never supported those kind of numbers anyway. And you'll see a few wags who are living just the way they lived when your friend Hardwycke first set foot on Peponi."

"It sounds interesting," I admitted.

"It is. I'll even provide you with a guide."

"One of your own men?"

"You're a valuable commodity, Matthew," he replied with a smile. "I've got to take good care of you."

"Why am I so valuable?"

"I told you before," he replied. "I'd like to spend the rest of my life here, but you never know what a new dictator will do. You're my insurance policy."

I considered his proposition. I *wanted* to see a park that had been virtually untouched over the years, and certainly having a security man as a driver and interpreter on an alien world would be more of a benefit than a handicap.

"Will I still be allowed to visit the other parks?" I asked at last.

"Certainly," replied Masterson. "I just want you to see one of our few remaining good parks first." He paused. "You know, Matthew, I have a feeling that we're going to become good friends."

"Oh?"

He smiled. "I can open a lot of doors for my friends," he continued.

"Whose doors?" I asked meaningfully.

"I could probably arrange an interview with Tonka."

"Dictators don't talk to the press."

"*This* one will—if I tell him it would be good for his image," said Masterson confidently.

"Why would he listen to you?"

"I told you before, Matthew: I'm the only person in the government who's not after his job, so I'm the only one he trusts." He paused. "Yes, I think I could arrange it—*if* I can review what you write."

"Why do you care?" I asked. "Good security men are in demand all over the galaxy. Surely you can get job offers without appearing in my book."

"I get job offers every month."

"Well, then?"

"Matthew, I have every intention of spending the rest of my life on Peponi," he said. "But if I should have to leave in a hurry, I'd like to know that I have lots of places to go." He stared at me. "That will depend not only on how *I* am treated in the book, but on how Tonka's government is treated."

"You'll both be treated fairly," I said.

"Good. That's all I ask."

I'd heard *that* before on a number of other worlds, but there was no sense arguing about whose notion of fairness would prevail.

Finally Masterson got up, moved around his desk, and walked me to the door.

"My man will be at the Royal first thing in the morning," he said. "In the meantime, think about what an interview with Tonka would mean for your book."

"I will," I said noncommittally.

"I *knew* we were going to be friends," he said as the door dilated to let me out.

Seventeen

"Well, here we are," said my companion, pulling the landcar up to a rustic lodge, which was surrounded by perhaps a dozen plastic domes.

I stepped out of the landcar and suddenly realized just how hot it was outside. A few avian raptors perched on the roof of the lodge, motionless in the burning sun, and the staff was moving as if in slow motion through the open-air restaurant and bar. The lodge and domes were shaded by a row of thorny, stunted desert trees, and the rock-hard ground was covered by sparse clumps of spiny grasses. About fifty yards from the bar was a water hole, and I was surprised to see that the water hadn't all evaporated. A number of small, colorful avians were standing at the shallow end, neither drinking nor searching for fish, and I got the distinct impression that they were simply trying to cool their feet. A distant mountain range was barely visible on the horizon.

There were three other landcars in the parking lot. One bore the imprimatur of the Republic Wildlife Fund, and I assumed it belonged to some ecological researcher. A second—dust-covered, rusted, and missing a back window— bore the mark of a company called Wildlife Holidays. The third, which had also seen better days, seemed to belong to a family on vacation, for I saw a number of toys scattered around the seats.

My guide was named Stan Gardner, and like so many of the Men currently on Peponi, he had come to fight the Kalakala, and had then decided to stay. He had become a professional hunter after the Emergency, but hunting animals simply didn't give him the thrill that he got from hunting sentient beings, and when Buko Pepon outlawed all hunting on the planet he became one of the most feared and hated game rangers on the Great Eastern Continent, tracking and hunting down poachers with even more skill than the poachers tracked and hunted down the animals. He had come to Masterson's attention about five years ago, and jumped at the chance to join Masterson's security team.

He was unfailingly polite to me, and his knowledge of the land and the animals was as thorough as one would expect from a man with his background, but I got the distinct impression that he wasn't exactly thrilled with his current assignment, and that he was eager to get back to the more exciting prospect of hunting down enemies of the state. He related some of his old hunting adventures as we were driving to the park, and admitted that his favorite part of the job was going into the bush after Thunderheads that his clients had wounded. I remembered Hardwycke's utter distaste for that aspect of hunting, *especially* when the animal was a Thunderhead. I eventually concluded that the difference between the two was that Hardwycke had hunted for money and Gardner had hunted for excitement, which made Hardwycke the easier of the two for me to understand.

Perhaps the only thing that came close to pleasing Gardner as much as the prospect of stalking an animal that had the capacity to kill him was, of all things, watching avians. He was never without his fieldglasses and his handful of avian field guides, and from the moment we passed Balimora he began pointing out and identifying the various species for me. When he came to one he didn't recognize, we stopped the landcar until he could find a likeness of it in a field guide. Then he would make a meticulous note next to the representation, entering the time, date, and location where he had seen it.

When we finally reached Keringera I didn't even bother to stop at my dome, but instead walked right up to the bar and ordered a cold beer. I looked around to see if Gardner wanted one, but he was deep in conversation with the native proprietor of the tiny gift shop. When he rejoined me a moment later at a shaded table, he explained that he was finding out where the game was at this time of year, since he hadn't been to Keringera since before Pepon's death.

It was so hot that we decided to wait for the sun to drop lower in the sky before taking the landcar out to search for animals, so we remained in the shade, sipping cold drinks and watching an endless parade of birds landing at the water hole.

Finally, as I was just about to nod off to sleep, I felt Gardner's hand on my arm.

"What is it?" I asked.

"Ngana's wildbuck," he said.

I looked out at the landscape, but couldn't see anything.

"Where?" I said, puzzled.

"About three hundred yards away, at two o'clock."

"Two o'clock?" I repeated, mystified.

"Twelve o'clock is straight ahead of you, nine and three are left and right," he explained.

I looked at two o'clock and still couldn't see anything.

"Here," he said, handing me his fieldglasses. "Try it with these."

I held them up to my eyes. They instantly read my optic disks and adjusted to my nearsightedness, then read my lens implants and readjusted to them, and finally enriched the reds and browns to adjust for a slight tendency I had toward color blindness, and suddenly a tiny written statement appeared in the middle of my field of vision, requesting the distance of the object I wished to study.

"Three hundred yards," I said, and the fieldglasses responded in a fraction of a second—and now, finally, I could see a tiny horned head sticking out from behind a bush.

"Lovely creature, isn't he?" said Gardner when he saw that I had finally spotted it. "Very delicate and very fast."

"How did you see it without your fieldglasses?" I asked, more impressed by his vision than by the wildbuck.

"The bush looked wrong," he answered.

"Wrong? In what way?"

He shrugged. "It seemed too substantial, so I assumed an animal was standing directly behind it. Then I saw its horns and I was able to identify the wildbuck from them."

"I can barely see the bush from here," I said. "I would never have guessed that there was anything behind it."

"It's a knack you pick up if you hunt long enough," he replied. "You just keep scanning the landscape until you see something that strikes you as wrong. Then you study it until you can figure out *why* it's wrong, and nine times out of ten you've spotted an animal. Not always the one you're after," he continued, "but even an antelope can kill you if he can get those horns into you."

"I'm impressed," I said.

"By the end of our second day in the park, you'll be spotting them yourself," he said reassuringly. "Perhaps not all of them, but the bigger ones."

Then a purple avian with yellow stripes on its underbelly landed by the water hole, and Gardner was off on an ecstasy of observation and identification.

There were no waiters, but the bartender kept coming by with more beer every ten or fifteen minutes, until I finally decided that if I had any more I'd soon be drunk. Gardner had no such problem, and I remembered what Hardwycke had told me about professional hunters: their most important trait was the ability to hold their liquor.

Eventually it began cooling off—or, to be more accurate, the heat became slightly more bearable—and we left the bar and returned to the landcar.

"Beautiful country," said Gardner admiringly as we began following a bumpy dirt track through the park. "Absolutely untouched. I must start coming up here more often."

"It seems rather empty, though," I said.

"Do you really think so?" he asked, amused.

"Don't tell me you can see any animals from here," I said disbelievingly.

"There are four Thunderheads at ten o'clock, about a quarter mile away," he said. "There's a Ngana's wildbuck dead ahead at about three hundred yards, and later tonight there will be a Bush Devil in that old tree at one o'clock."

"How do you know that?" I asked.

He brought the landcar to a stop and pointed to a barely visible carcass wedged in between two branches. "That's the way he keeps it safe from the scavengers," he explained. "He'll be sleeping now, probably in a cave, but he'll be back tonight for the rest of it."

"Let me try to spot the Thunderheads," I said, reaching for the fieldglasses.

"We'll drive closer and you won't need those," he said, indicating the glasses.

He turned to his left and began driving slowly toward a thick stand of bushes, never seeming to approach it directly, but always coming closer and closer, until we heard an angry bellow and a huge Thunderhead broke cover and began charging us. Gardner gunned the motor, but waited until the Thunderhead was about thirty yards away before he began driving off.

We drove for another two hours, and saw literally hundreds of animals, including a family of Treetops, that rare northern herbivore that towers some twenty feet above the ground and feeds itself by standing on its back legs, supporting its front legs on the branches, and grazing off the tops of trees.

"Good Landship territory," remarked Gardner as we finally turned the landcar back toward the lodge.

"Everyone tells me that most Landship hunts were equipped in Balimora," I said, "but it still puzzles me: how could this sparse, barren landscape support Landships?"

"You'd be surprised at what this landscape can support," he replied. "Most of the animals are well adapted for life here. For example, neither the Ngana's wildbuck nor the Treetop ever has to drink; they get all the water they need from the moisture on the plants they eat. Same with the Bush Devils: they drink when water's available, but during the dry season they can get enough from the bellies of the animals they kill."

"How did the Landships survive here without water?" I asked.

"Oh, there's water," he replied. "Most of it is beneath the surface, but the Landships were big enough and strong enough to dig down to it, especially with those prehensile lips of theirs." He paused, looking out at the bleak countryside. "One of the things I love about this place is that anything that can live here *deserves* to live. It's totally different from the Siboni Plains, where there's food and water everywhere —or at least, there used to be."

"What's changed there?" I asked. "I heard about the Silvercoats, but I assumed that just meant there was more food for everything else."

"The Silvercoats *were* the food for a few thousand Demon-cats and Nightkillers," he replied. "Now there are hardly any predators left. And at the rate the Siboni are moving their Beefcakes into the park, it won't be too long before it looks just like this one. The difference is that Keringera was *meant* to look this way." He paused. "I gather that things are even worse on the Great Western Continent. Buko Pepon created a model game park there for the Sentabels, complete with first-class tourist accommodations, and now it's a desert." He briefly turned to me as he continued driving. "This planet has a pretty fragile ecology, Matthew. It doesn't take much to ruin it."

"So I gather."

"They say that the wags lived in harmony with their environment for millennia before Man showed up," continued Gardner, "but as far as I can tell that's just not true. They were destroying their farmland long before colonization; we just showed them how to do it faster."

"Then maybe we should leave and let them go back to doing it slowly," I suggested.

He shook his head. "It's too late now. We're probably the only thing that stands between them and anarchy."

"Didn't they have problems back before Edward Ngana landed here?" I asked.

He shrugged. "I really couldn't say. But I'll tell you what they didn't have: modern weapons. If there's a Sentabel left on Peponi ten years from now, I'll be surprised. The only reason the government hasn't wiped out the Siboni yet is because the Siboni still live like savages and won't come to the cities—but one of these days the government is going to want all those Siboni game parks for farmland, and from that moment on the Siboni's days will be numbered."

"You don't sound like you have much hope for Peponi," I said.

"Not much," he agreed. "Another Buko Pepon might slow things down for a generation, but he couldn't stop what's going to happen."

"What *is* going to happen?"

"They'll destroy the land and kill each other off until they're finally back in balance with their environment again."

"And then?"

"Who knows?" he said with a shrug. "They're not Men, and whatever kind of society they ultimately develop isn't going to be anything that makes sense to Men." He paused. "That's the whole problem with Peponi right now—we've convinced them to be like us, and they're *not* like us. They're tribal, and we've told them that they have to have a president who represents all of them; they're farmers and hunters, and we've helped them kill off most of their animals and introduced Beefcakes and sugar berries, which are destroying the land; they're covered with fur and they wear human clothing in tropical climates because our missionaries taught them that it was sinful to go naked. They speak some three hundred different tongues, and yet the official language of Peponi is Terran." He swerved to avoid hitting a small rodentlike animal that had waddled in front of the landcar. "It's not a good situation, and it's only going to get worse."

"And yet you've chosen to spend most of your adult life here," I pointed out. "Why?"

"Why not?" he replied. "I live better here than I would anywhere else, and I enjoy my work."

"Does it bother you that you have privileges that are denied to the natives more than three decades after Independence?" I asked.

"Should it?"

"You tell me," I said. "Should it?"

He considered my question for a moment. "No," he said at last. "Half of them are one generation out of the bush; the rest are still *in* the bush. Giving them the privileges of citizens of the Republic doesn't *make* them Republic citizens. They'd have been better off if we'd never opened this planet up, but we did, and I'm not about to feel guilty because of something that occurred more than half a century before I was even born." He paused. "I'll accept my special prerogatives because they're here for the taking; if someone removes them, I'll find another world on which to live and work."

I was about to make a comment when he pointed out a Bush Devil sleeping in a tree. Then a small herd of Willowbucks sped across the road right in front of us, and before long I was once more thoroughly engrossed in watching the animals.

It was almost dark when we pulled into the lodge's parking lot, and we had a pleasant dinner. A cool breeze had sprung up, and a number of animals came down in twos and threes to drink at the water hole.

"Masterson was right," I said as some Treecrawlers and Chatterboxes began chasing each other across the grounds of the lodge, finally feeling energetic now that the sun had gone down. "This is a lovely place."

"It is *now*," agreed Gardner. "Masterson told me he came up here about ten years ago and the place was a shambles. The wags had just taken it over, and most of the furniture was broken, there wasn't any parking lot, and the water was putting all the tourists into the hospital."

"The water?"

He smiled. "I hope you don't think you're drinking the same untreated stuff that's in the water hole," he said. "The water up here has enough parasites in it to wipe out whole planetary populations, and the wags never thought to boil it and treat it with chemicals before making it available to the guests. Which reminds me," he added; "you'll find a container of water by your bed when you go to your dome. That's the only water you should drink; don't even brush your teeth with the stuff that comes out of the tap in your bathroom. Sometimes I wonder how Fuentes and Dunnegan and some of those early hunters survived."

He paused for a moment. "You know, speaking of the water hole, *that's* new, too. Masterson tells me that when he came up here he spent an entire afternoon in the bar and never saw an avian or an animal, so he got whoever was president at the time—Colonel Zigoza, I think it was—to order them to dig a water hole here and run a pipe out to it from the main well. *Now* the tourists have something to see during the heat of the day."

"Masterson said that there was a very primitive tribe living somewhere near here," I remarked. "Is there any chance that we can see them tomorrow?"

"No problem at all," replied Gardner. "They're the Bal Fosi tribe. There used to be about a thousand of them; they're down under two hundred now." He paused. "I should warn you, though: we'll probably run into about fifty alien anthropologists. The Bal Fosi are primitive even by Peponi standards, and scientists just can't seem to resist studying them."

"How do they survive up here?" I asked. "The Bal Fosi, I mean, not the scientists."

"There's a freshwater lake about one hundred and twenty miles from here. They live on the shores, and they fish with their spears. From what I hear, they've also started keeping a small Beefcake that was bred for desert life." He smiled. "It should be quite a sight. Every morning all these scientists come out of their air-cooled domes, cook their breakfasts, and hop into their landcars so they can drive over and watch a bunch of people sitting around in loincloths and eating raw fish."

"You would think that their very presence would alter the way the Bal Fosi live," I said.

"When did that ever bother scientists?" responded Gardner with a grin. Suddenly he sat upright. "Have you ever seen a Demoncat before?" he asked.

"Only in books."

"Then take a look at the water hole, and don't make any loud noises."

I turned and saw a huge, red catlike carnivore crouched over the water's edge, lapping it up into a mouth that contained two rows of long, wicked-looking teeth. It must have weighed close to seven hundred pounds, yet the overall impression I got from its rippling muscles was one of litheness and agility.

The Demoncat drank for another minute or two and then, slowly, it turned its head until it was staring directly into my eyes.

"Uh . . . Mr. Gardner?" I said uneasily.

"Stan," he corrected me.

"Stan, I think he's looking at me."

"Why not? You're looking at him."

It suddenly occurred to me that the two-foot stone wall that lined the outdoor restaurant was not much of a barrier.

"What do we do if he comes this way?" I asked nervously.

"He won't," said Gardner.

"But *if* he does."

"Look at his belly," pointed out Gardner. "He's already eaten close to eighty pounds. He won't be hungry for another two days."

"He doesn't have to be hungry," I said, half-expecting the Demoncat to get up and charge me. "Just irritable."

Gardner grinned and pointed to a uniformed native who was standing at the bar with a sonic rifle trained on the huge animal. "He probably hasn't had to fire that thing in the past five years, but if the Demoncat charges he'll scare it off. It wouldn't do to have the animals eating the tourists."

The Demoncat remained motionless for another minute, then strode majestically off into the night.

"Well," said Gardner, "now you've seen your first Demoncat."

"I was frightened for a minute there," I admitted.

"Hard to believe that the Siboni used to hunt them with spears, isn't it?"

"That thing was *big*!" I continued. "I mean, I thought they were about the size of a Bush Devil."

Gardner chuckled. "They're not as quick or as vicious, but they're about three times as large. A Bush Devil that size could probably have brought down a Sabrehorn—*and* pulled it up into a tree."

The adrenaline was still racing through my body, and I ordered a drink to calm me down.

"Did you ever have to go into the bush after a wounded Demoncat?" I asked Gardner.

"A couple of times," he said. "They're not as nasty as Thunderheads or Bush Devils, though. Usually they just want to get away so they can lie up and tend to their wounds." He paused. "I'd much rather go after an armed wag any day."

I stared at him for a moment and realized that, in many ways, I understood the alien Buko Pepon better than I would ever understand this member of my own race.

Finally he stood up.

"Well, Matthew," he said, "if we're going to visit the Bal Fosi tomorrow and still see some more of the park, we'd better get an early start."

"Fine," I said, getting to my feet. "I really enjoyed myself today, Stan."

"I'm glad to hear it," replied Gardner. He paused. "By the way, have you considered where else you'll be going after you've seen the various parks?"

"I've never been to the Great Western Continent," I said.

"I thought I'd like to see Bakatula and some of the other cities there, and maybe visit what's left of the Sentabels' game park, since I've heard so much about it."

He stopped walking and turned to me. "Did you clear that with Masterson?" he asked.

"No," I said. "I haven't even mentioned it to him."

"I don't think he'll approve of it."

"Why not?"

"Tonka is having some problems on the Great Western Continent," he answered.

"That's no concern of mine," I said.

"I think it might be," said Gardner seriously.

"Why?"

"Because I don't think we can protect you if you insist on going there."

Eighteen

The Bal Fosi were a disappointment. They may have been primitive a few years earlier, but they had been the subject of so much recent attention that they were as sophisticated as any other tribe I had met. A couple of the fishermen even wore Republic timepieces along with their loincloths.

And if the Bal Fosi were a disappointment, Mount Pekana was a tragedy. Tens of thousands of acres of Mike Wesley's beloved forest had been cut down, and except for an occasional rodent or avian, the only living creatures atop the mountain were the endless herds of Beefcakes that grazed on every newly-uncovered piece of ground.

We then journeyed down to the Siboni Plains. The park held the largest concentration of animals I had seen on Peponi, though the great herds of Hardwycke's day were a distant memory. Thousands of tourists, mostly human, were staying in the well-kept lodges. They raced out each morning at sunrise for a glimpse of a Thunderhead or a small family of Dashers, they raced back for lunch, and they raced out again after the heat of the day for another look. They were crammed into overcrowded minibuses, which kept in touch with each other by radio, so that when one of them found an interesting animal, soon a dozen more minibuses joined the first one, like the scavengers surrounding a carnivore on a kill.

It took half a day of arguing with Gardner and another two hours over the vidphone with Masterson before I was finally permitted to travel to the Great Western Continent, and then only on the condition that Gardner would accompany me everywhere I went. I agreed to their restrictions, and two days later I stepped out of the commercial plane and stood, for the first time, on Peponi's other major continent.

The Sentabels' game park was as bad as I had been led to believe, but, perhaps because I was expecting it, it made less of an impression on me than a number of other things I saw. We drove past a number of derelict and deserted factories, some of which had never been completed. The roads, covered with perhaps half an inch of paving material, were in abysmal condition, far worse than the dirt roads of the game parks, since once they began buckling they constituted a very real danger to life and limb.

The poverty was endemic, but even more alarming was the fact that a number of villages were not only deserted but had been burned to the ground. Gardner initially suggested that the Sentabels had made war on one of the smaller tribes, but that didn't explain the tank tracks and shell casings I saw on the ground. It was obvious to me that the army had been systematically destroying the villages, and finally he admitted that Tonka had been forced to "react rather firmly" to the opposition.

"That's as nice a euphemism for genocide as I've heard," I replied.

"The alternative was to let them secede and create a separate country," he replied, unperturbed.

"Why doesn't he allow it?" I asked. "The land is practically worthless, the expense of keeping an army here is exorbitant, and the people obviously don't want to be governed by a government that sits in Berengi."

"If Tonka wants to remain in office, he can't show any signs of weakness," answered Gardner.

"And slaughtering innocent people is a sign of strength?"

"You're not dealing with Men here. These tribes were slaughtering each other for thousands of years before we came on the scene, and they'll be doing it long after we leave."

"How many Sentabels has Tonka exterminated?"

"You'll have to ask Tonka or Masterson."

During the next three days, I found out that the Sentabels were the least of Tonka's—and Peponi's—problems on the Great Western Continent.

We visited Lake Pepon, which had formerly been Lake Ramirez, and it was totally polluted. Eight large factories were pouring toxic waste into the lake day and night; all the fish had died in the past three years, and the water was no longer safe for drinking or bathing. Despite that, I saw literally hundreds of native females washing clothes in it, and each was accompanied by wading and swimming children.

The second biggest lake in the area, Lake Bago Baja (formerly Lake Fuentes) had a different problem. It provided the drinking water for all of Bakatula and its surrounding villages. No factories polluted the lake, but the local farmers had created so many irrigation channels leading from it to their land that it was now less than half the size it had been at Independence, and Gardner told me that experts were now predicting that it would be nothing more than a swamp in another decade.

The city of Bakatula itself was yet another time bomb waiting to explode. The original ten or twelve buildings had been erected by colonists almost seventy years ago, but because the farmland on the Great Western Continent was so poor, Bakatula had never become the counterpart of Berengi that its founders had envisioned, and most of the rest of the city —except for two new (and nearly empty) hotels which seemed totally out of place—had been built by the Sentabels and other tribes. The streets were narrow and winding, frequently turning back on themselves. There seemed no master plan, no overview governing the structure of the city. There was no residential section, no commercial section, no parks, nothing but a haphazard arrangement of totally dissimilar structures that were used for whatever purpose the current owners wished. As often as not, they were deserted and in varying states of decay. Pepon's struggle against tribalism obviously hadn't reached Bakatula; the Sentabels and Morari controlled all the jobs, and members of other tribes were confined to the poorest section of the city, where crime and drug use were omnipresent.

Bakatula was a seaport, and the government had initially spent an enormous amount of money building a number of deepwater docks—but there were no ships sailing Peponi's oceans, and as a result the docks had fallen into disrepair. There were hundreds of small fishing vessels, but many fishermen preferred to drop explosive charges into the water, which not only killed more fish than could be processed before they rotted, but destroyed the coral-like barrier and allowed a number of huge predatory fish to approach to within ten or fifteen yards of the coast, where they thrived by feeding on the native swimmers.

The people were riddled with disease, as might be expected from Bakatula's lack of sanitation. There was only one hospital, and it had been closed due to a lack of trained doctors. I later found out that there were only seventeen doctors on the entire continent, and only eighty-four on the planet.

(There were human doctors too, of course, but they invariably limited their practices to human patients.)

Both Pepon and Tonka had done their best to combat illiteracy, but while they had shown some progress on their own continent, there was none at all here. The only schools I saw outside of Bakatula were a handful of tiny, one-room buildings that were run by human missionaries. Most of the families needed their children to tend the Beefcakes while the females worked the land.

The land itself was so poor that there were very few permanent farms. The natives would force a few crops from the soil and move on, or else the Beefcakes would begin grazing and leave a lifeless field behind them. As a result, almost all the tribes I saw were at least semi-nomadic, making an endless round of their lands, hoping each new tract would have recovered from its previous misuse.

Now and then, when he felt it was safe, Gardner let me stop and speak to the people. Most were very bitter about the government: It was killing their people, it was corrupt, it only cared for the Bogoda, it was the tool of the Republic, it was trying to keep all the good land for itself, it taxed the Sentabels more than the Kia or the Sorotoba, it tortured its political enemies, it bought elections. Every one of them wanted to see Tonka thrown out of office, and many of them told me exactly what they'd like to do to the President and "his human masters." I decided that if only half of the charges they made had any truth to them, Peponi was in even worse shape than I had been led to believe.

Finally, when my brief tour of the continent was finished, we drove to the one functioning airport—we had seen two abandoned ones and one that had never been completed—and, since we had a couple of hours before we were due to take off for Berengi, Gardner drove me through Bariola, a suburb of Bakatula.

It was as if we had entered an entirely different world. The houses were large and impressive, the streets were well-paved and immaculate, the vehicles were recent models imported from nearby worlds, the handful of stores and shops were doing an excellent business.

"This is where the politicians live," he explained when I commented on this surprising display of affluence.

"How do they stop the masses from rioting and looting them?" I asked.

"Their security forces are unobtrusive, but we've been under observation ever since we pulled off the main highway and entered Bariola."

"Still, given the conditions here, you'd think they would try to hide their wealth, rather than flaunt it."

"You still don't understand the Peponi mindset, Matthew," said Gardner. "Their kings and chiefs have been extorting money—or whatever used to pass for money—from them since time began. They *expect* them to be wealthy. In their eyes, an impoverished leader is an incompetent leader, and *that* would encourage some wag in Bakatula to try to depose him."

"It doesn't make sense," I said.

"It does to *them*."

When we reached the airport, a human security guard pulled Gardner over and whispered something to him. He nodded and returned to me.

"We'll be going in a private plane," he announced. "It takes off in about twenty minutes."

"Why the change in plans?" I asked.

"We think one of the wags on the commercial flight is being sent to Berengi to assassinate Tonka." He paused. "We'll grab him when the plane lands, but there's no sense taking any chances with your safety. When he realizes that we know who he is, he might settle for killing a couple of Men instead."

"Will they take him while he's still on the plane, or wait for him to get off?" I asked.

He shrugged. "That's up to Masterson."

"Why don't they just pick him up here, as long as they know who he is?"

"He hasn't broken any laws."

"He won't have broken any when you grab him in Berengi," I said. I stared at him. "What's the real reason?"

"The real reason," said Gardner, "is that we can control what gets reported in Berengi. There's no sense giving other wags the same idea. Does that satisfy you?"

I made no reply, and a few minutes later we boarded the small private plane that was to take us to Berengi. We took off and banked to the left, and as I looked out my window I was able to see first Bakatula and then the dusty, barren countryside.

"Take a good look, Matthew," said Gardner, "and remember it well." He paused. "That's Berengi and the Great Eastern Continent in another twenty years."

"I hope you're wrong," I said.

"So do I," he said sincerely. "But I'm not."

The flight took almost seven hours, including a refueling stop in the Connectors, and Ian Masterson was waiting for us when we landed in Berengi.

"Welcome back, Matthew," he said. "I hope you had a pleasant flight."

"It was all right."

"And an interesting trip?"

"Very."

"Good," he said. "You must tell me all about it. Why don't I take you out to dinner?"

"Right now?"

"I know you haven't eaten since the Connectors," he said. "Don't worry about your luggage. Stan will see that it gets to the Royal." He turned to Gardner. "I'll speak with you after I return."

Gardner nodded and walked off, while Masterson put an arm around my shoulder like a long-lost friend.

"It's good to see you again, Matthew."

"Did you catch your would-be assassin?" I asked.

"Of course."

"*Was* he here to kill the President?"

"Ask me tomorrow. We're questioning him right now."

"I'd like to sit in on the interrogation," I said.

He smiled. "I think not, Matthew."

"*That* brutal?"

"That efficient."

He walked me to the main exit and signaled for his private vehicle, which arrived a moment later. We drove to The Cutlery, an outdoor restaurant on the outskirts of town that owned the only game ranch on the planet and supplied all its own needs. It was owned and frequented entirely by humans.

"Well, Matthew," said Masterson after he had ordered a Silvercoat steak and I had ordered a sampler of Silvercoat, Dasher, and two types of wildbuck, "now that you've been on the planet for more than a week, what are your thoughts?"

"I think the ghosts of Commodore Quincy and Buko Pepon must both be weeping bitter tears," I said.

Masterson smiled. "I rather think they're both laughing their heads off, since they passed from the scene before the *real* problems manifested themselves."

"*You're* still on the scene," I said. "Do *you* think these problems are soluble?"

"All problems are capable of solution," he responded. "Our job is to keep our fingers in the dike until the solution comes along."

"What kind of solution do you anticipate?" I asked.

He shrugged. "Who knows? It could be anything from a planetary plague to another Johnny Ramsey."

"You mean another Buko Pepon."

He shook his head. "This planet's problems aren't going to be solved by any wag, no matter how talented he is. Peponi needs someone in the Republic, someone with power, to fall in love with it."

"Someone with money, you mean."

"No. You've seen what happens to the money they send here, Matthew. Half of it goes right into Tonka's pocket, and the rest gets divided up among the other politicians. No, we need someone with the power and the enthusiasm to totally remake Peponi."

"It's already been done," I said. "They called it colonialism."

"And Peponi was better off then than now."

"Why don't you stop the first five natives you see on the street and ask them if they agree with you?" I suggested.

"Why don't we ask them when the population reaches six billion and every last one of them is starving?" he shot back. "It's only a century or two away, Matthew."

"I know."

"Still, Nature has a way of fighting back. It sounds cruel, but something that wiped out three-quarters of the population would be the best thing that could happen to the planet."

"That's a little too cataclysmic for my taste," I said. "Peponi can feed itself right now. It's just a matter of education."

"This isn't Lodin XI or the Canphor Twins we're talking about, Matthew. These people had never seen a wheel one hundred and fifty years ago. Peponi is a world that's one generation removed from the bush, and it's faced with overwhelming problems."

Our meals arrived just then, and we let the subject drop while we began eating. I didn't like Silvercoat any better now than when Buko Pepon had offered me some fourteen years ago, but the Dasher was acceptable and the two species of wildbuck were excellent.

"How did you like the Keringera park, Matthew?" asked Masterson.

"It was wonderful," I said. "Not at all what I anticipated. I suppose after hearing Hardwycke speak about the endless herds of game, I was expecting to see more animals, but there was a certain austere beauty to the place that appeals to me."

"I knew you'd like it," he said with a satisfied expression. "There aren't many places like that left on Peponi these days. Did you get to visit the Bal Fosi people?"

"We drove there," I said, "but there were so many landcars and scientists taking holos that I felt like . . ." I searched for the proper example.

"Like you were a tourist on the Siboni Plains, and you were in one of twenty minibuses that were surrounding a Demoncat on a kill?" he suggested.

"Exactly!" I said.

"Oh, well," he said with a sigh. "When I first met them, they were a primitive and unspoiled people. Of course," he added, "when I first met the Siboni, they were a proud, arrogant race of warriors. Now they hang around the gates of the game parks and cadge money in exchange for posing for holographs. Times change." He paused thoughtfully. "I suppose that's why I admire the Bogoda. They seem to be the one tribe that tries to adapt to change."

"But you serve a Begau," I pointed out.

"I serve the Presidency," he replied. "Whoever happens to hold it is a matter of complete indifference to me."

"As long as he lets you keep your job."

"True."

We sat in silence for a few minutes.

"Have you given any further thought to our discussion, Matthew?" he asked at last.

"I have."

"And?"

"I want to see Tonka, but I'm not going to let you write my book for me."

"I'm no writer," he said, amused. "I just want to look at it."

"And change what you don't like."

He leaned forward and lowered his voice. "I'll be perfectly frank with you, Matthew," he said. "The way things are going on this planet, I don't expect *any* wag to hold the Presidency for more than three years—which means Tonka's already on borrowed time. The only reason he's still here is because each side is afraid of a civil war if they put somebody from their own tribe in power. Even so, he can't hang on much longer." Masterson paused. "I've got a good ten or twelve years left, Matthew. I'm good at my job, damned good, and if I can't do it here, I want to do it somewhere else."

"So you've said."

"I want to stay on Peponi. I really do. But if I have to leave, I've got to be sure that your book isn't going to make me a pariah throughout the Republic."

"Let's be totally honest," I replied. "We both know that you're not looking for work as the security chief of a bank or a large corporation. For better or worse, you supply security to politicians and governments." He opened his mouth to say something, but I held up my hand. "I won't let you dictate or edit my book, or any section of it. But what if I give you my word that nothing I write will in any way hinder you from being offered a position comparable to the one you now hold?"

He stared at me distrustfully. "What you're saying is that ten or eleven dictators who read the book will like me and everyone else will hate me."

"*I* don't hate you," I said. "I don't like your job, but I recognize the necessity for it." I paused. "I want to meet with Tonka, but that's my best offer. Take it or leave it."

He continued staring at me, as if trying to make up his

mind. Finally he sighed, and the tension seemed to melt from his body.

"The day after tomorrow," he said. "I'll set it up and get back to you."

"Thank you, Ian."

"I hope, for both our sakes, that you're not lying to me," he said.

Nineteen

I spent the next day preparing for my interview with Tonka. I reread all the research material I had gathered on him, reviewed his finances, and listened to holographic recreations of his major speeches. Then, since I hadn't heard from Masterson yet, I walked from the Royal to Berengi's bustling downtown area to do a little shopping.

Before I had covered the mile that separated the venerable Royal from the Equator Hotel (which was in the midst of yet another renovation, its eighth to date), I was accosted, at one-block intervals, by seven different young natives. Each explained to me, in perfect Terran, that he was a student from the Great Western Continent who would be sent back home to almost certain extermination if he could not raise the necessary funds for his tuition so that he could remain at Buko Pepon University here in Berengi. I gave a couple of credits to the first of them, but when I started hearing the same sad story repeated almost word-for-word, I simply increased my speed and walked past the next six, barely suppressing a grin when I was able to see the mark of the Bogoda on the last one's bead necklace.

It was a new scam since the last time I had been on Peponi, and it seemed to be working very well. Everywhere I went, gullible tourists were handing over money so that these poor "Great Western students" wouldn't be returned to their homeland to face certain genocide. Eventually, I knew, the spaceliners would warn their passengers about this newest refinement of the beggar's art before they disembarked, and shortly thereafter the poor downtrodden students would vanish, to be instantly replaced by poor downtrodden orphans or poor downtrodden noncommunicable disease carriers or whatever else seemed to appeal most to the compassion of the tourists.

The first eight shops I passed carried nothing but low-priced and cheaply-made tourist items, but the ninth had some exquisite Baroni wood sculptures in the window, and I quickly entered the store, glad to be out of the sun and the reach of the street beggars.

Everything seemed to be on sale, and as I was examining a delicate carving of a Sabrehorn, the middle-aged auburn-haired human proprietor walked over to me.

"Gorgeous piece, isn't it?" he said.

"It's beautiful," I agreed.

"It's on sale," he announced. "It's been marked down from seven thousand credits to three thousand."

"That's not much for a Baroni sculpture," I said suspiciously.

"I know what you're thinking," he said quickly. "I can supply a certificate of authentication with it."

"Then why is it so inexpensive?" I asked.

"This is my going-out-of-business sale."

"Why?" I asked. "You have a prime location and an excellent selection of stock."

"I'm getting off this damned planet," he said bitterly. "I put up with a little of this and a little of that, with higher taxes for humans and with all the wags I have to pay off to stay in business, but this latest ruling . . ." He shook his head. "I know when I'm not wanted. There's a lot of worlds out there; I don't have to stay here."

"What ruling are you talking about?" I asked.

"When Buko Pepon was in charge, he did everything he could to attract human businessmen. He didn't care what world we were citizens of, as long as we'd come here and invest our money. But now that bastard Tonka has declared that only Peponi citizens can own their own businesses; if you don't have a Peponi passport, you can't own more than forty-nine percent of any business."

"If you're going to live here, why don't you just apply for citizenship?" I asked.

"It used to cost fifty credits to become a Peponi citizen when the Old Man was running things. Do you know what Tonka is charging?"

"No."

"Thirty thousand credits!" snapped the man. "It's extortion, plain and simple, and I'm not going to pay it—and I'm also not going to give fifty-one percent of my business to some wag who will put forty members of his family on the payroll and steal half the stock!" He paused for breath. "Come back tomorrow and that Sabrehorn will be five hundred credits less—if it's still here."

"Where will you go from here?" I asked.

He shrugged. "I don't know. But it's damned well going to be a Republic world. I've learned my lesson. I've been robbed by one alien world; I'm not going to give another one the chance."

I finally decided to buy the Sabrehorn, then went back outside and continued window-shopping. I stopped for a cold drink at the Equator Hotel's bar and carried it out to a table near the Message Tree, where I sat down and watched the bustle of activity surrounding me. There were natives in tribal attire, natives in human garb, natives in rags, tourists with holo cameras, human businessmen walking briskly from one appointment to another, even a pair of Canphorites. It seemed like any other cosmopolitan city, and at that moment I had a difficult time convincing myself that Peponi faced any problems that it couldn't solve. Then I recalled what I had seen during the previous week, and I realized that Berengi was the showplace of the planet precisely because it differed so much from all the other cities. The city's inhabitants had been yanked from one existence and thrust into another, and, despite their occasional complaints, they were doing their best to adapt to it.

My heart went out to them, these Bogoda and Sorotoba and Kia who had grown up on a very small patch of ground and were now being forced to live in a very large galaxy. I wished them well, and hoped they would overcome the obstacles that they faced, but even as I watched them bustle around this unlikely city on this unlikely world, I had a sinking feeling that the odds against them were too high.

Finally I got up and walked back to the Royal. Masterson had left a message that my meeting with Tonka was set for ten o'clock the next morning, so I made an early night of it.

I walked to the President's mansion the next morning, arrived about half an hour early, had one of the officers on duty tell Tonka that I was in the lobby, and spent the next few minutes studying the artwork that was on display. There was a permanent sign posted that Buko Pepon's body lay in an ornate freestanding mausoleum in the next room, watched over around the clock by an honor guard, and I stopped in for a moment to pay my respects. Then I returned to the lobby, and a few minutes later I was summoned to Tonka's office.

Two handsomely-uniformed officers escorted me to the lift and rode up to the fourth floor with me. Then one remained behind while the other led me to the office door, which dilated to let me through.

The office had been redecorated since Pepon's time, and the three huge holographs of Pepon had been replaced by three even larger holos of Tonka. Also new was the security scanner that examined everyone walking through the doorway.

Nathan Kibi Tonka was seated at his desk, clad in a very expensive human outfit. He had aged considerably, and seemed heavier than when I had last seen him.

"Hello, Matthew," he said, remaining seated.

"Good morning, Mr. President," I replied.

"Call me Nathan, please," he said. "After all, we're old friends." He paused. "You're looking prosperous."

"So are you," I said. "I see that you no longer wear your Begau tribal outfit."

"I am now President of all the people. Won't you please sit down, Matthew?"

I sat on the chair he had indicated.

"I want you to know that I give very few interviews to off-worlders," he said. "I have agreed to this one because of my friendship for you and my high regard for the books you have written about Peponi."

"I appreciate that, sir," I said.

"Nathan," he corrected me.

"I feel uneasy calling a planetary president by his first name," I said.

He shrugged. "Whatever you wish." He paused while I set up my recording device and activated it. "Where shall we begin, Matthew?"

"Fourteen years ago, on the trip we took to Balimora, we

discussed what you thought were the major problems facing Peponi. Do you recall that conversation, sir?"

"Vaguely," he replied. "But I have no difficulty recalling the problems. They were overpopulation, and the destruction of the environment, correct?"

I nodded in agreement. "I wonder if you can tell me what steps you've taken to combat them?"

He sighed deeply. "I told you back then that they were not simple problems. However, I don't think even *I* realized how complex they were until I took office." He paused. "To combat our population growth, I have offered tax incentives to any family that produces three children or less, and there are heavy penalties for those families producing four children or more. I have also authorized some ten million credits for the dissemination of birth control information among the tribes of the Great Western Continent."

"Have you noticed any improvement?"

"Not as much as I would like, but there has definitely been a leveling off of our population growth."

"Can your office supply me with any figures to corroborate that?" I asked.

"I'm afraid not," he replied. "We're in the midst of a planetary census, and the final figures won't be available for another year."

The fact that he couldn't support his claim didn't surprise me. Tax penalties were meaningless to a family that didn't make enough money to pay any taxes in the first place; and as for the birth control clinics on the Great Western Continent, if they existed at all, I could just imagine the Sentabels' reaction to being singled out for a population decrease: they would assume this was a new scheme to weaken them, and would immediately start producing even more children.

Still, I couldn't be too argumentative. Pepon had truly wanted an honest book; Tonka had agreed to the interview only because Masterson had urged him to do so, and he could call it off whenever he felt like it.

"What about the environment, sir?" I asked.

"I understand that you went back to Mount Pekana."

"Yes, I did."

"Then you know what they're doing up there."

"They're destroying it. In ten or twenty years all the soil will have eroded."

He nodded. "I know." He stared directly at me. "But you *must* know that my hands are tied."

"You're the President," I said. "Can't you do something?"

"My Presidency is the result of a compromise between the Bogoda and the Kia," he said. "If I seem to be favoring one over the other, I'll be out of office within a week." He paused. "I happen to think that I'm a very good President, so I have to put up with the situation, as distasteful as I find it."

"What about the environmental degradation that is taking place all over the planet on lands that *aren't* owned by the Bogoda or the Kia?"

"You've been misinformed, Matthew," he said sincerely. "We're actually in the process of reclaiming land that has been abused."

"I don't want to contradict you, Mr. President," I said, "but I've been to the Great Western Continent, and it's in the process of becoming another dust bowl."

He shrugged. "Well, the *Sentabels*," he said contemptuously. "What can one do with them?"

"I saw what your army was doing with them."

"My army has done nothing but restore peace in the face of civil disorder perpetrated by our enemies."

"Are the Sentabels your enemies?" I asked.

He pointed to the recording device. "Deactivate that thing!"

I reached forward and turned it off.

He glared at me, the slits of his pupils dilating and contracting. "Are you trying to make me sound like a genocidal maniac?" he demanded.

"No, sir," I said. "I'm merely trying to get your responses to various situations that I've observed on Peponi."

"Of course we're killing the Sentabels! They're trying to secede and form their own government, they've sabotaged all my efforts to improve conditions on the Great Western Continent, they've murdered my representatives, they've refused to pay their taxes, they've even tried to organize an army! What would you have me do?"

"It's not for me to say, sir," I replied. "I'm just trying to get *your* answers."

"They're a cancer on the face of Peponi," he said firmly. "And when you find a cancer, you cut it out."

"I also saw a Senoba village that had been burned down."

"The Senoba are lackeys of the Sentabels!" He continued glaring at me. "I will answer no more questions on the subject. You're treading on very dangerous ground, Matthew."

"All right," I said. "The subject is closed." I indicated the recording device. "May I?"

He stared at it for a moment and finally nodded.

"Thank you," I said, activating it again. "I had an interesting discussion with a human shopkeeper in downtown Berengi yesterday."

"Oh?"

"He was selling off his stock, preparatory to leaving the planet. He told me that you've passed a new law stating that no non-citizen can own more than forty-nine percent of a Peponi business."

"That's true."

"Would you care to tell me why?"

"Whatever the future holds for Peponi, it is essential that we are in control of our own destiny," he said. "That is what being an independent world means. Yet if you look around you, you will see that the largest hotels, the major oil refineries, many of the biggest farms, and most of the import houses were owned by off-world corporations. They had the power of economic life and death over Peponi, since if they decided to leave, our economy and our balance of trade would collapse. Therefore, I decided that no non-citizen could own a majority of any business on Peponi, which ensures that these businesses will never leave us."

"But I understand that the Vainmill Syndicate divested themselves of all their Peponi holdings more than a year ago."

"*They* did," said Tonka with a smile, "but their hotels, their bank, and their factories remain."

"And what happens if a business wants to remain?"

"Then we make them a fair offer for fifty-one percent of their stock."

"And if they refuse it?"

"Then we insist than they prove ownership by a Peponi citizen, or we confiscate it."

I leaned over and deactivated the recording device.

"Which Peponi citizen gets the fifty-one percent of each company?"

"From the fact that you turned off the device, I think you can guess."

"You own fifty-one percent of *all* these businesses?" I asked.

"Not quite fifty-one percent, and not quite all," he replied. "But enough." He paused. "Do you remember, Matthew, that I once told you why no one resented Buko Pepon's wealth? The chief is *supposed* to be the richest member of the tribe—and I am the chief of the entire planet."

I was startled by his admission of great wealth, just as I had been startled when Pepon acknowledged his own wealth, and I realized once again how different the Peponi mindset was from Man's.

"How much are you worth?"

He shrugged. "You would have to ask my accountants."

"Where are they?"

"On Deluros VIII."

"I thought it was illegal for a Peponi citizen to invest money off the planet," I said.

"It is," he agreed. "But it is not illegal for a stock transference to take place on Deluros."

"I know that you love this planet as much as Pepon did," I said. "He invested all his money here. Why don't you?"

He sighed. "Look around you, Matthew. Peponi is rife with corruption. I invest *some* of my money here, but I won't line the pockets of the Bogoda and Kia and Sorotoba officials with it. When the time comes that I know that the money will benefit the people, I'll bring every credit of it back here."

"If you're waiting for corruption to vanish from Peponi, you'll be waiting a long time."

"I have infinite patience," he replied.

"At twelve percent per annum, I suppose *I* could have infinite patience too," I said, and he chuckled appreciatively.

I reactivated the device.

"The reason this shopkeeper was leaving the planet," I continued, "was because he is not a Peponi citizen. He was willing to become one, but the fee for an application for citizenship has been raised from fifty credits to thirty thousand, and he feels as if he's being extorted: he must either give up fifty-one percent of his business, or he must pay thirty thousand credits to keep what was his in the first place. Have you an answer for him, Mr. President?"

"Yes, I do," said Tonka. "When we first announced that we were considering passing a law that off-world ownership would be limited to forty-nine percent, a number of corporate officers immediately applied for Peponi citizenship, and we discovered that the Republic was allowing them to retain their former citizenship as well. This, in effect, allowed them to circumvent our desires for a mere fifty credits. *That* is why we raised the citizenship fee to thirty thousand credits. As for your shopkeeper, he is an unfortunate victim of a regulation that was passed to stop huge corporations from flouting our laws. If you will give me his name, I will do what I can to see that an exception is made in his case."

I paused, trying to decide if his offer was sincere. I doubted it, but I decided to accept it anyway. "I don't have his name," I replied at last, "but I'll send it by tomorrow."

"I am not promising anything, you understand," continued Tonka. "We must draw the line somewhere. But I will look into it." He smiled. "Next question?"

"What happened to Buko Pepon's farms in the Greenlands?" I asked.

"They are in good, competent hands."

"His family's?"

"Good, competent hands," repeated Tonka firmly. "Next question?"

"I understand you have had to build two new prisons in Berengi," I said. "Why?"

"Why does one build prisons anywhere?" he said. "To hold prisoners, of course."

"What kind of prisoners?"

"Those who break the law. What other kind are there?"

"There are political prisoners."

He shook his head. "No, Matthew. A prisoner, by definition, is a lawbreaker. A political prisoner is merely a lawbreaker who broke a particular law."

"Such as?"

"Treason."

"You've had to build two new jails to hold prisoners convicted of treason?"

"*I* did not say that."

"It's no secret that you've imprisoned more than two hundred of your countrymen for supposedly plotting to overthrow the government."

"The two new jails hold one thousand five hundred prisoners each. Two hundred political prisoners is a very small percentage of that."

"Are you saying that you have *only* two hundred political prisoners?"

"No, Matthew, *you* are saying it."

"How many *do* you have?"

He stared coldly at me. "I choose not to answer that question."

"May I ask why not?"

"Because treason is a very sensitive subject," he replied, clasping his hands together on the desk. "I can see no reason to discuss it. Any publicity given it would simply encourage others to consider committing treasonable acts against the government."

"If they knew that three thousand political prisoners are currently sitting in Berengi jail cells, wouldn't it *discourage* them?" I suggested.

"I did not say that we have three thousand political prisoners!" he shot back angrily.

I decided to stop pressing him for the number before he got so mad that he terminated the interview.

"What becomes of them, however many there are?"

"Most of them are awaiting trial," he said. "After that their fate is out of my hands. The President may not interfere with the judicial process on Peponi."

"How long have some of them been waiting to go to trial?" I asked.

"Some of them have been waiting less than a week," he replied. "One is a Sentabel who was sent here to assassinate me, and was apprehended only two days ago. I believe that you are familiar with the case."

"How long have some of the others been waiting?" I persisted.

"More than a week," he said. "Next question?"

"Buko Pepon never jailed any political prisoners. Could you perhaps compare your—?"

"I said: Next question," he interrupted harshly.

"All right," I said, scanning my notes. "You have been forced to devalue your currency twice since taking office. Do you anticipate having to do so again?"

"Probably, if we cannot keep inflation under fifteen percent."

"Why does Peponi have such a high inflation rate?"

"The government must initiate many projects to develop Peponi's assets, and of course we must print enough money to pay our bills. The more money we print, the higher the inflation rate."

"What would some of those projects be?" I asked.

"More roads, more water preservation projects, a major airport in the Greenlands, more and better schools, various desert reclamation projects, dams, the creation of more game parks and tourist facilities . . . the list goes on and on."

"Why do you need more game parks?" I asked. "You seem unable to properly manage the ones you have now."

He reached over and deactivated the recorder.

"The interview is over, Matthew," he said. "I agreed to it because Ian Masterson urged me to, but I find your questions offensive."

"I didn't ask them with the intention of offending you," I said sincerely.

"I know," he replied, more weary than angered. "But I read your biography of Pepon, and I know that whoever reads this book will be comparing me to him—*very* unfavorably, I might add."

"He was a difficult leader to follow."

"He was *impossible* to follow," said Tonka bitterly. "He was like a god to the people. He made mistakes, just like any other leader, but no one ever criticized him—and he had the good fortune to die at exactly the right time. What would he have done with the Sentabels? How could he, who owned thousands of Beefcakes, convince the people that their Beefcakes were destroying the land? How would he have reacted to the demands that Republic investors make upon me? He was an old man, and he gave us stability and a sense of worth, but he didn't *solve* anything!"

Tonka paused, and when he spoke again he was more in control of himself. "Take the parks you asked about. Of course we can't manage the ones we have. But we need the revenues from tourism. What am I to do? Close all the parks until I can educate the entire planet about the importance of the environment, and then reopen them and hope that tourists will come back? Of course not. So I will open new parks, and hope that we can stay one step ahead of disaster until the people finally realize what must be done. Then, hopefully, we can begin reclaiming and restocking the old parks."

"It's a tough job," I said. "I don't envy you."

"It's a balancing act," he answered. "I have a tenth of Pepon's power and ten times his problems."

"I'll bet the life of a fisherman looks pretty tempting sometimes," I said.

"It was a tranquil, pleasant life," he responded. "There are times," he added with a wry smile, "when it seems even more tranquil and pleasant in retrospect."

"I have one last, unofficial, off-the-record question to ask of you," I said as I got up to leave.

"What is it?"

"Would you have accepted the Presidency if you had known what to expect?"

"I'm here, and I'm doing the very best job I can," he replied. "That is a very hypothetical question."

"But I notice that you didn't answer it," I said.

"I know."

Twenty

I had walked about half the distance from the President's mansion to the Royal Hotel when Ian Masterson pulled his landcar up to the curb next to me and invited me to get in.

"Thanks," I said, climbing into the passenger's seat. "I was getting tired."

"What have you got there?" he asked, indicating the package I was carrying.

I pulled out the Baroni wood sculpture I had purchased and held it up for him to see.

"Lovely piece," he commented.

"Isn't it?" I replied. "And I got it at a lovely price."

"From the guy who's going out of business?"

"How did you know about him?" I asked, surprised.

"Tonka summoned me to his office after you left." He

paused. "That's why I came after you. He wants you off the planet tonight."

"Why?"

"He thinks you're out to sabotage him with this book."

"Didn't you tell him I wasn't?"

He sighed. "Look, Matthew," he said, "I already put my job on the line by getting you the interview. If I'd argued in favor of letting you stay, we'd *both* be leaving Peponi tonight." He paused. "Besides, you've seen enough and heard enough so you can write the book, haven't you?"

"Yes, I suppose so," I said.

Suddenly he took a hard left, and a moment later we were driving out of town on Independence Highway.

"This isn't the way to the Royal Hotel," I said.

"I know."

"But my luggage is there!"

"Don't worry about it," said Masterson. "Stan Gardner will take it to the spaceport for you." He reached into a pocket and withdrew a spaceliner ticket. "Which reminds me—here's your ticket, courtesy of the President's Office."

"Thanks," I said, staring at it. "I don't take off for another four hours. Where are we going?"

"I thought I'd treat you to lunch," said Masterson.

"I wasn't aware that there were any restaurants in this direction," I said.

"There aren't."

We drove in silence for another five minutes, and then passed through the gates of the Berengi Park, a small game reserve on the outskirts of the city.

We turned onto a bumpy dirt track, drove through a small forest, and emerged on a rolling plain. Small groups of Silvercoats and Willowbucks watched us curiously, but we sped by them and finally came to a large water hole that was surrounded by colorful avians. Masterson pulled the landcar into the shade of a tree, then opened the doors and windows, reached into a cooler that he kept in the back of the car, and withdrew two containers of beer and some sandwiches.

"I thought you might like to have your last Peponi meal in pleasant surroundings," he said. "And it's on the way to the spaceport."

"It *is* lovely," I said, looking out at the water hole as a huge Water Pig broke the surface, bellowed once, and then submerged again.

"I often come here for breakfast," confided Masterson. "I park under this tree, pull out a container of coffee, and just relax for an hour or two before going to my office."

"I'm surprised that there isn't anyone else here."

"The tourists want to see the bigger parks, and the natives are too busy trying to make a living to bother coming here," he answered. "There will be a little traffic here in the afternoon, but I've usually got the place to myself in the mornings." He paused and looked out at the water hole and the plain beyond it. "I don't know what I'd do without this place. You sit here at the dawn of a new day, and you can almost forget that the rest of the planet is such a mess." He pointed off to the right. "Half a century ago there used to be a herd of Silvercoats out there even bigger than the one that used to migrate to the Siboni Plains."

"I assume they're gone now?"

He nodded. "Berengi got too big, and blocked their migration route. You know, animals can recover from most disasters, including poaching—but start destroying their habitat and you've written their epitaph."

"I thought poaching killed off the Landship and the Sabrehorn," I said.

"Only because the poachers knew where to find them. Take away ninety percent of *any* animal's range, and there's no way he can hide from poachers. Hardwycke and his friends took a million eyestones a year out of Peponi and didn't do half the damage to the Landship population that the farmers did."

I took a sip of my beer. "I'm all turned around," I said at last. "Where is Berengi from here?"

"Just about five miles behind us," he said. "If you climb to the top of that rise," he said, indicating a small hill, "you can see a couple of the taller buildings." He paused. "That's why I parked down here. For an hour a day I can pretend they don't exist."

"But they do."

"I know." He paused. "By the way, what did you think of your old friend?"

"Tonka?"

"Yes."

"Before I spoke with him, I had just about made up my mind that he was a villainous petty tyrant who imprisoned his enemies and kept all his money on Deluros in case he had to leave in a hurry."

"He *does* imprison his enemies, and most of his money *is* on Deluros," said Masterson wryly.

"I know. But he's not an evil man."

"He's not a *man* at all."

"You know what I mean," I said. "He cares about Peponi as much as Buko Pepon did." I paused. "But the job is too big for him."

"I think it's too big for anyone these days."

"Perhaps."

"Even the Old Man couldn't have solved the problems Peponi is facing."

"I agree," I said. "He had wisdom and compassion, and I think he'd do a better job than Tonka, but I don't think he could have done anything except slow down the inevitable."

"It's a shame," said Masterson, opening his beer and taking a long swallow.

"Yes it is," I said, unwrapping a sandwich.

"It's not Tonka's fault, either," added Masterson.

"Whose fault is it?" I asked.

"Ours."

I smiled. "Yours and mine?"

"Man's." He paused. "They didn't have population problems before we came here. They never heard of poaching. They made war with spears instead of bombs. They didn't have any debt because they didn't have any currency. Their cities weren't overcrowded and crime-infested, because they didn't have any cities. *We* did all that for them. And you want to know something else?" he continued. "It wasn't the Commodore Quincys who did it. It was all the people like Hardwycke and Amanda Pickett who fell in love with this place, decided it was almost Paradise, and tried, with that odious paternalism of theirs, to show the wags how to make it perfect." He sighed. "So the wags listened, and they tried, and the Hardwyckes and Picketts went back to live in the Republic, and this is what's left."

"I knew Hardwycke and Pickett," I said, "and I think you're misjudging them. They loved Peponi."

"You know who loves Peponi?" Masterson said angrily. "*I* love Peponi! If you love a world, you stay on it and you fight for it. It's not perfect, and it never will be, but I'm trying to make it the best world it can be."

"They tried too," I said.

He shook his head. "They tried to make it something it wasn't. I'm trying to help Tonka make it something it can be." He paused. "Every one of them—Fuentes and Hardwycke and Pickett and the rest—came out here with a totally unrealistic golden dream of what Peponi was. Read your own books, Matthew. Hardwycke thought it was Paradise when Fuentes first set foot on it, and Amanda Pickett thought it must have been Paradise when Hardwycke was here, and even Mike Wesley thought it must have been just about perfect when Amanda was a colonist. But do you know something, Matthew? It was never Paradise. The first ten Men to settle here died of disease. The eleventh was killed by a Demoncat.

The twelfth was tortured to death by the Siboni. Do you think *they* thought it was Paradise?"

"No."

"The Republic is filled with Men who left Peponi when it turned out to be just a world, instead of an early glimpse of Heaven. Maybe if enough of them had stayed behind, they might have created what they wanted and my job wouldn't be necessary." Masterson sighed deeply. "Or maybe not. What's Paradise for half a million Men isn't exactly Paradise for the hundred million wags that the Men think were born to serve their every need." He stopped and turned to me. "I'm sorry, Matthew. Sometimes I talk too much. It's a bad habit for a person in my profession."

"I wish you'd talk a little more," I said. "I found it very interesting."

He grimaced and looked out at the pond, where four Water Pigs were splashing around playfully and a number of avians were squawking out their annoyance.

"Talking never cured anything," he said. "You're going to go home and write a book about how Peponi is going straight to hell, and I'm going to go back to my office and find out who's been added to Tonka's enemy list."

"And yet you stay when so many others have left."

"I stay," he replied. "The colonists looked back and thought they saw Paradise, and they were wrong. Buko Pepon looked ahead and thought he could see it, and he was wrong too." He gave me an embarrassed smile. "But me, I come here every morning, and even though I know everything that's wrong with Peponi and everything that's going to happen to it, I sit here alone for an hour or so, and it *seems* like Paradise."

"You're as much of a romantic as they were," I said, returning his smile.

He shook his head. "I'm not trying to remake the rest of the world, Matthew. I take my hour a day, and then I go back to my desk. I do things I never thought I'd be able to do, for

politicians I don't especially like . . . but as long as I know
that hour a day is waiting for me, I do what I have to do. I
suppose it's a case of diminished expectations."

"Or realistic ones," I replied.

"Well," he said, activating the landcar, "I guess we'd better
be on our way."

"Thank you for sharing this spot with me."

"It's here for anyone who'll make the effort to find it," he
replied.

"Maybe someday they will," I said.

"Maybe," he replied doubtfully.

Twenty-one

It took me about six months to write *Peponi After Pepon*, and the book was moderately successful. Then I received an assignment to cover the civil war on Doxloter II, and after that I wrote books about Foster VI and Bailiwick, two other worlds that had recently attained their independence from the Republic.

During the time that I was busy with other projects, I made every effort to keep up with events on Peponi. Tonka had remained in office for three years after I left, and was now living in exile on Deluros VIII. His successor, a Kia, had been assassinated within a month of taking office, and after the military took control of the government for a year, a general election was held and a young Bogoda politician, distantly related to Buko Pepon, was elected to the Presidency.

I never heard from Ian Masterson again, but I read that he

had died on the job some six years after I left. There were no details concerning the cause of his death.

When I was finally able to set aside a couple of months for a vacation, I decided to go back to Peponi to visit the Keringera Game Park and spend a little time in Berengi, but my visa application was denied. No reason was given, but I was told, unofficially, that my presence on Peponi was no longer desired.

I used that vacation to begin writing my first novel, an epic about men like Fuentes and Hakira and August Hardwycke during the early days of Peponi. Much to my surprise, it sold far better than my nonfiction, and I embarked on a new literary career. My second novel was a fictionalization of the life of Amanda Pickett, and my third was set during the Kalakala Emergency.

After my novels began selling well on Peponi, the new government—the fourth since Tonka's departure—officially invited me to visit the planet. I was tempted, for I often wondered if anyone still sat beneath the tree overlooking the water hole in Berengi Park, but I finally elected not to go. I would have been just one more Man looking for a tiny piece of the Paradise which the inhabitants of Peponi must ultimately find for themselves.